THE L·O·S·T COLONY

BOOK NO. 3

Last RIGHTS

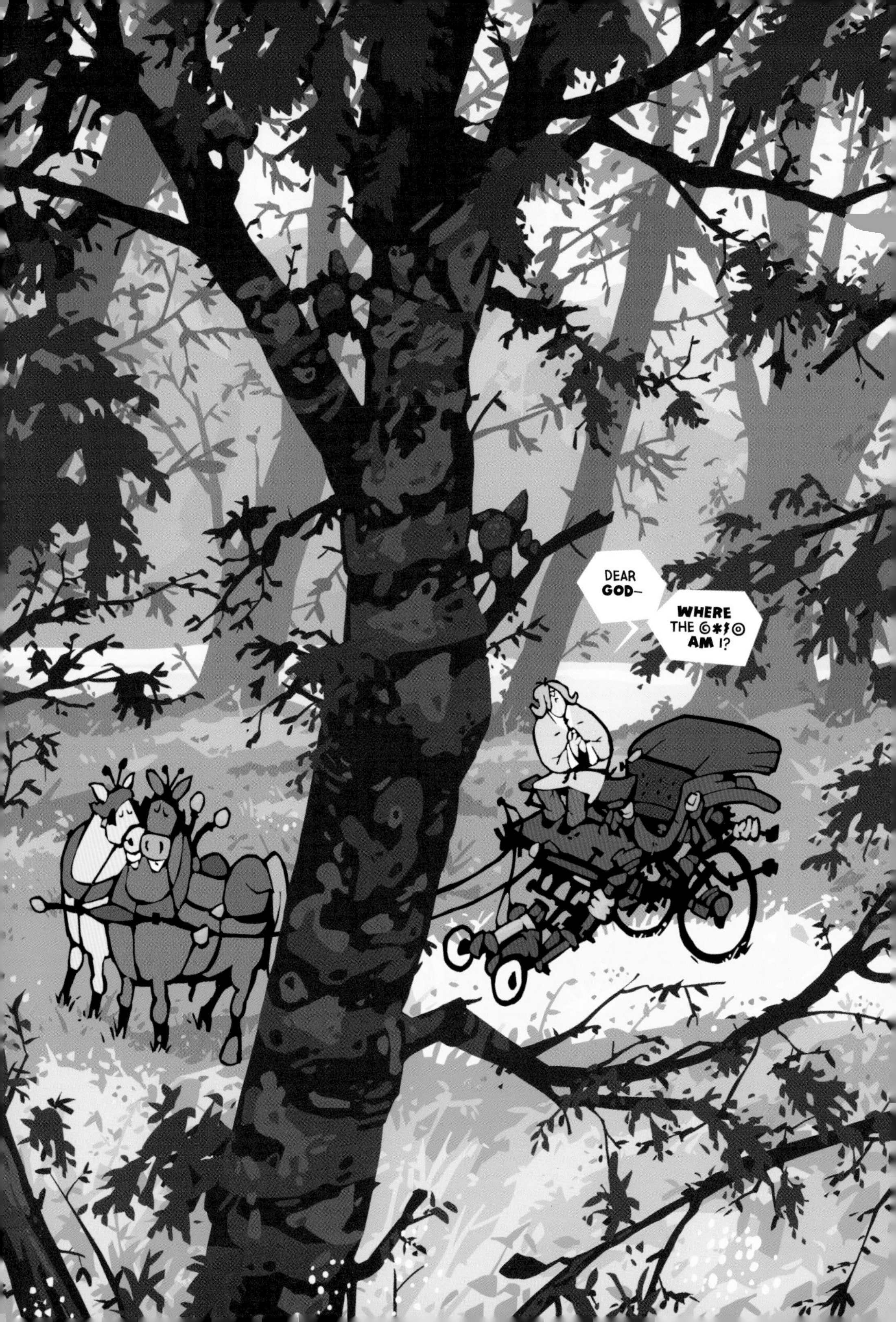
DEAR GOD–
WHERE THE ©*$© AM I?

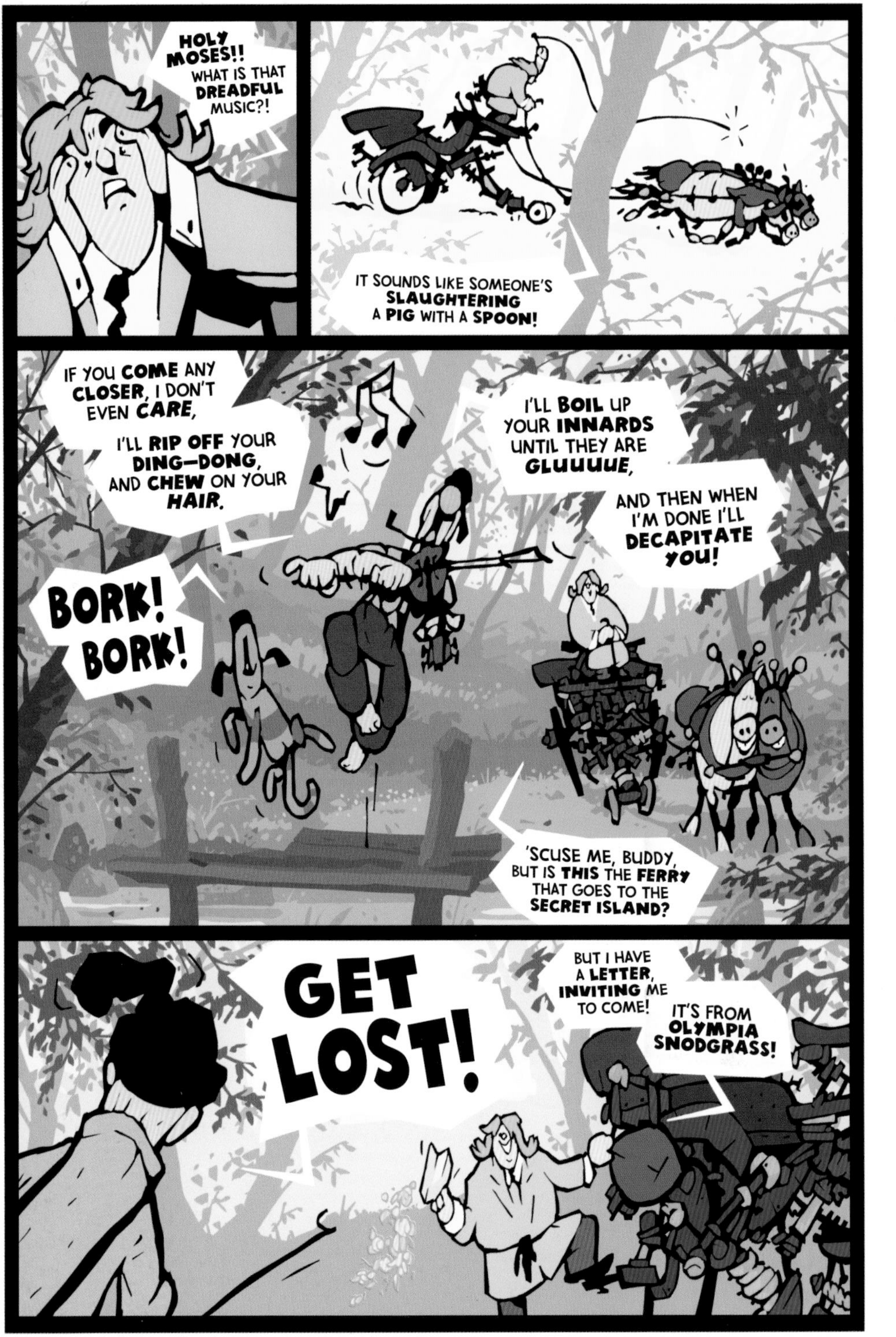
HOLY MOSES!! WHAT IS THAT DREADFUL MUSIC?!
IT SOUNDS LIKE SOMEONE'S SLAUGHTERING A PIG WITH A SPOON!
IF YOU COME ANY CLOSER, I DON'T EVEN CARE,
I'LL RIP OFF YOUR DING-DONG, AND CHEW ON YOUR HAIR.
I'LL BOIL UP YOUR INNARDS UNTIL THEY ARE GLUUUUE,
AND THEN WHEN I'M DONE I'LL DECAPITATE YOU!
BORK! BORK!
'SCUSE ME, BUDDY, BUT IS THIS THE FERRY THAT GOES TO THE SECRET ISLAND?
GET LOST!
BUT I HAVE A LETTER, INVITING ME TO COME!
IT'S FROM OLYMPIA SNODGRASS!

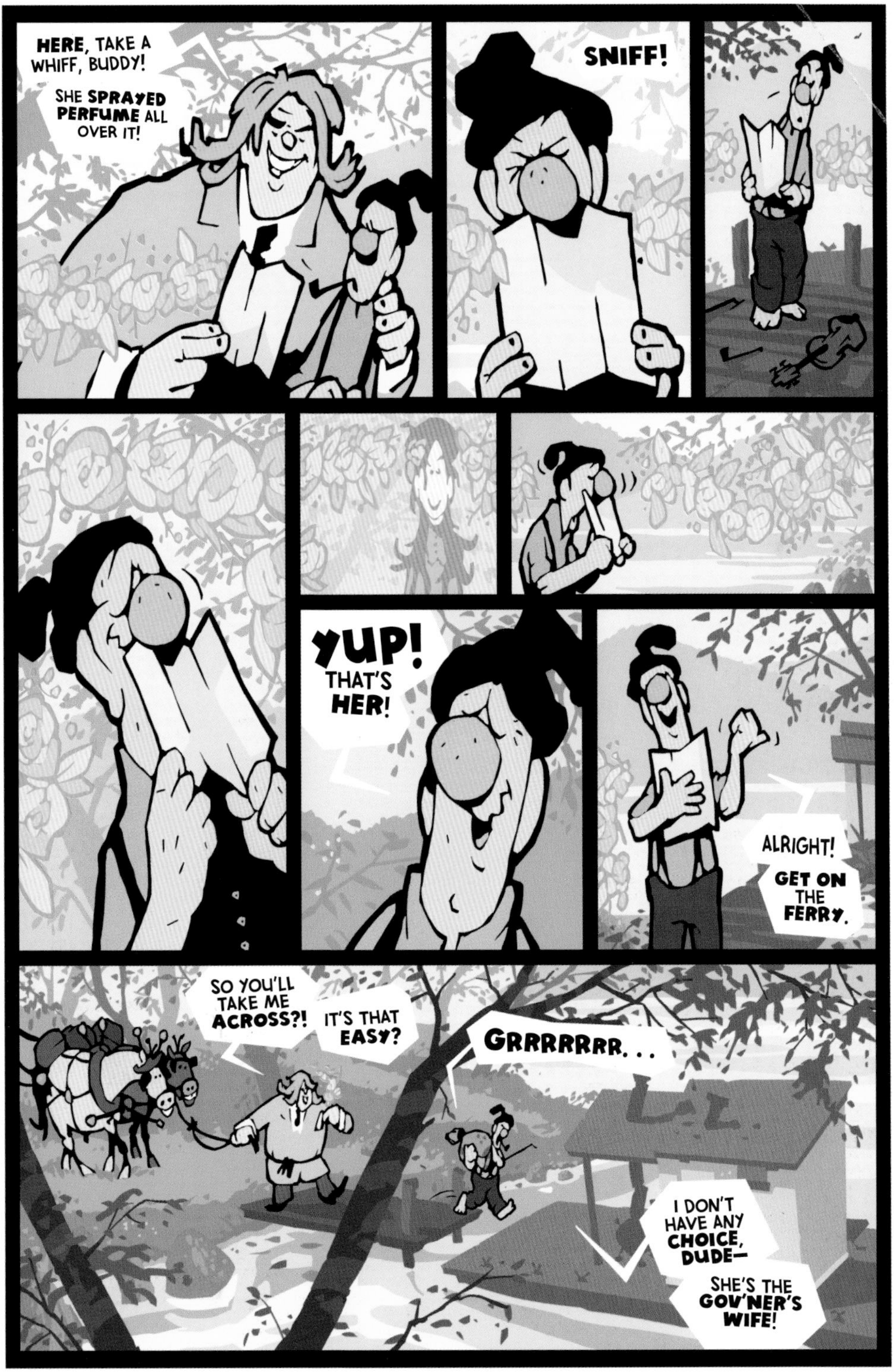
HERE, TAKE A WHIFF, BUDDY!
SHE SPRAYED PERFUME ALL OVER IT!
SNIFF!
YUP! THAT'S HER!
ALRIGHT!
GET ON THE FERRY.
SO YOU'LL TAKE ME ACROSS?!
IT'S THAT EASY?
GRRRRRRR. . .
I DON'T HAVE ANY CHOICE, DUDE—
SHE'S THE GOV'NER'S WIFE!

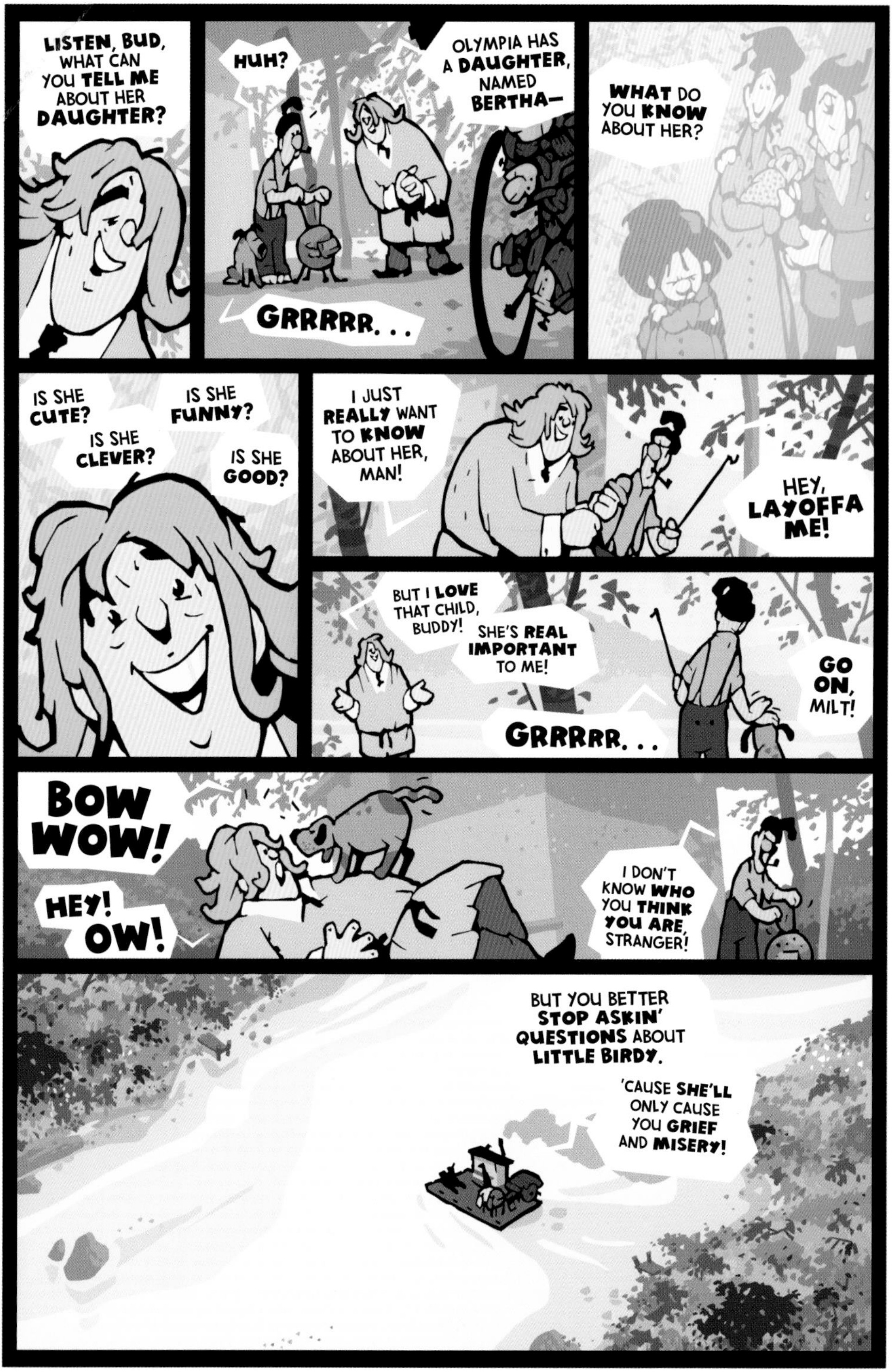

LISTEN, BUD, WHAT CAN YOU TELL ME ABOUT HER DAUGHTER?
HUH?
OLYMPIA HAS A DAUGHTER, NAMED BERTHA—
GRRRRR. . .
WHAT DO YOU KNOW ABOUT HER?
IS SHE CUTE?
IS SHE FUNNY?
IS SHE CLEVER?
IS SHE GOOD?
I JUST REALLY WANT TO KNOW ABOUT HER, MAN!
HEY, LAYOFFA ME!
BUT I LOVE THAT CHILD, BUDDY!
SHE'S REAL IMPORTANT TO ME!
GO ON, MILT!
GRRRRR. . .
BOW WOW!
HEY! OW!
I DON'T KNOW WHO YOU THINK YOU ARE, STRANGER!
BUT YOU BETTER STOP ASKIN' QUESTIONS ABOUT LITTLE BIRDY.
'CAUSE SHE'LL ONLY CAUSE YOU GRIEF AND MISERY!

THE LOST COLONY

BOOK 3

of Last RIGHTS

Grady Klein

ADMIT ONE

GRUDGINGLY READER

NO. 3

DO NOT TRESPASS

:01

First Second

NEW YORK & LONDON

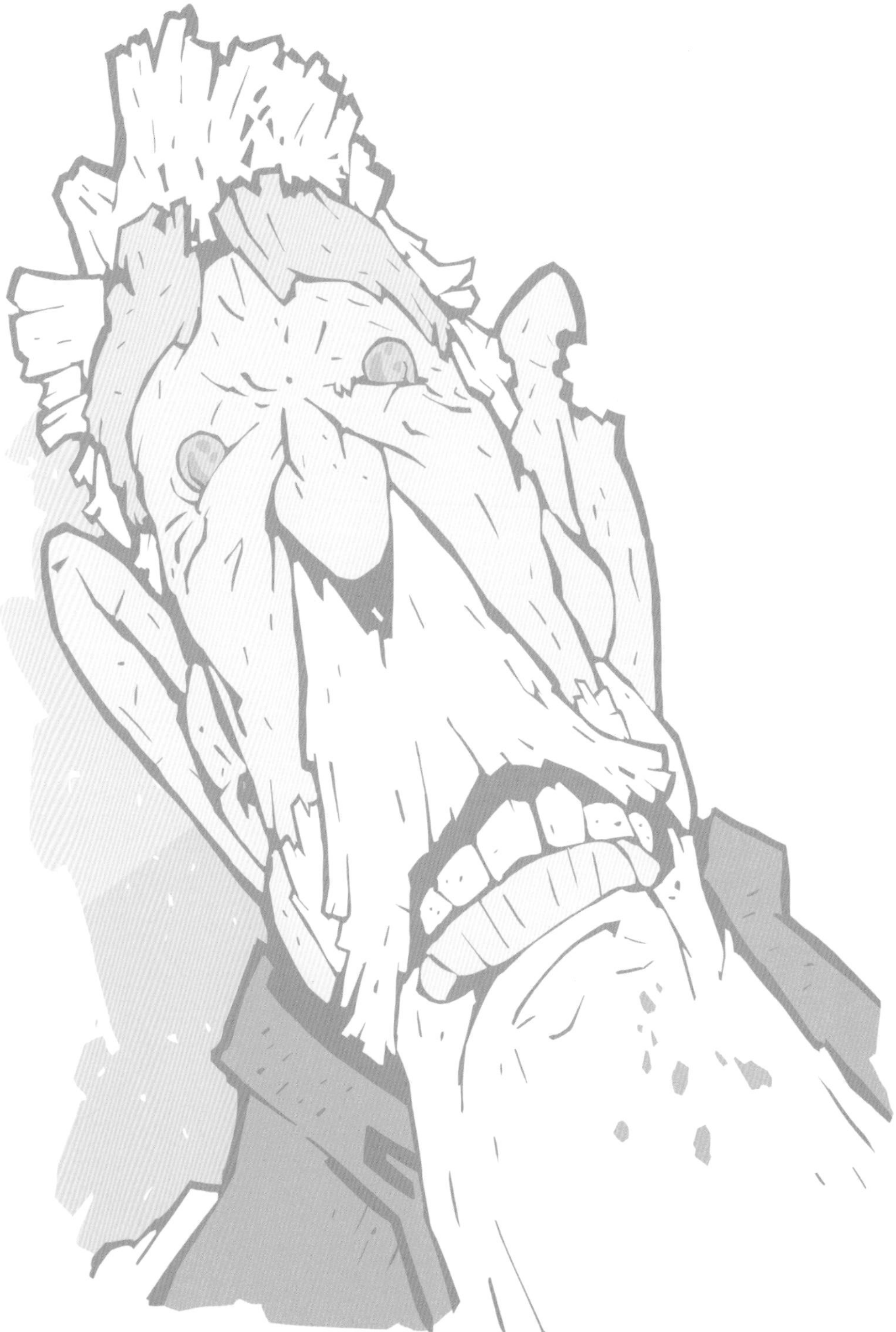

CHAPTER ONE
A Memory Best FORGOTTEN.

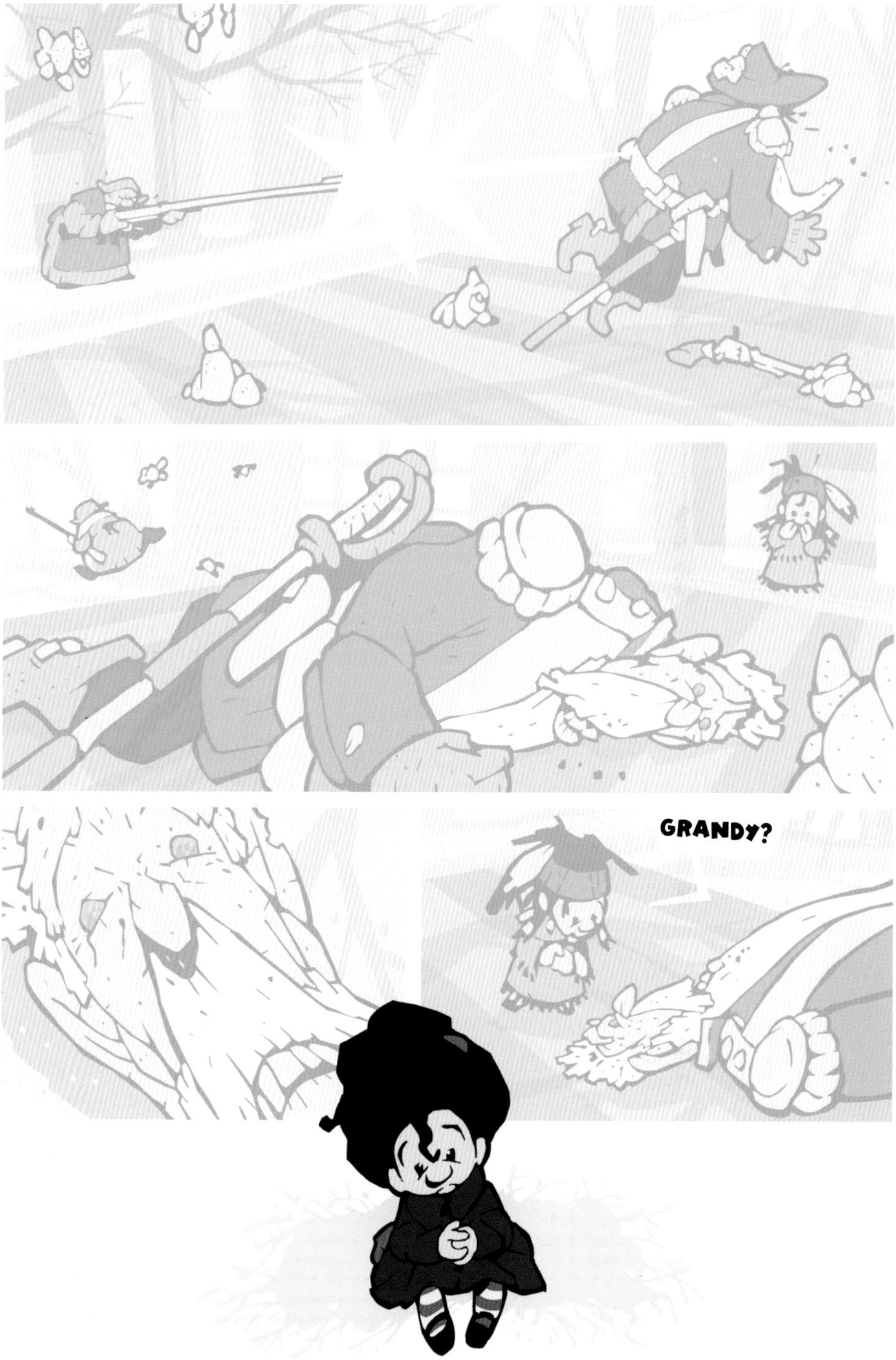
GRANDY?

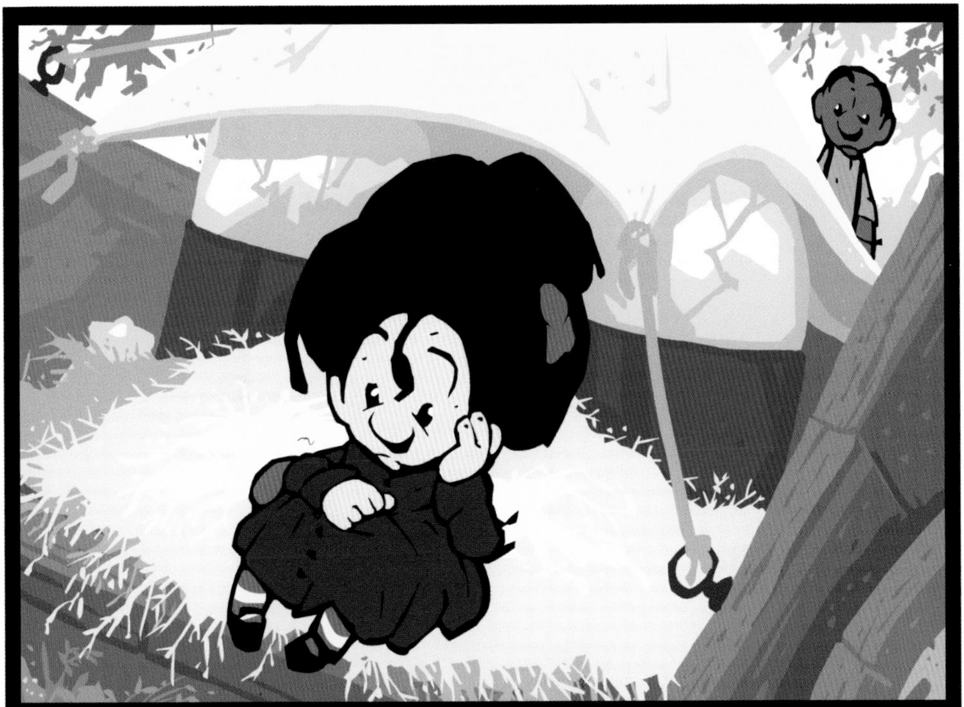

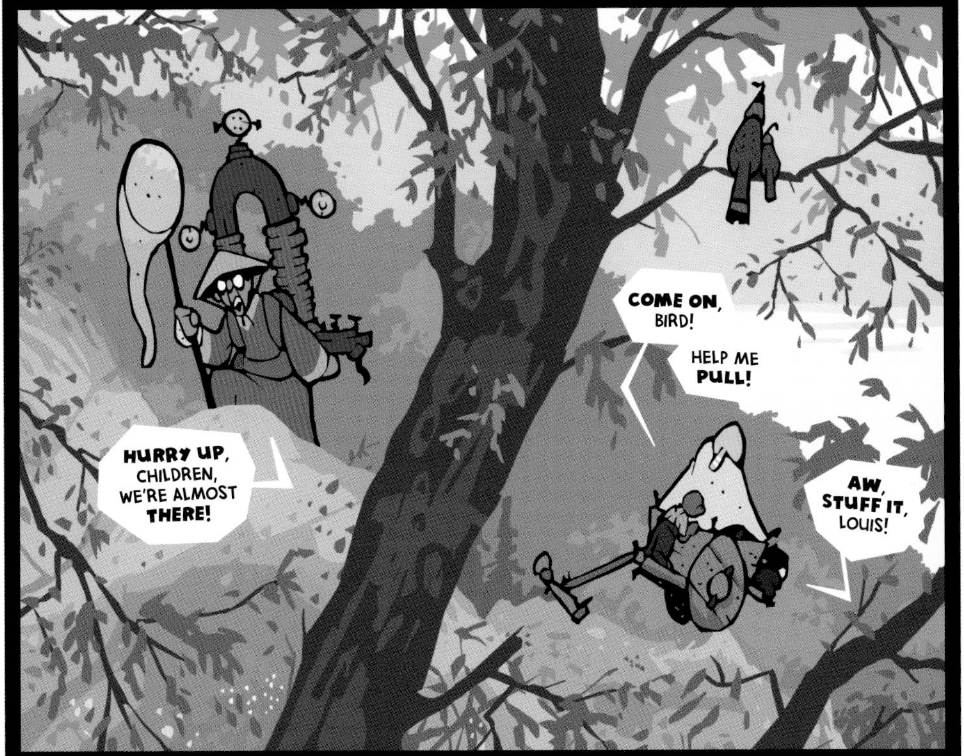
HURRY UP, CHILDREN, WE'RE ALMOST THERE!
COME ON, BIRD!
HELP ME PULL!
AW, STUFF IT, LOUIS!

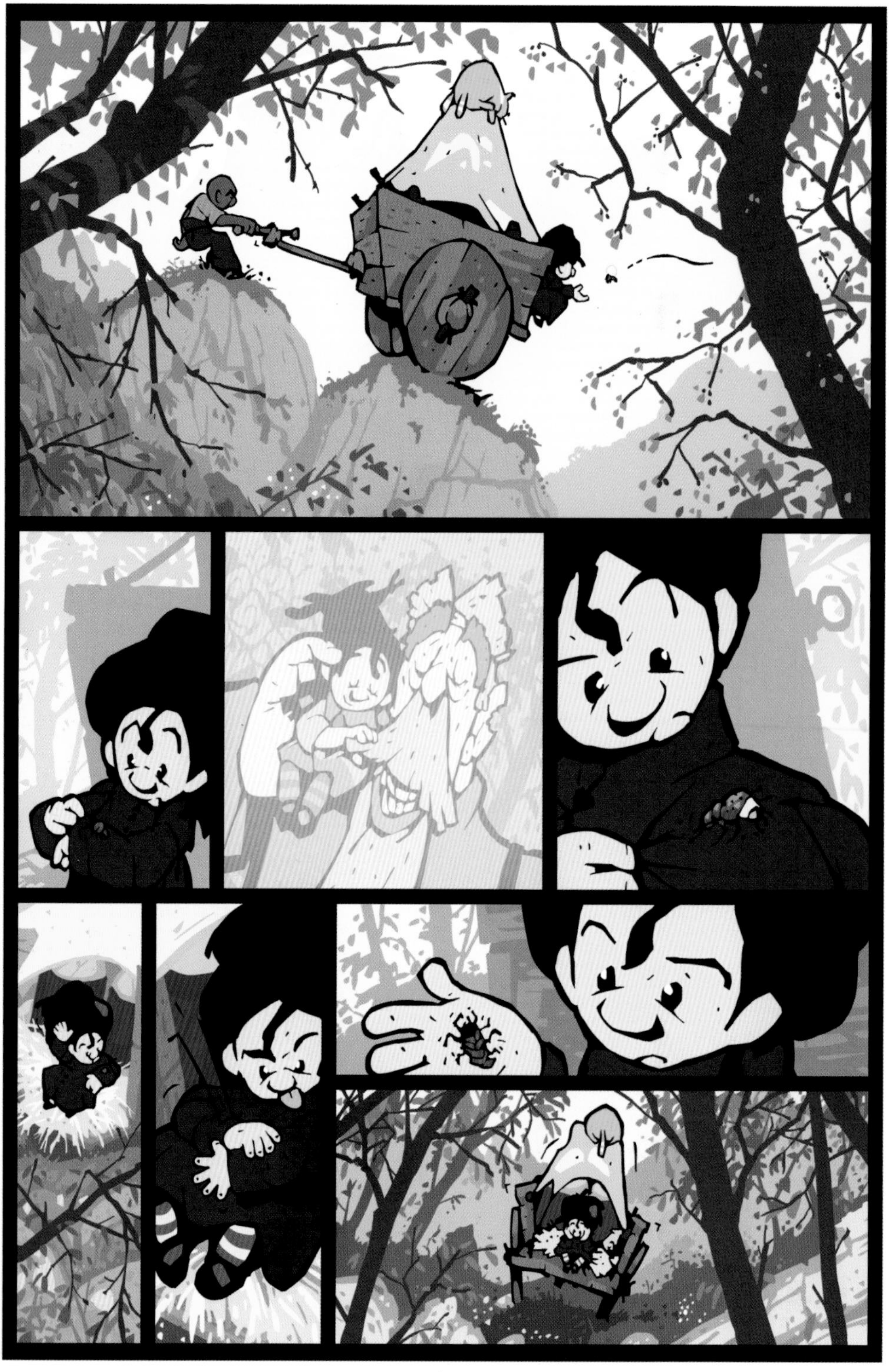

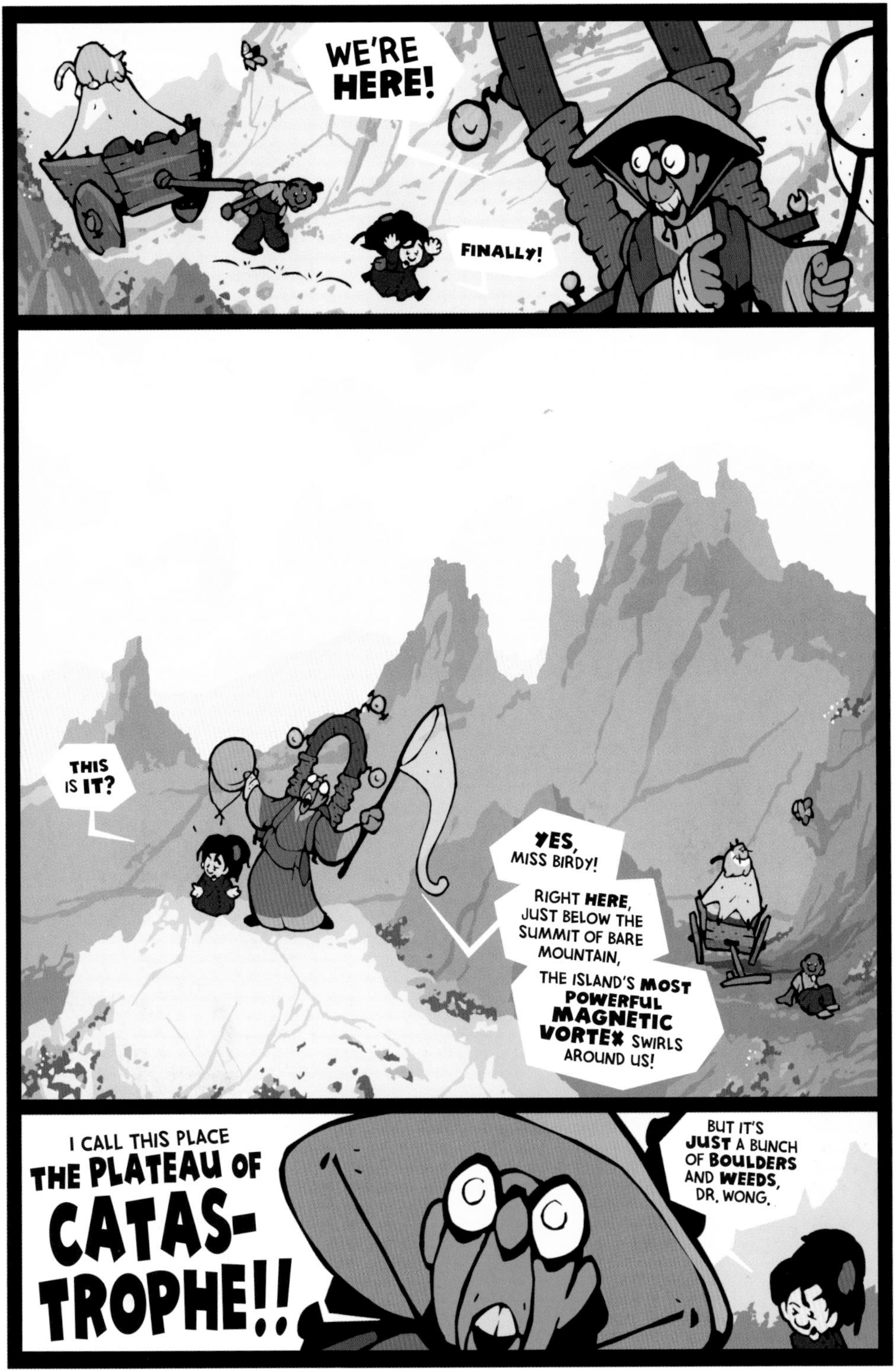
WE'RE HERE!
FINALLY!
THIS IS IT?
YES, MISS BIRDY!
RIGHT HERE, JUST BELOW THE SUMMIT OF BARE MOUNTAIN,
THE ISLAND'S MOST POWERFUL MAGNETIC VORTEX SWIRLS AROUND US!
I CALL THIS PLACE THE PLATEAU OF CATAS-TROPHE!!
BUT IT'S JUST A BUNCH OF BOULDERS AND WEEDS, DR. WONG.

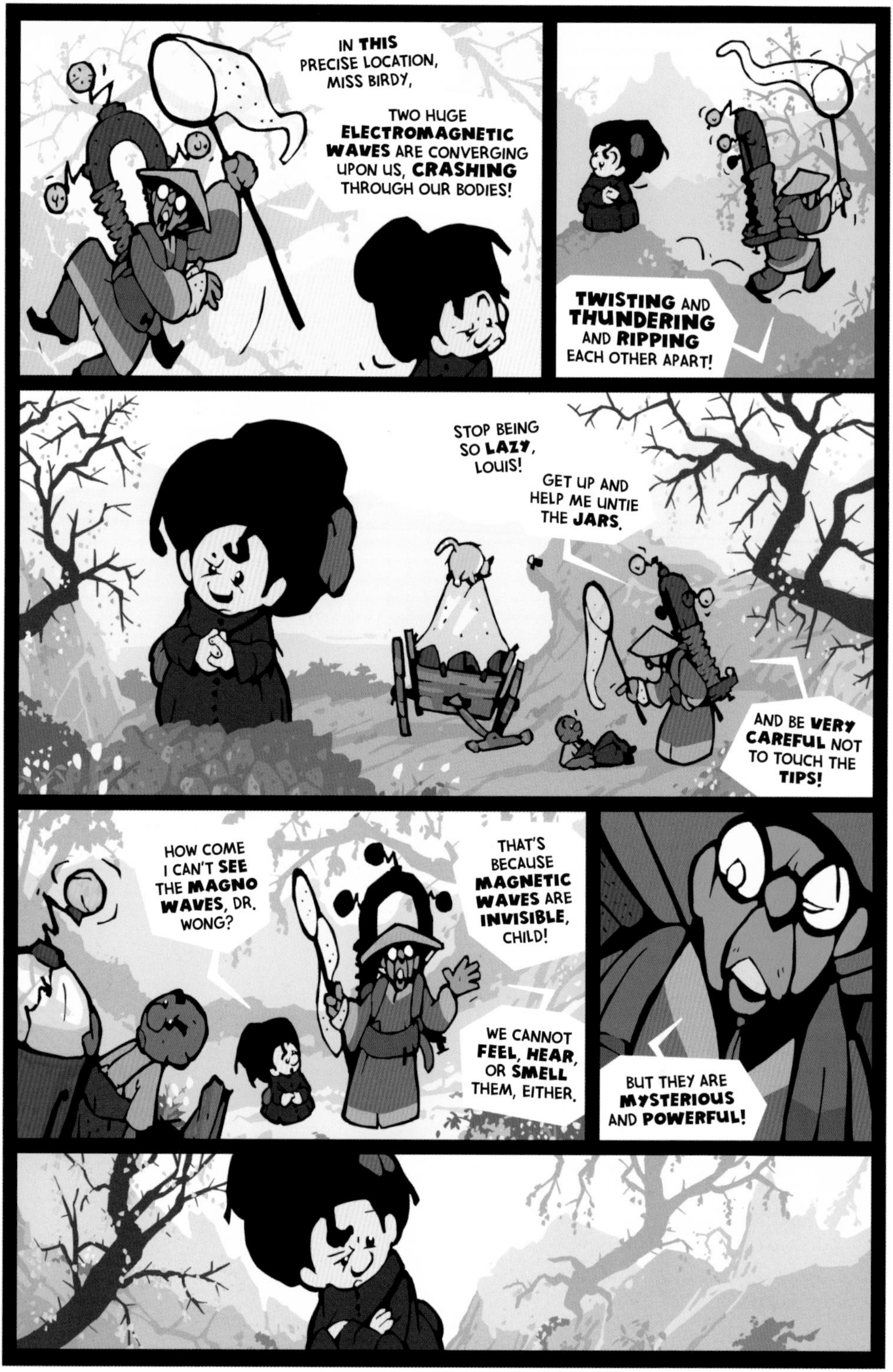
IN THIS PRECISE LOCATION, MISS BIRDY,
TWO HUGE ELECTROMAGNETIC WAVES ARE CONVERGING UPON US, CRASHING THROUGH OUR BODIES!
TWISTING AND THUNDERING AND RIPPING EACH OTHER APART!
STOP BEING SO LAZY, LOUIS!
GET UP AND HELP ME UNTIE THE JARS.
AND BE VERY CAREFUL NOT TO TOUCH THE TIPS!
HOW COME I CAN'T SEE THE MAGNO WAVES, DR. WONG?
THAT'S BECAUSE MAGNETIC WAVES ARE INVISIBLE, CHILD!
WE CANNOT FEEL, HEAR, OR SMELL THEM, EITHER.
BUT THEY ARE MYSTERIOUS AND POWERFUL!

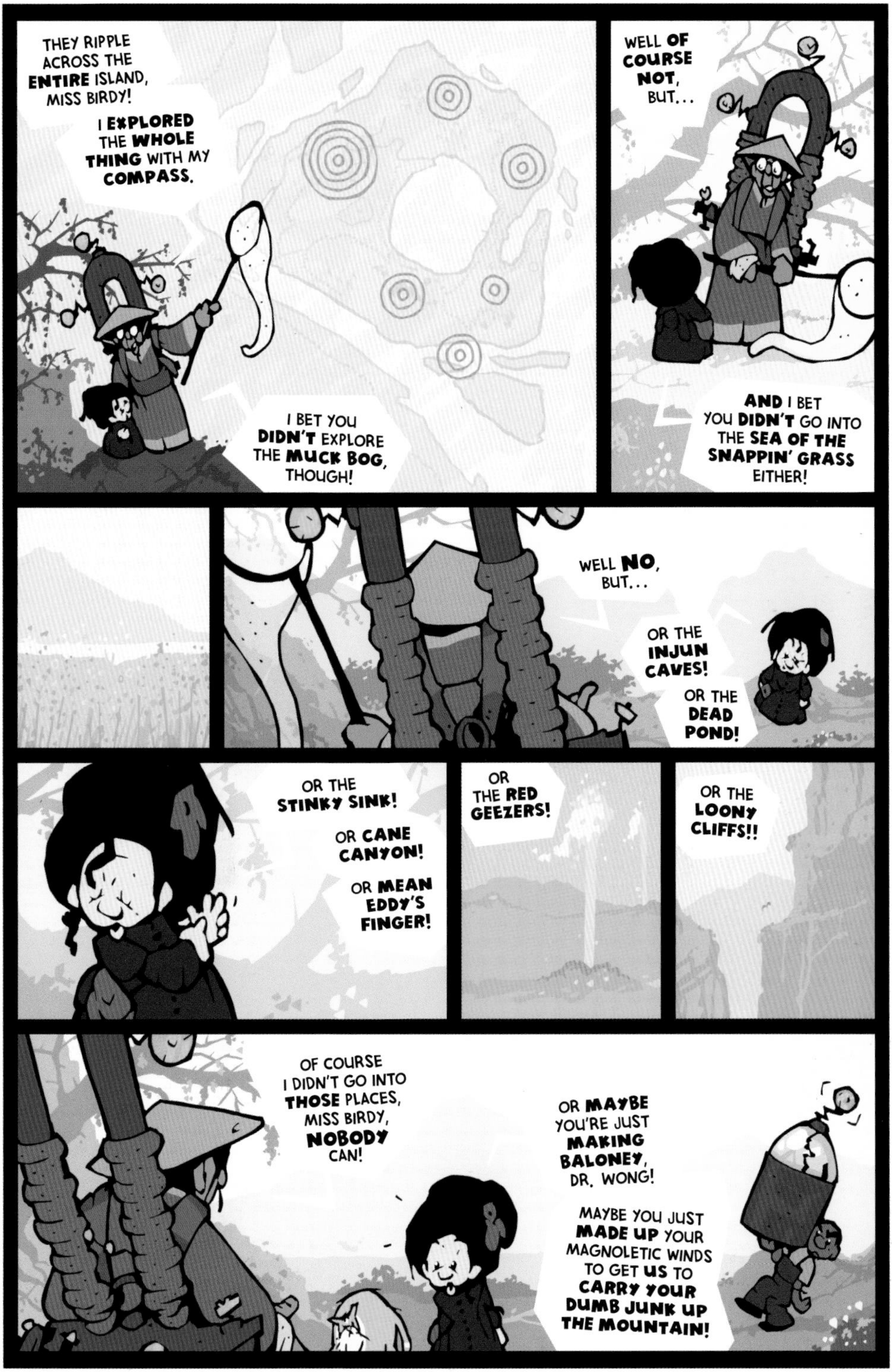

THEY RIPPLE ACROSS THE ENTIRE ISLAND, MISS BIRDY!
I EXPLORED THE WHOLE THING WITH MY COMPASS.
I BET YOU DIDN'T EXPLORE THE MUCK BOG, THOUGH!
WELL OF COURSE NOT, BUT...
AND I BET YOU DIDN'T GO INTO THE SEA OF THE SNAPPIN' GRASS EITHER!
WELL NO, BUT...
OR THE INJUN CAVES!
OR THE DEAD POND!
OR THE STINKY SINK!
OR CANE CANYON!
OR MEAN EDDY'S FINGER!
OR THE RED GEEZERS!
OR THE LOONY CLIFFS!!
OF COURSE I DIDN'T GO INTO THOSE PLACES, MISS BIRDY, NOBODY CAN!
OR MAYBE YOU'RE JUST MAKING BALONEY, DR. WONG!
MAYBE YOU JUST MADE UP YOUR MAGNOLETIC WINDS TO GET US TO CARRY YOUR DUMB JUNK UP THE MOUNTAIN!

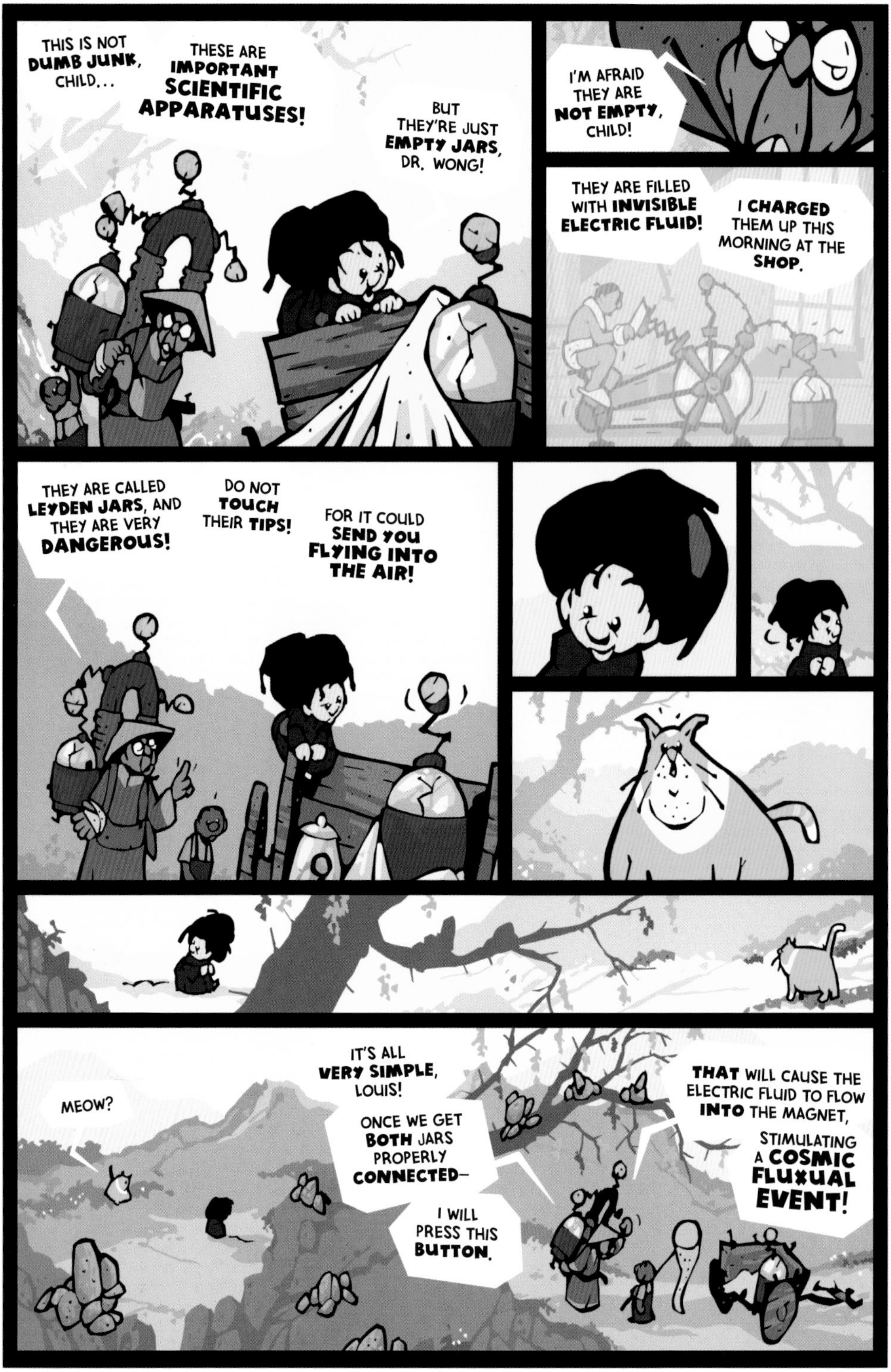
THIS IS NOT DUMB JUNK, CHILD...
THESE ARE IMPORTANT SCIENTIFIC APPARATUSES!
BUT THEY'RE JUST EMPTY JARS, DR. WONG!
I'M AFRAID THEY ARE NOT EMPTY, CHILD!
THEY ARE FILLED WITH INVISIBLE ELECTRIC FLUID!
I CHARGED THEM UP THIS MORNING AT THE SHOP.
THEY ARE CALLED LEYDEN JARS, AND THEY ARE VERY DANGEROUS!
DO NOT TOUCH THEIR TIPS!
FOR IT COULD SEND YOU FLYING INTO THE AIR!
MEOW?
IT'S ALL VERY SIMPLE, LOUIS!
ONCE WE GET BOTH JARS PROPERLY CONNECTED—
I WILL PRESS THIS BUTTON.
THAT WILL CAUSE THE ELECTRIC FLUID TO FLOW INTO THE MAGNET,
STIMULATING A COSMIC FLUXUAL EVENT!

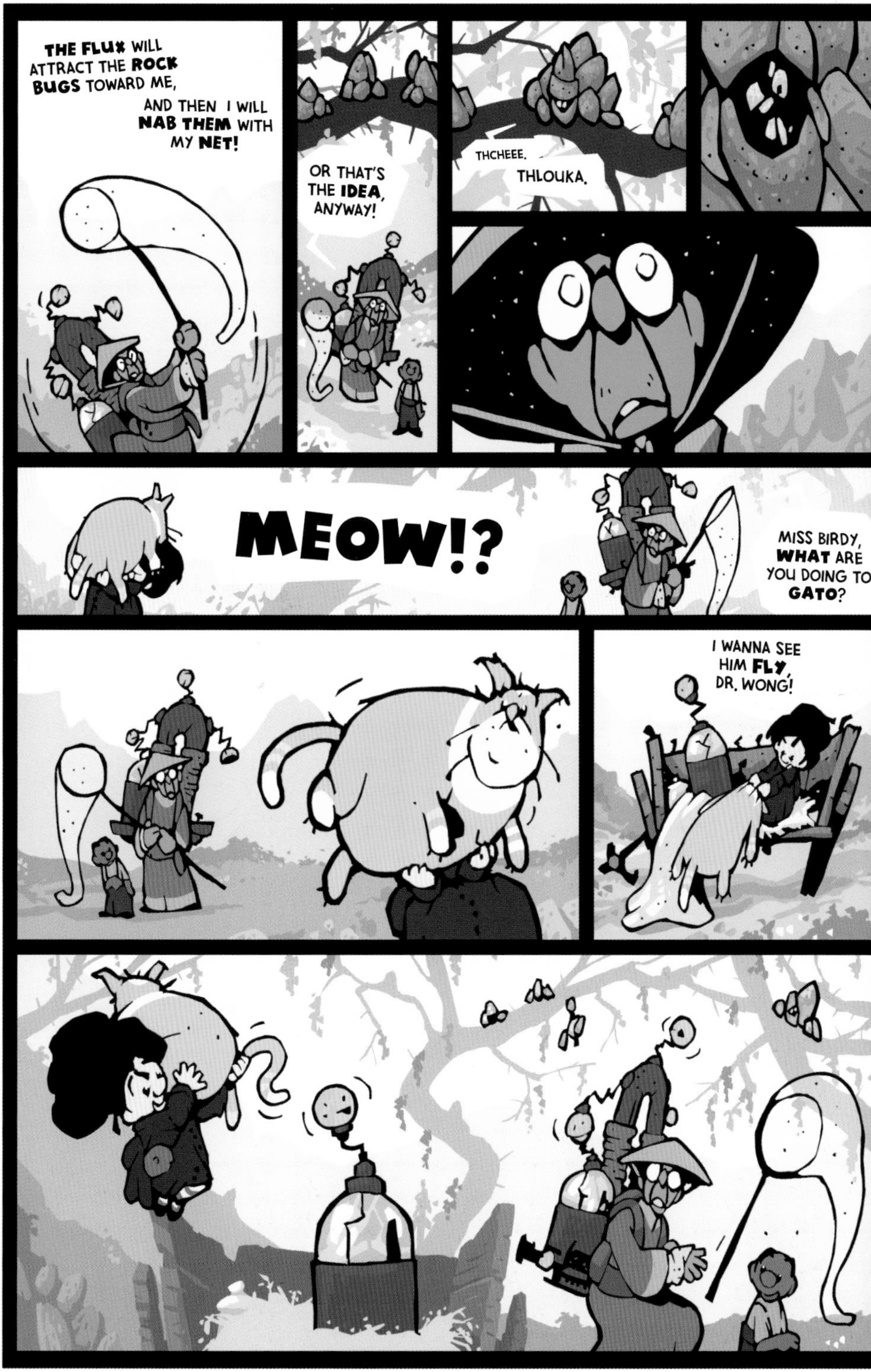
THE FLUX WILL ATTRACT THE ROCK BUGS TOWARD ME,
AND THEN I WILL NAB THEM WITH MY NET!
OR THAT'S THE IDEA, ANYWAY!
THCHEEE.
THLOUKA.
MEOW!?
MISS BIRDY, WHAT ARE YOU DOING TO GATO?
I WANNA SEE HIM FLY, DR. WONG!

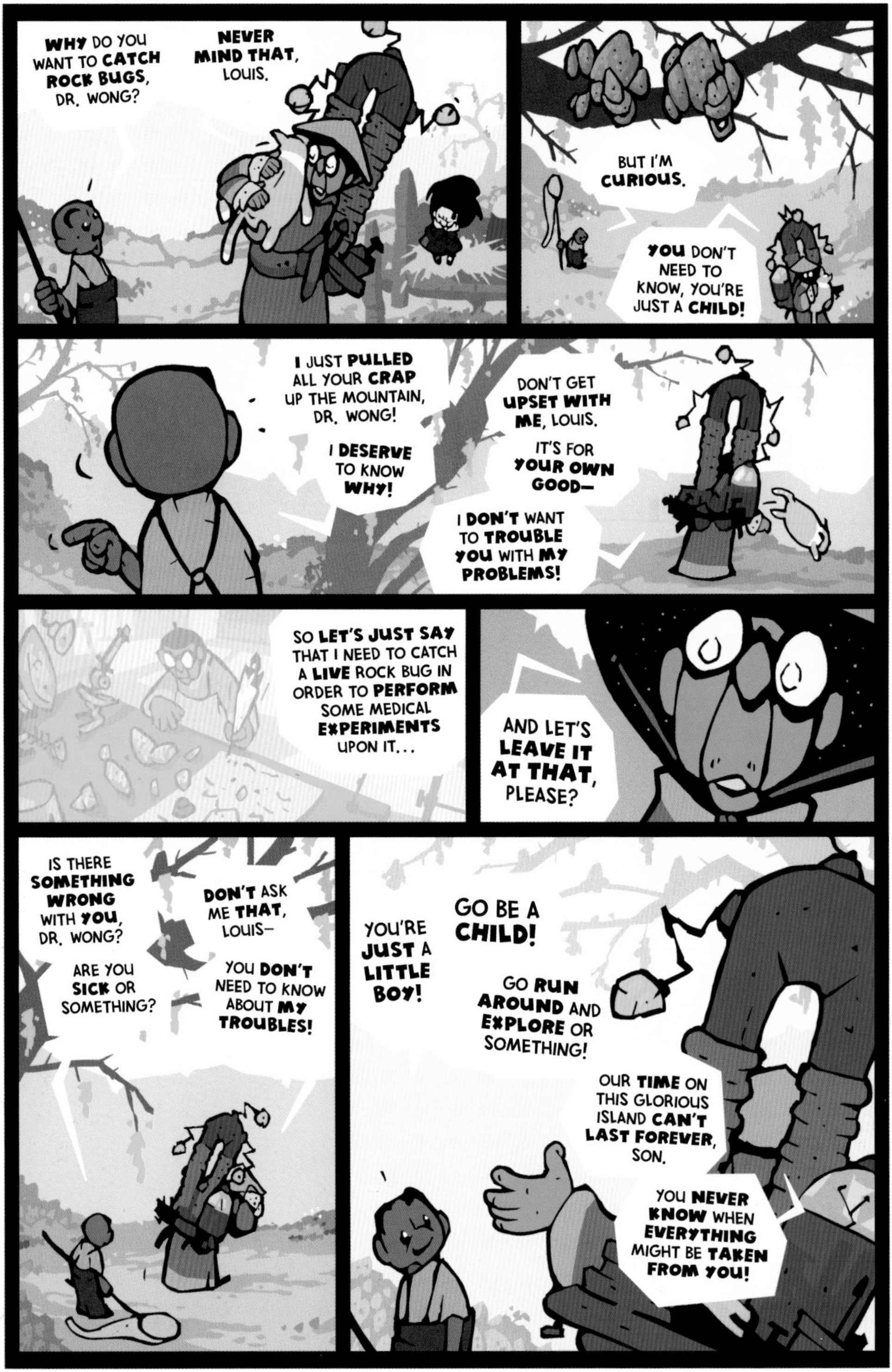
WHY DO YOU WANT TO CATCH ROCK BUGS, DR. WONG?
NEVER MIND THAT, LOUIS.
BUT I'M CURIOUS.
YOU DON'T NEED TO KNOW, YOU'RE JUST A CHILD!
I JUST PULLED ALL YOUR CRAP UP THE MOUNTAIN, DR. WONG!
I DESERVE TO KNOW WHY!
DON'T GET UPSET WITH ME, LOUIS.
IT'S FOR YOUR OWN GOOD—
I DON'T WANT TO TROUBLE YOU WITH MY PROBLEMS!
SO LET'S JUST SAY THAT I NEED TO CATCH A LIVE ROCK BUG IN ORDER TO PERFORM SOME MEDICAL EXPERIMENTS UPON IT...
AND LET'S LEAVE IT AT THAT, PLEASE?
IS THERE SOMETHING WRONG WITH YOU, DR. WONG?
ARE YOU SICK OR SOMETHING?
DON'T ASK ME THAT, LOUIS—
YOU DON'T NEED TO KNOW ABOUT MY TROUBLES!
YOU'RE JUST A LITTLE BOY!
GO BE A CHILD!
GO RUN AROUND AND EXPLORE OR SOMETHING!
OUR TIME ON THIS GLORIOUS ISLAND CAN'T LAST FOREVER, SON.
YOU NEVER KNOW WHEN EVERYTHING MIGHT BE TAKEN FROM YOU!

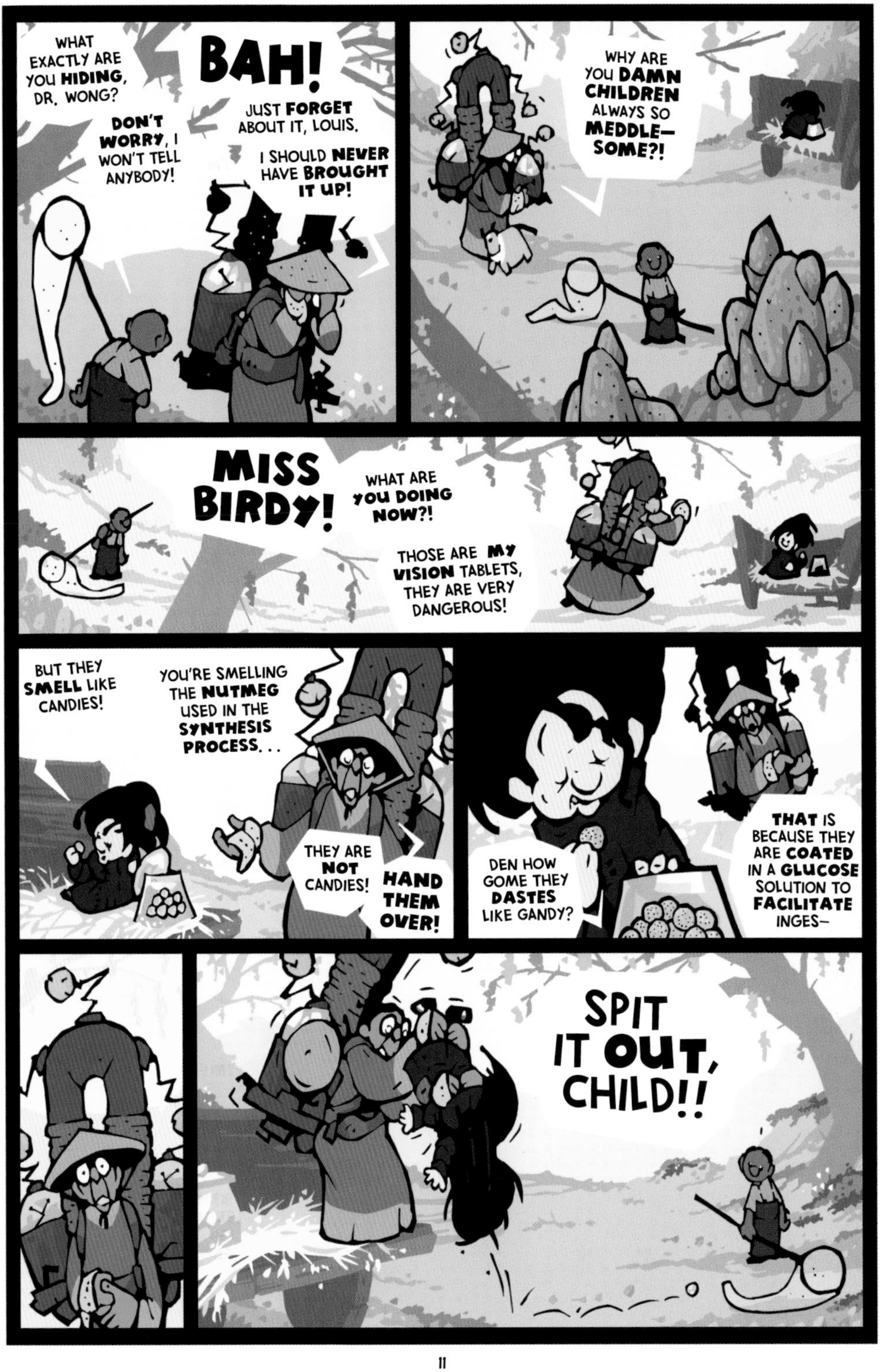
WHAT EXACTLY ARE YOU HIDING, DR. WONG?
DON'T WORRY, I WON'T TELL ANYBODY!
BAH!
JUST FORGET ABOUT IT, LOUIS.
I SHOULD NEVER HAVE BROUGHT IT UP!
WHY ARE YOU DAMN CHILDREN ALWAYS SO MEDDLE-SOME?!
MISS BIRDY!
WHAT ARE YOU DOING NOW?!
THOSE ARE MY VISION TABLETS, THEY ARE VERY DANGEROUS!
BUT THEY SMELL LIKE CANDIES!
YOU'RE SMELLING THE NUTMEG USED IN THE SYNTHESIS PROCESS. . .
THEY ARE NOT CANDIES!
HAND THEM OVER!
DEN HOW GOME THEY DASTES LIKE GANDY?
THAT IS BECAUSE THEY ARE COATED IN A GLUCOSE SOLUTION TO FACILITATE INGES–
SPIT IT OUT, CHILD!!

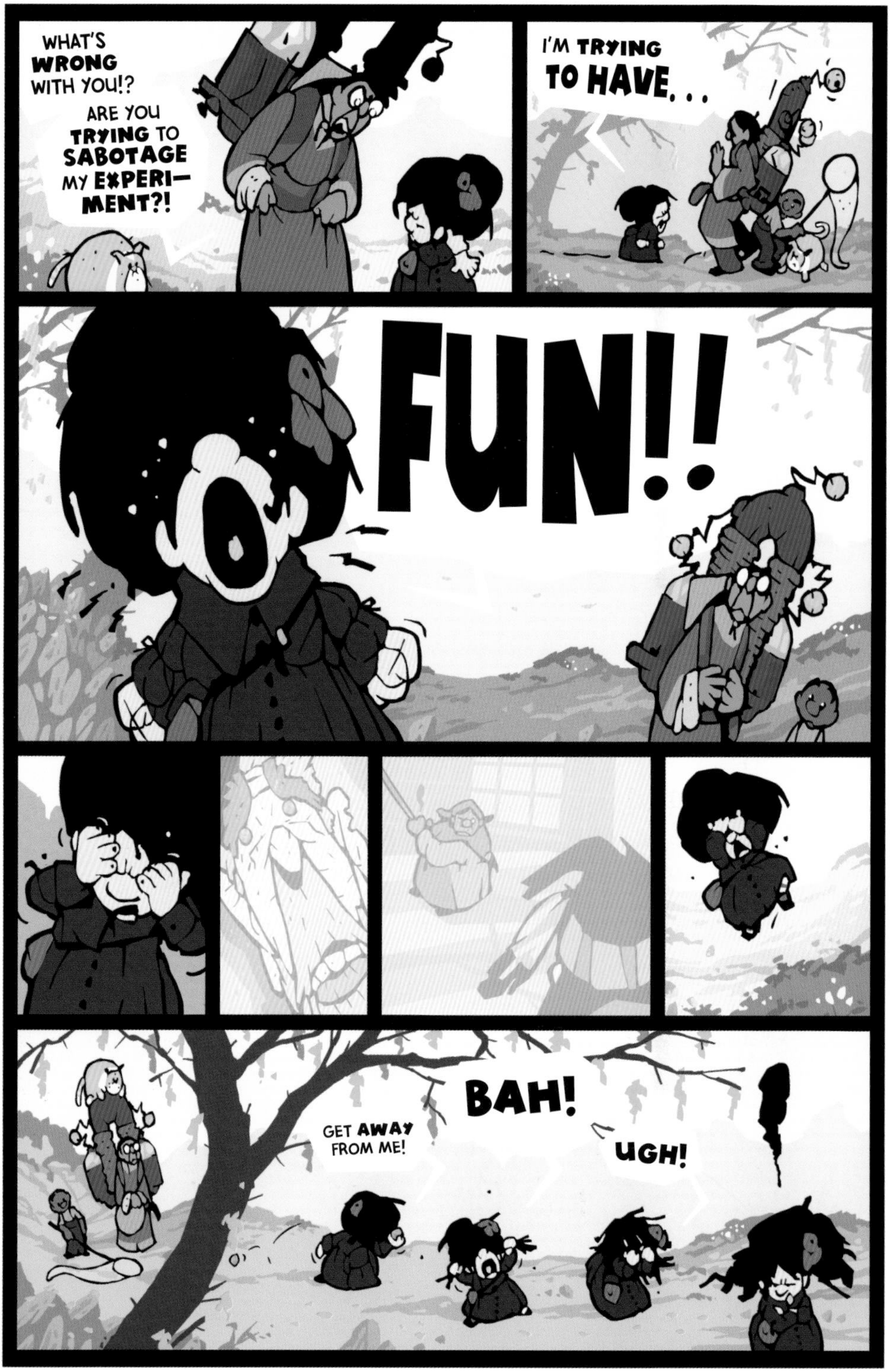
WHAT'S WRONG WITH YOU!? ARE YOU TRYING TO SABOTAGE MY EXPERI-MENT?!
I'M TRYING TO HAVE. . .
FUN!!
GET AWAY FROM ME!
BAH!
UGH!

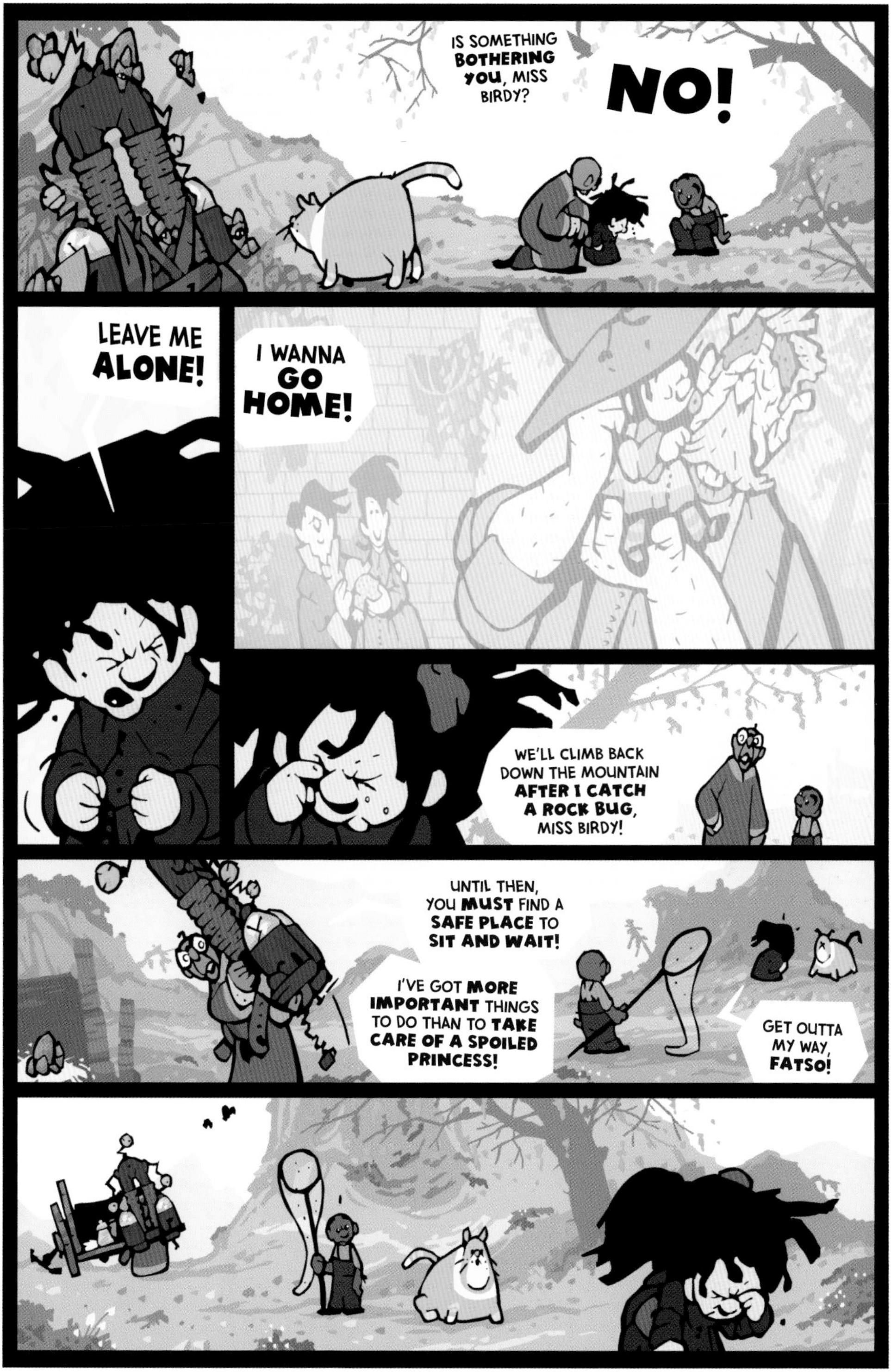
IS SOMETHING BOTHERING YOU, MISS BIRDY?
NO!
LEAVE ME ALONE!
I WANNA GO HOME!
WE'LL CLIMB BACK DOWN THE MOUNTAIN AFTER I CATCH A ROCK BUG, MISS BIRDY!
UNTIL THEN, YOU MUST FIND A SAFE PLACE TO SIT AND WAIT!
I'VE GOT MORE IMPORTANT THINGS TO DO THAN TO TAKE CARE OF A SPOILED PRINCESS!
GET OUTTA MY WAY, FATSO!

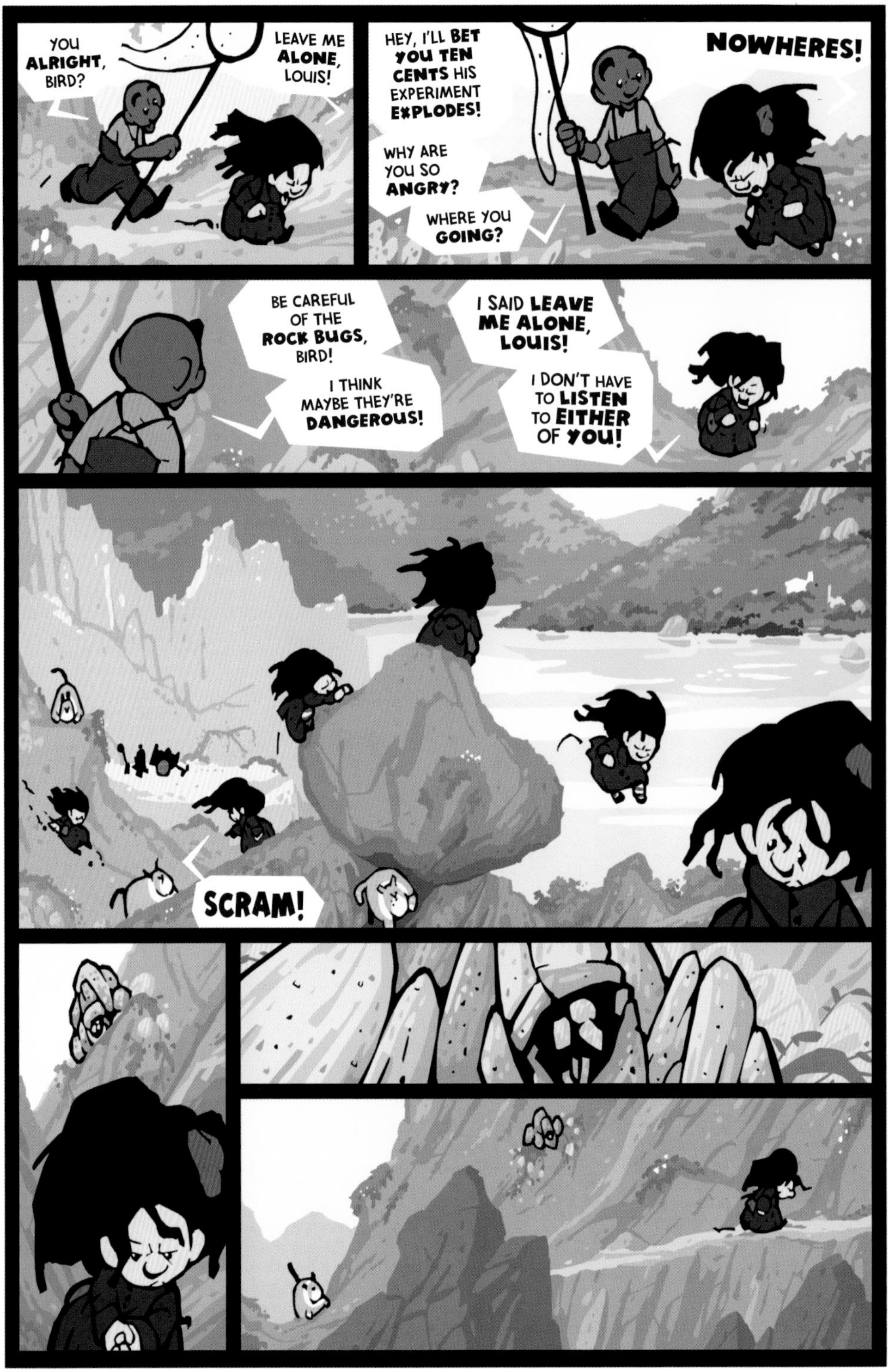
YOU ALRIGHT, BIRD?
LEAVE ME ALONE, LOUIS!
HEY, I'LL BET YOU TEN CENTS HIS EXPERIMENT EXPLODES!
WHY ARE YOU SO ANGRY?
WHERE YOU GOING?
NOWHERES!
BE CAREFUL OF THE ROCK BUGS, BIRD!
I THINK MAYBE THEY'RE DANGEROUS!
I SAID LEAVE ME ALONE, LOUIS!
I DON'T HAVE TO LISTEN TO EITHER OF YOU!
SCRAM!

CHAPTER TWO
What You Can See from the Mountaintop.

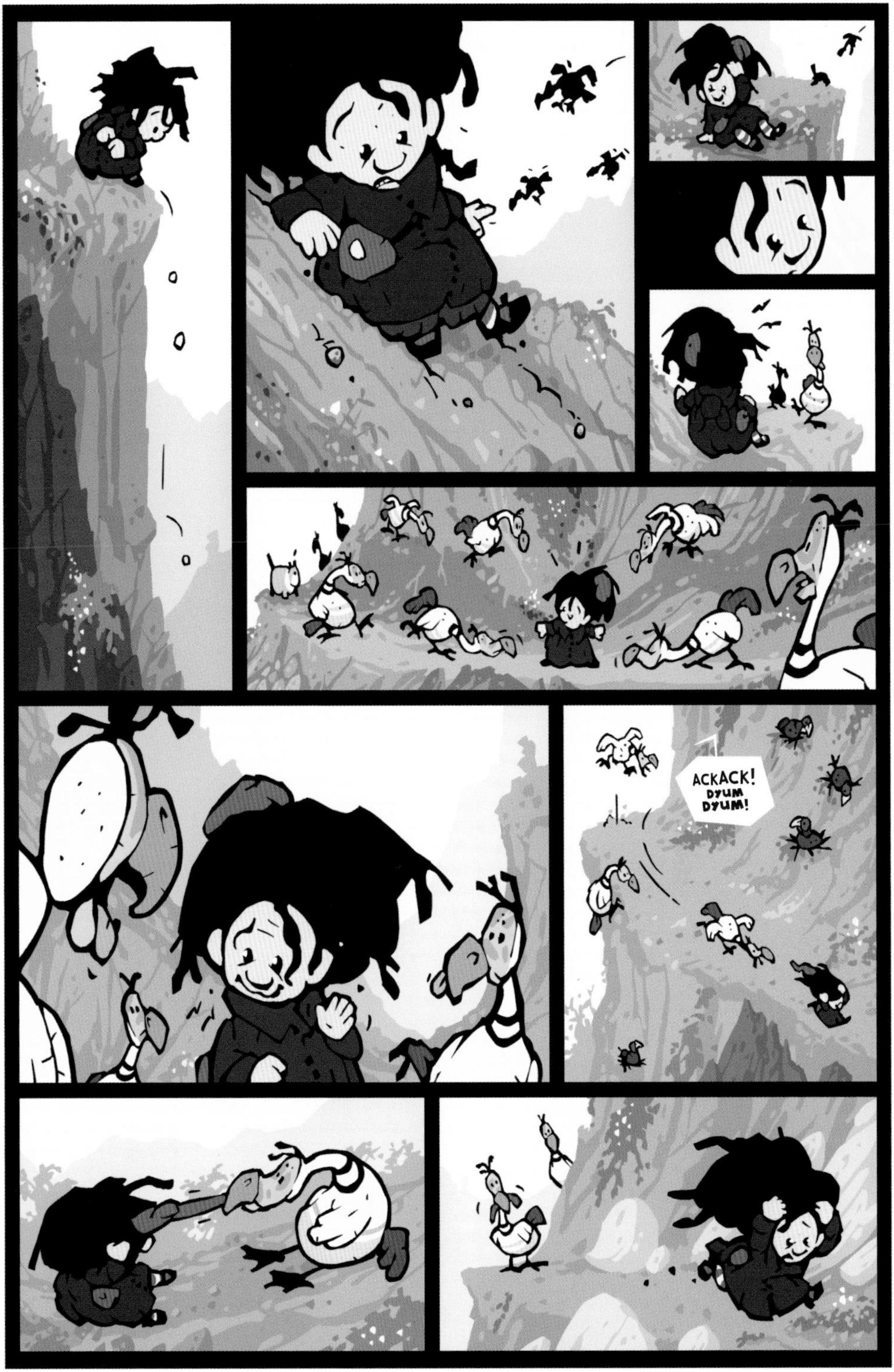
ACKACK!
DYUM
DYUM!

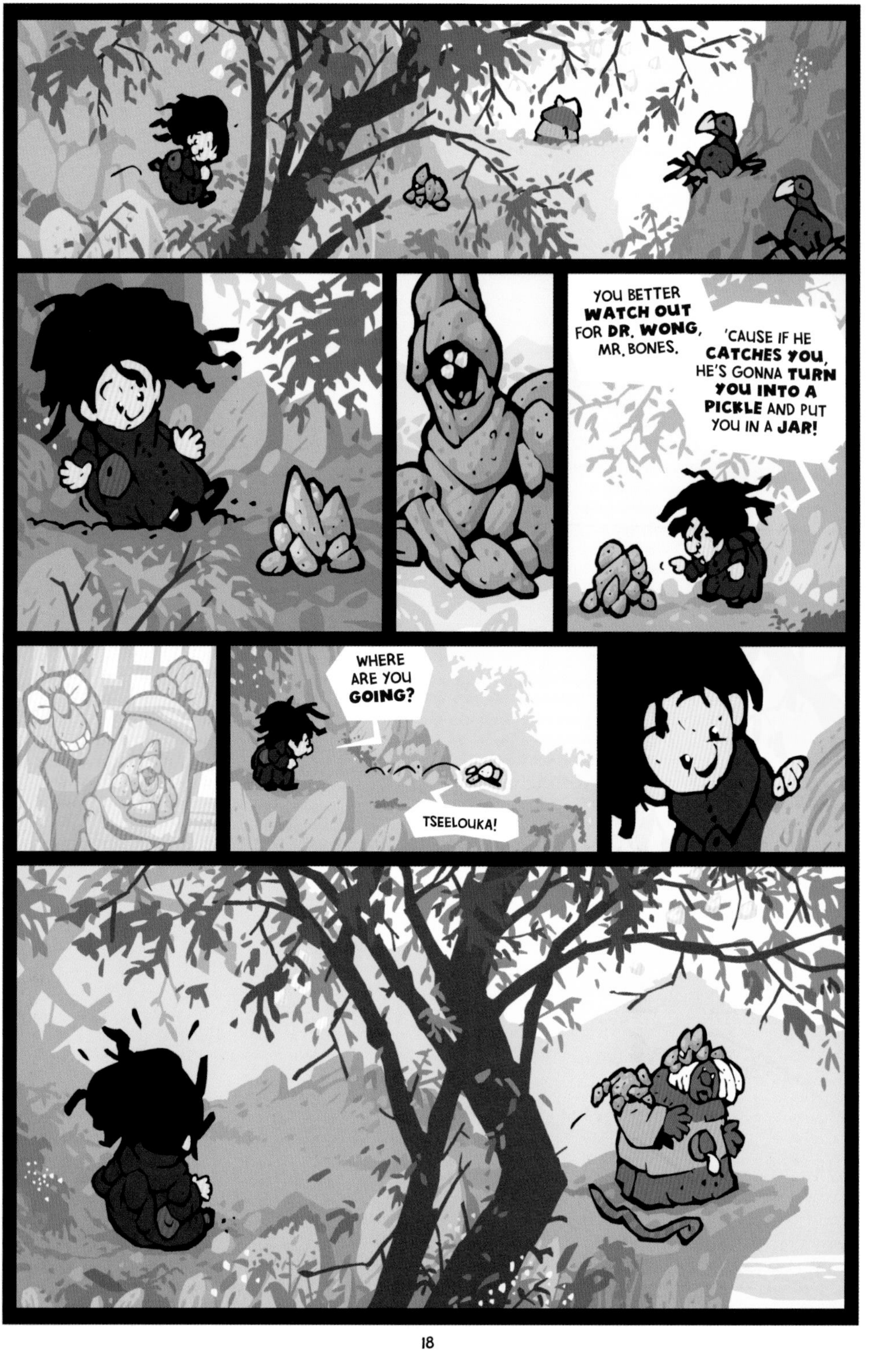
YOU BETTER WATCH OUT FOR DR. WONG, MR. BONES.
'CAUSE IF HE CATCHES YOU, HE'S GONNA TURN YOU INTO A PICKLE AND PUT YOU IN A JAR!
WHERE ARE YOU GOING?
TSEELOUKA!

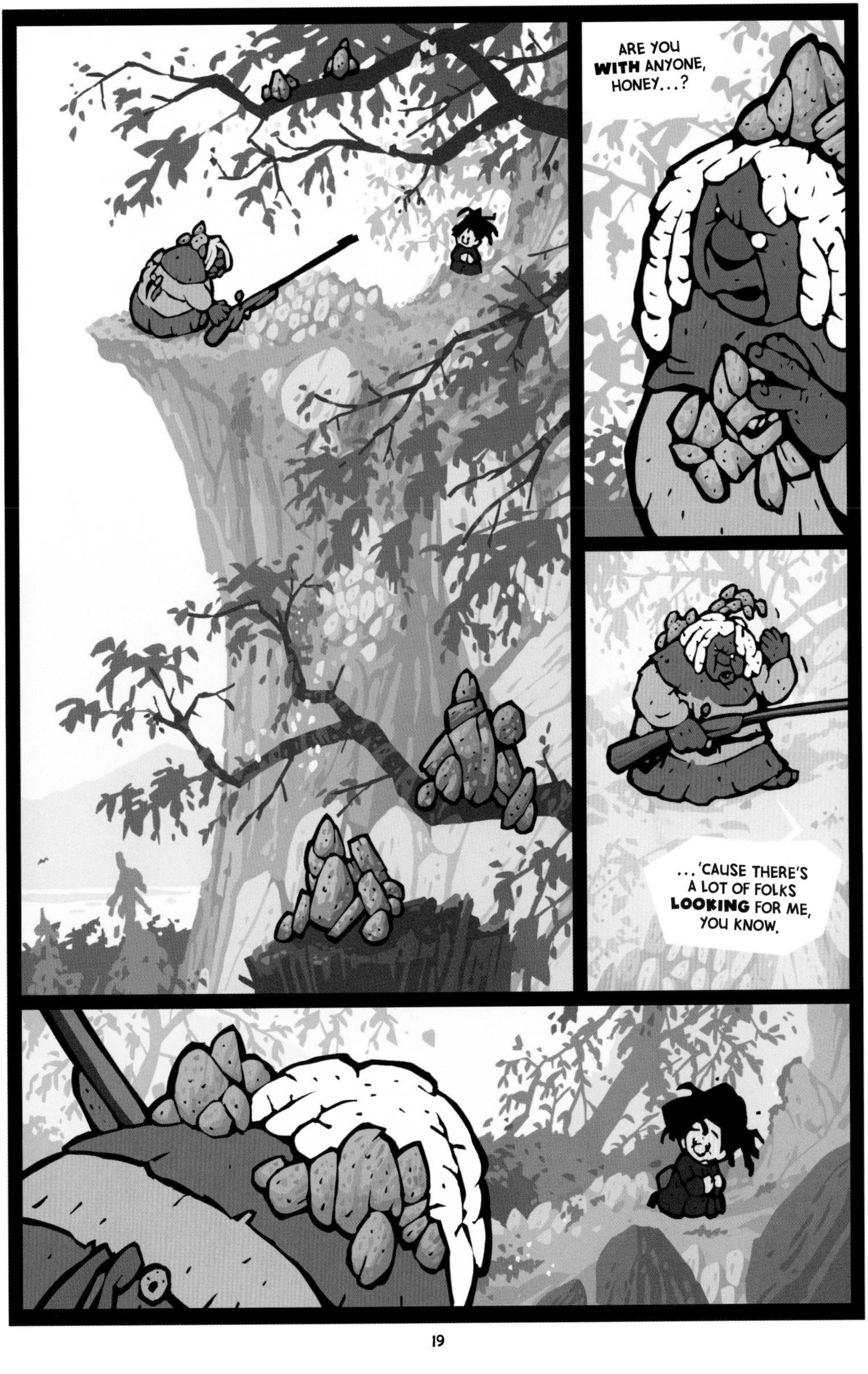
ARE YOU **WITH** ANYONE, HONEY...?
...'CAUSE THERE'S A LOT OF FOLKS **LOOKING** FOR ME, YOU KNOW.

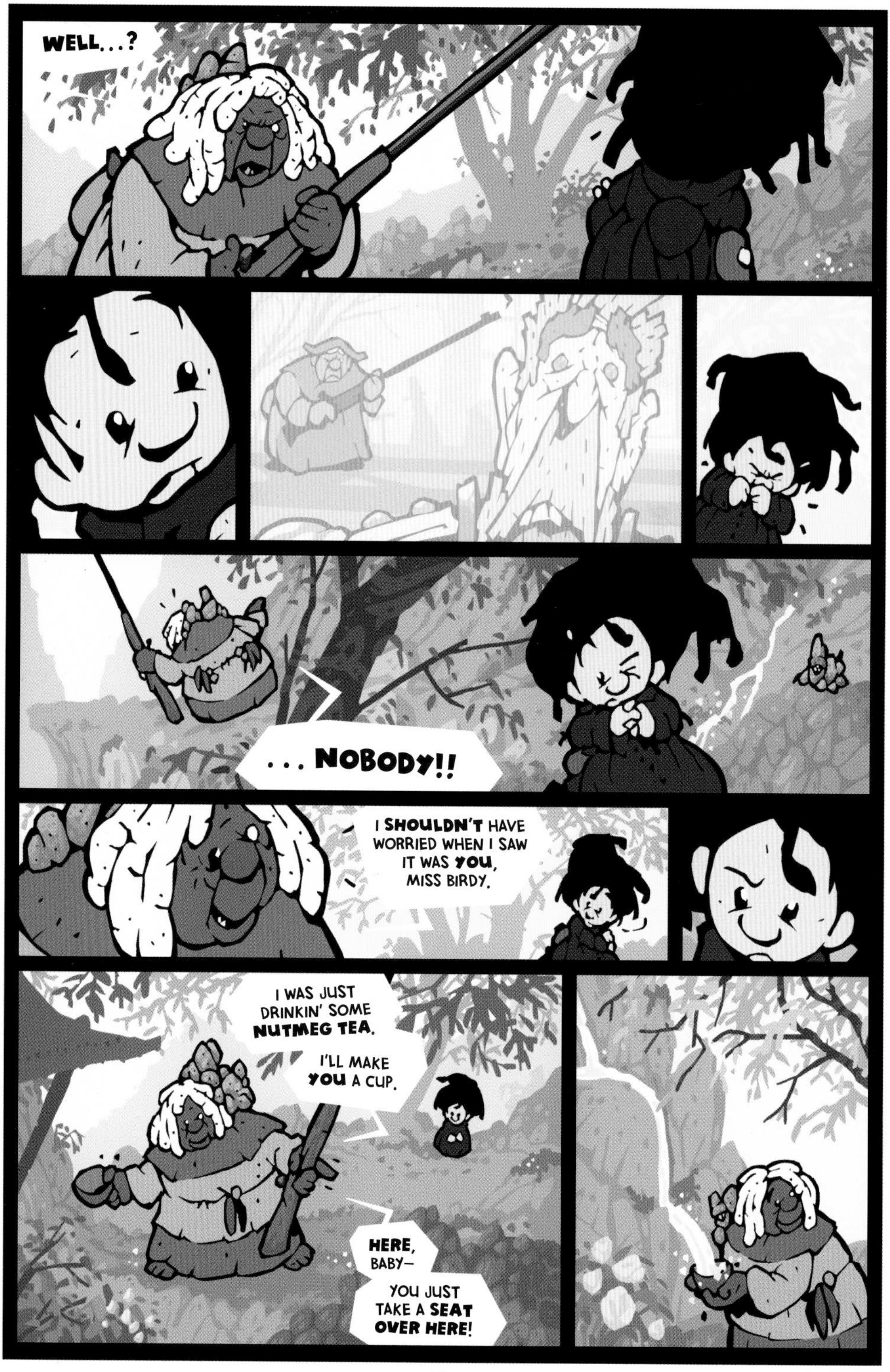
WELL...?
...NOBODY!!
I SHOULDN'T HAVE WORRIED WHEN I SAW IT WAS YOU, MISS BIRDY.
I WAS JUST DRINKIN' SOME NUTMEG TEA.
I'LL MAKE YOU A CUP.
HERE, BABY—
YOU JUST TAKE A SEAT OVER HERE!

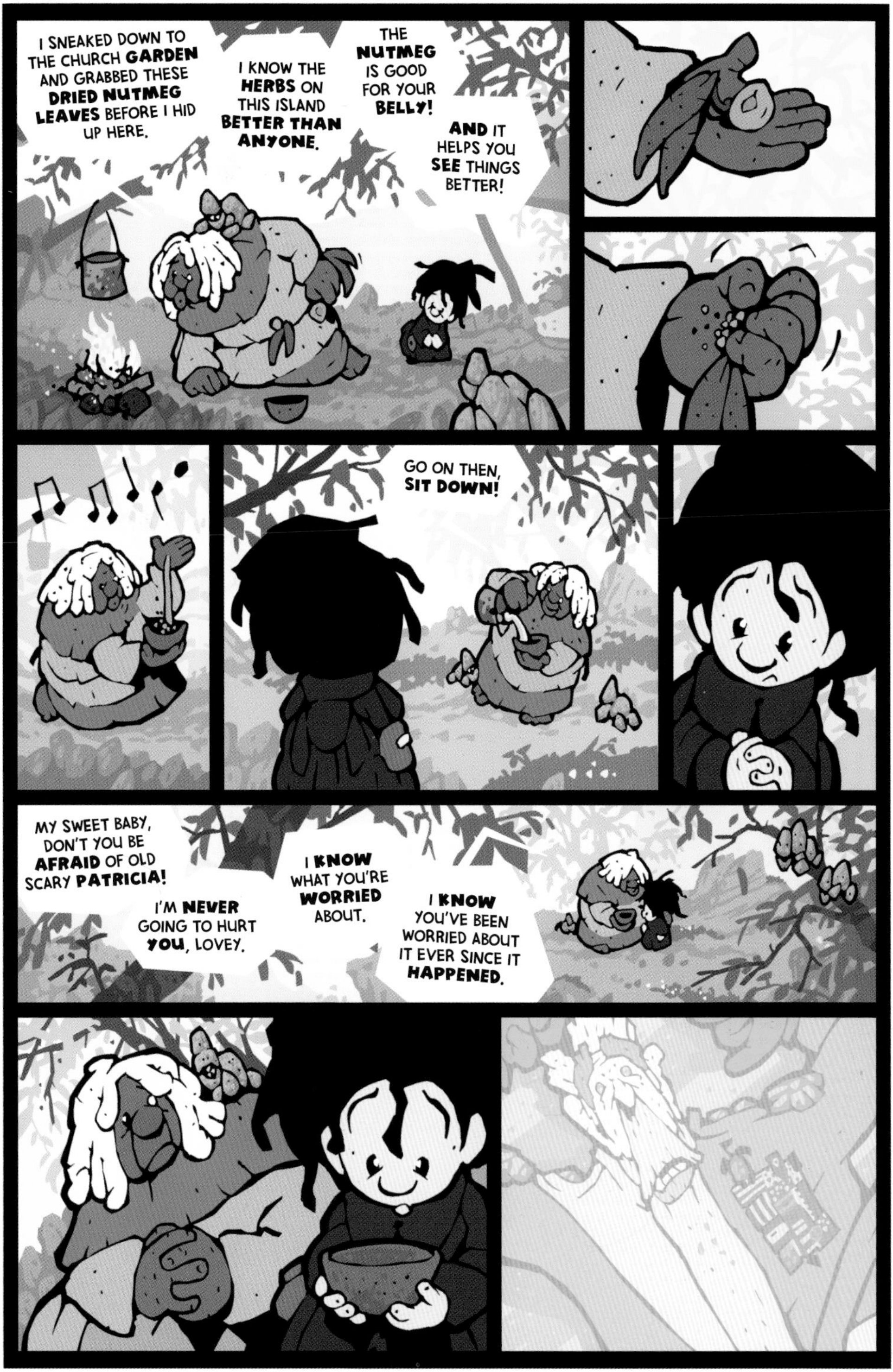
I SNEAKED DOWN TO THE CHURCH GARDEN AND GRABBED THESE DRIED NUTMEG LEAVES BEFORE I HID UP HERE.
I KNOW THE HERBS ON THIS ISLAND BETTER THAN ANYONE.
THE NUTMEG IS GOOD FOR YOUR BELLY!
AND IT HELPS YOU SEE THINGS BETTER!
GO ON THEN, SIT DOWN!
MY SWEET BABY, DON'T YOU BE AFRAID OF OLD SCARY PATRICIA!
I'M NEVER GOING TO HURT YOU, LOVEY.
I KNOW WHAT YOU'RE WORRIED ABOUT.
I KNOW YOU'VE BEEN WORRIED ABOUT IT EVER SINCE IT HAPPENED.

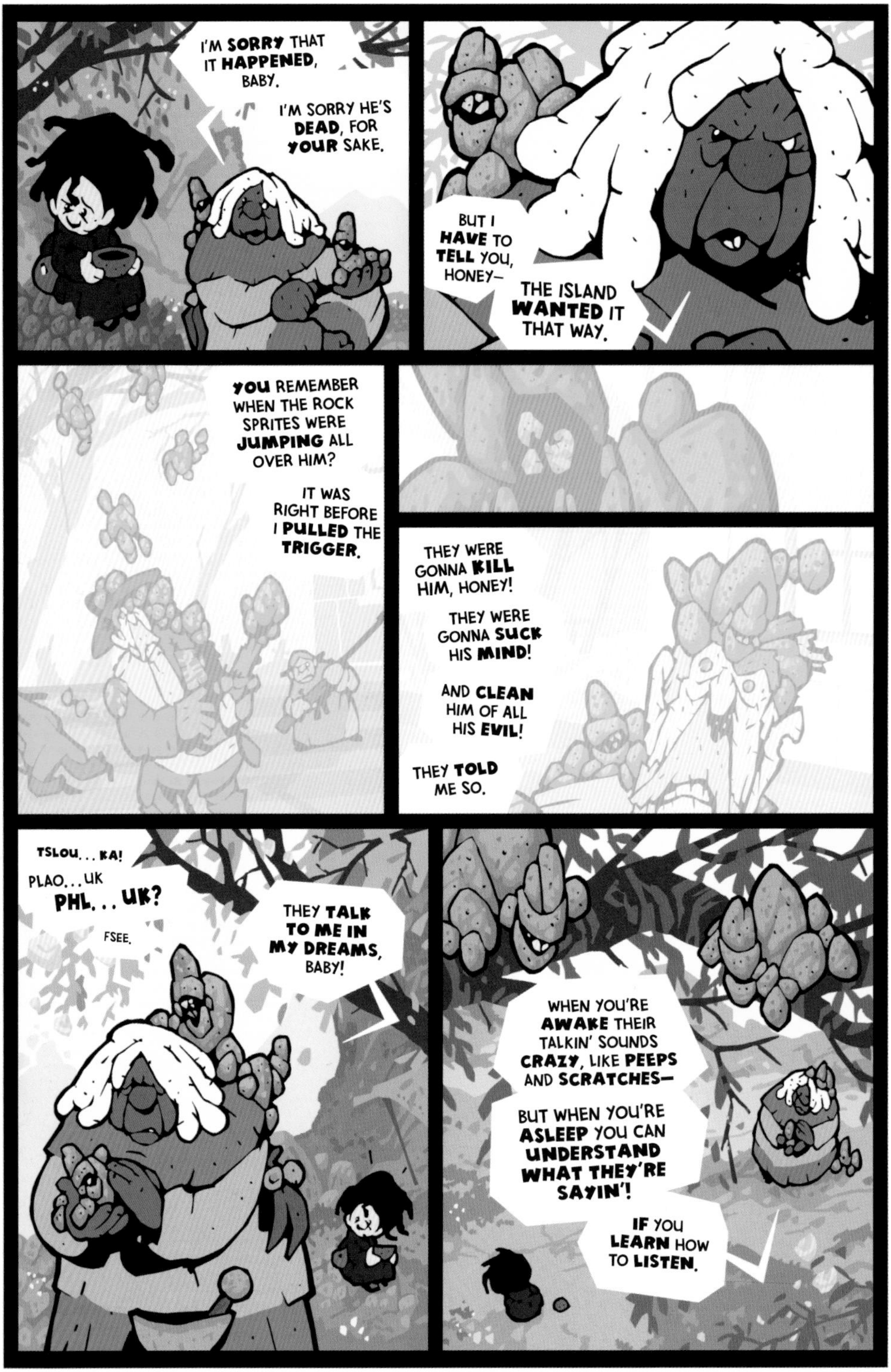
I'M SORRY THAT IT HAPPENED, BABY.
I'M SORRY HE'S DEAD, FOR YOUR SAKE.
BUT I HAVE TO TELL YOU, HONEY—
THE ISLAND WANTED IT THAT WAY.
YOU REMEMBER WHEN THE ROCK SPRITES WERE JUMPING ALL OVER HIM?
IT WAS RIGHT BEFORE I PULLED THE TRIGGER.
THEY WERE GONNA KILL HIM, HONEY!
THEY WERE GONNA SUCK HIS MIND!
AND CLEAN HIM OF ALL HIS EVIL!
THEY TOLD ME SO.
TSLOU...KA!
PLAO...UK
PHL...UK?
FSEE.
THEY TALK TO ME IN MY DREAMS, BABY!
WHEN YOU'RE AWAKE THEIR TALKIN' SOUNDS CRAZY, LIKE PEEPS AND SCRATCHES—
BUT WHEN YOU'RE ASLEEP YOU CAN UNDERSTAND WHAT THEY'RE SAYIN'!
IF YOU LEARN HOW TO LISTEN.

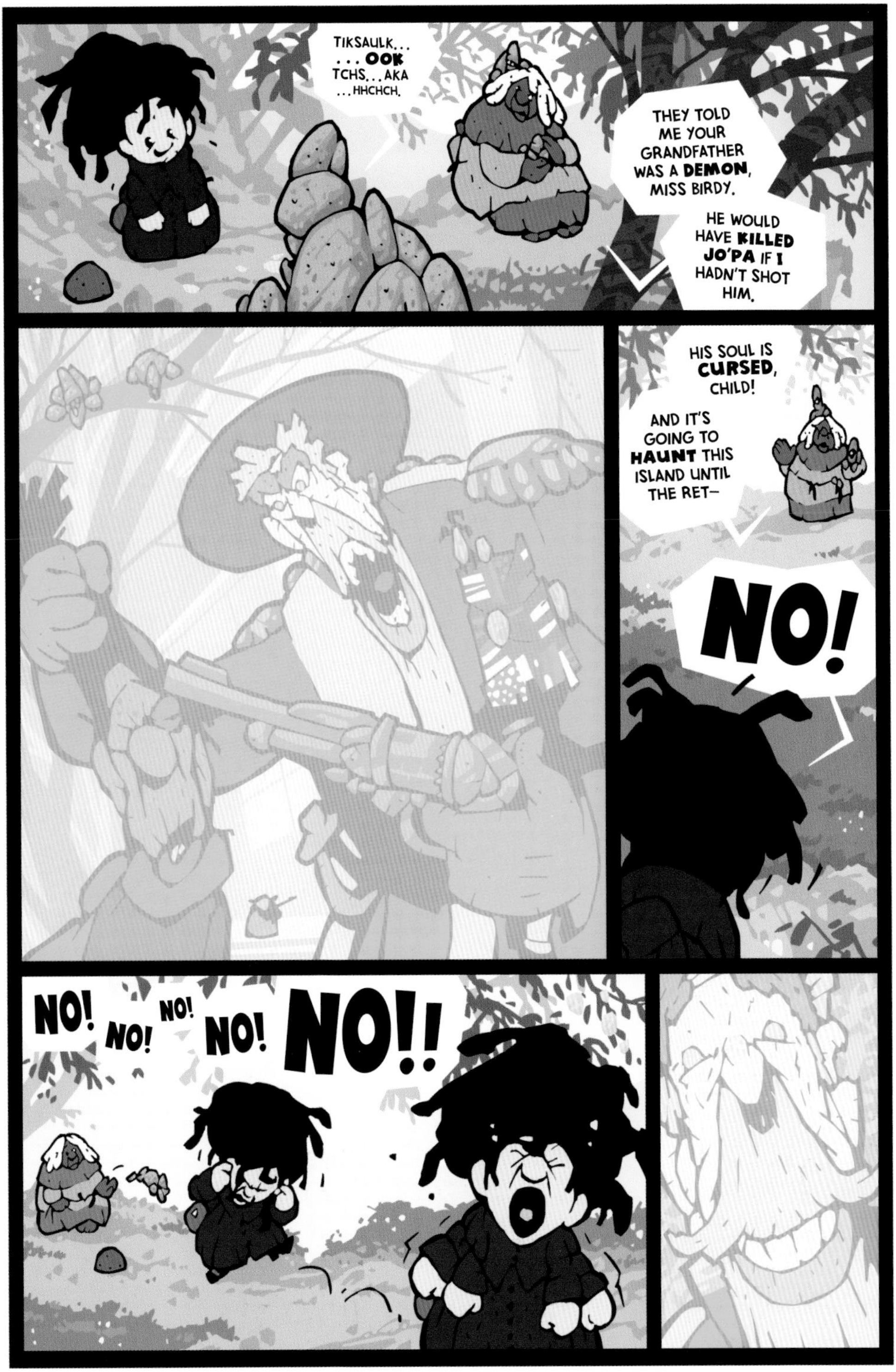
TIKSAULK... ...OOK TCHS...AKA ...HHCHCH.
THEY TOLD ME YOUR GRANDFATHER WAS A DEMON, MISS BIRDY.
HE WOULD HAVE KILLED JO'PA IF I HADN'T SHOT HIM.
HIS SOUL IS CURSED, CHILD!
AND IT'S GOING TO HAUNT THIS ISLAND UNTIL THE RET—
NO!
NO! NO! NO! NO! NO!!

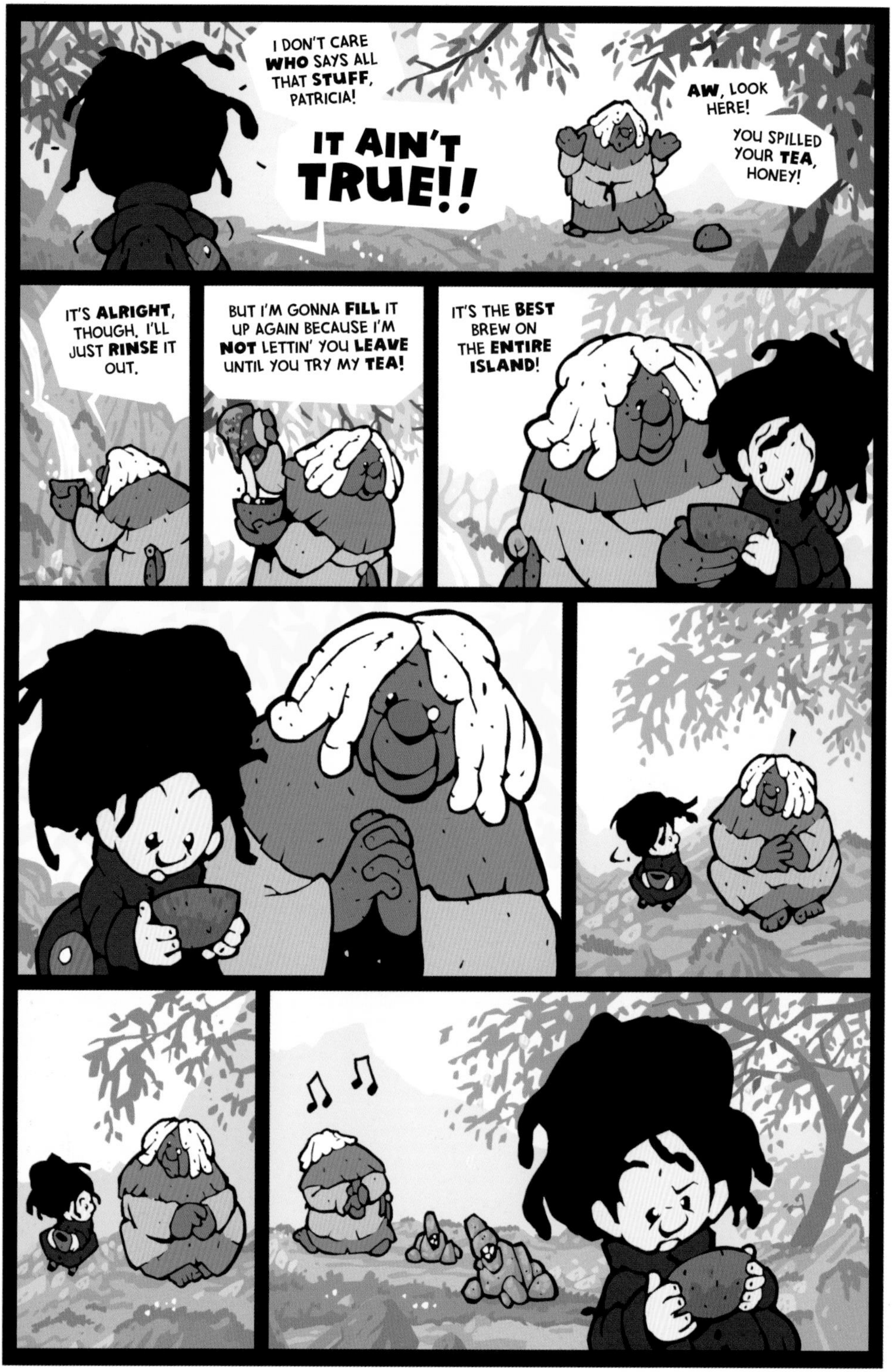
I DON'T CARE WHO SAYS ALL THAT STUFF, PATRICIA!
IT AIN'T TRUE!!
AW, LOOK HERE!
YOU SPILLED YOUR TEA, HONEY!
IT'S ALRIGHT, THOUGH. I'LL JUST RINSE IT OUT.
BUT I'M GONNA FILL IT UP AGAIN BECAUSE I'M NOT LETTIN' YOU LEAVE UNTIL YOU TRY MY TEA!
IT'S THE BEST BREW ON THE ENTIRE ISLAND!

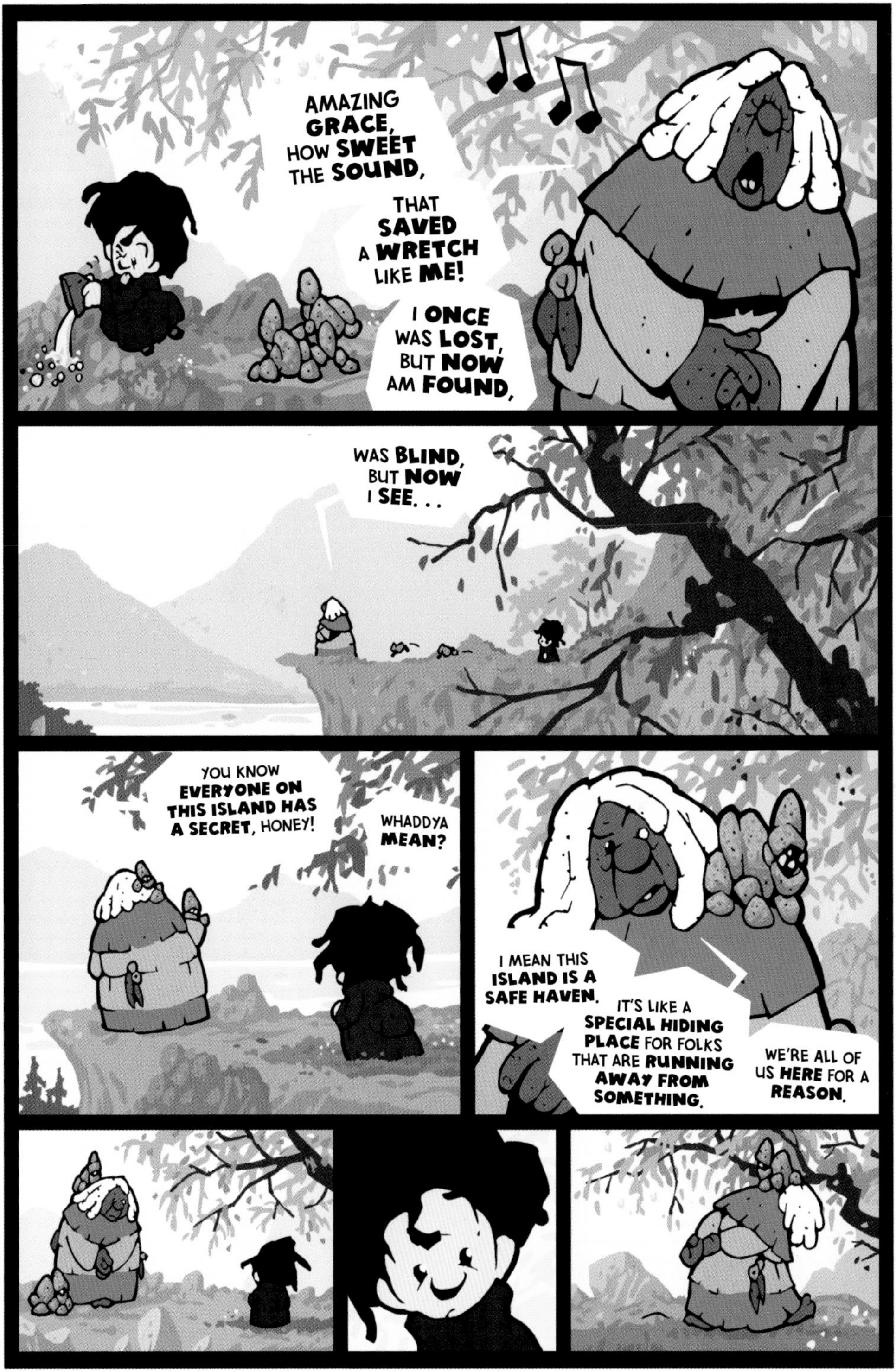
AMAZING GRACE, HOW SWEET THE SOUND,
THAT SAVED A WRETCH LIKE ME!
I ONCE WAS LOST, BUT NOW AM FOUND,
WAS BLIND, BUT NOW I SEE. . .
YOU KNOW EVERYONE ON THIS ISLAND HAS A SECRET, HONEY!
WHADDYA MEAN?
I MEAN THIS ISLAND IS A SAFE HAVEN.
IT'S LIKE A SPECIAL HIDING PLACE FOR FOLKS THAT ARE RUNNING AWAY FROM SOMETHING.
WE'RE ALL OF US HERE FOR A REASON.

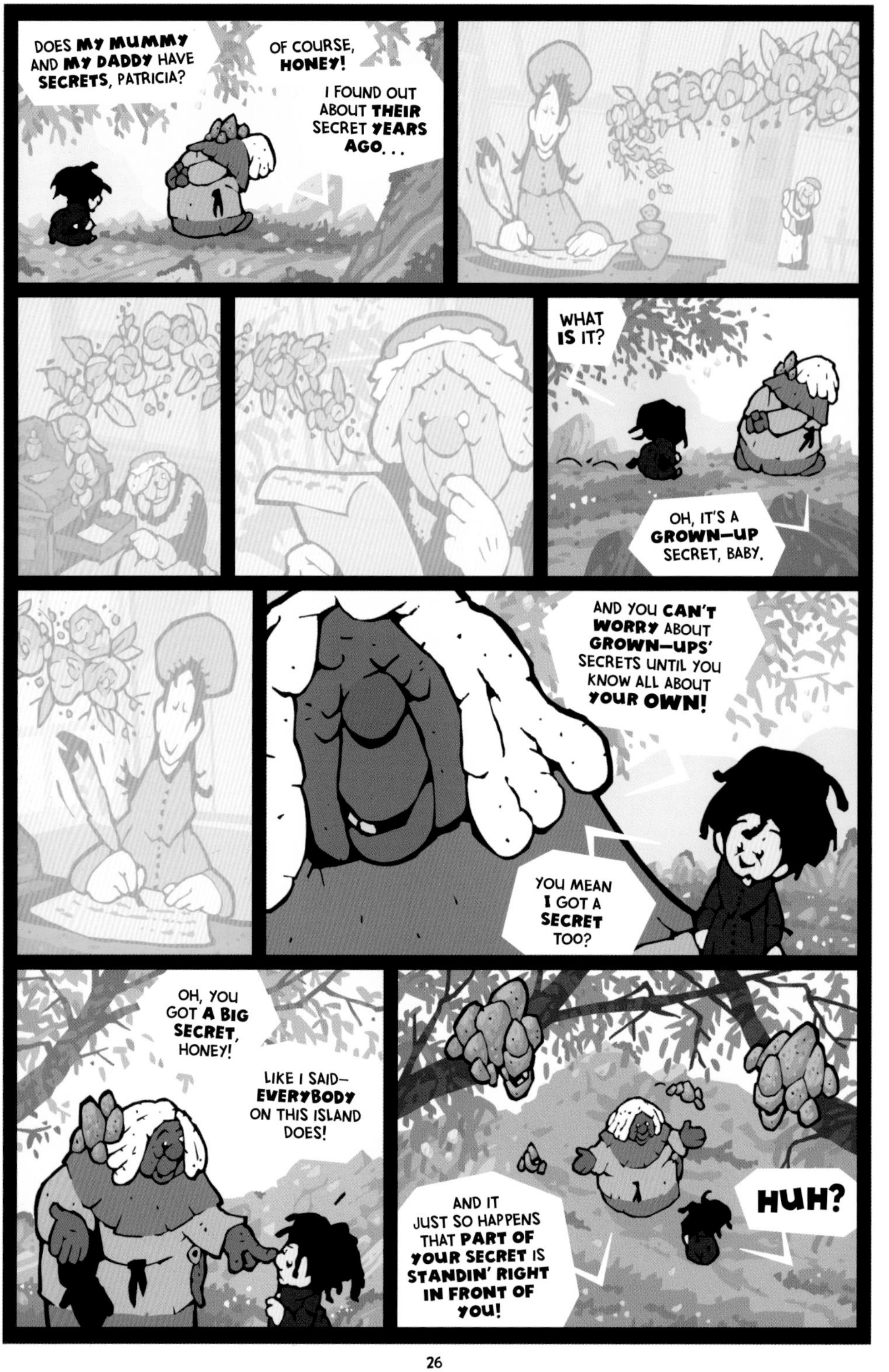
DOES MY MUMMY AND MY DADDY HAVE SECRETS, PATRICIA?
OF COURSE, HONEY!
I FOUND OUT ABOUT THEIR SECRET YEARS AGO. . .
WHAT IS IT?
OH, IT'S A GROWN-UP SECRET, BABY.
AND YOU CAN'T WORRY ABOUT GROWN-UPS' SECRETS UNTIL YOU KNOW ALL ABOUT YOUR OWN!
YOU MEAN I GOT A SECRET TOO?
OH, YOU GOT A BIG SECRET, HONEY!
LIKE I SAID— EVERYBODY ON THIS ISLAND DOES!
AND IT JUST SO HAPPENS THAT PART OF YOUR SECRET IS STANDIN' RIGHT IN FRONT OF YOU!
HUH?

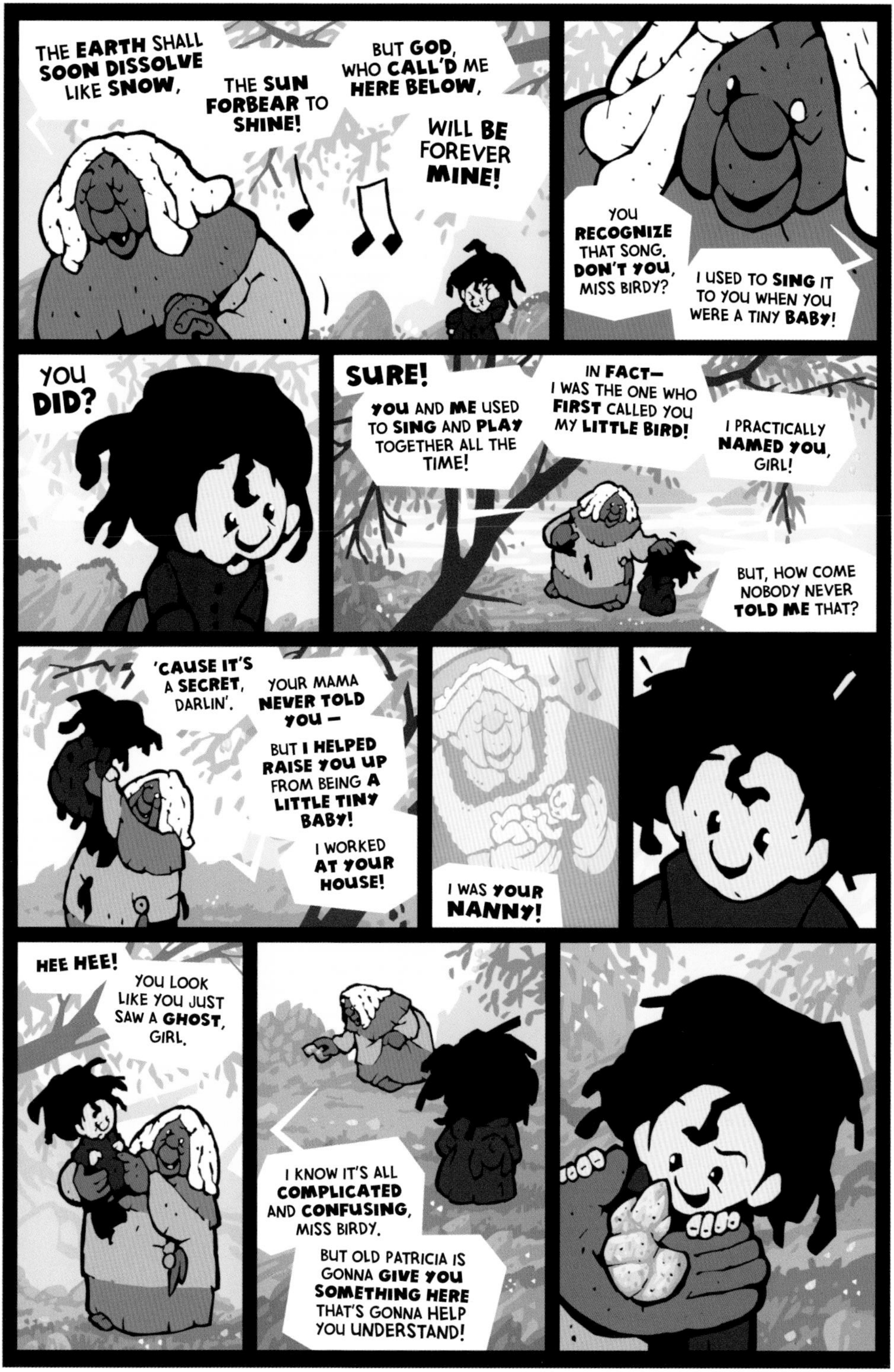
THE EARTH SHALL SOON DISSOLVE LIKE SNOW,
THE SUN FORBEAR TO SHINE!
BUT GOD, WHO CALL'D ME HERE BELOW,
WILL BE FOREVER MINE!
YOU RECOGNIZE THAT SONG, DON'T YOU, MISS BIRDY?
I USED TO SING IT TO YOU WHEN YOU WERE A TINY BABY!
YOU DID?
SURE!
YOU AND ME USED TO SING AND PLAY TOGETHER ALL THE TIME!
IN FACT— I WAS THE ONE WHO FIRST CALLED YOU MY LITTLE BIRD!
I PRACTICALLY NAMED YOU, GIRL!
BUT, HOW COME NOBODY NEVER TOLD ME THAT?
'CAUSE IT'S A SECRET, DARLIN'.
YOUR MAMA NEVER TOLD YOU —
BUT I HELPED RAISE YOU UP FROM BEING A LITTLE TINY BABY!
I WORKED AT YOUR HOUSE!
I WAS YOUR NANNY!
HEE HEE!
YOU LOOK LIKE YOU JUST SAW A GHOST, GIRL.
I KNOW IT'S ALL COMPLICATED AND CONFUSING, MISS BIRDY.
BUT OLD PATRICIA IS GONNA GIVE YOU SOMETHING HERE THAT'S GONNA HELP YOU UNDERSTAND!

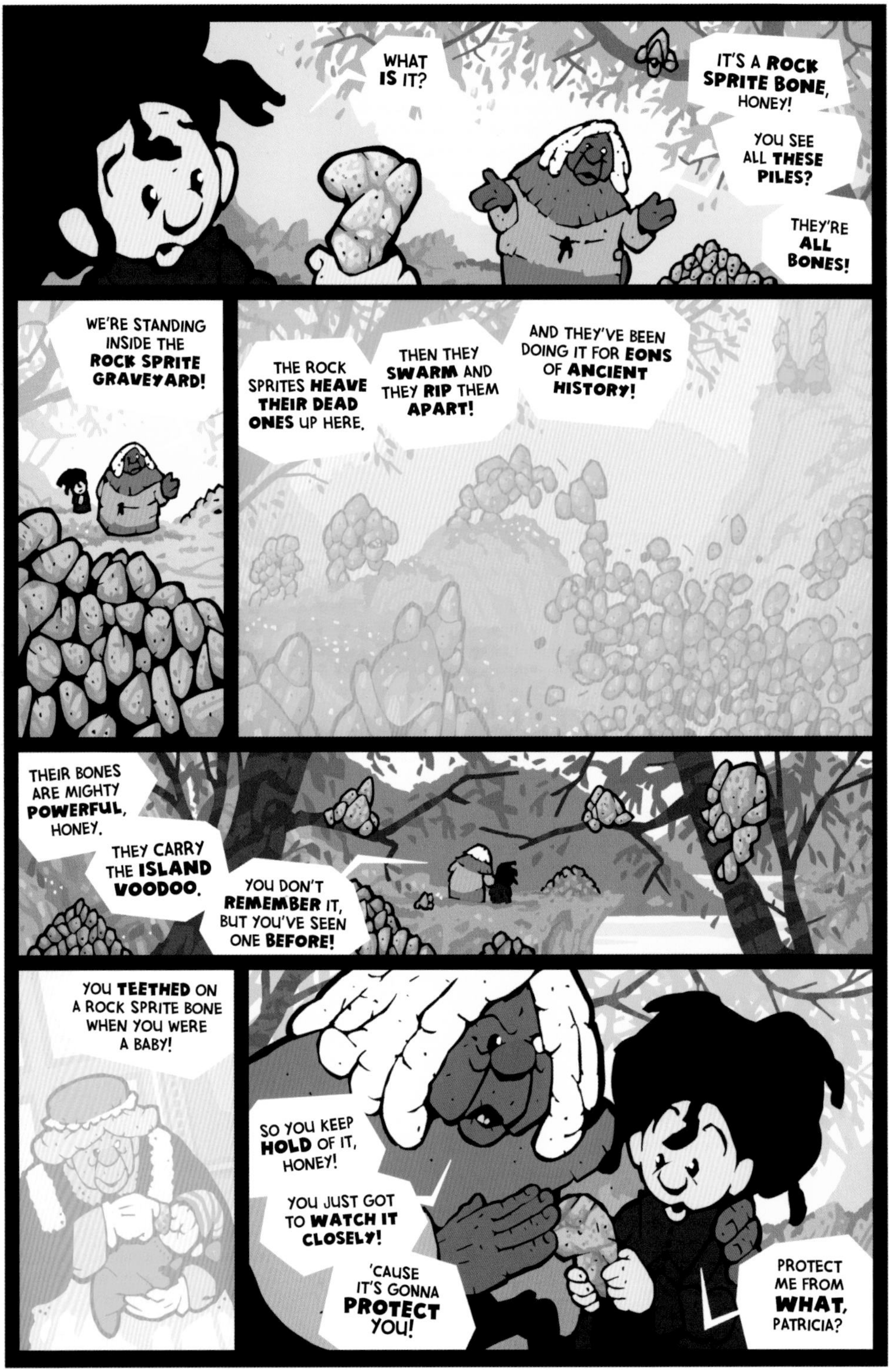
WHAT IS IT?
IT'S A ROCK SPRITE BONE, HONEY!
YOU SEE ALL THESE PILES?
THEY'RE ALL BONES!
WE'RE STANDING INSIDE THE ROCK SPRITE GRAVEYARD!
THE ROCK SPRITES HEAVE THEIR DEAD ONES UP HERE.
THEN THEY SWARM AND THEY RIP THEM APART!
AND THEY'VE BEEN DOING IT FOR EONS OF ANCIENT HISTORY!
THEIR BONES ARE MIGHTY POWERFUL, HONEY.
THEY CARRY THE ISLAND VOODOO.
YOU DON'T REMEMBER IT, BUT YOU'VE SEEN ONE BEFORE!
YOU TEETHED ON A ROCK SPRITE BONE WHEN YOU WERE A BABY!
SO YOU KEEP HOLD OF IT, HONEY!
YOU JUST GOT TO WATCH IT CLOSELY!
'CAUSE IT'S GONNA PROTECT YOU!
PROTECT ME FROM WHAT, PATRICIA?

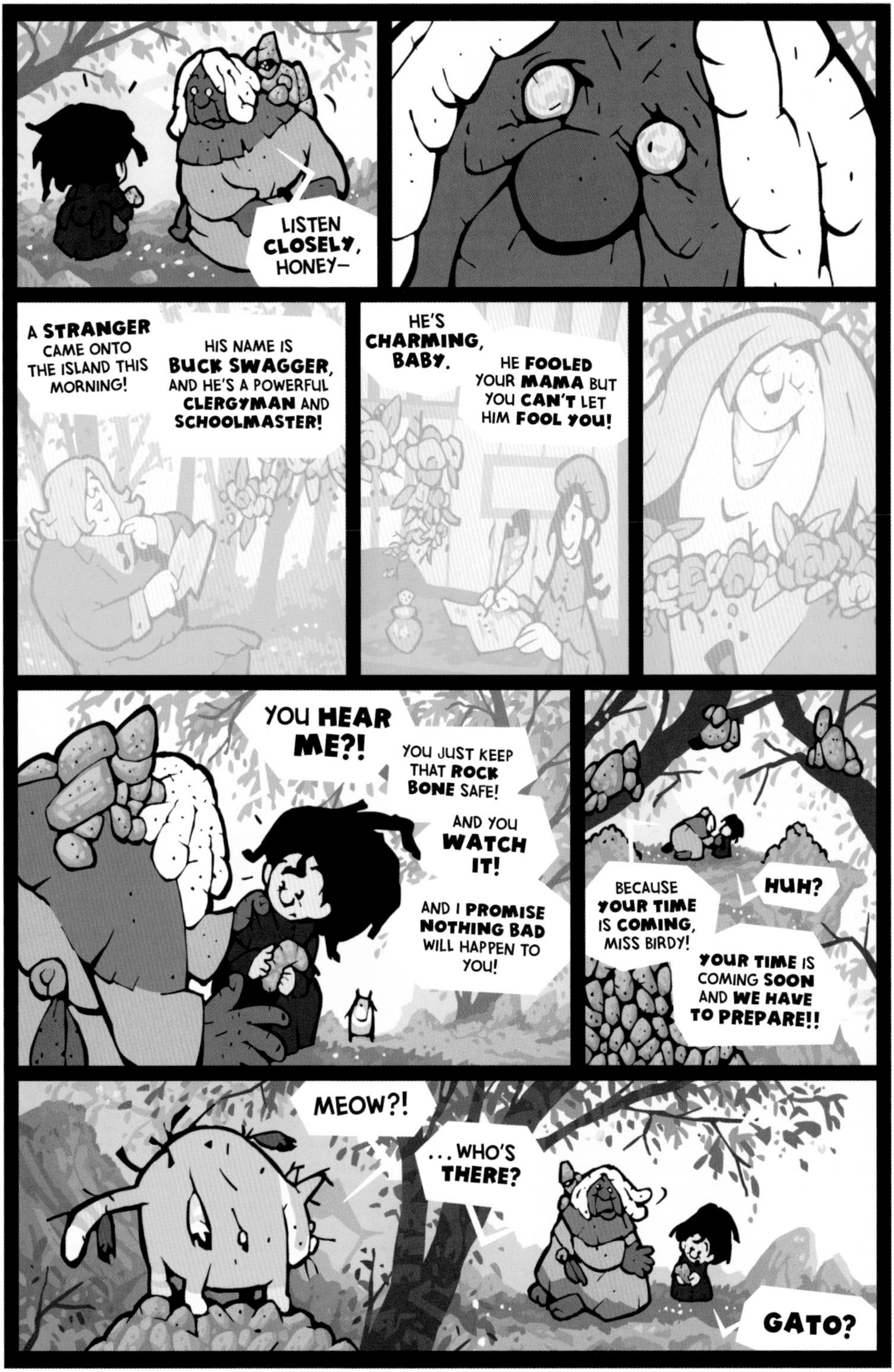
LISTEN CLOSELY, HONEY—
A STRANGER CAME ONTO THE ISLAND THIS MORNING!
HIS NAME IS BUCK SWAGGER, AND HE'S A POWERFUL CLERGYMAN AND SCHOOLMASTER!
HE'S CHARMING, BABY.
HE FOOLED YOUR MAMA BUT YOU CAN'T LET HIM FOOL YOU!
YOU HEAR ME?!
YOU JUST KEEP THAT ROCK BONE SAFE!
AND YOU WATCH IT!
AND I PROMISE NOTHING BAD WILL HAPPEN TO YOU!
BECAUSE YOUR TIME IS COMING, MISS BIRDY!
HUH?
YOUR TIME IS COMING SOON AND WE HAVE TO PREPARE!!
MEOW?!
...WHO'S THERE?
GATO?

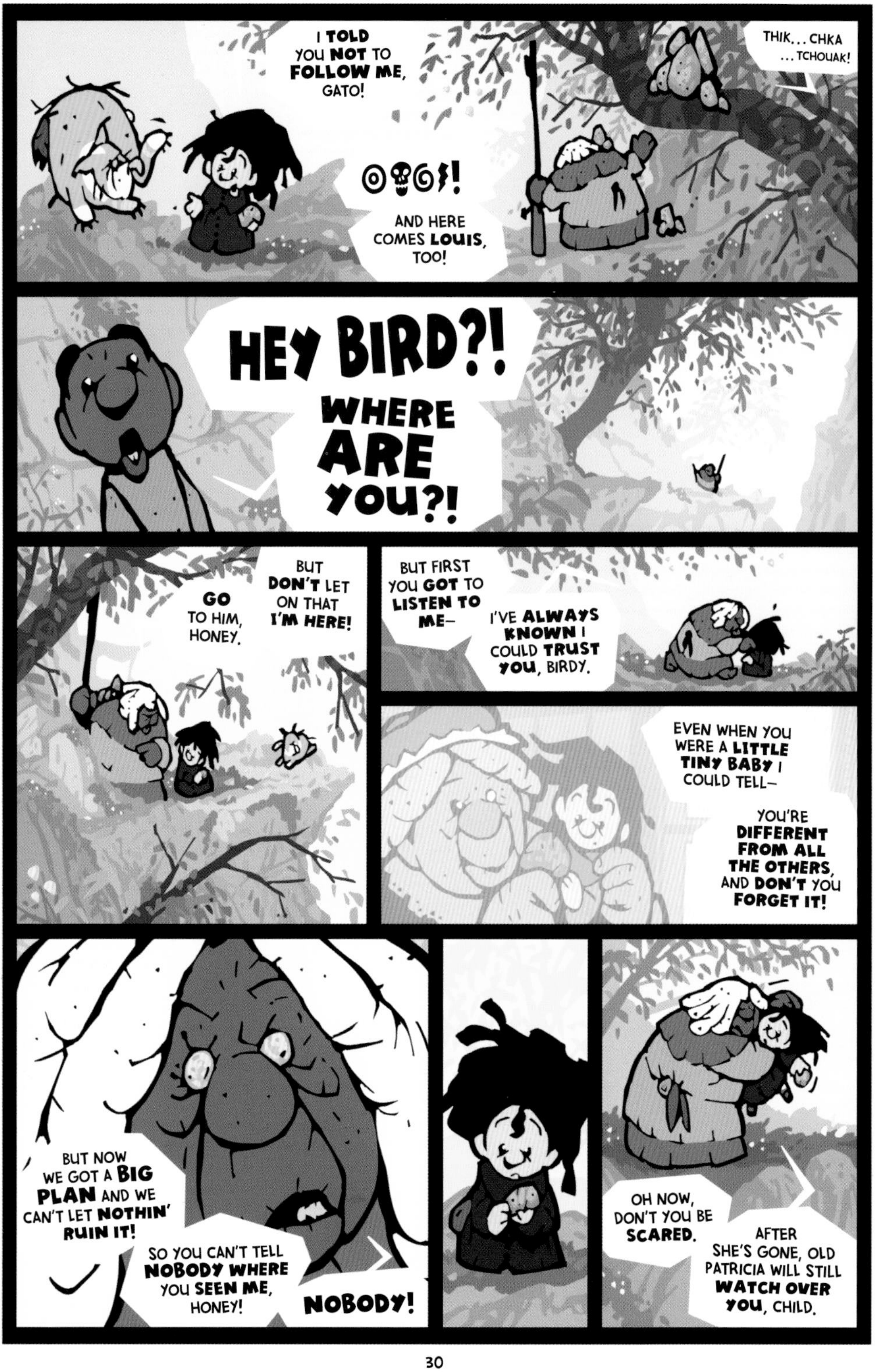
I TOLD YOU NOT TO FOLLOW ME, GATO!
THIK... CHKA ...TCHOUAK!
AND HERE COMES LOUIS, TOO!
HEY BIRD?!
WHERE ARE YOU?!
GO TO HIM, HONEY.
BUT DON'T LET ON THAT I'M HERE!
BUT FIRST YOU GOT TO LISTEN TO ME—
I'VE ALWAYS KNOWN I COULD TRUST YOU, BIRDY.
EVEN WHEN YOU WERE A LITTLE TINY BABY I COULD TELL—
YOU'RE DIFFERENT FROM ALL THE OTHERS, AND DON'T YOU FORGET IT!
BUT NOW WE GOT A BIG PLAN AND WE CAN'T LET NOTHIN' RUIN IT!
SO YOU CAN'T TELL NOBODY WHERE YOU SEEN ME, HONEY!
NOBODY!
OH NOW, DON'T YOU BE SCARED.
AFTER SHE'S GONE, OLD PATRICIA WILL STILL WATCH OVER YOU, CHILD.

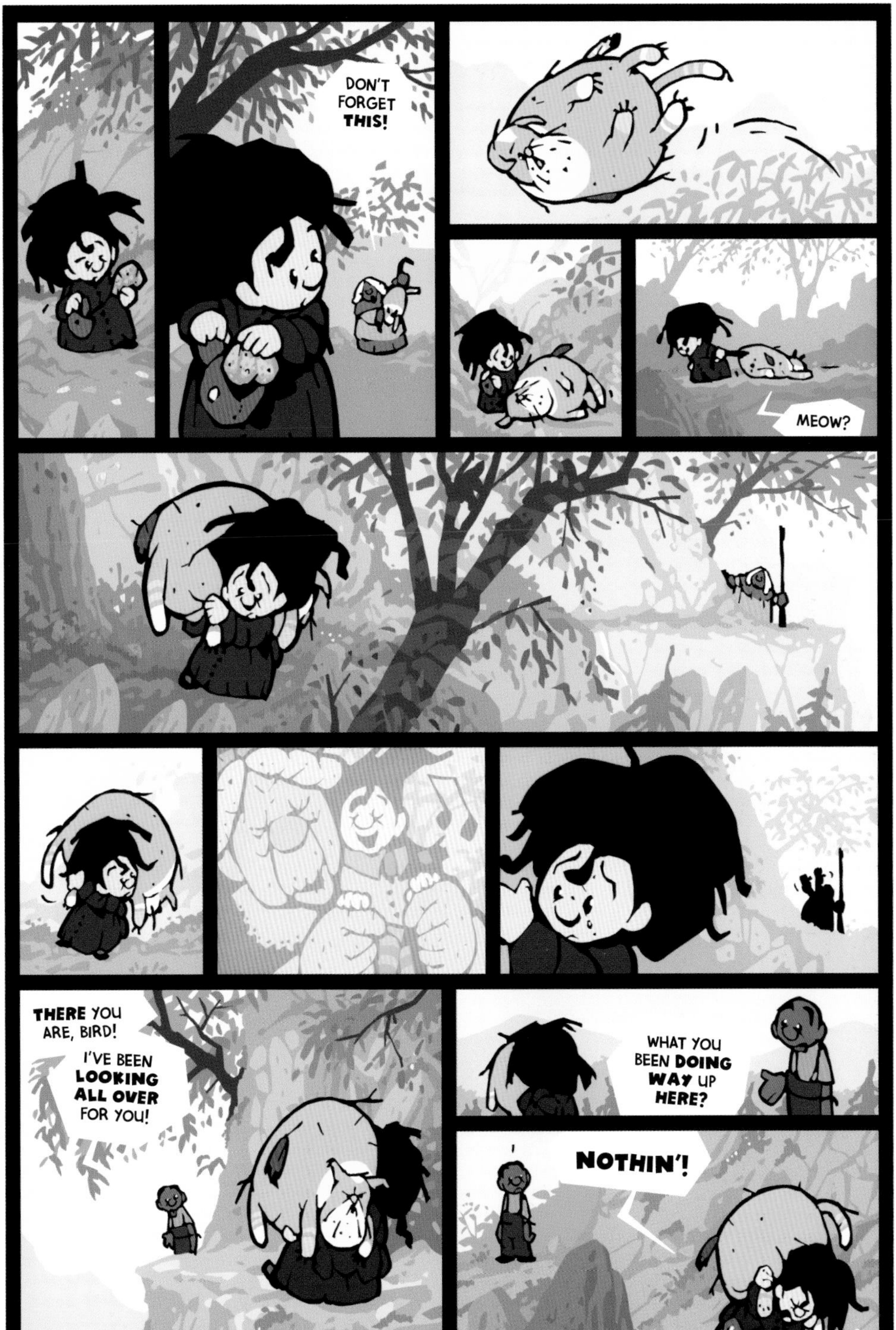
DON'T FORGET THIS!
MEOW?
THERE YOU ARE, BIRD!
I'VE BEEN LOOKING ALL OVER FOR YOU!
WHAT YOU BEEN DOING WAY UP HERE?
NOTHIN'!

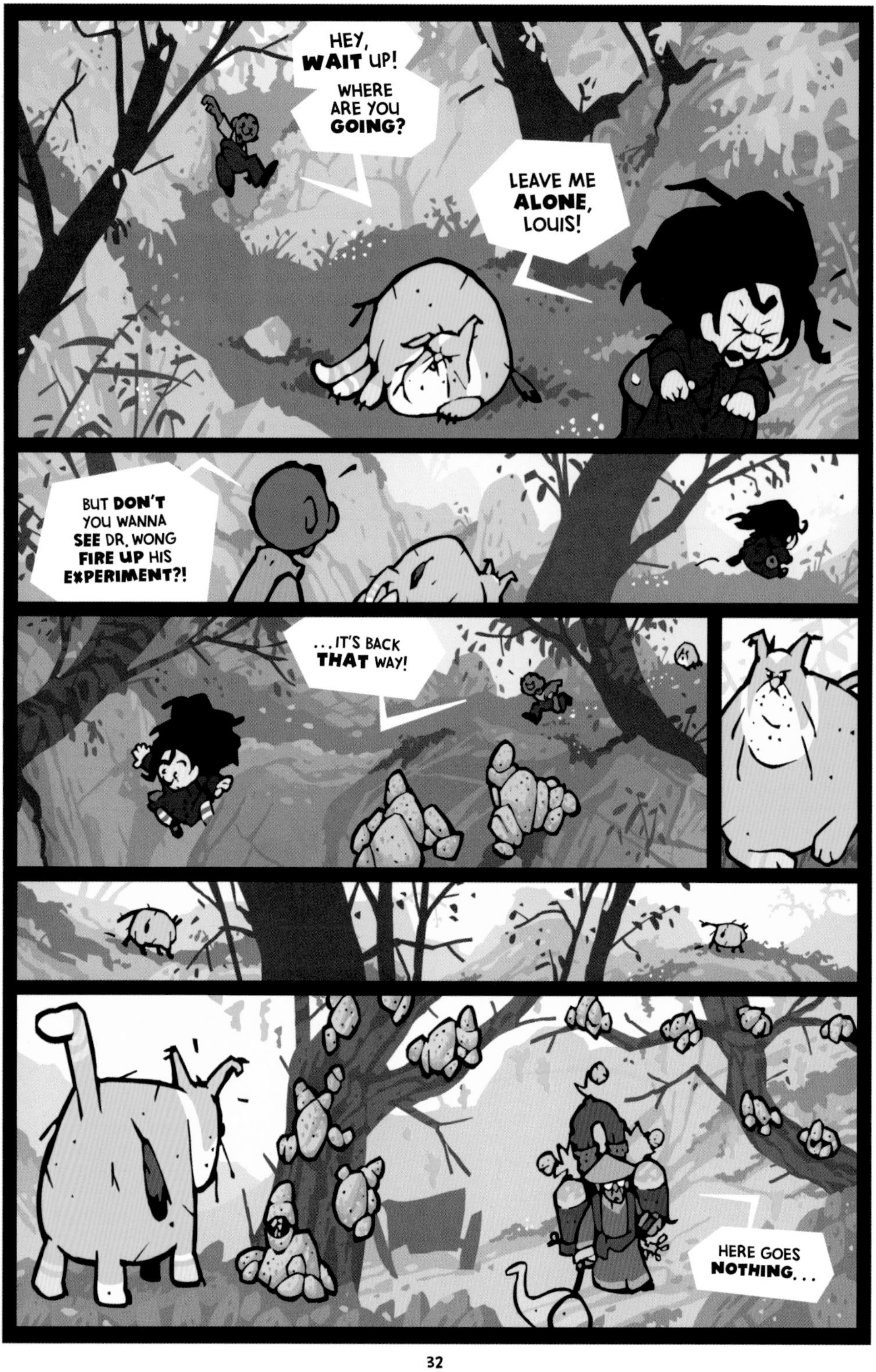
HEY, WAIT UP!
WHERE ARE YOU GOING?
LEAVE ME ALONE, LOUIS!
BUT DON'T YOU WANNA SEE DR. WONG FIRE UP HIS EXPERIMENT?!
...IT'S BACK THAT WAY!
HERE GOES NOTHING...

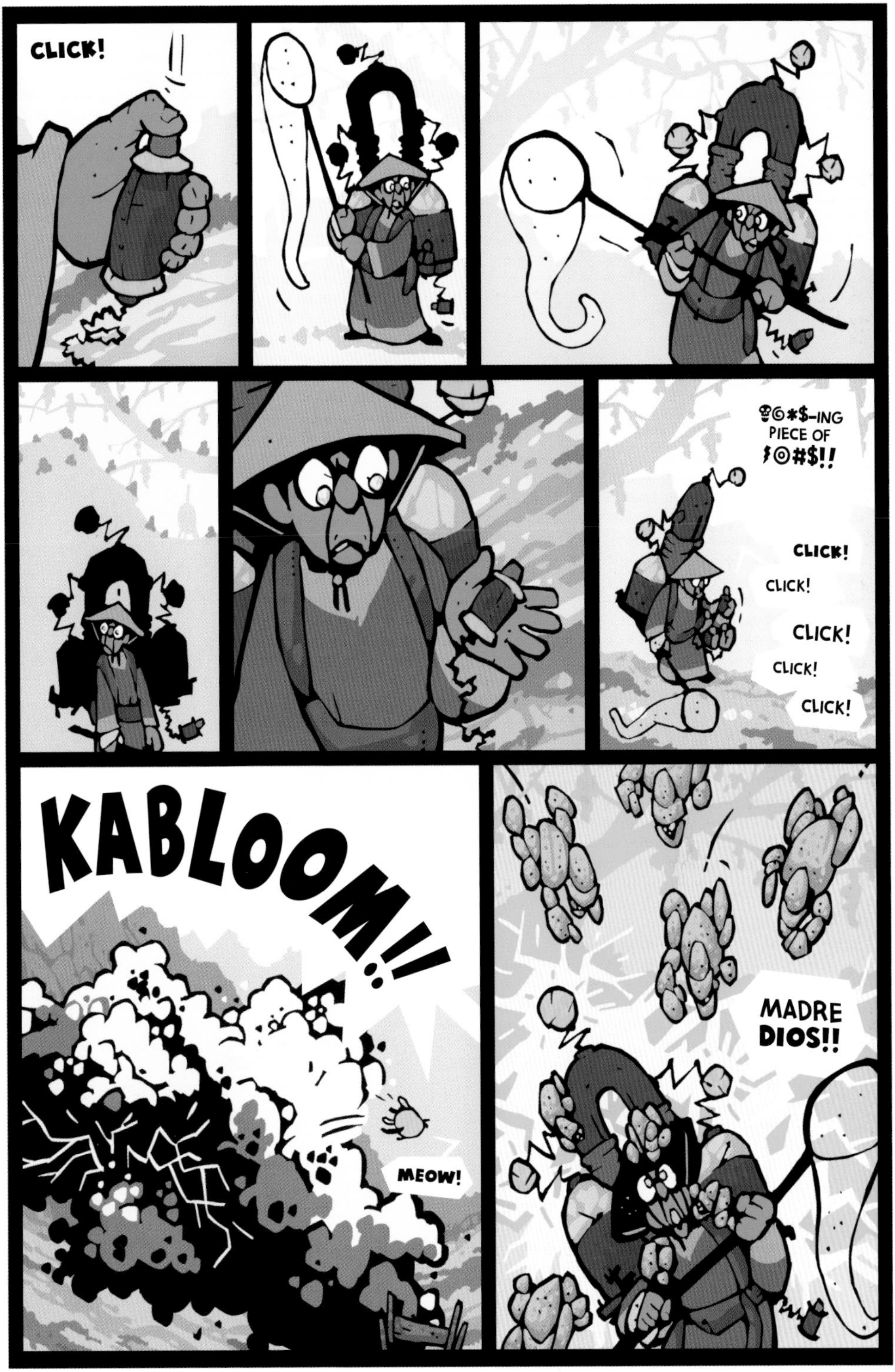
CLICK!
☠©*$-ING
PIECE OF
ϟ◎#$!!
CLICK!
CLICK!
CLICK!
CLICK!
CLICK!
KABLOOM!!
MEOW!
MADRE
DIOS!!

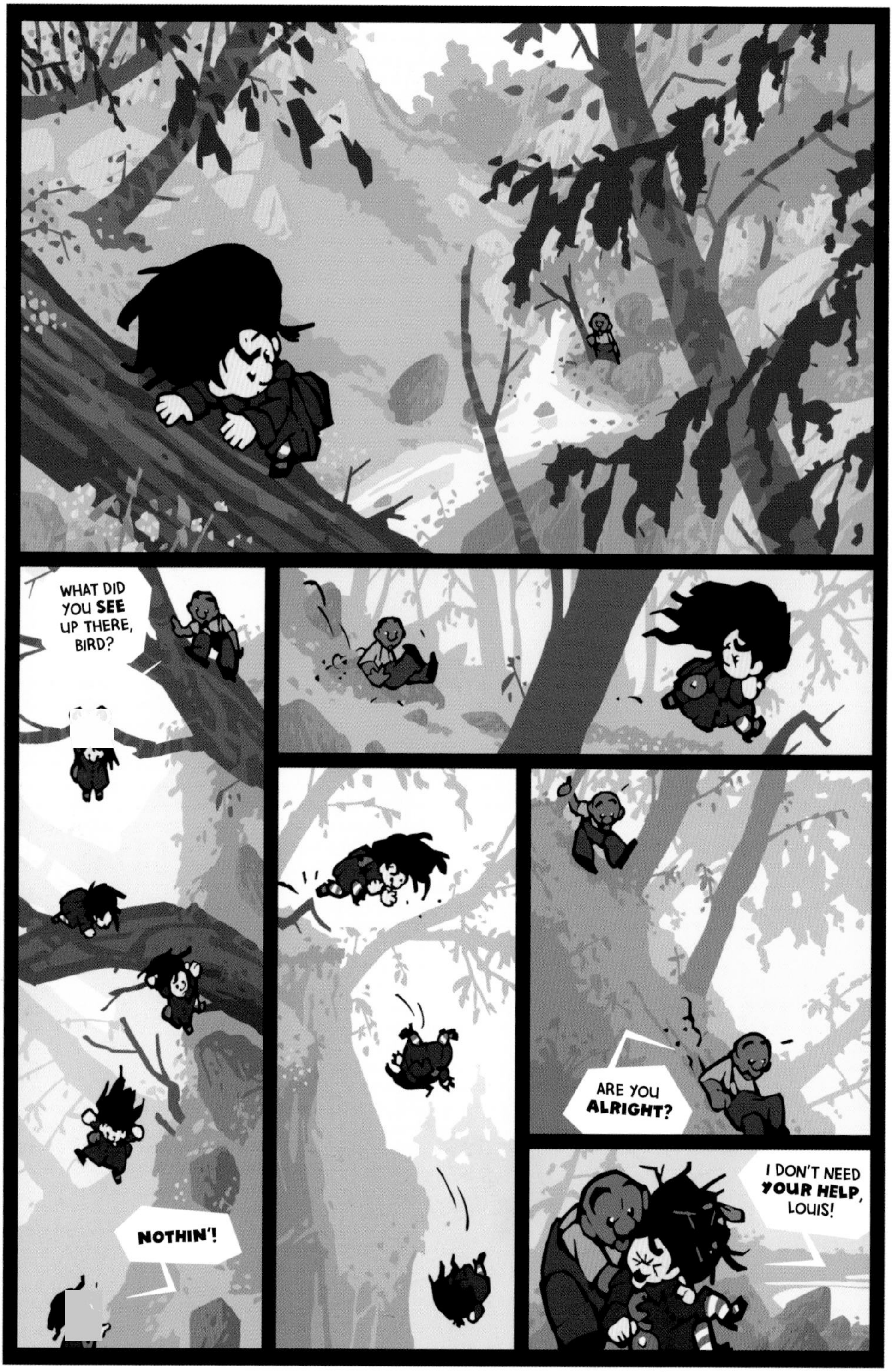
WHAT DID YOU **SEE** UP THERE, BIRD?
NOTHIN'!
ARE YOU **ALRIGHT?**
I DON'T NEED **YOUR HELP**, LOUIS!

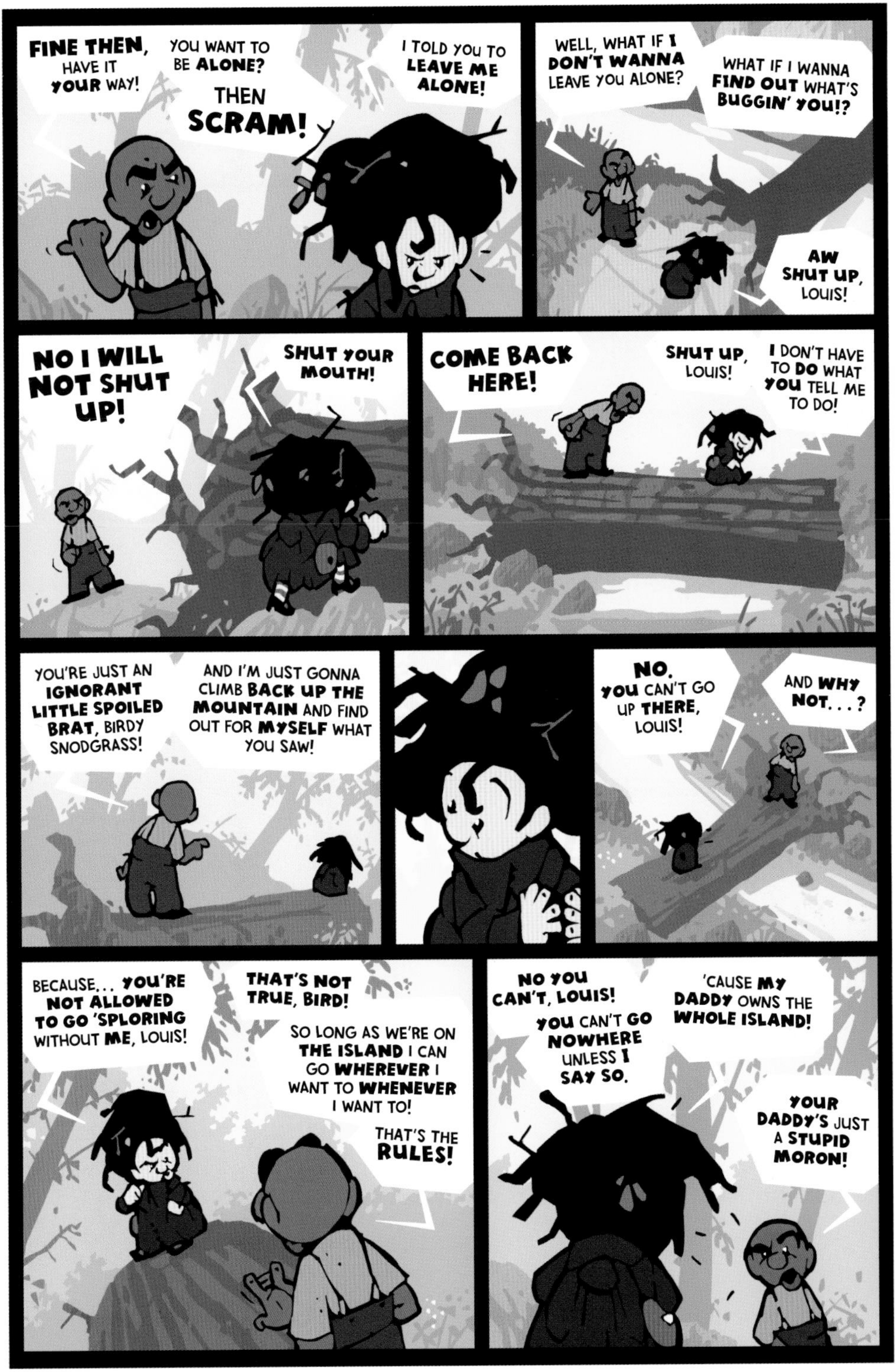
FINE THEN, HAVE IT YOUR WAY!
YOU WANT TO BE ALONE?
THEN SCRAM!
I TOLD YOU TO LEAVE ME ALONE!
WELL, WHAT IF I DON'T WANNA LEAVE YOU ALONE?
WHAT IF I WANNA FIND OUT WHAT'S BUGGIN' YOU!?
AW SHUT UP, LOUIS!
NO I WILL NOT SHUT UP!
SHUT YOUR MOUTH!
COME BACK HERE!
SHUT UP, LOUIS!
I DON'T HAVE TO DO WHAT YOU TELL ME TO DO!
YOU'RE JUST AN IGNORANT LITTLE SPOILED BRAT, BIRDY SNODGRASS!
AND I'M JUST GONNA CLIMB BACK UP THE MOUNTAIN AND FIND OUT FOR MYSELF WHAT YOU SAW!
NO. YOU CAN'T GO UP THERE, LOUIS!
AND WHY NOT. . . ?
BECAUSE. . . YOU'RE NOT ALLOWED TO GO 'SPLORING WITHOUT ME, LOUIS!
THAT'S NOT TRUE, BIRD!
SO LONG AS WE'RE ON THE ISLAND I CAN GO WHEREVER I WANT TO WHENEVER I WANT TO!
THAT'S THE RULES!
NO YOU CAN'T, LOUIS!
YOU CAN'T GO NOWHERE UNLESS I SAY SO.
'CAUSE MY DADDY OWNS THE WHOLE ISLAND!
YOUR DADDY'S JUST A STUPID MORON!

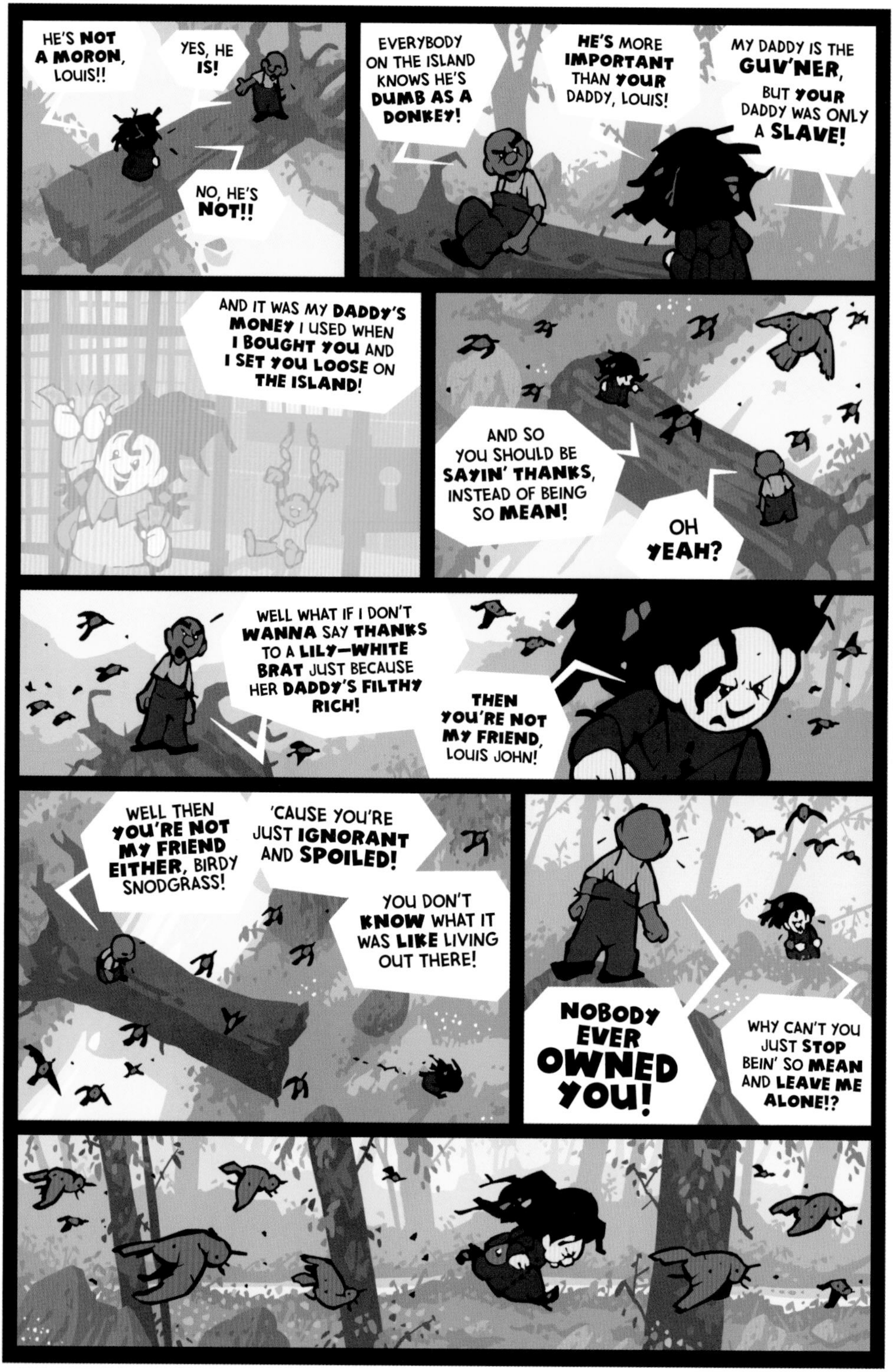
HE'S NOT A MORON, LOUIS!!
YES, HE IS!
NO, HE'S NOT!!
EVERYBODY ON THE ISLAND KNOWS HE'S DUMB AS A DONKEY!
HE'S MORE IMPORTANT THAN YOUR DADDY, LOUIS!
MY DADDY IS THE GUV'NER,
BUT YOUR DADDY WAS ONLY A SLAVE!
AND IT WAS MY DADDY'S MONEY I USED WHEN I BOUGHT YOU AND I SET YOU LOOSE ON THE ISLAND!
AND SO YOU SHOULD BE SAYIN' THANKS, INSTEAD OF BEING SO MEAN!
OH YEAH?
WELL WHAT IF I DON'T WANNA SAY THANKS TO A LILY-WHITE BRAT JUST BECAUSE HER DADDY'S FILTHY RICH!
THEN YOU'RE NOT MY FRIEND, LOUIS JOHN!
WELL THEN YOU'RE NOT MY FRIEND EITHER, BIRDY SNODGRASS!
'CAUSE YOU'RE JUST IGNORANT AND SPOILED!
YOU DON'T KNOW WHAT IT WAS LIKE LIVING OUT THERE!
NOBODY EVER OWNED YOU!
WHY CAN'T YOU JUST STOP BEIN' SO MEAN AND LEAVE ME ALONE!?

CHAPTER THREE
Holy %#$!*

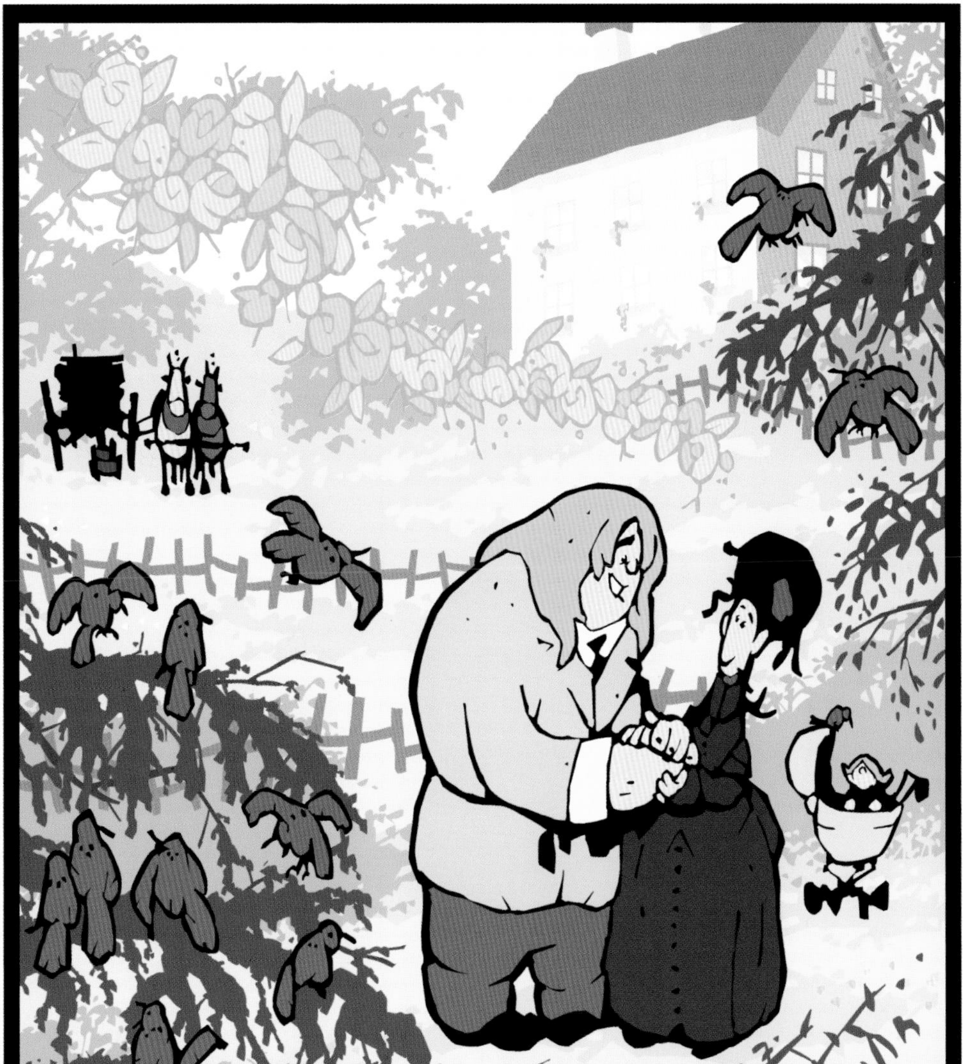

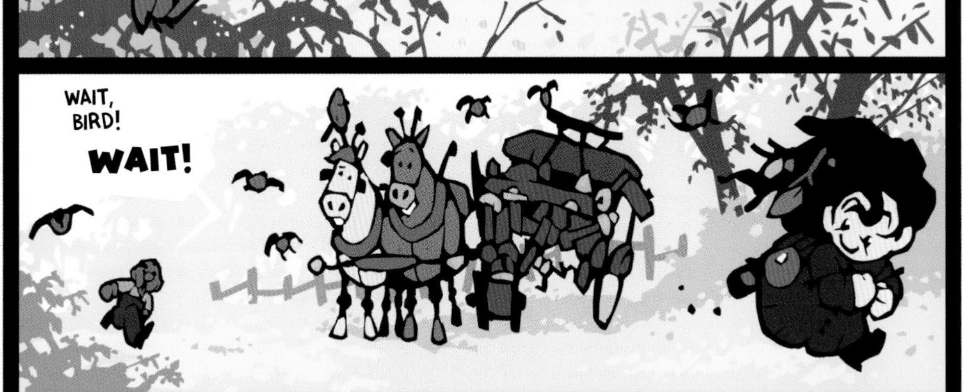
WAIT, BIRD!
WAIT!

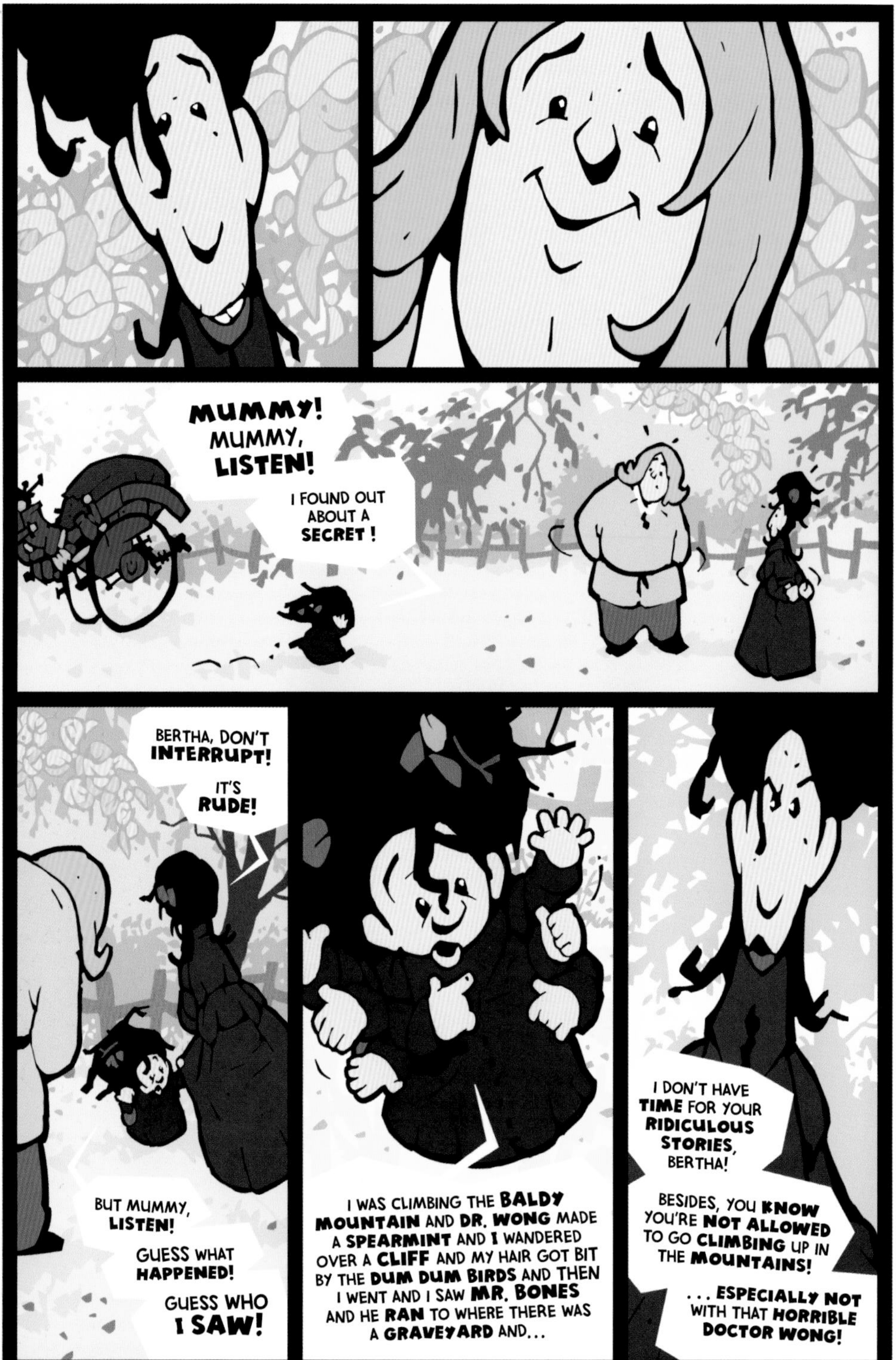
MUMMY! MUMMY, LISTEN!
I FOUND OUT ABOUT A SECRET !
BERTHA, DON'T INTERRUPT!
IT'S RUDE!
BUT MUMMY, LISTEN!
GUESS WHAT HAPPENED!
GUESS WHO I SAW!
I WAS CLIMBING THE BALDY MOUNTAIN AND DR. WONG MADE A SPEARMINT AND I WANDERED OVER A CLIFF AND MY HAIR GOT BIT BY THE DUM DUM BIRDS AND THEN I WENT AND I SAW MR. BONES AND HE RAN TO WHERE THERE WAS A GRAVEYARD AND...
I DON'T HAVE TIME FOR YOUR RIDICULOUS STORIES, BERTHA!
BESIDES, YOU KNOW YOU'RE NOT ALLOWED TO GO CLIMBING UP IN THE MOUNTAINS!
... ESPECIALLY NOT WITH THAT HORRIBLE DOCTOR WONG!

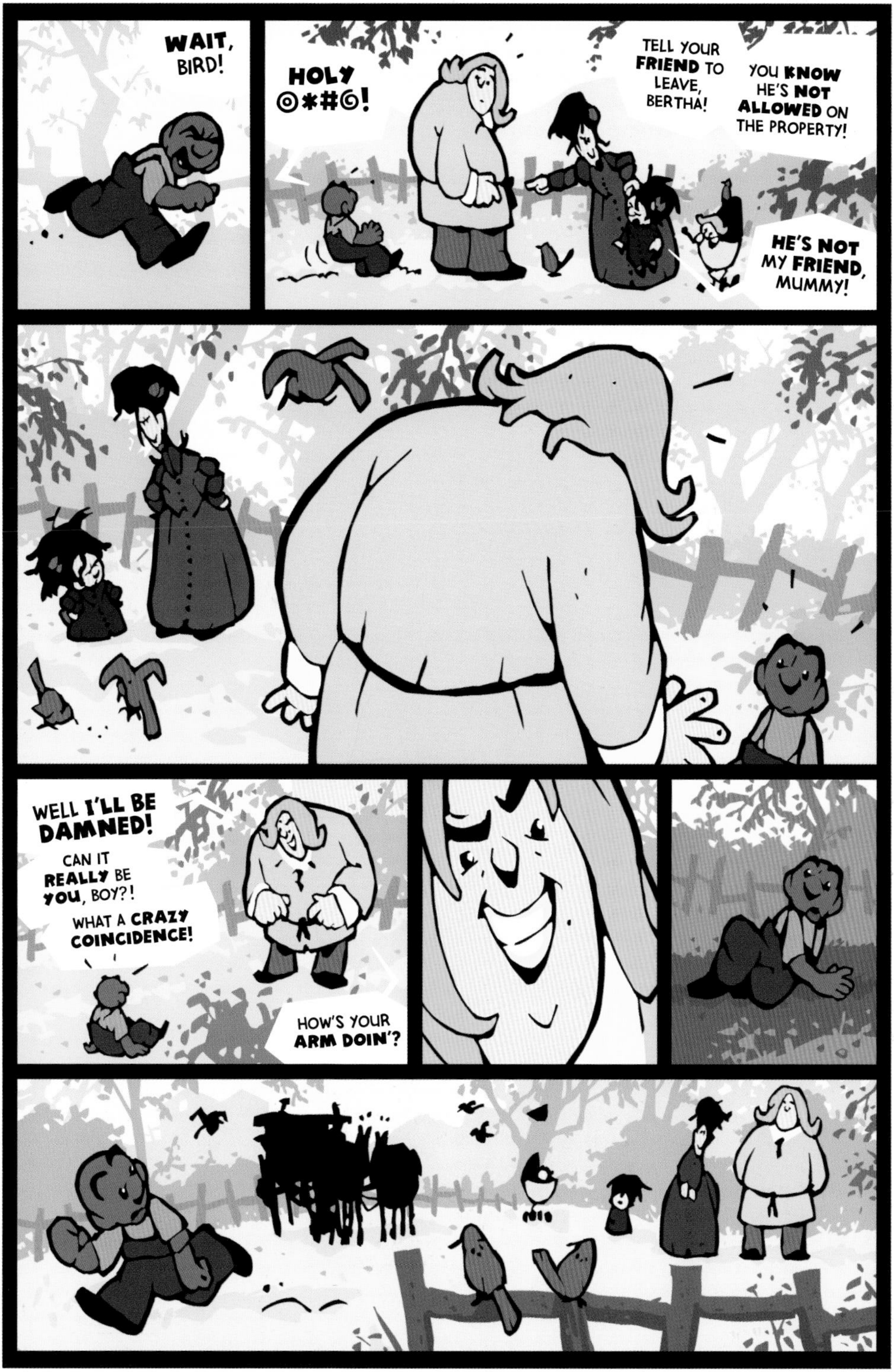
WAIT, BIRD!
HOLY ◎✱#◎!
TELL YOUR FRIEND TO LEAVE, BERTHA!
YOU KNOW HE'S NOT ALLOWED ON THE PROPERTY!
HE'S NOT MY FRIEND, MUMMY!
WELL I'LL BE DAMNED!
CAN IT REALLY BE YOU, BOY?!
WHAT A CRAZY COINCIDENCE!
HOW'S YOUR ARM DOIN'?

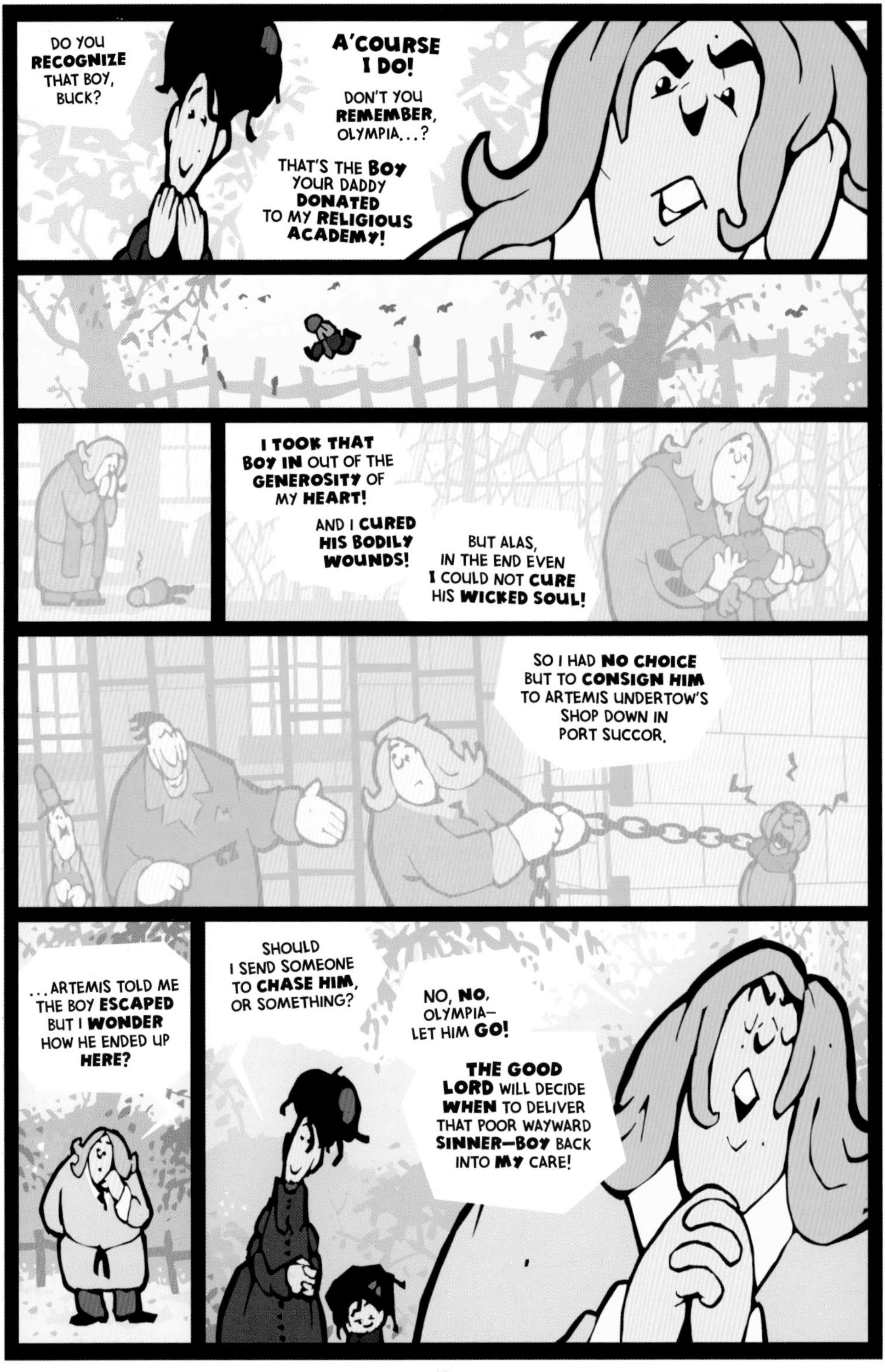
DO YOU RECOGNIZE THAT BOY, BUCK?
A'COURSE I DO!
DON'T YOU REMEMBER, OLYMPIA...?
THAT'S THE BOY YOUR DADDY DONATED TO MY RELIGIOUS ACADEMY!
I TOOK THAT BOY IN OUT OF THE GENEROSITY OF MY HEART!
AND I CURED HIS BODILY WOUNDS!
BUT ALAS, IN THE END EVEN I COULD NOT CURE HIS WICKED SOUL!
SO I HAD NO CHOICE BUT TO CONSIGN HIM TO ARTEMIS UNDERTOW'S SHOP DOWN IN PORT SUCCOR.
...ARTEMIS TOLD ME THE BOY ESCAPED BUT I WONDER HOW HE ENDED UP HERE?
SHOULD I SEND SOMEONE TO CHASE HIM, OR SOMETHING?
NO, NO, OLYMPIA— LET HIM GO!
THE GOOD LORD WILL DECIDE WHEN TO DELIVER THAT POOR WAYWARD SINNER—BOY BACK INTO MY CARE!

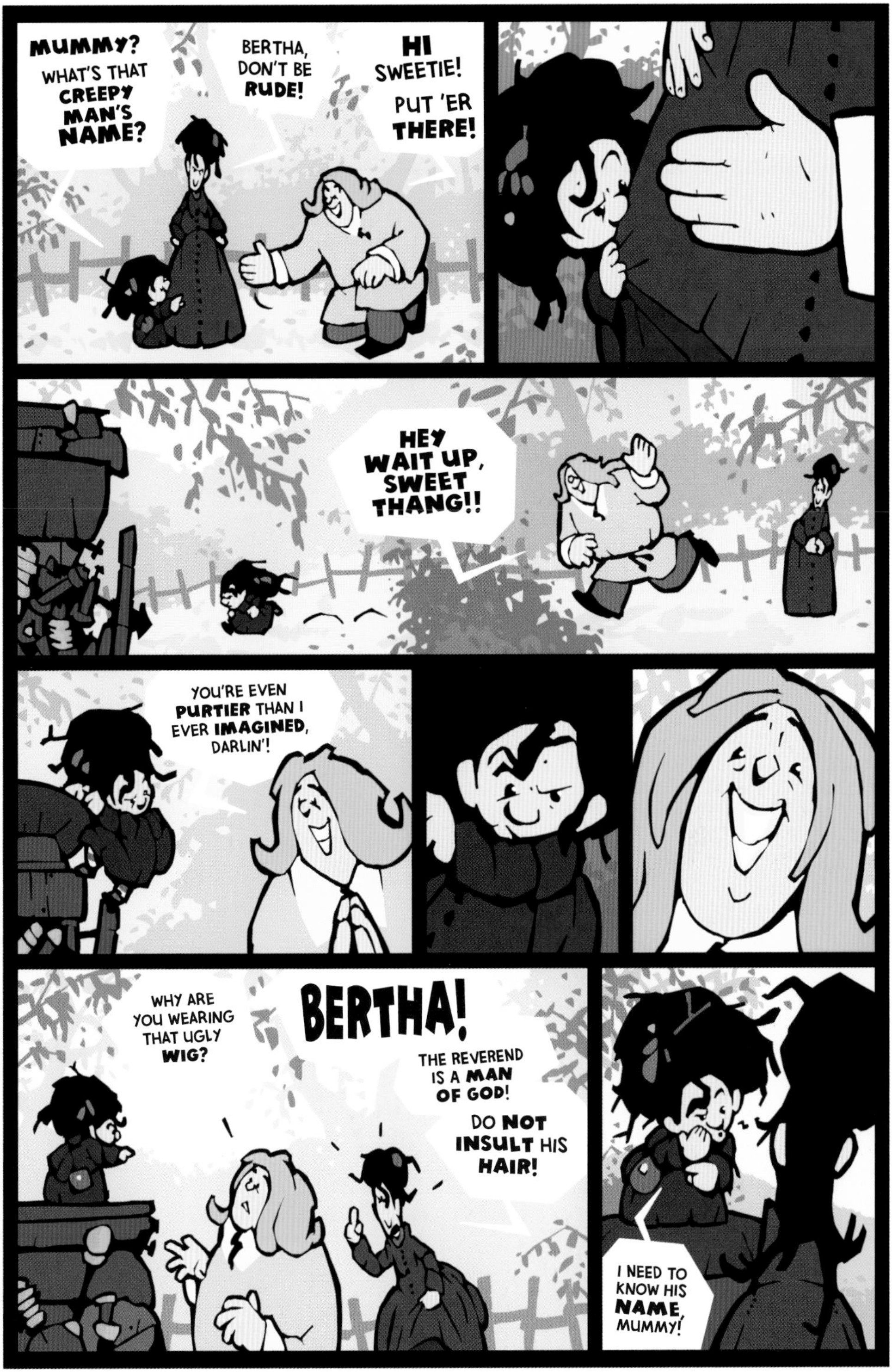
MUMMY? WHAT'S THAT CREEPY MAN'S NAME?
BERTHA, DON'T BE RUDE!
HI SWEETIE!
PUT 'ER THERE!
HEY WAIT UP, SWEET THANG!!
YOU'RE EVEN PURTIER THAN I EVER IMAGINED, DARLIN'!
WHY ARE YOU WEARING THAT UGLY WIG?
BERTHA!
THE REVEREND IS A MAN OF GOD!
DO NOT INSULT HIS HAIR!
I NEED TO KNOW HIS NAME, MUMMY!

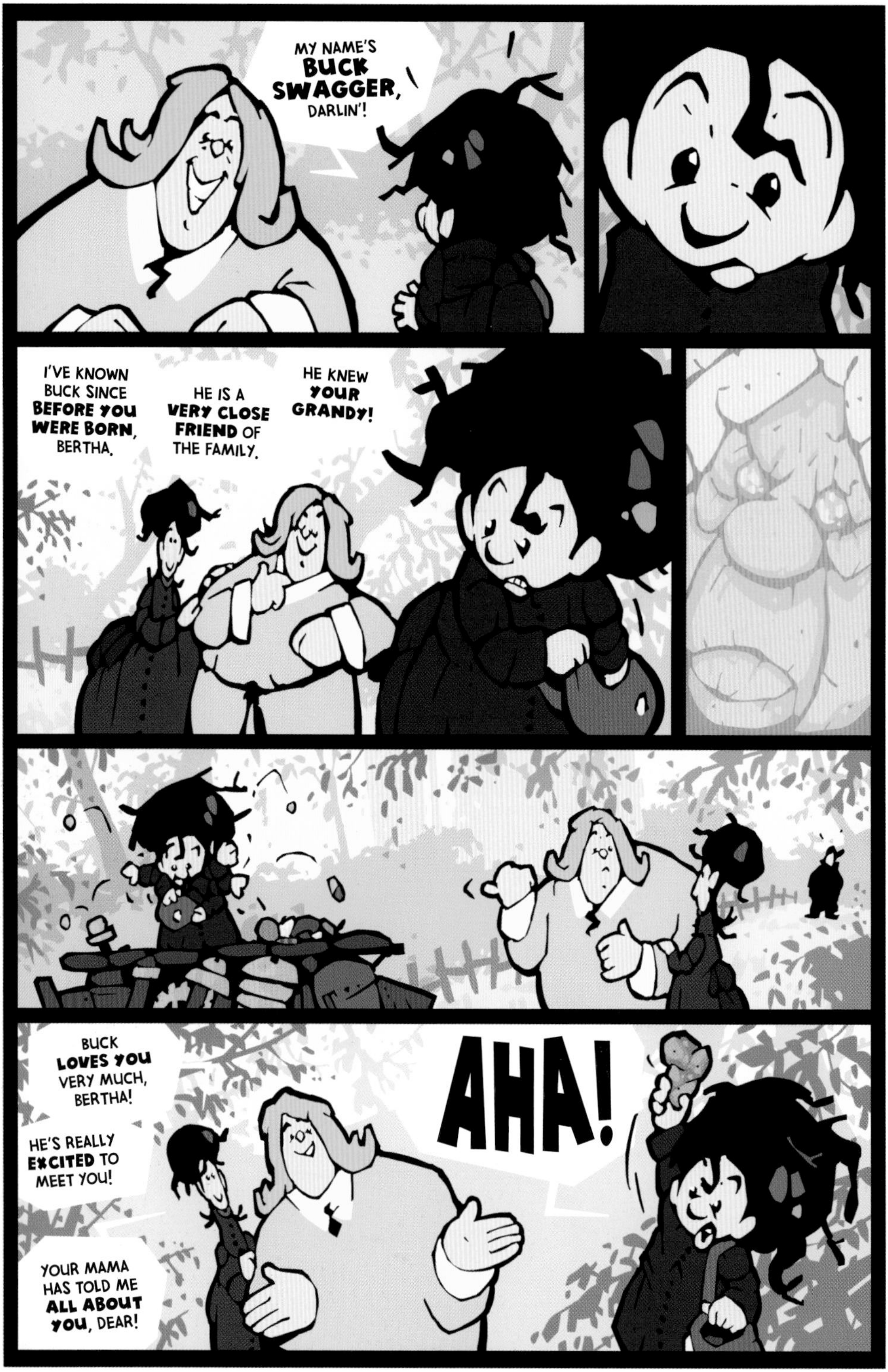
MY NAME'S BUCK SWAGGER, DARLIN'!
I'VE KNOWN BUCK SINCE BEFORE YOU WERE BORN, BERTHA.
HE IS A VERY CLOSE FRIEND OF THE FAMILY.
HE KNEW YOUR GRANDY!
BUCK LOVES YOU VERY MUCH, BERTHA!
HE'S REALLY EXCITED TO MEET YOU!
YOUR MAMA HAS TOLD ME ALL ABOUT YOU, DEAR!
AHA!

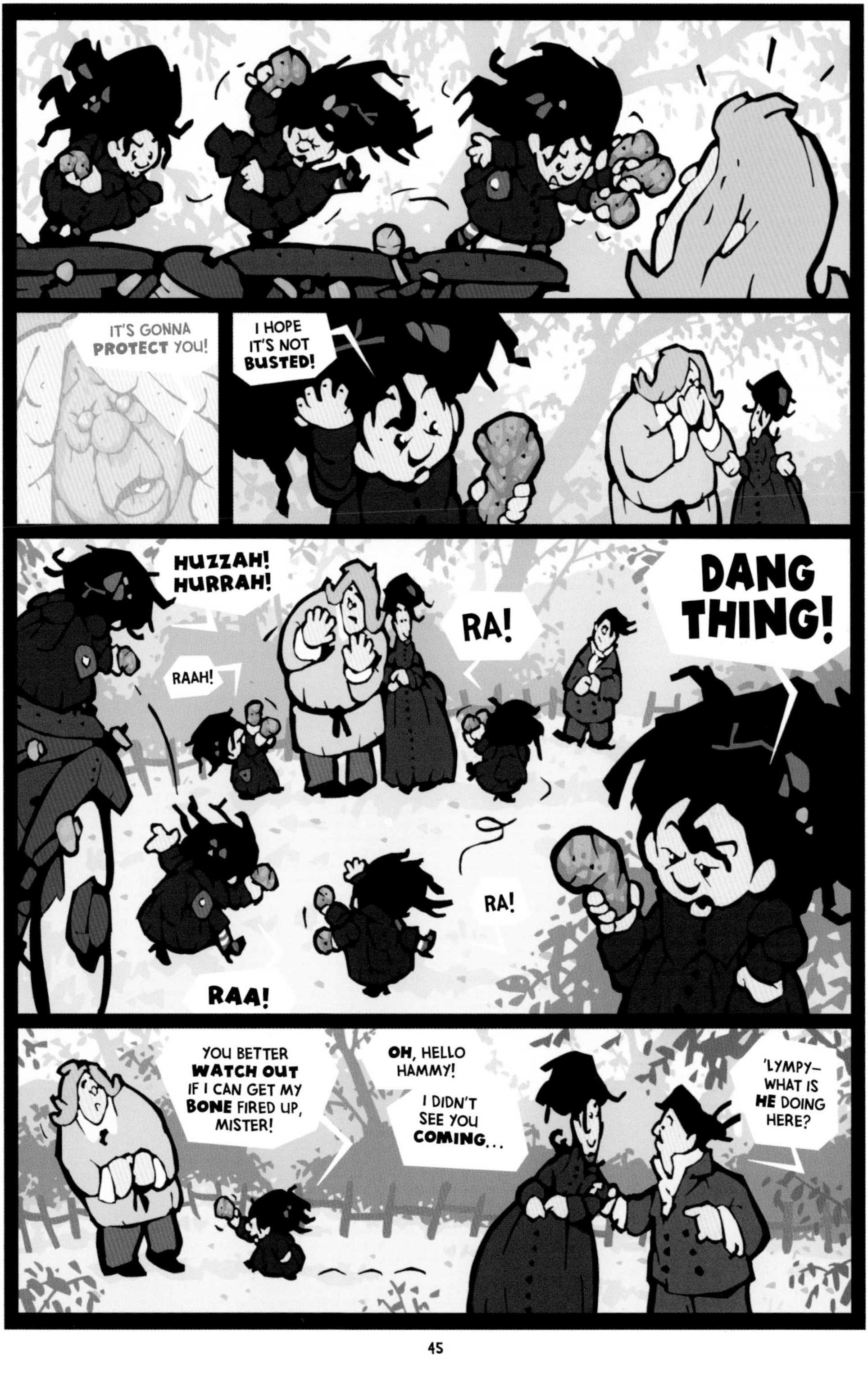
IT'S GONNA PROTECT YOU!
I HOPE IT'S NOT BUSTED!
HUZZAH! HURRAH!
RAAH!
RA!
DANG THING!
RA!
RAA!
YOU BETTER WATCH OUT IF I CAN GET MY BONE FIRED UP, MISTER!
OH, HELLO HAMMY!
I DIDN'T SEE YOU COMING...
'LYMPY— WHAT IS HE DOING HERE?

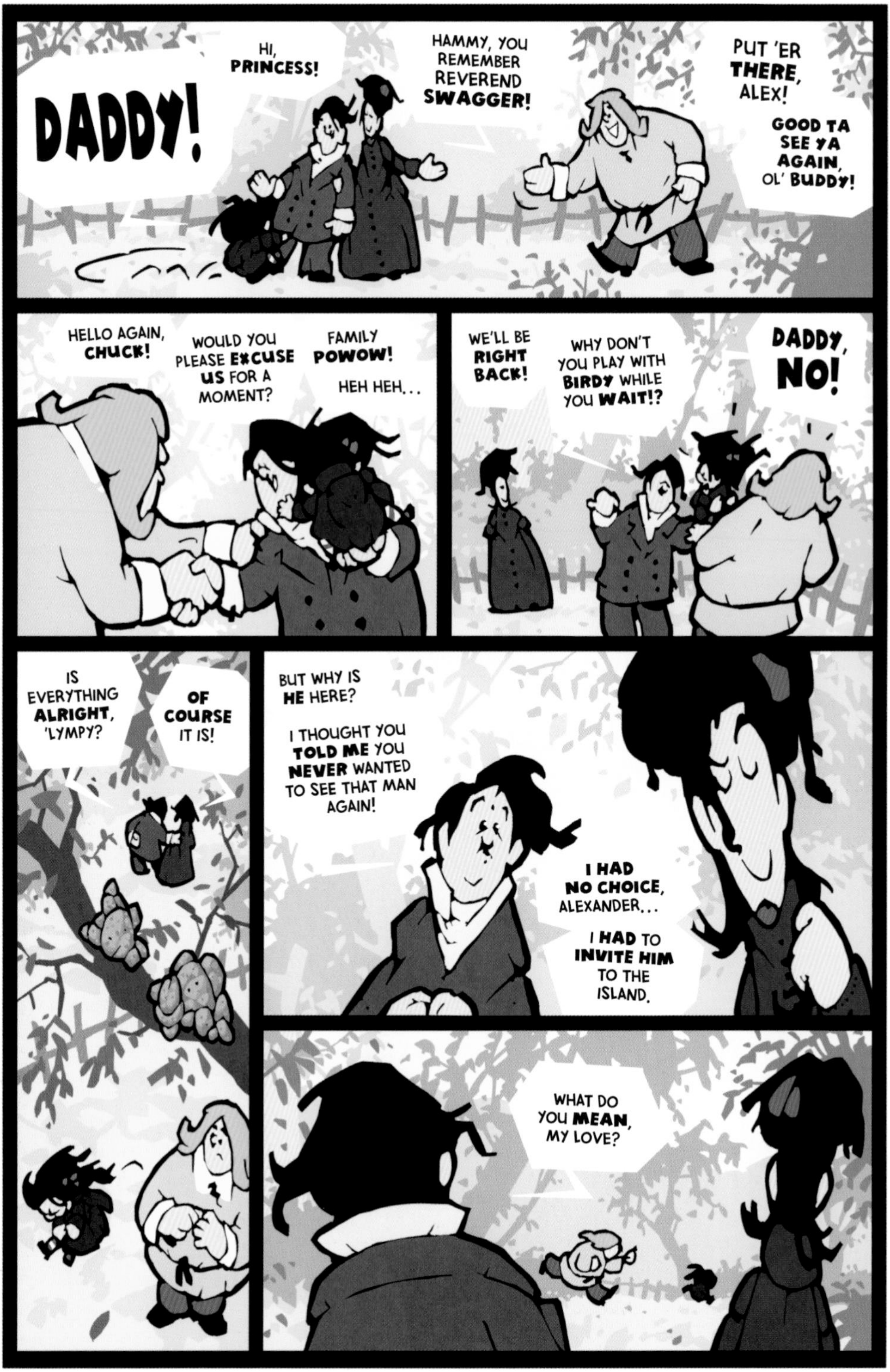
DADDY!
HI, PRINCESS!
HAMMY, YOU REMEMBER REVEREND SWAGGER!
PUT 'ER THERE, ALEX!
GOOD TA SEE YA AGAIN, OL' BUDDY!
HELLO AGAIN, CHUCK!
WOULD YOU PLEASE EXCUSE US FOR A MOMENT?
FAMILY POWOW!
HEH HEH...
WE'LL BE RIGHT BACK!
WHY DON'T YOU PLAY WITH BIRDY WHILE YOU WAIT!?
DADDY, NO!
IS EVERYTHING ALRIGHT, 'LYMPY?
OF COURSE IT IS!
BUT WHY IS HE HERE?
I THOUGHT YOU TOLD ME YOU NEVER WANTED TO SEE THAT MAN AGAIN!
I HAD NO CHOICE, ALEXANDER...
I HAD TO INVITE HIM TO THE ISLAND.
WHAT DO YOU MEAN, MY LOVE?

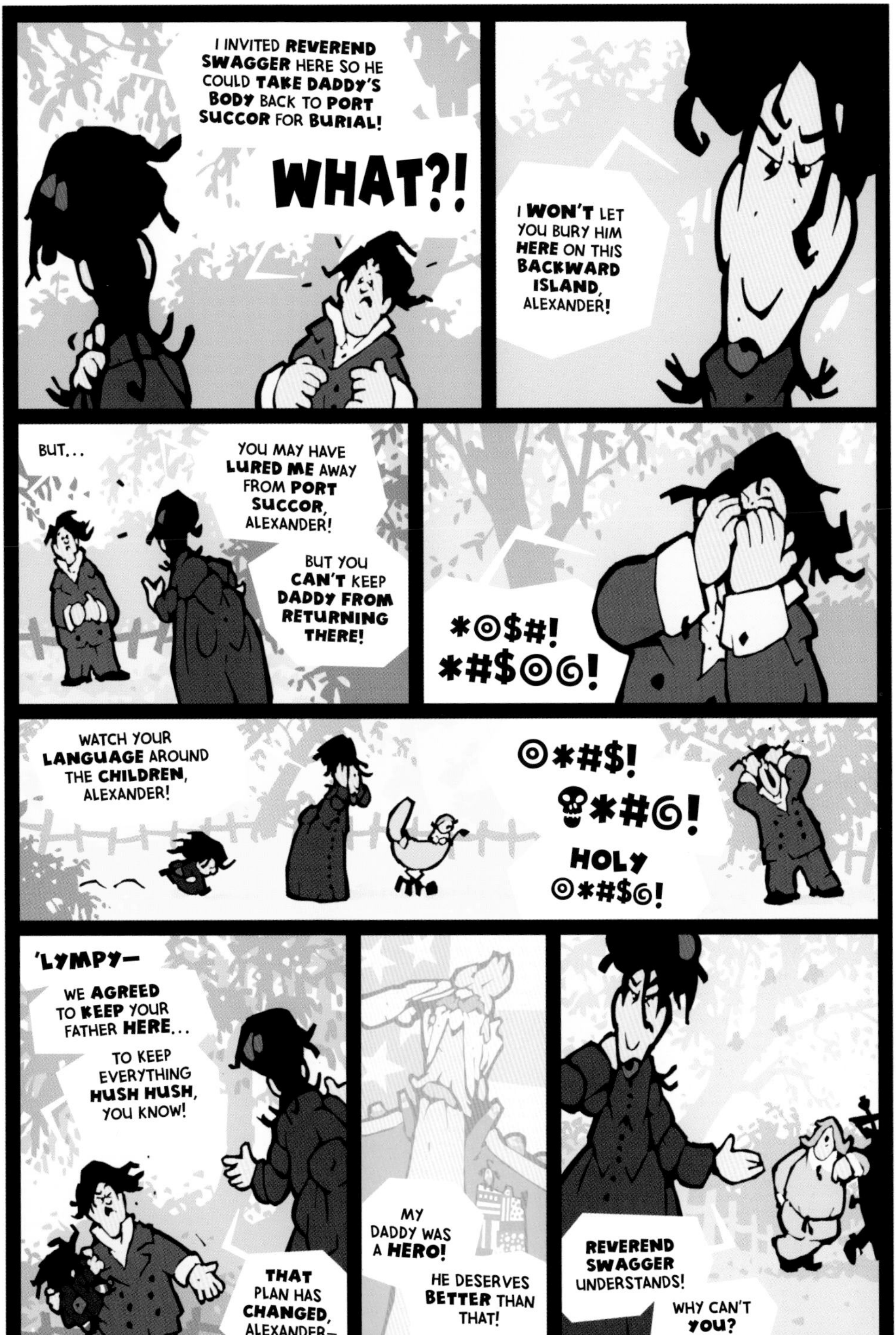

I INVITED REVEREND SWAGGER HERE SO HE COULD TAKE DADDY'S BODY BACK TO PORT SUCCOR FOR BURIAL!
WHAT?!
I WON'T LET YOU BURY HIM HERE ON THIS BACKWARD ISLAND, ALEXANDER!
BUT...
YOU MAY HAVE LURED ME AWAY FROM PORT SUCCOR, ALEXANDER!
BUT YOU CAN'T KEEP DADDY FROM RETURNING THERE!
*@$#! *#$@@!
WATCH YOUR LANGUAGE AROUND THE CHILDREN, ALEXANDER!
@*#$!
*#@!
HOLY @*#$@!
'LYMPY—
WE AGREED TO KEEP YOUR FATHER HERE...
TO KEEP EVERYTHING HUSH HUSH, YOU KNOW!
THAT PLAN HAS CHANGED, ALEXANDER—
MY DADDY WAS A HERO!
HE DESERVES BETTER THAN THAT!
REVEREND SWAGGER UNDERSTANDS!
WHY CAN'T YOU?

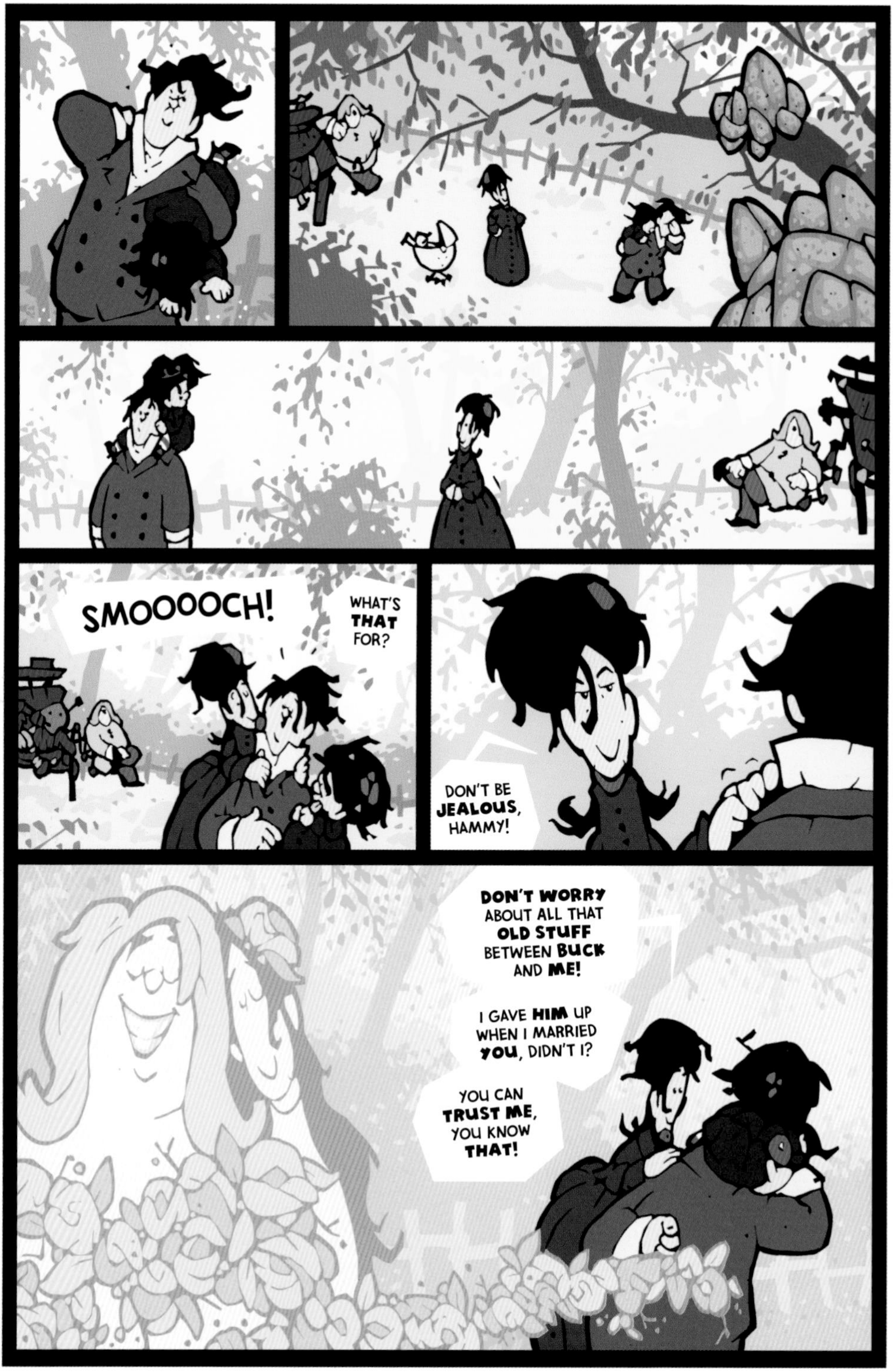
SMOOOCH!
WHAT'S **THAT** FOR?
DON'T BE **JEALOUS**, HAMMY!
DON'T WORRY ABOUT ALL THAT **OLD STUFF** BETWEEN **BUCK** AND **ME!**
I GAVE **HIM** UP WHEN I MARRIED **YOU**, DIDN'T I?
YOU CAN **TRUST ME**, YOU KNOW **THAT!**

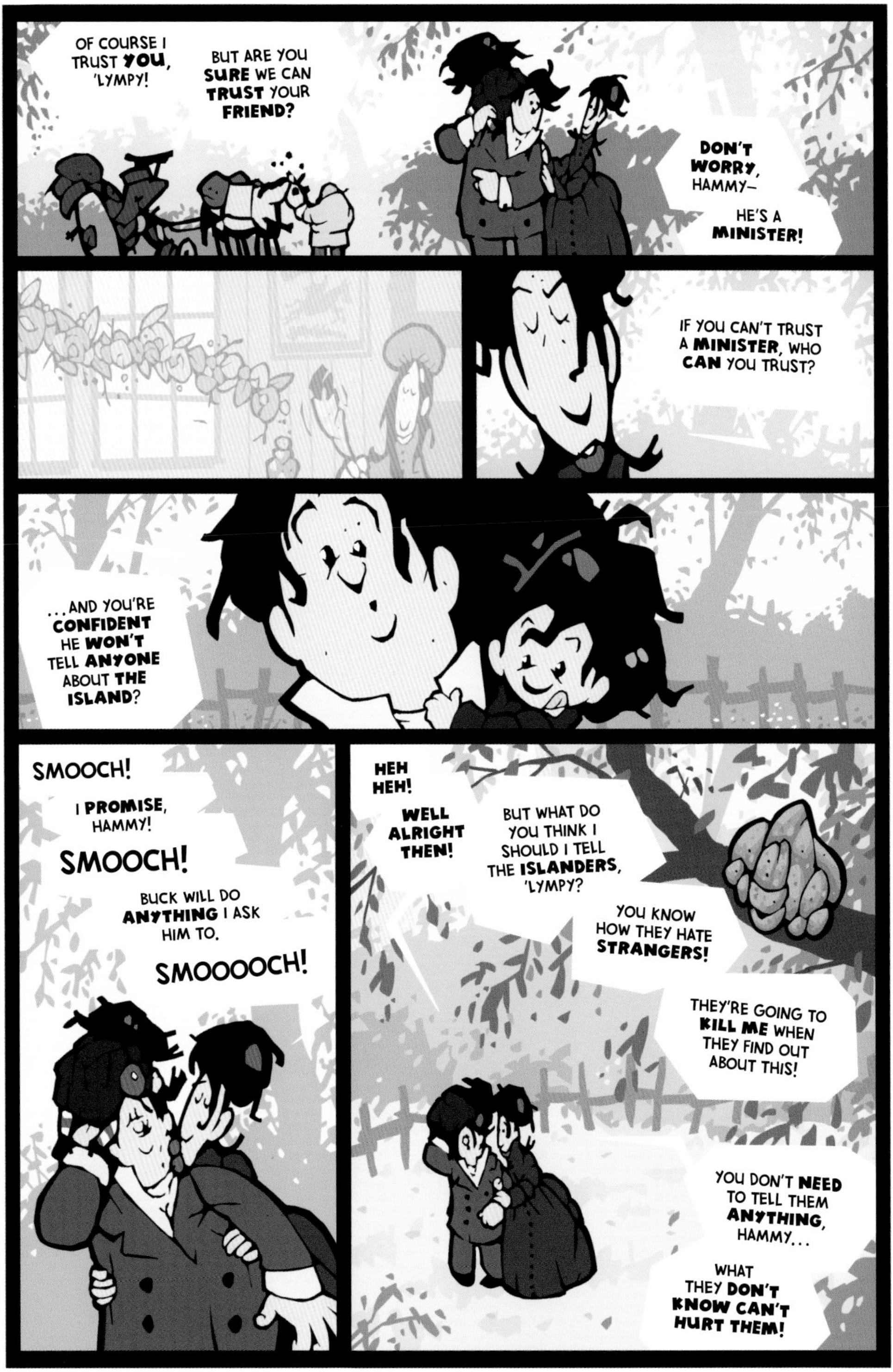
OF COURSE I TRUST **YOU**, 'LYMPY!
BUT ARE YOU **SURE** WE CAN **TRUST** YOUR **FRIEND?**
DON'T WORRY, HAMMY–
HE'S A **MINISTER!**
IF YOU CAN'T TRUST A **MINISTER**, WHO **CAN** YOU TRUST?
...AND YOU'RE **CONFIDENT** HE **WON'T** TELL **ANYONE** ABOUT **THE ISLAND**?
SMOOCH!
I **PROMISE**, HAMMY!
SMOOCH!
BUCK WILL DO **ANYTHING** I ASK HIM TO.
SMOOOOCH!
HEH HEH!
WELL ALRIGHT THEN!
BUT WHAT DO YOU THINK I SHOULD I TELL THE **ISLANDERS**, 'LYMPY?
YOU KNOW HOW THEY HATE **STRANGERS!**
THEY'RE GOING TO **KILL ME** WHEN THEY FIND OUT ABOUT THIS!
YOU DON'T **NEED** TO TELL THEM **ANYTHING**, HAMMY...
WHAT THEY **DON'T KNOW CAN'T HURT THEM!**

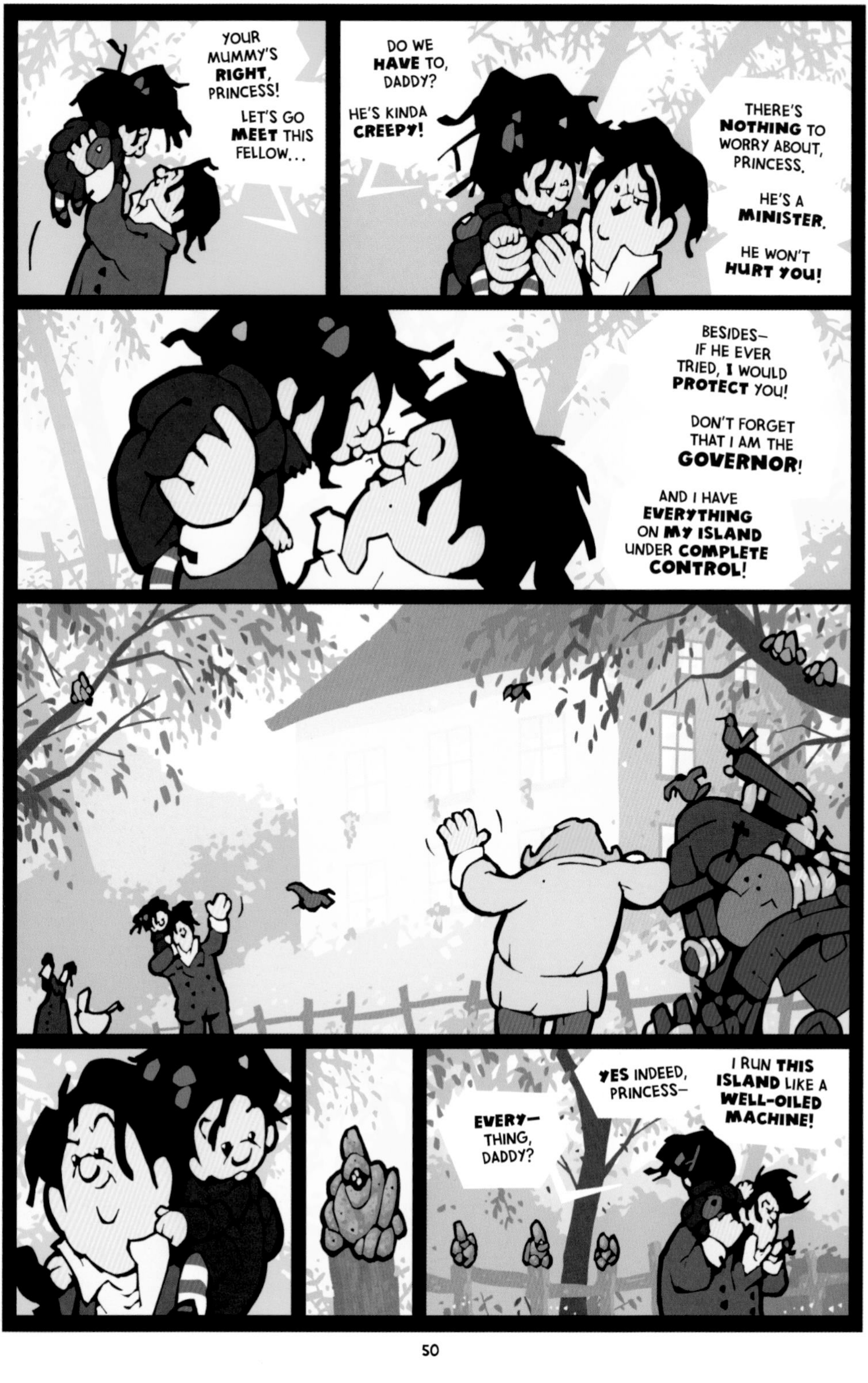
YOUR MUMMY'S RIGHT, PRINCESS!
LET'S GO MEET THIS FELLOW...
DO WE HAVE TO, DADDY?
HE'S KINDA CREEPY!
THERE'S NOTHING TO WORRY ABOUT, PRINCESS.
HE'S A MINISTER.
HE WON'T HURT YOU!
BESIDES— IF HE EVER TRIED, I WOULD PROTECT YOU!
DON'T FORGET THAT I AM THE GOVERNOR!
AND I HAVE EVERYTHING ON MY ISLAND UNDER COMPLETE CONTROL!
EVERY— THING, DADDY?
YES INDEED, PRINCESS—
I RUN THIS ISLAND LIKE A WELL-OILED MACHINE!

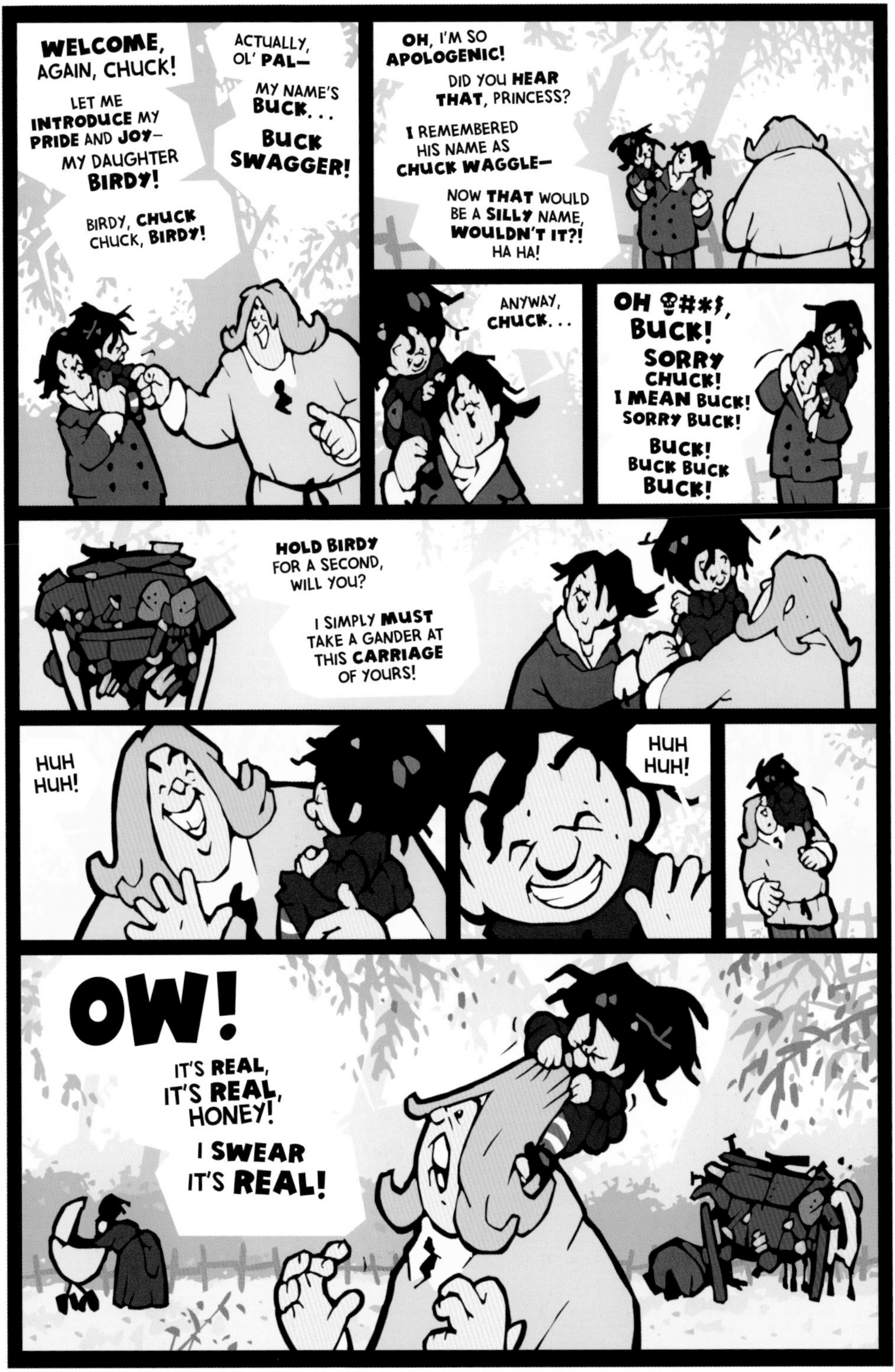
WELCOME, AGAIN, CHUCK!
LET ME INTRODUCE MY PRIDE AND JOY— MY DAUGHTER BIRDY!
BIRDY, CHUCK CHUCK, BIRDY!
ACTUALLY, OL' PAL—
MY NAME'S BUCK. . .
BUCK SWAGGER!
OH, I'M SO APOLOGENIC!
DID YOU HEAR THAT, PRINCESS?
I REMEMBERED HIS NAME AS CHUCK WAGGLE—
NOW THAT WOULD BE A SILLY NAME, WOULDN'T IT?! HA HA!
ANYWAY, CHUCK. . .
OH ☠#*$, BUCK!
SORRY CHUCK! I MEAN BUCK! SORRY BUCK!
BUCK! BUCK BUCK BUCK!
HOLD BIRDY FOR A SECOND, WILL YOU?
I SIMPLY MUST TAKE A GANDER AT THIS CARRIAGE OF YOURS!
HUH HUH!
HUH HUH!
OW!
IT'S REAL, IT'S REAL, HONEY!
I SWEAR IT'S REAL!

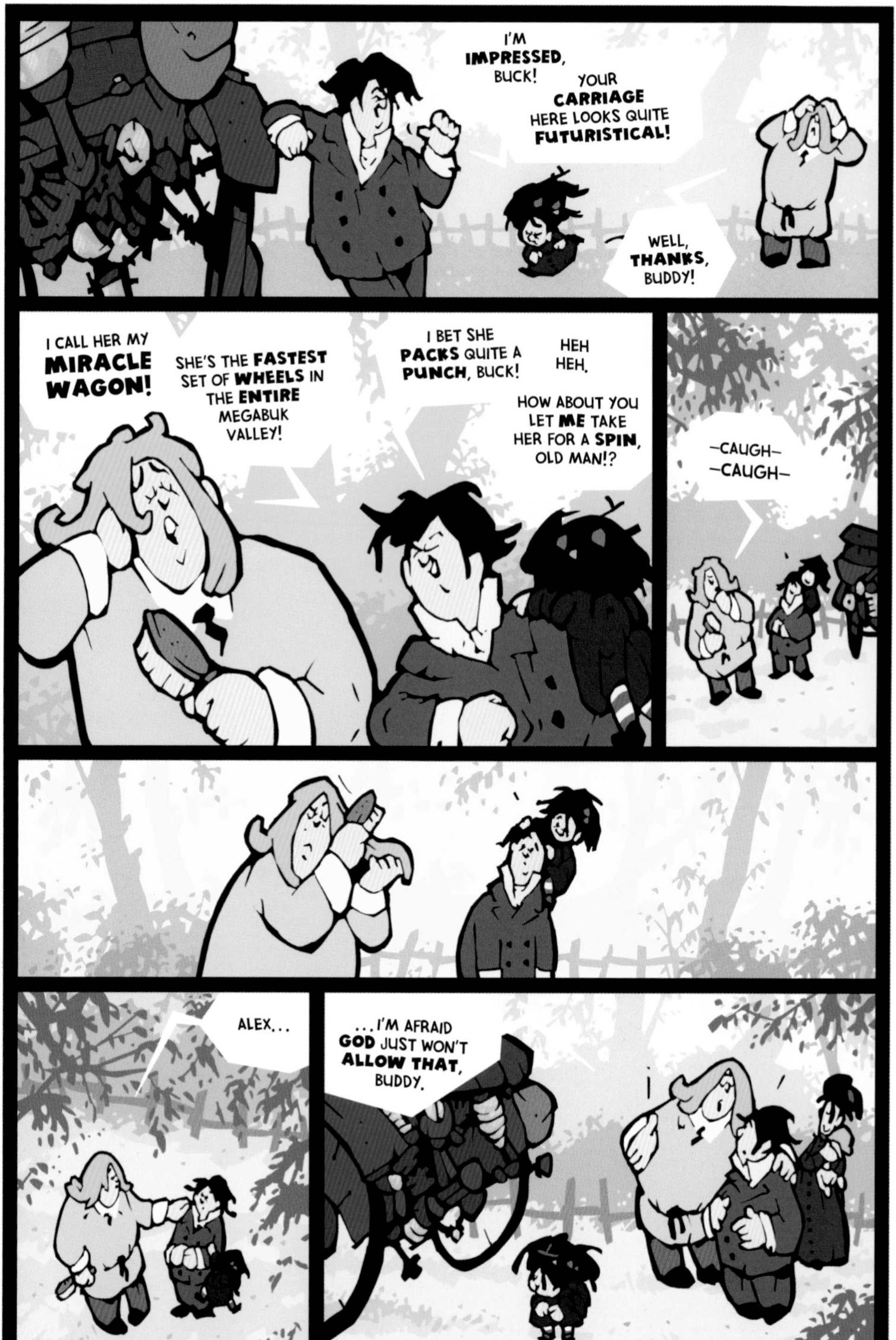

I'M **IMPRESSED**, BUCK!
YOUR **CARRIAGE** HERE LOOKS QUITE **FUTURISTICAL!**
WELL, **THANKS**, BUDDY!
I CALL HER MY **MIRACLE WAGON!**
SHE'S THE **FASTEST** SET OF **WHEELS** IN THE **ENTIRE** MEGABUK VALLEY!
I BET SHE **PACKS** QUITE A **PUNCH**, BUCK!
HEH HEH.
HOW ABOUT YOU LET **ME** TAKE HER FOR A **SPIN**, OLD MAN!?
-CAUGH-
-CAUGH-
ALEX,...
...I'M AFRAID **GOD** JUST WON'T **ALLOW THAT**, BUDDY.

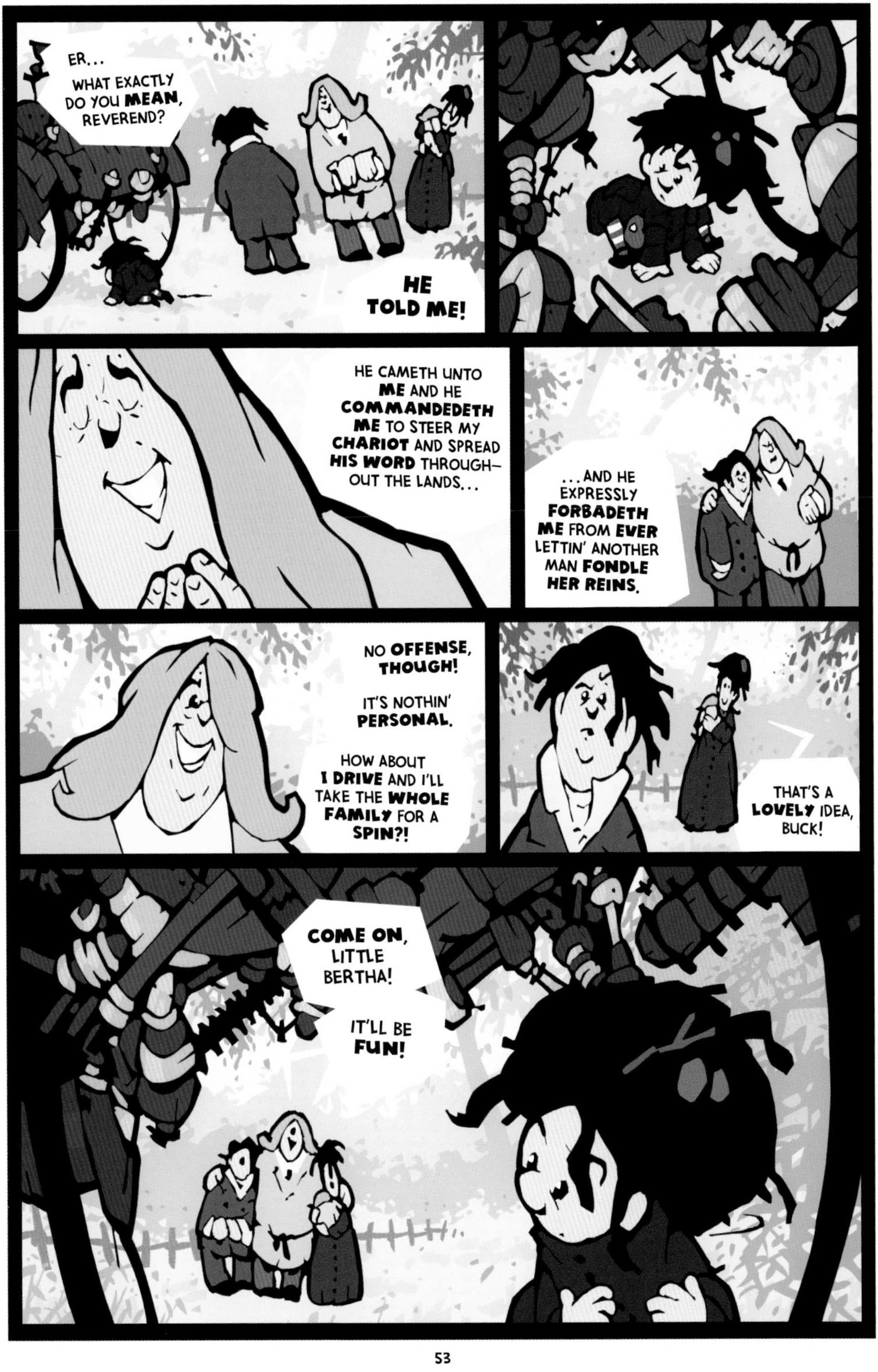
ER...
WHAT EXACTLY DO YOU MEAN, REVEREND?
HE TOLD ME!
HE CAMETH UNTO ME AND HE COMMANDEDETH ME TO STEER MY CHARIOT AND SPREAD HIS WORD THROUGH-OUT THE LANDS...
...AND HE EXPRESSLY FORBADETH ME FROM EVER LETTIN' ANOTHER MAN FONDLE HER REINS.
NO OFFENSE, THOUGH!
IT'S NOTHIN' PERSONAL.
HOW ABOUT I DRIVE AND I'LL TAKE THE WHOLE FAMILY FOR A SPIN?!
THAT'S A LOVELY IDEA, BUCK!
COME ON, LITTLE BERTHA!
IT'LL BE FUN!

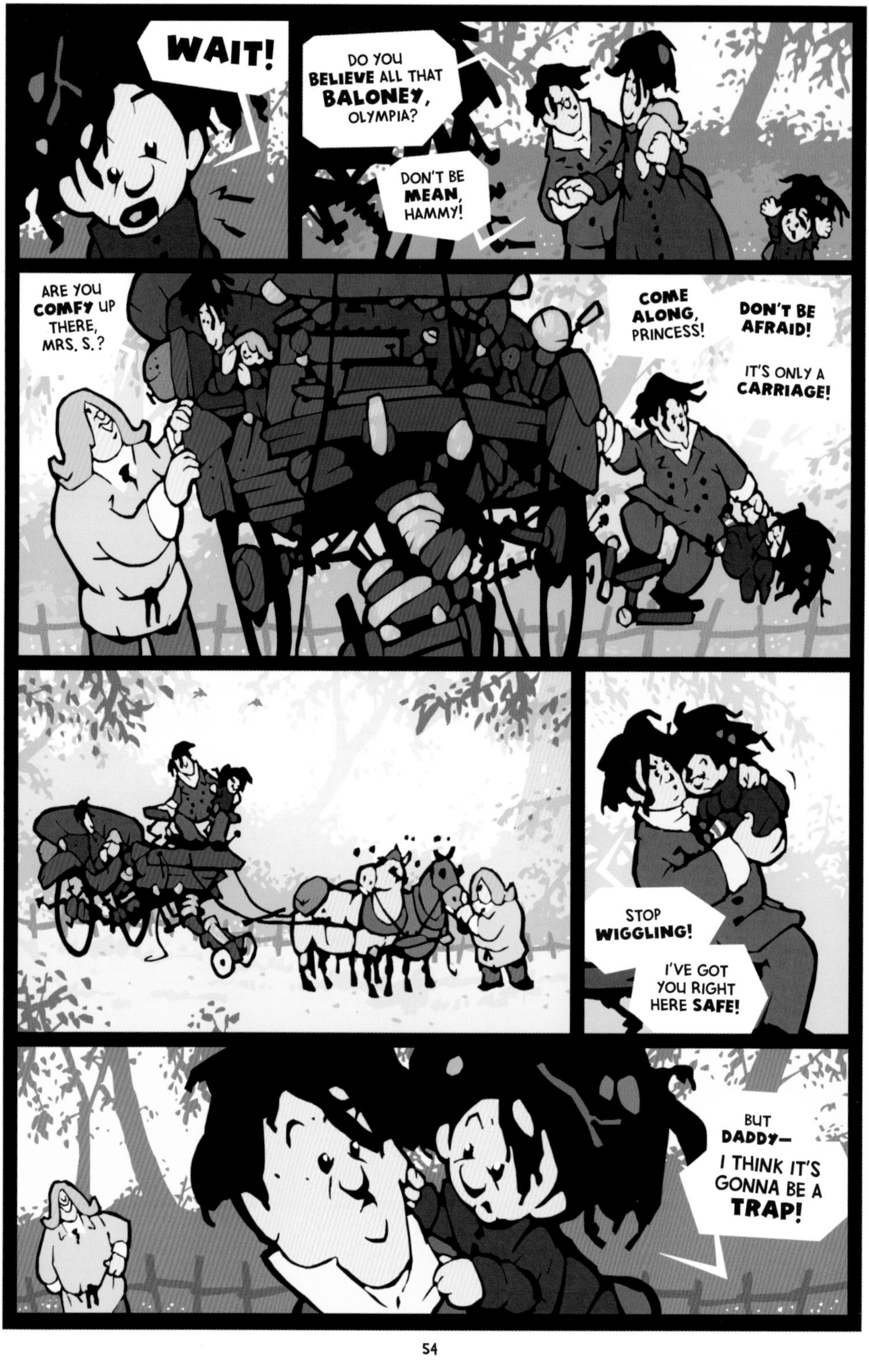
WAIT!
DO YOU BELIEVE ALL THAT BALONEY, OLYMPIA?
DON'T BE MEAN, HAMMY!
ARE YOU COMFY UP THERE, MRS. S.?
COME ALONG, PRINCESS!
DON'T BE AFRAID!
IT'S ONLY A CARRIAGE!
STOP WIGGLING!
I'VE GOT YOU RIGHT HERE SAFE!
BUT DADDY—
I THINK IT'S GONNA BE A TRAP!

CHAPTER FOUR
❧ *Welcome to* PARADISE! ❧

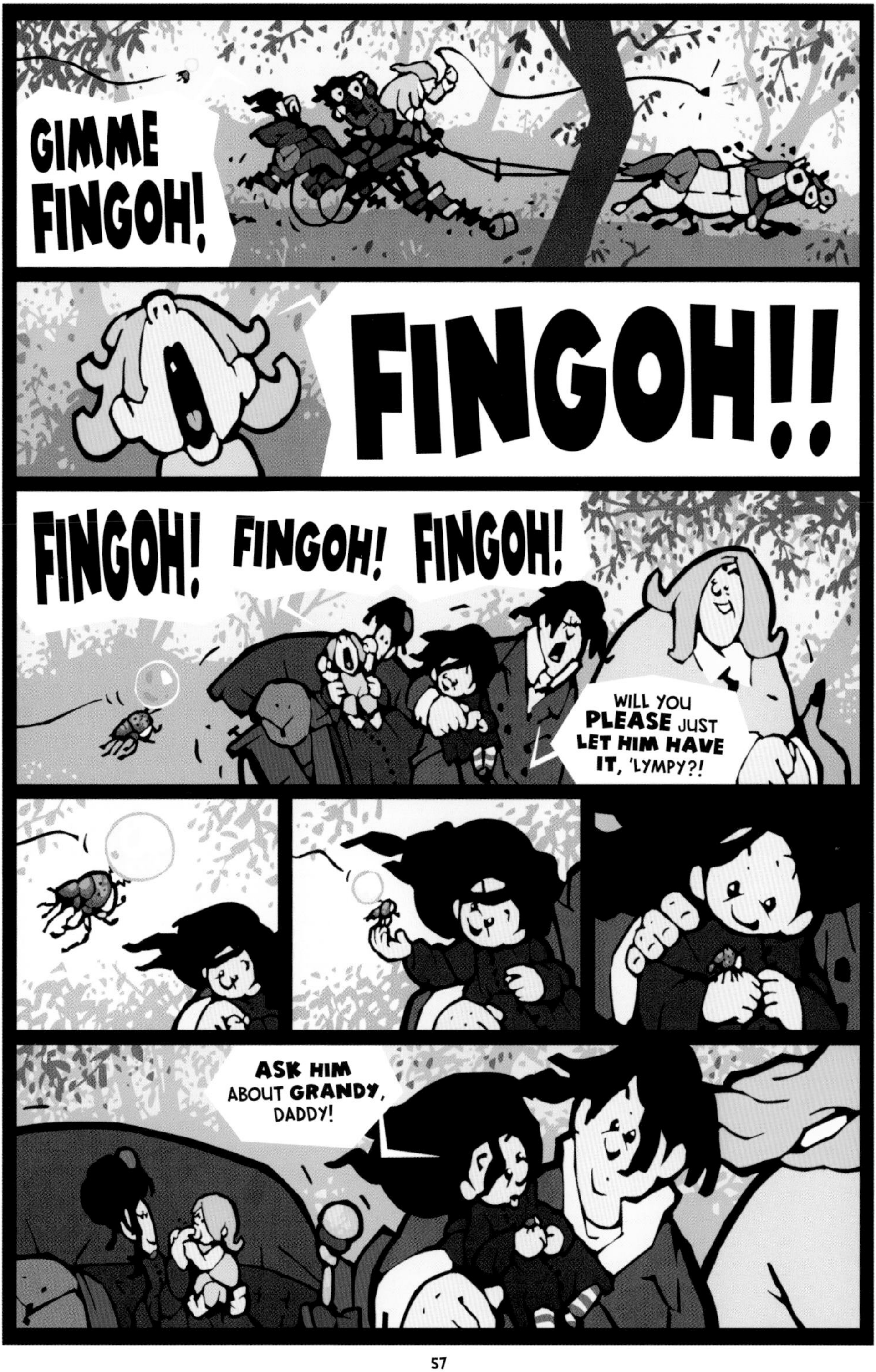
GIMME FINGOH!
FINGOH!!
FINGOH! FINGOH! FINGOH!
WILL YOU PLEASE JUST LET HIM HAVE IT, 'LYMPY?!
ASK HIM ABOUT GRANDY, DADDY!

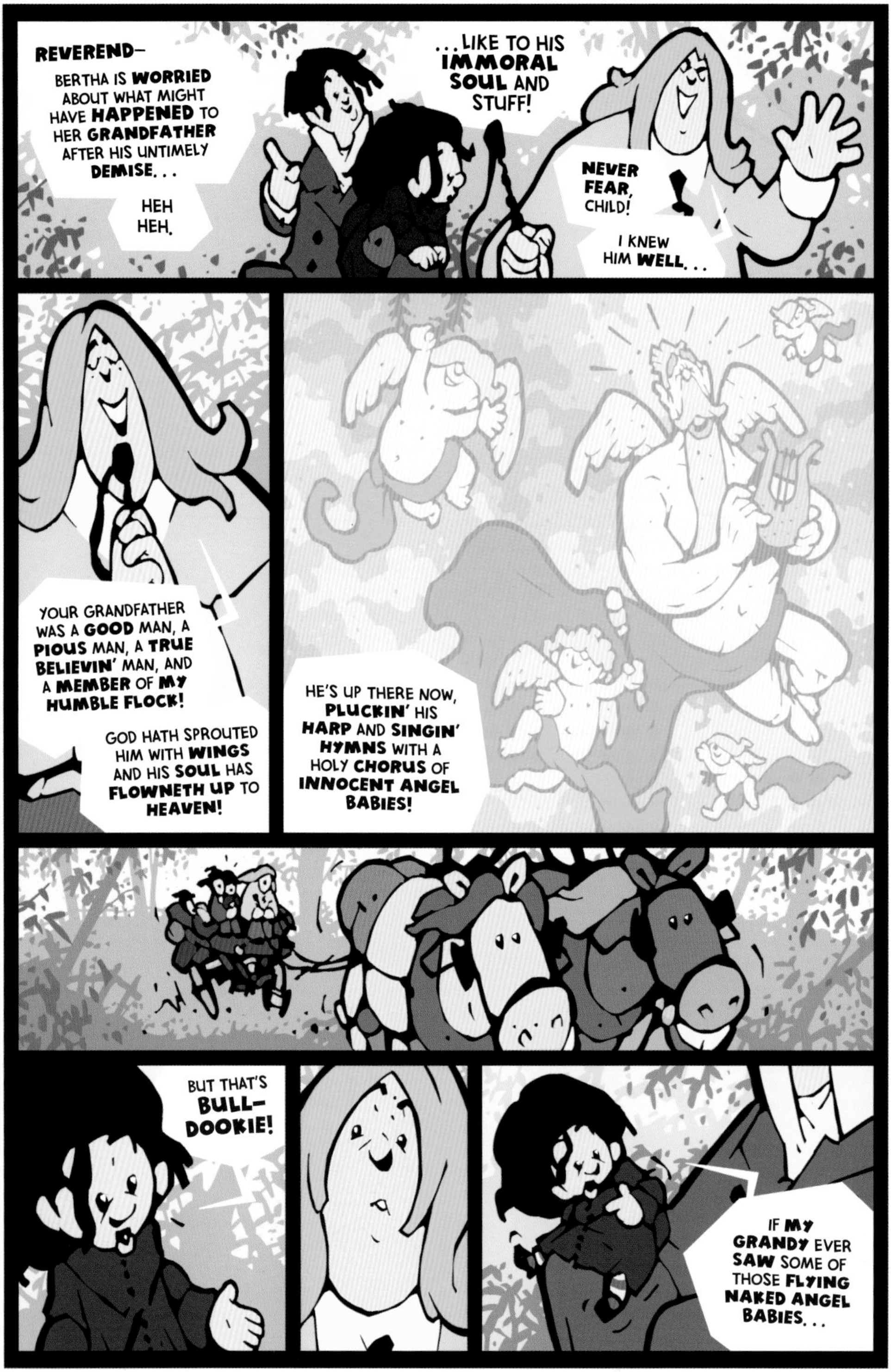
REVEREND–
BERTHA IS WORRIED ABOUT WHAT MIGHT HAVE HAPPENED TO HER GRANDFATHER AFTER HIS UNTIMELY DEMISE. . .
HEH HEH.
. . . LIKE TO HIS IMMORAL SOUL AND STUFF!
NEVER FEAR, CHILD!
I KNEW HIM WELL. . .
YOUR GRANDFATHER WAS A GOOD MAN, A PIOUS MAN, A TRUE BELIEVIN' MAN, AND A MEMBER OF MY HUMBLE FLOCK!
GOD HATH SPROUTED HIM WITH WINGS AND HIS SOUL HAS FLOWNETH UP TO HEAVEN!
HE'S UP THERE NOW, PLUCKIN' HIS HARP AND SINGIN' HYMNS WITH A HOLY CHORUS OF INNOCENT ANGEL BABIES!
BUT THAT'S BULL-DOOKIE!
IF MY GRANDY EVER SAW SOME OF THOSE FLYING NAKED ANGEL BABIES. . .

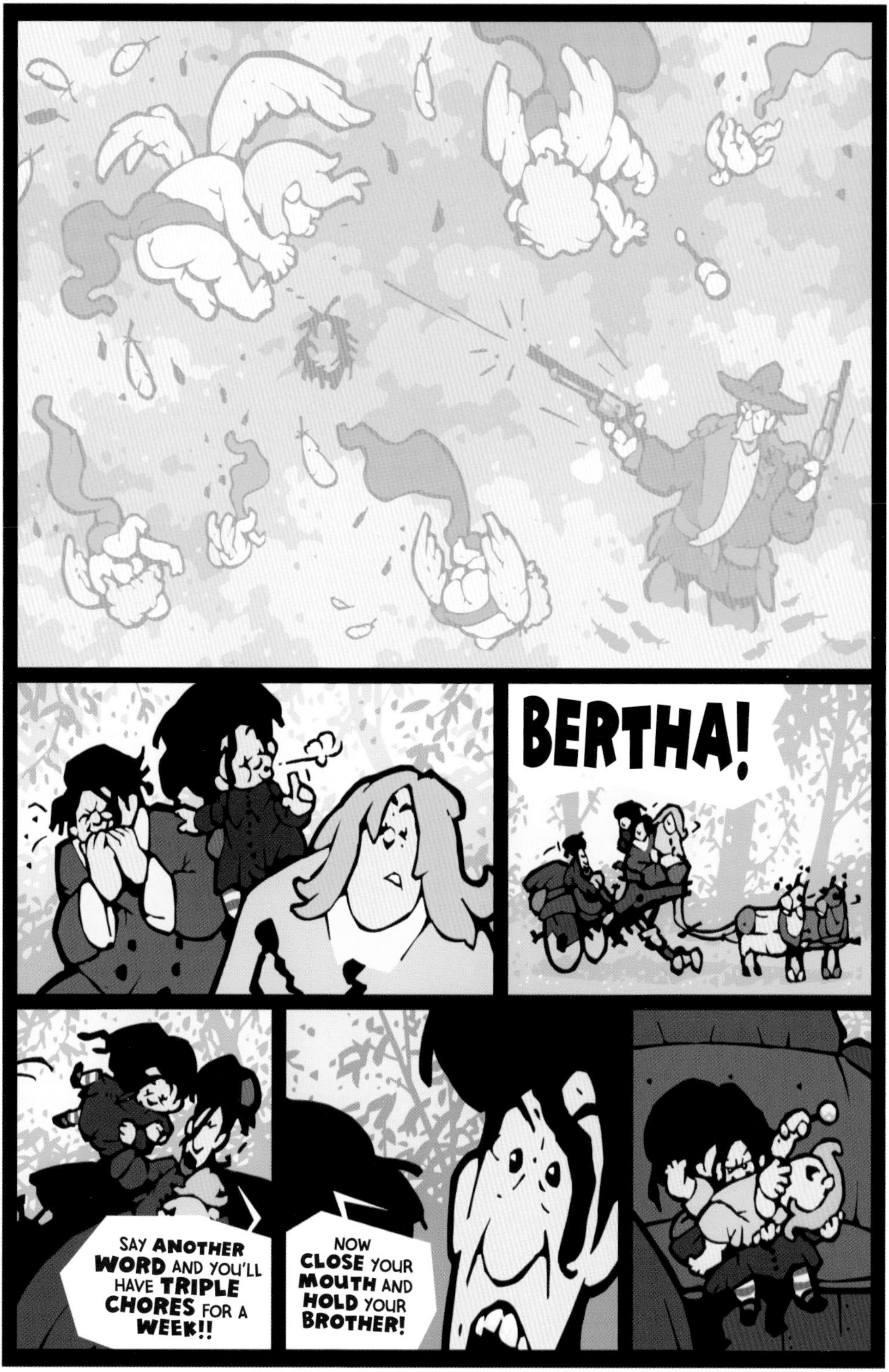
BERTHA!
SAY ANOTHER WORD AND YOU'LL HAVE TRIPLE CHORES FOR A WEEK!!
NOW CLOSE YOUR MOUTH AND HOLD YOUR BROTHER!

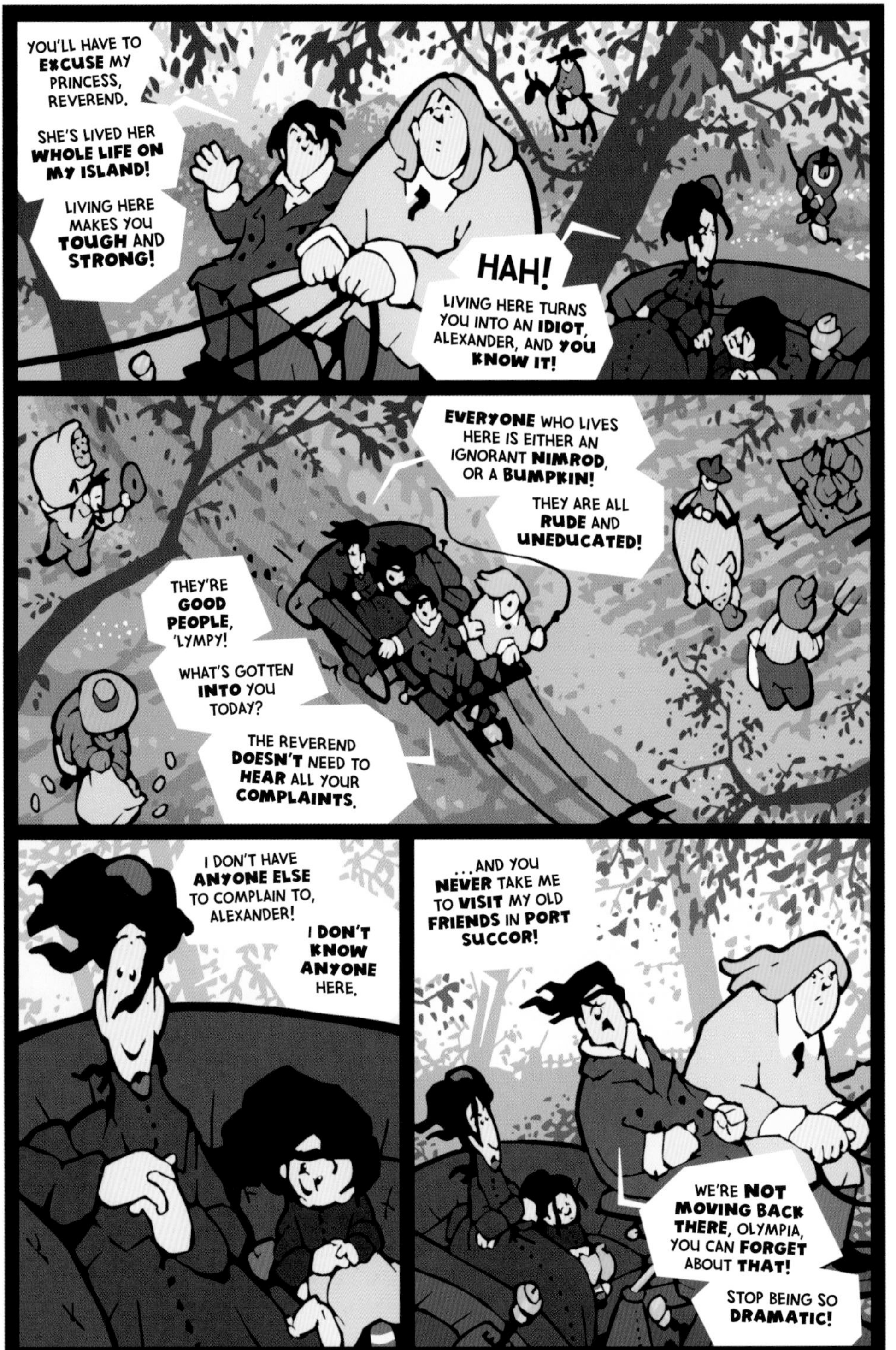
YOU'LL HAVE TO EXCUSE MY PRINCESS, REVEREND.
SHE'S LIVED HER WHOLE LIFE ON MY ISLAND!
LIVING HERE MAKES YOU TOUGH AND STRONG!
HAH!
LIVING HERE TURNS YOU INTO AN IDIOT, ALEXANDER, AND YOU KNOW IT!
EVERYONE WHO LIVES HERE IS EITHER AN IGNORANT NIMROD, OR A BUMPKIN!
THEY ARE ALL RUDE AND UNEDUCATED!
THEY'RE GOOD PEOPLE, 'LYMPY!
WHAT'S GOTTEN INTO YOU TODAY?
THE REVEREND DOESN'T NEED TO HEAR ALL YOUR COMPLAINTS.
I DON'T HAVE ANYONE ELSE TO COMPLAIN TO, ALEXANDER!
I DON'T KNOW ANYONE HERE.
...AND YOU NEVER TAKE ME TO VISIT MY OLD FRIENDS IN PORT SUCCOR!
WE'RE NOT MOVING BACK THERE, OLYMPIA, YOU CAN FORGET ABOUT THAT!
STOP BEING SO DRAMATIC!

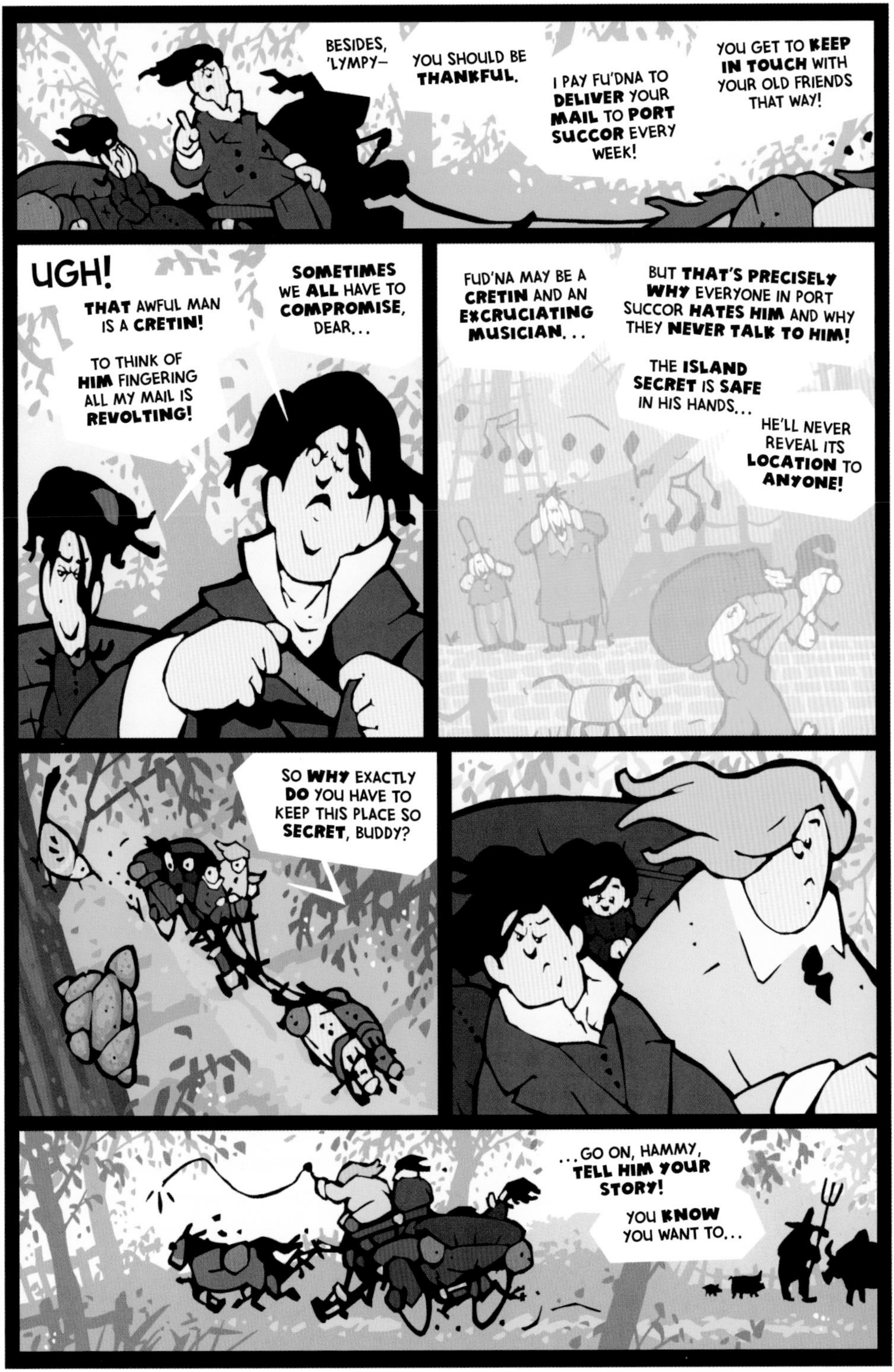
BESIDES, 'LYMPY—
YOU SHOULD BE THANKFUL.
I PAY FU'DNA TO DELIVER YOUR MAIL TO PORT SUCCOR EVERY WEEK!
YOU GET TO KEEP IN TOUCH WITH YOUR OLD FRIENDS THAT WAY!
UGH!
THAT AWFUL MAN IS A CRETIN!
TO THINK OF HIM FINGERING ALL MY MAIL IS REVOLTING!
SOMETIMES WE ALL HAVE TO COMPROMISE, DEAR...
FUD'NA MAY BE A CRETIN AND AN EXCRUCIATING MUSICIAN...
BUT THAT'S PRECISELY WHY EVERYONE IN PORT SUCCOR HATES HIM AND WHY THEY NEVER TALK TO HIM!
THE ISLAND SECRET IS SAFE IN HIS HANDS...
HE'LL NEVER REVEAL ITS LOCATION TO ANYONE!
SO WHY EXACTLY DO YOU HAVE TO KEEP THIS PLACE SO SECRET, BUDDY?
...GO ON, HAMMY, TELL HIM YOUR STORY!
YOU KNOW YOU WANT TO...

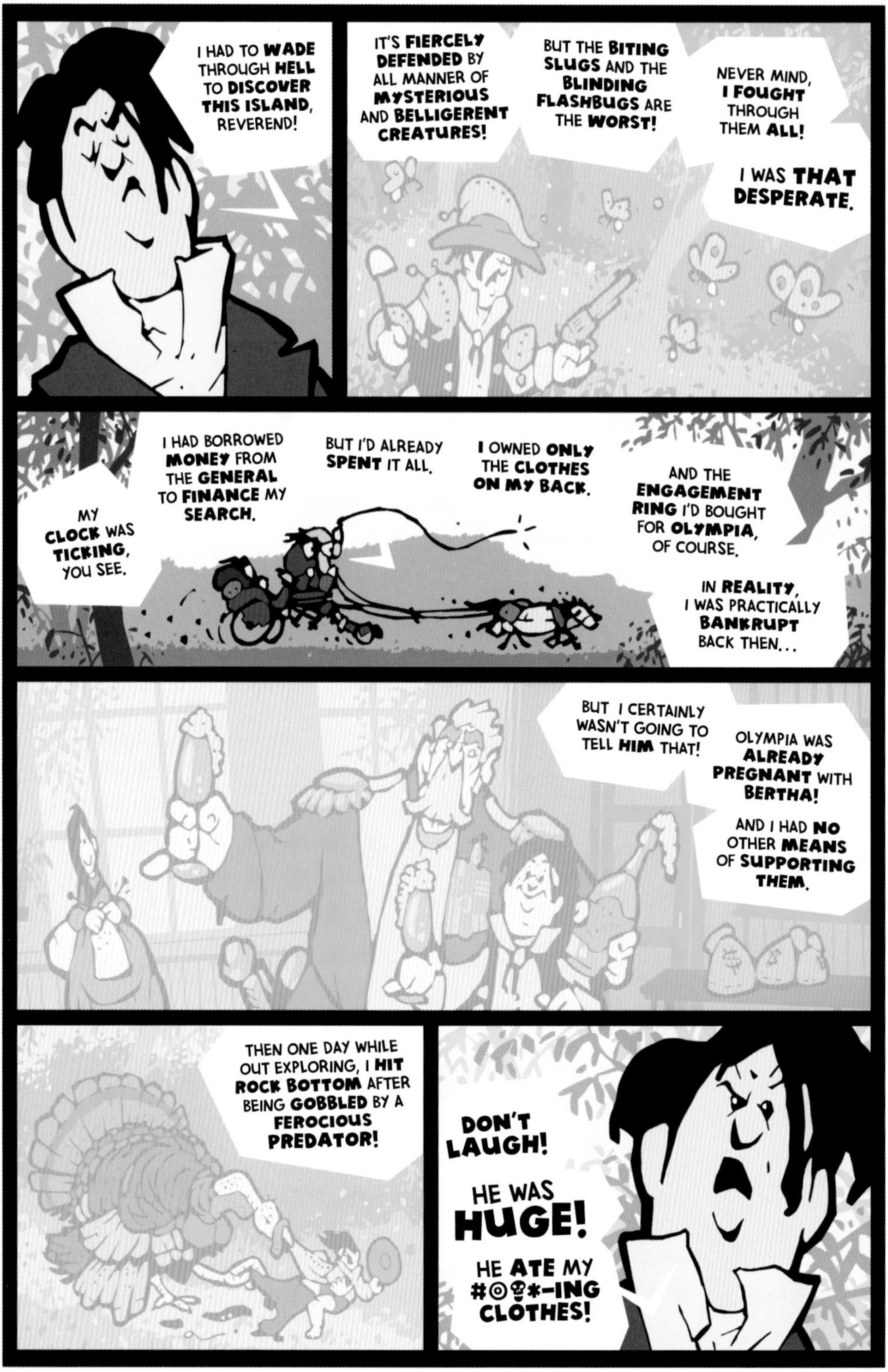
I HAD TO WADE THROUGH HELL TO DISCOVER THIS ISLAND, REVEREND!
IT'S FIERCELY DEFENDED BY ALL MANNER OF MYSTERIOUS AND BELLIGERENT CREATURES!
BUT THE BITING SLUGS AND THE BLINDING FLASHBUGS ARE THE WORST!
NEVER MIND, I FOUGHT THROUGH THEM ALL!
I WAS THAT DESPERATE.
MY CLOCK WAS TICKING, YOU SEE.
I HAD BORROWED MONEY FROM THE GENERAL TO FINANCE MY SEARCH.
BUT I'D ALREADY SPENT IT ALL.
I OWNED ONLY THE CLOTHES ON MY BACK.
AND THE ENGAGEMENT RING I'D BOUGHT FOR OLYMPIA, OF COURSE.
IN REALITY, I WAS PRACTICALLY BANKRUPT BACK THEN...
BUT I CERTAINLY WASN'T GOING TO TELL HIM THAT!
OLYMPIA WAS ALREADY PREGNANT WITH BERTHA!
AND I HAD NO OTHER MEANS OF SUPPORTING THEM.
THEN ONE DAY WHILE OUT EXPLORING, I HIT ROCK BOTTOM AFTER BEING GOBBLED BY A FEROCIOUS PREDATOR!
DON'T LAUGH!
HE WAS HUGE!
HE ATE MY #@☠*-ING CLOTHES!

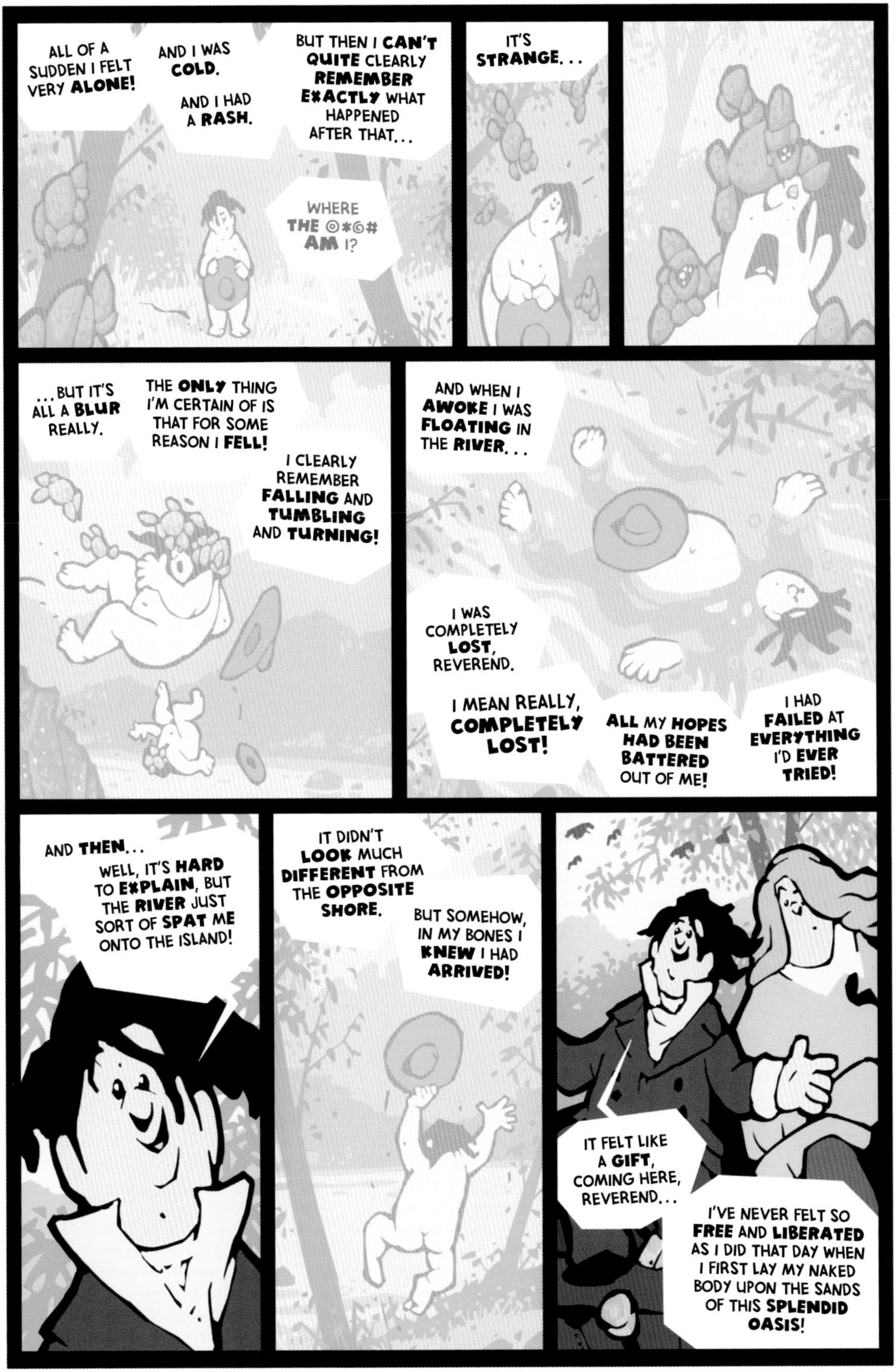
ALL OF A SUDDEN I FELT VERY ALONE!
AND I WAS COLD.
AND I HAD A RASH.
BUT THEN I CAN'T QUITE CLEARLY REMEMBER EXACTLY WHAT HAPPENED AFTER THAT...
WHERE THE @*©# AM I?
IT'S STRANGE...
...BUT IT'S ALL A BLUR REALLY.
THE ONLY THING I'M CERTAIN OF IS THAT FOR SOME REASON I FELL!
I CLEARLY REMEMBER FALLING AND TUMBLING AND TURNING!
AND WHEN I AWOKE I WAS FLOATING IN THE RIVER...
I WAS COMPLETELY LOST, REVEREND.
I MEAN REALLY, COMPLETELY LOST!
ALL MY HOPES HAD BEEN BATTERED OUT OF ME!
I HAD FAILED AT EVERYTHING I'D EVER TRIED!
AND THEN...
WELL, IT'S HARD TO EXPLAIN, BUT THE RIVER JUST SORT OF SPAT ME ONTO THE ISLAND!
IT DIDN'T LOOK MUCH DIFFERENT FROM THE OPPOSITE SHORE.
BUT SOMEHOW, IN MY BONES I KNEW I HAD ARRIVED!
IT FELT LIKE A GIFT, COMING HERE, REVEREND...
I'VE NEVER FELT SO FREE AND LIBERATED AS I DID THAT DAY WHEN I FIRST LAY MY NAKED BODY UPON THE SANDS OF THIS SPLENDID OASIS!

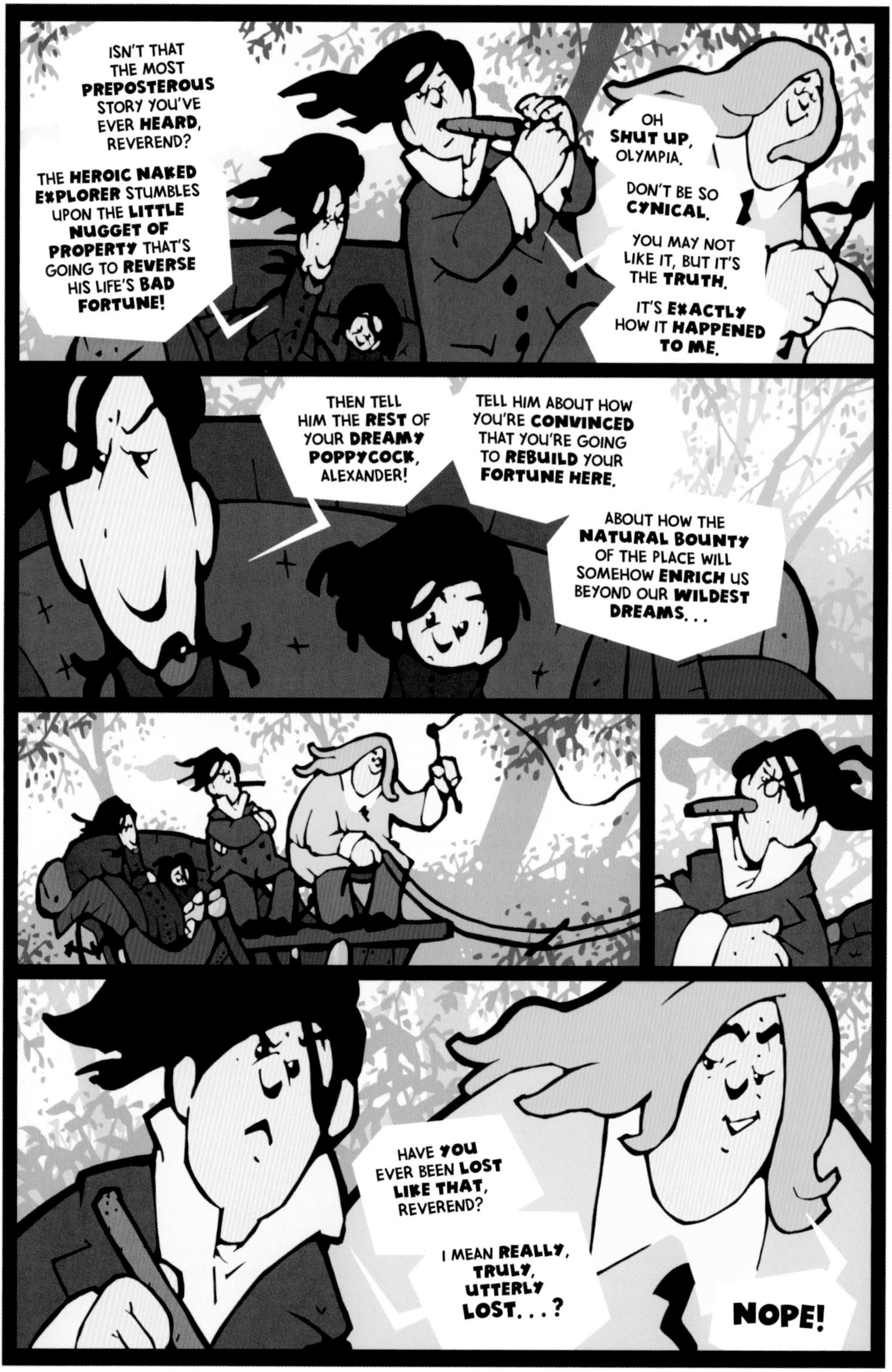
ISN'T THAT THE MOST PREPOSTEROUS STORY YOU'VE EVER HEARD, REVEREND?
THE HEROIC NAKED EXPLORER STUMBLES UPON THE LITTLE NUGGET OF PROPERTY THAT'S GOING TO REVERSE HIS LIFE'S BAD FORTUNE!
OH SHUT UP, OLYMPIA.
DON'T BE SO CYNICAL.
YOU MAY NOT LIKE IT, BUT IT'S THE TRUTH.
IT'S EXACTLY HOW IT HAPPENED TO ME.
THEN TELL HIM THE REST OF YOUR DREAMY POPPYCOCK, ALEXANDER!
TELL HIM ABOUT HOW YOU'RE CONVINCED THAT YOU'RE GOING TO REBUILD YOUR FORTUNE HERE.
ABOUT HOW THE NATURAL BOUNTY OF THE PLACE WILL SOMEHOW ENRICH US BEYOND OUR WILDEST DREAMS. . .
HAVE YOU EVER BEEN LOST LIKE THAT, REVEREND?
I MEAN REALLY, TRULY, UTTERLY LOST. . . ?
NOPE!

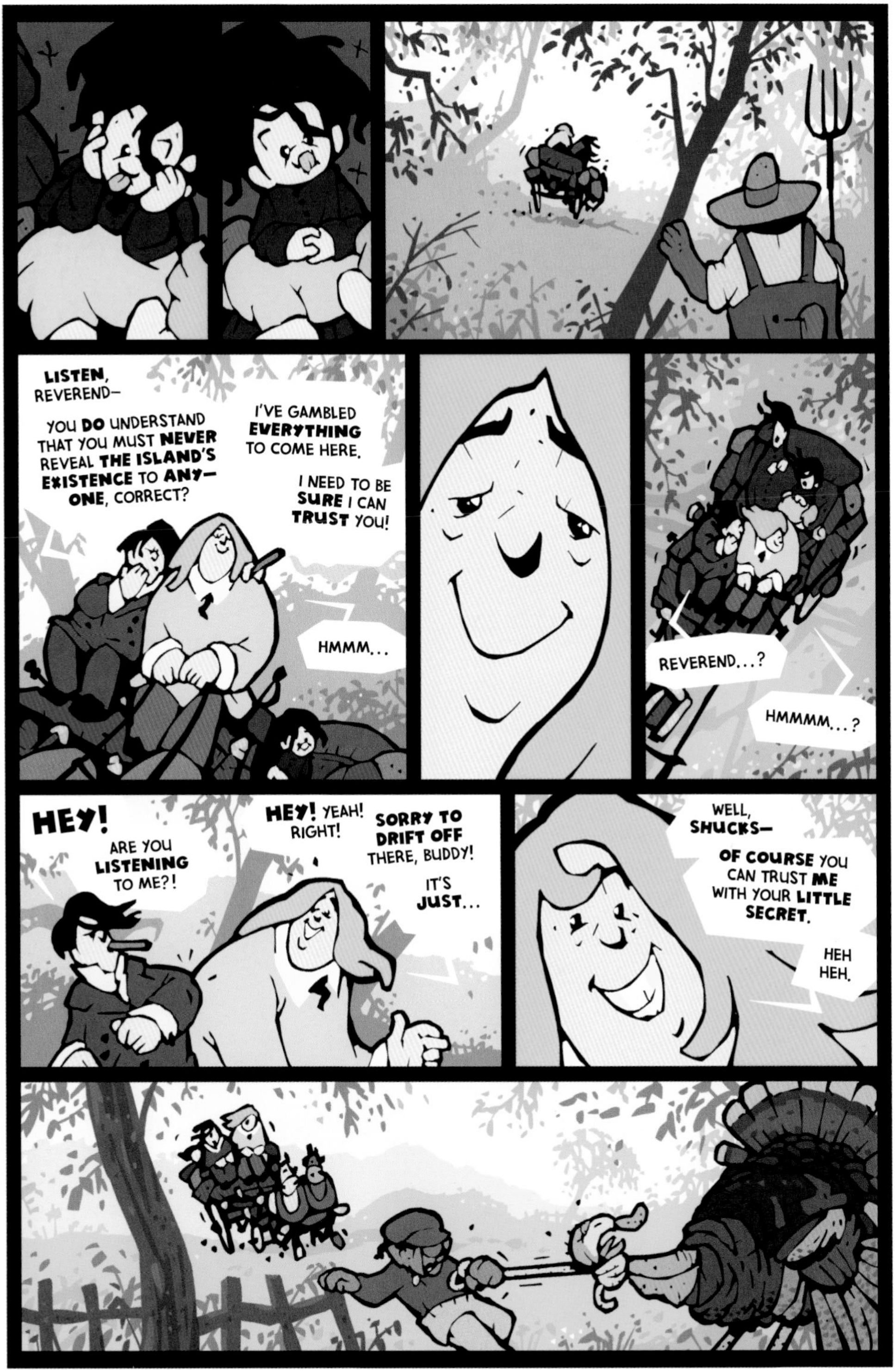

LISTEN, REVEREND—
YOU DO UNDERSTAND THAT YOU MUST NEVER REVEAL THE ISLAND'S EXISTENCE TO ANY-ONE, CORRECT?
I'VE GAMBLED EVERYTHING TO COME HERE.
I NEED TO BE SURE I CAN TRUST YOU!
HMMM...
REVEREND...?
HMMMM...?
HEY! ARE YOU LISTENING TO ME?!
HEY! YEAH! RIGHT!
SORRY TO DRIFT OFF THERE, BUDDY!
IT'S JUST...
WELL, SHUCKS—
OF COURSE YOU CAN TRUST ME WITH YOUR LITTLE SECRET.
HEH HEH.

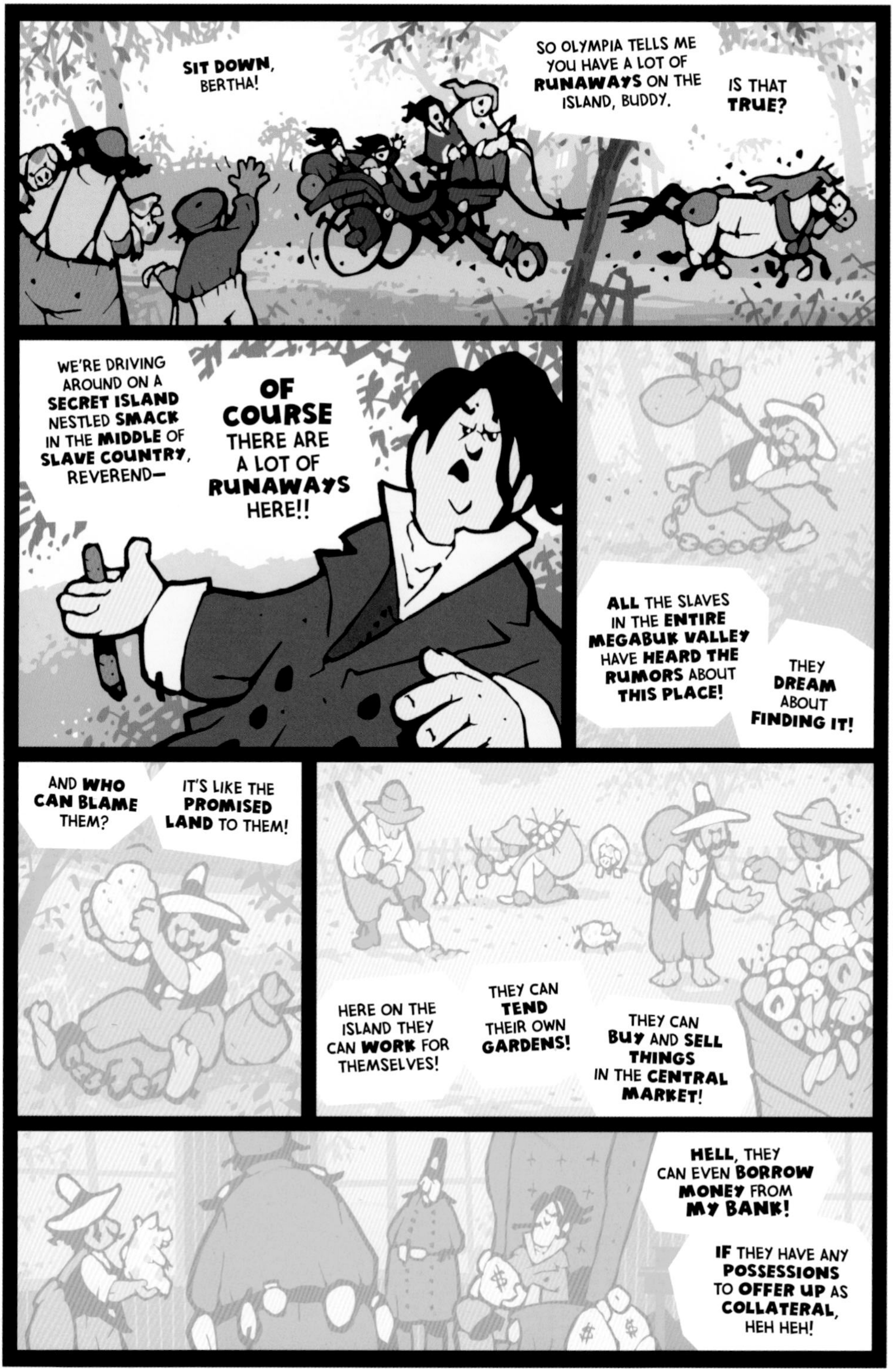

SIT DOWN, BERTHA!
SO OLYMPIA TELLS ME YOU HAVE A LOT OF RUNAWAYS ON THE ISLAND, BUDDY.
IS THAT TRUE?
WE'RE DRIVING AROUND ON A SECRET ISLAND NESTLED SMACK IN THE MIDDLE OF SLAVE COUNTRY, REVEREND—
OF COURSE THERE ARE A LOT OF RUNAWAYS HERE!!
ALL THE SLAVES IN THE ENTIRE MEGABUK VALLEY HAVE HEARD THE RUMORS ABOUT THIS PLACE!
THEY DREAM ABOUT FINDING IT!
AND WHO CAN BLAME THEM?
IT'S LIKE THE PROMISED LAND TO THEM!
HERE ON THE ISLAND THEY CAN WORK FOR THEMSELVES!
THEY CAN TEND THEIR OWN GARDENS!
THEY CAN BUY AND SELL THINGS IN THE CENTRAL MARKET!
HELL, THEY CAN EVEN BORROW MONEY FROM MY BANK!
IF THEY HAVE ANY POSSESSIONS TO OFFER UP AS COLLATERAL, HEH HEH!

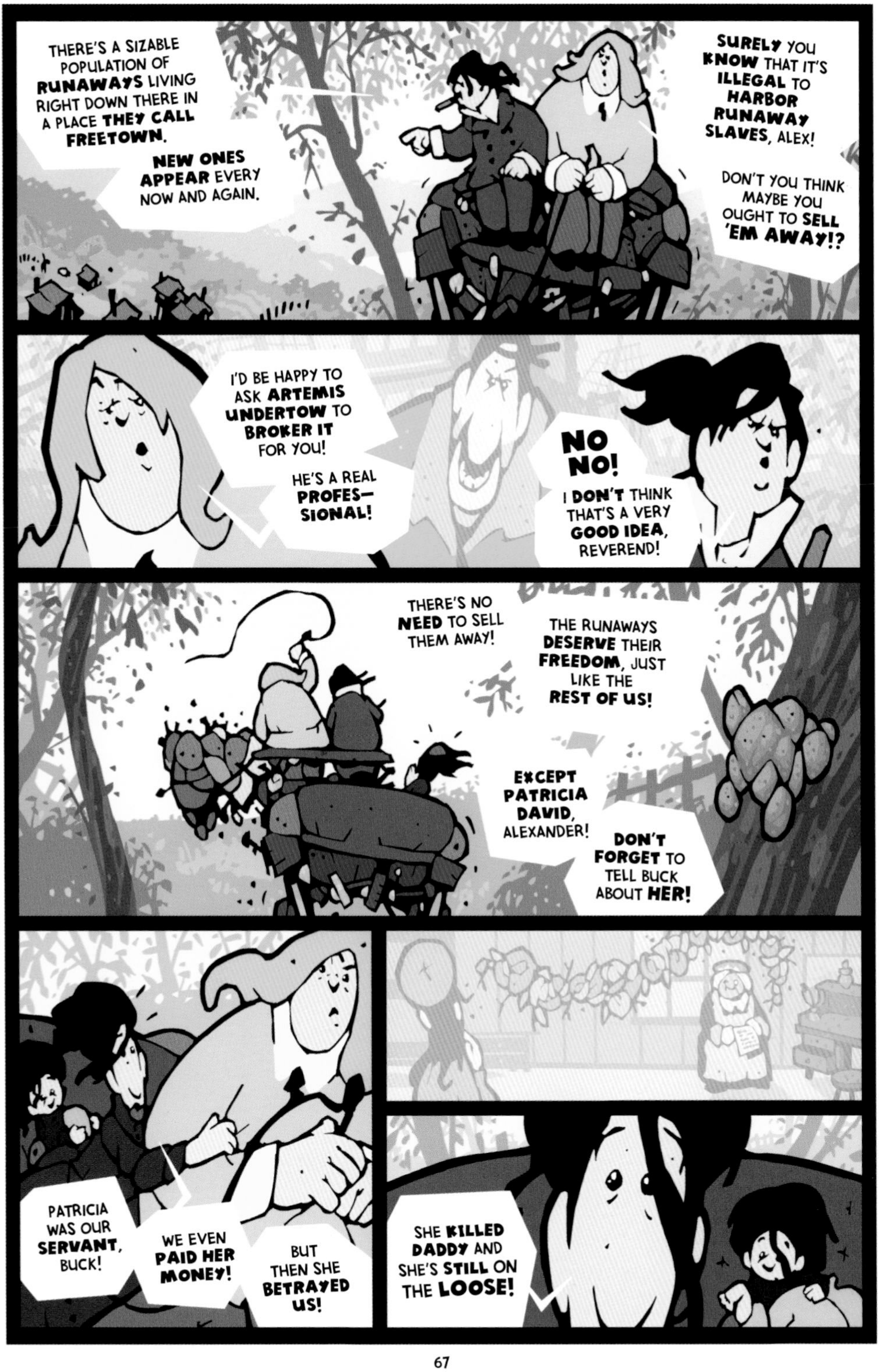

THERE'S A SIZABLE POPULATION OF RUNAWAYS LIVING RIGHT DOWN THERE IN A PLACE THEY CALL FREETOWN.
NEW ONES APPEAR EVERY NOW AND AGAIN.
SURELY YOU KNOW THAT IT'S ILLEGAL TO HARBOR RUNAWAY SLAVES, ALEX!
DON'T YOU THINK MAYBE YOU OUGHT TO SELL 'EM AWAY!?
I'D BE HAPPY TO ASK ARTEMIS UNDERTOW TO BROKER IT FOR YOU!
HE'S A REAL PROFES-SIONAL!
NO NO!
I DON'T THINK THAT'S A VERY GOOD IDEA, REVEREND!
THERE'S NO NEED TO SELL THEM AWAY!
THE RUNAWAYS DESERVE THEIR FREEDOM, JUST LIKE THE REST OF US!
EXCEPT PATRICIA DAVID, ALEXANDER!
DON'T FORGET TO TELL BUCK ABOUT HER!
PATRICIA WAS OUR SERVANT, BUCK!
WE EVEN PAID HER MONEY!
BUT THEN SHE BETRAYED US!
SHE KILLED DADDY AND SHE'S STILL ON THE LOOSE!

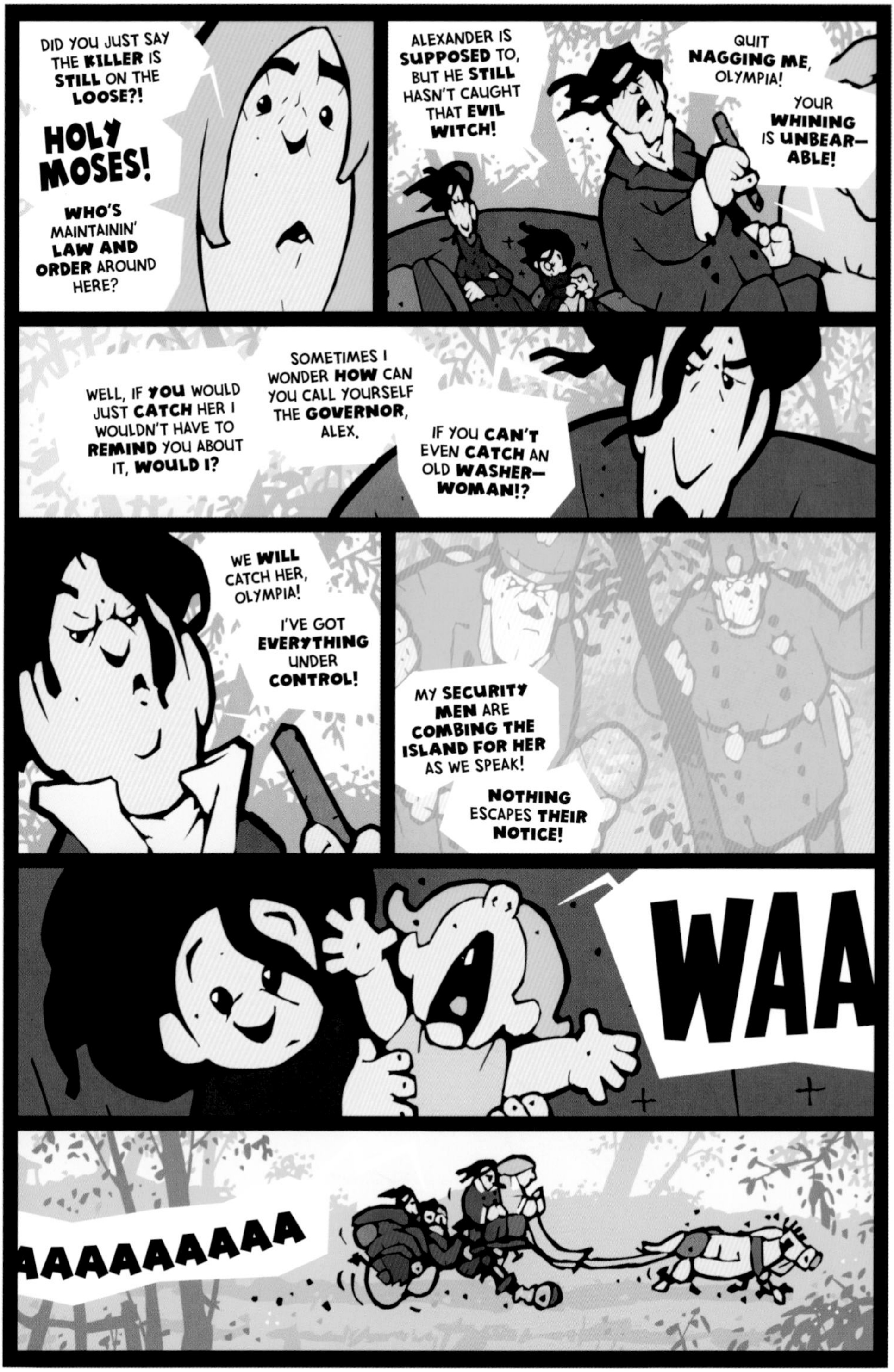
DID YOU JUST SAY THE KILLER IS STILL ON THE LOOSE?!
HOLY MOSES!
WHO'S MAINTAININ' LAW AND ORDER AROUND HERE?
ALEXANDER IS SUPPOSED TO, BUT HE STILL HASN'T CAUGHT THAT EVIL WITCH!
QUIT NAGGING ME, OLYMPIA!
YOUR WHINING IS UNBEAR-ABLE!
WELL, IF YOU WOULD JUST CATCH HER I WOULDN'T HAVE TO REMIND YOU ABOUT IT, WOULD I?
SOMETIMES I WONDER HOW CAN YOU CALL YOURSELF THE GOVERNOR, ALEX.
IF YOU CAN'T EVEN CATCH AN OLD WASHER-WOMAN!?
WE WILL CATCH HER, OLYMPIA!
I'VE GOT EVERYTHING UNDER CONTROL!
MY SECURITY MEN ARE COMBING THE ISLAND FOR HER AS WE SPEAK!
NOTHING ESCAPES THEIR NOTICE!
WAA
AAAAAAAAA

CHAPTER FIVE

What's Hiding *in Dr. Wong's Shop?*

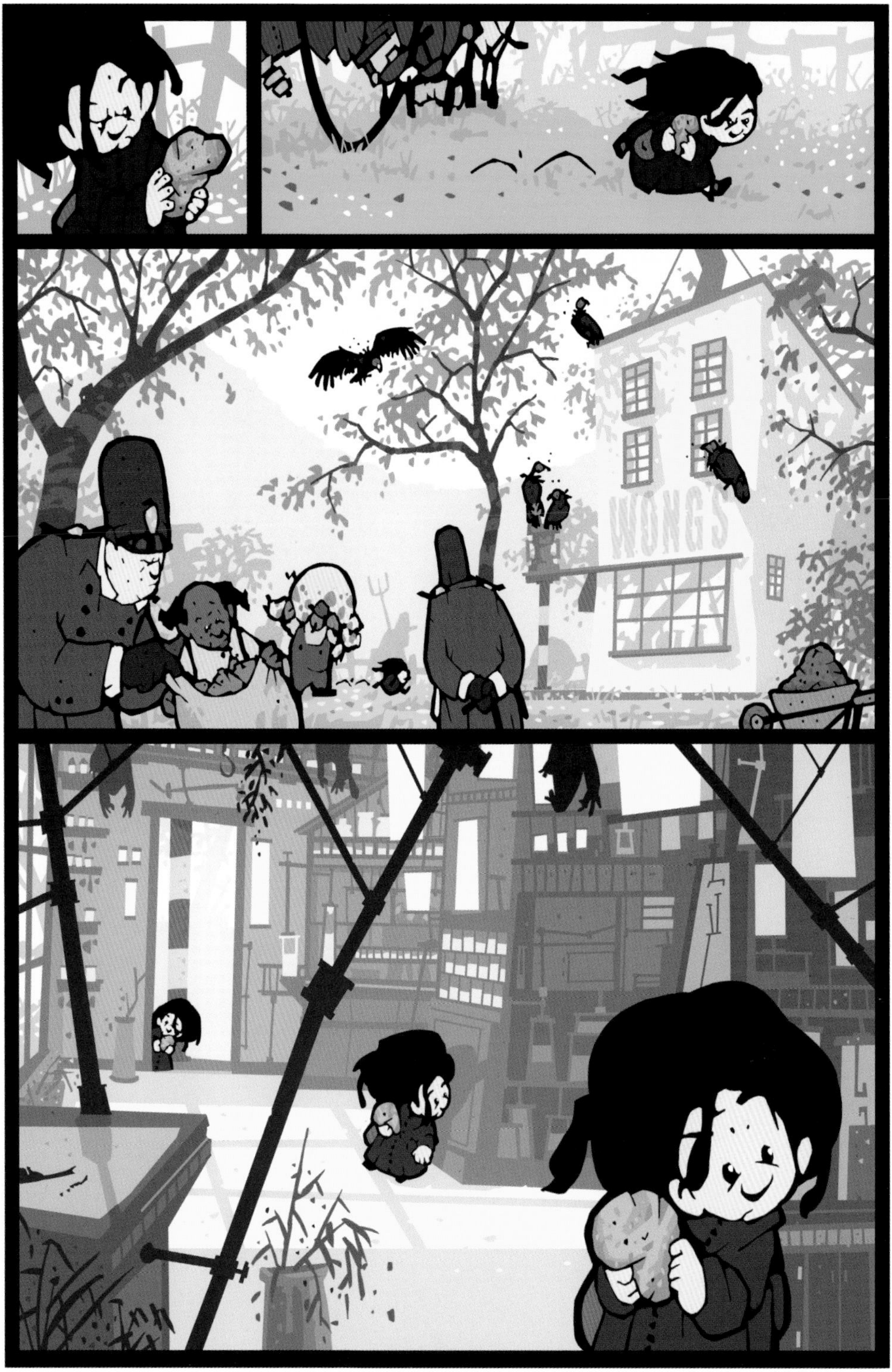
WONGS

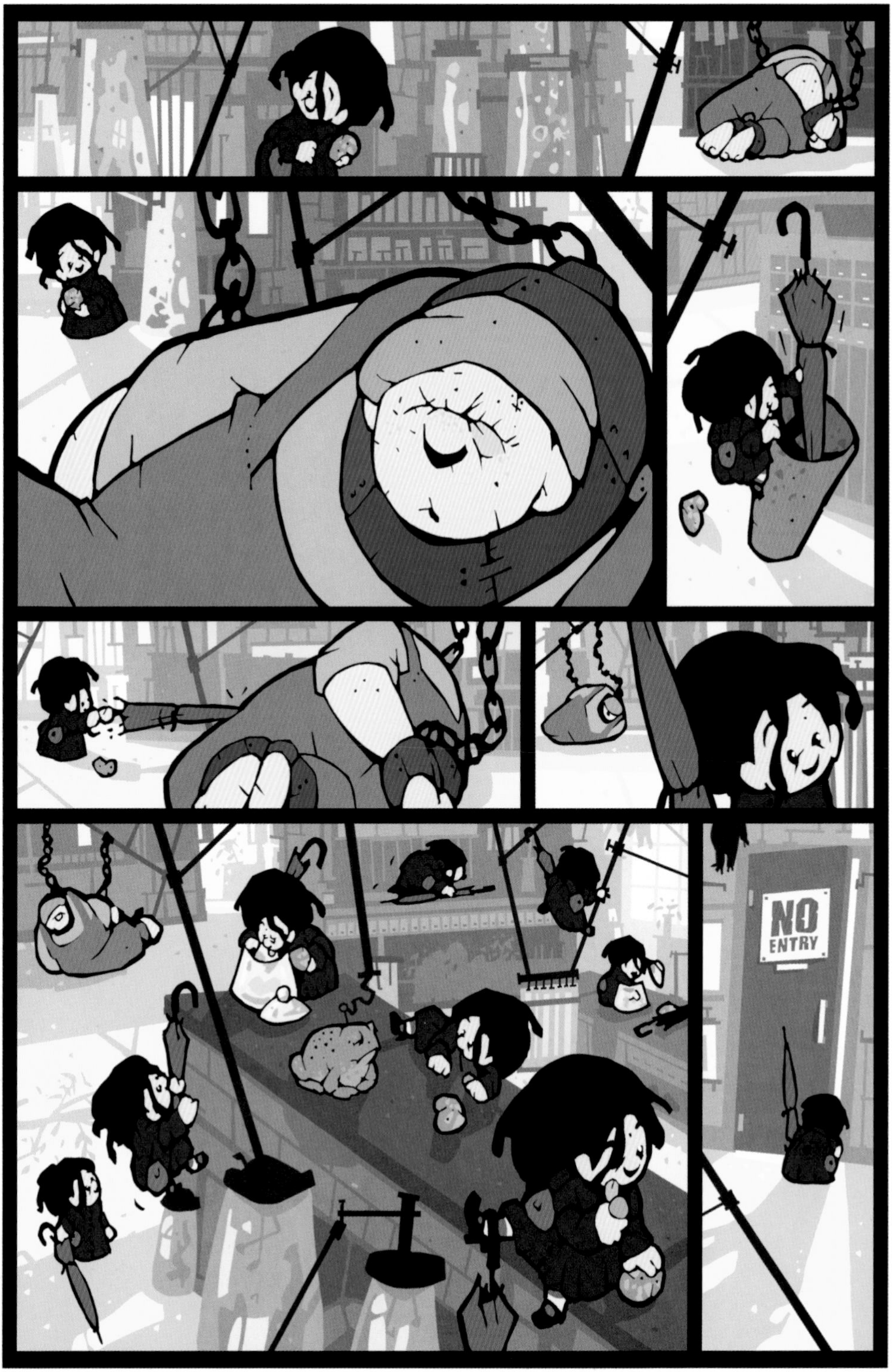
NO ENTRY

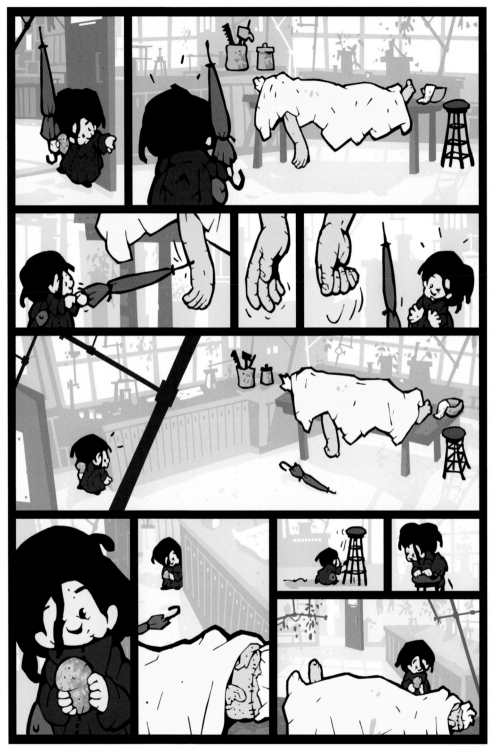

73

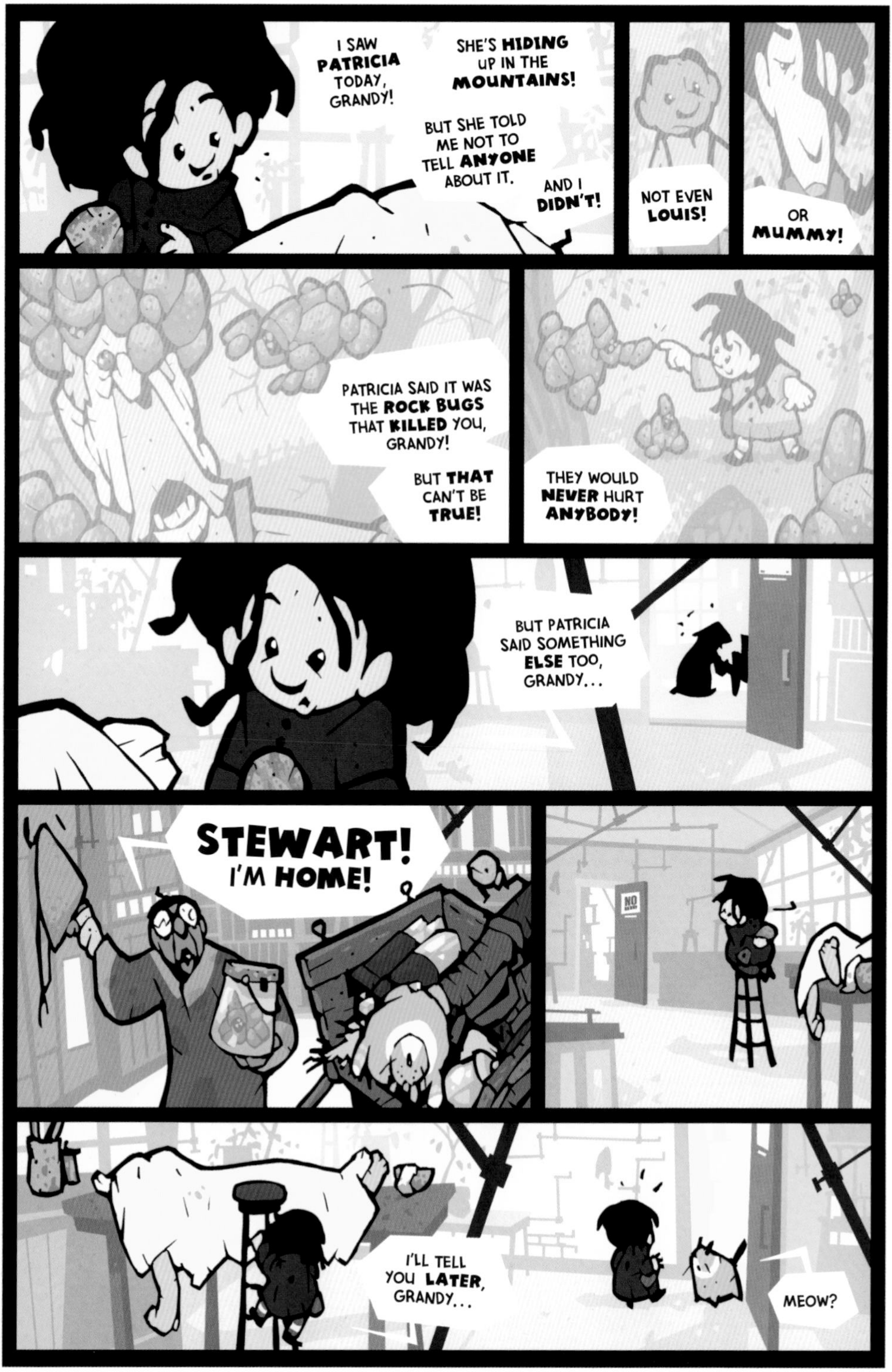
I SAW PATRICIA TODAY, GRANDY!
SHE'S HIDING UP IN THE MOUNTAINS!
BUT SHE TOLD ME NOT TO TELL ANYONE ABOUT IT.
AND I DIDN'T!
NOT EVEN LOUIS!
OR MUMMY!
PATRICIA SAID IT WAS THE ROCK BUGS THAT KILLED YOU, GRANDY!
BUT THAT CAN'T BE TRUE!
THEY WOULD NEVER HURT ANYBODY!
BUT PATRICIA SAID SOMETHING ELSE TOO, GRANDY...
STEWART! I'M HOME!
NO
I'LL TELL YOU LATER, GRANDY...
MEOW?

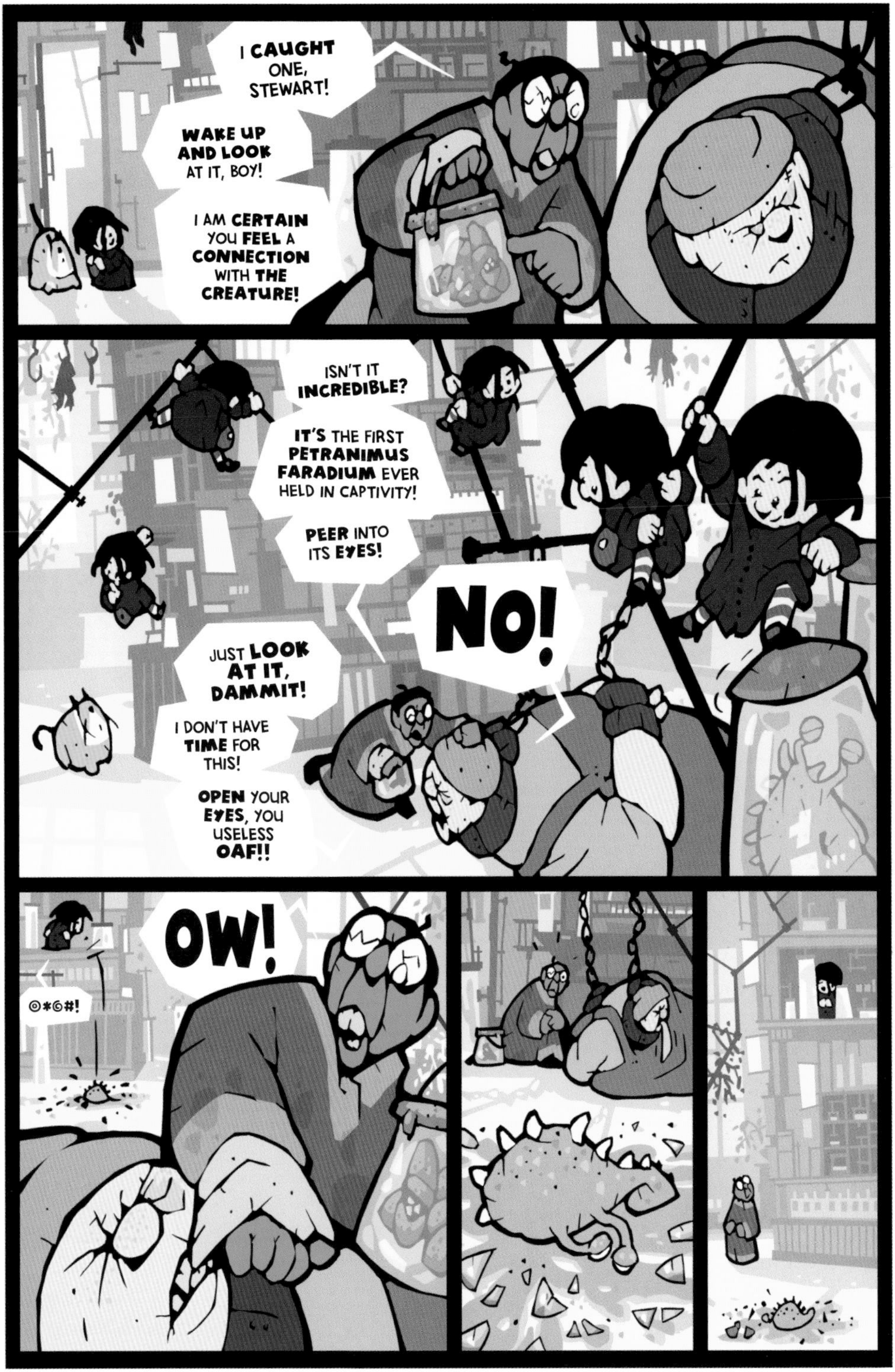
I CAUGHT ONE, STEWART!
WAKE UP AND LOOK AT IT, BOY!
I AM CERTAIN YOU FEEL A CONNECTION WITH THE CREATURE!
ISN'T IT INCREDIBLE?
IT'S THE FIRST PETRANIMUS FARADIUM EVER HELD IN CAPTIVITY!
PEER INTO ITS EYES!
NO!
JUST LOOK AT IT, DAMMIT!
I DON'T HAVE TIME FOR THIS!
OPEN YOUR EYES, YOU USELESS OAF!!
OW!
@*©#!

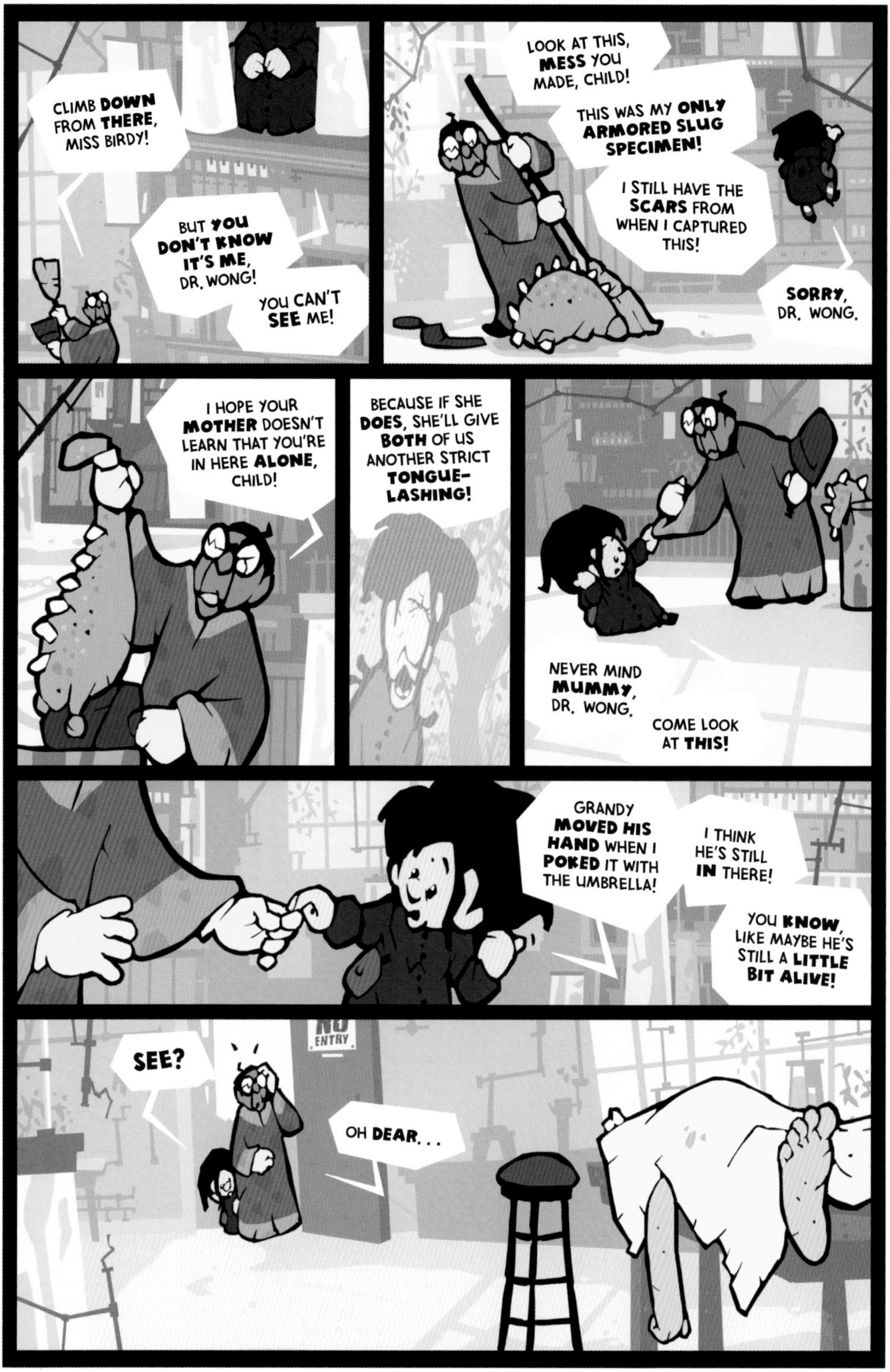
CLIMB DOWN FROM THERE, MISS BIRDY!
BUT YOU DON'T KNOW IT'S ME, DR. WONG!
YOU CAN'T SEE ME!
LOOK AT THIS, MESS YOU MADE, CHILD!
THIS WAS MY ONLY ARMORED SLUG SPECIMEN!
I STILL HAVE THE SCARS FROM WHEN I CAPTURED THIS!
SORRY, DR. WONG.
I HOPE YOUR MOTHER DOESN'T LEARN THAT YOU'RE IN HERE ALONE, CHILD!
BECAUSE IF SHE DOES, SHE'LL GIVE BOTH OF US ANOTHER STRICT TONGUE-LASHING!
NEVER MIND MUMMY, DR. WONG.
COME LOOK AT THIS!
GRANDY MOVED HIS HAND WHEN I POKED IT WITH THE UMBRELLA!
I THINK HE'S STILL IN THERE!
YOU KNOW, LIKE MAYBE HE'S STILL A LITTLE BIT ALIVE!
SEE?
NO ENTRY
OH DEAR. . .

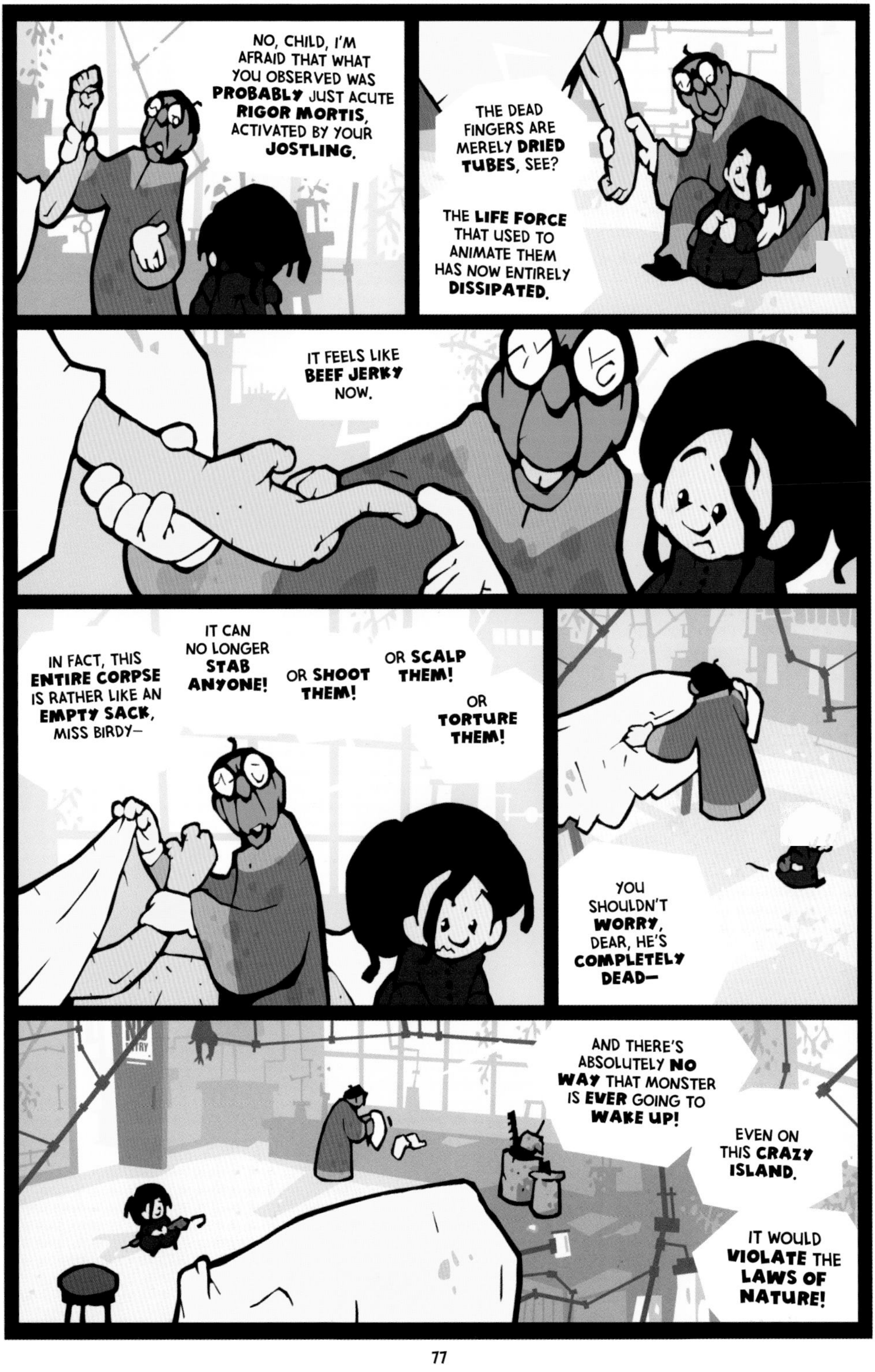
NO, CHILD, I'M AFRAID THAT WHAT YOU OBSERVED WAS PROBABLY JUST ACUTE RIGOR MORTIS, ACTIVATED BY YOUR JOSTLING.
THE DEAD FINGERS ARE MERELY DRIED TUBES, SEE?
THE LIFE FORCE THAT USED TO ANIMATE THEM HAS NOW ENTIRELY DISSIPATED.
IT FEELS LIKE BEEF JERKY NOW.
IN FACT, THIS ENTIRE CORPSE IS RATHER LIKE AN EMPTY SACK, MISS BIRDY—
IT CAN NO LONGER STAB ANYONE!
OR SHOOT THEM!
OR SCALP THEM!
OR TORTURE THEM!
YOU SHOULDN'T WORRY, DEAR, HE'S COMPLETELY DEAD—
AND THERE'S ABSOLUTELY NO WAY THAT MONSTER IS EVER GOING TO WAKE UP!
EVEN ON THIS CRAZY ISLAND.
IT WOULD VIOLATE THE LAWS OF NATURE!

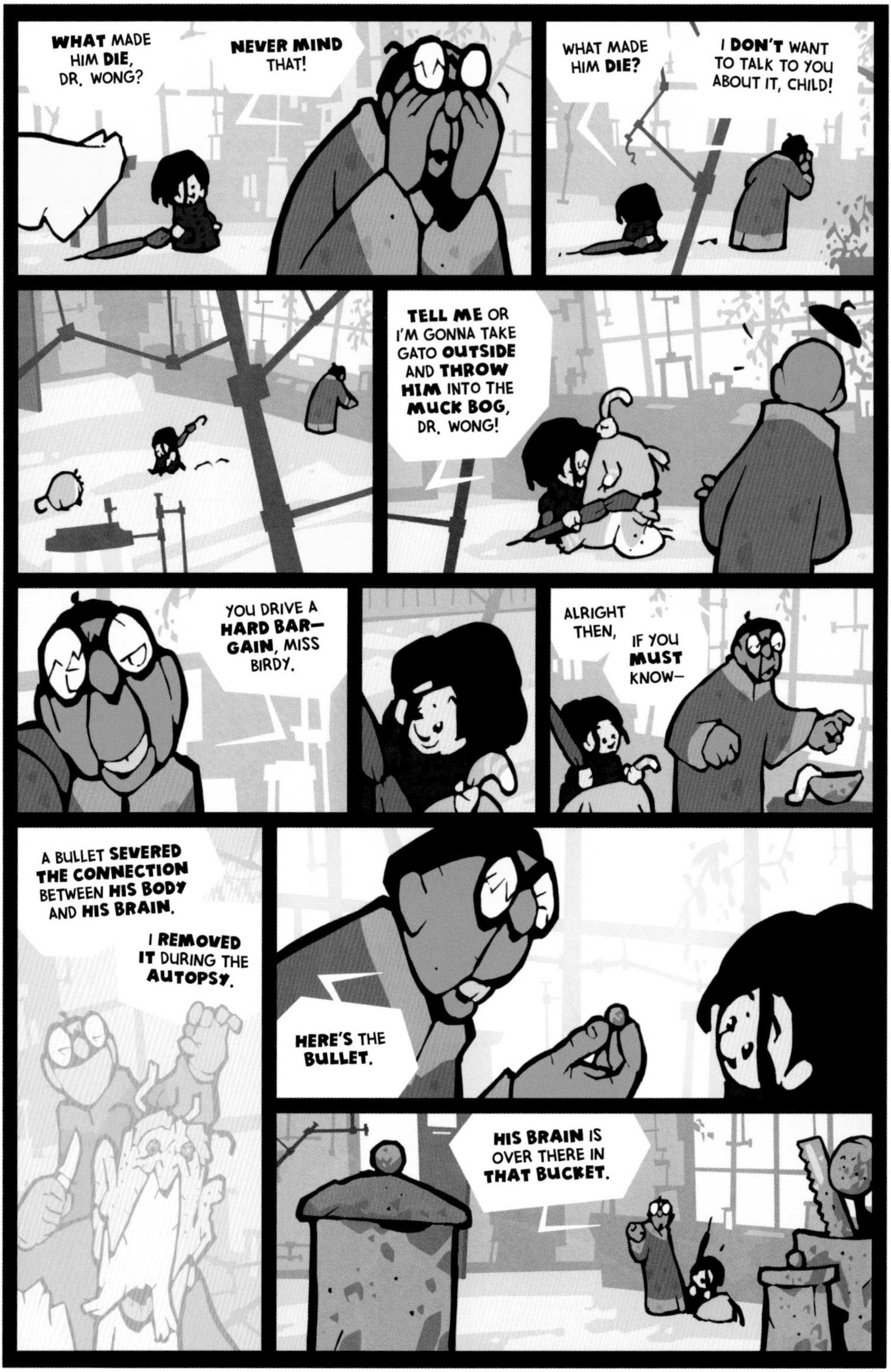
WHAT MADE HIM DIE, DR. WONG?
NEVER MIND THAT!
WHAT MADE HIM DIE?
I DON'T WANT TO TALK TO YOU ABOUT IT, CHILD!
TELL ME OR I'M GONNA TAKE GATO OUTSIDE AND THROW HIM INTO THE MUCK BOG, DR. WONG!
YOU DRIVE A HARD BAR-GAIN, MISS BIRDY.
ALRIGHT THEN,
IF YOU MUST KNOW–
A BULLET SEVERED THE CONNECTION BETWEEN HIS BODY AND HIS BRAIN.
I REMOVED IT DURING THE AUTOPSY.
HERE'S THE BULLET.
HIS BRAIN IS OVER THERE IN THAT BUCKET.

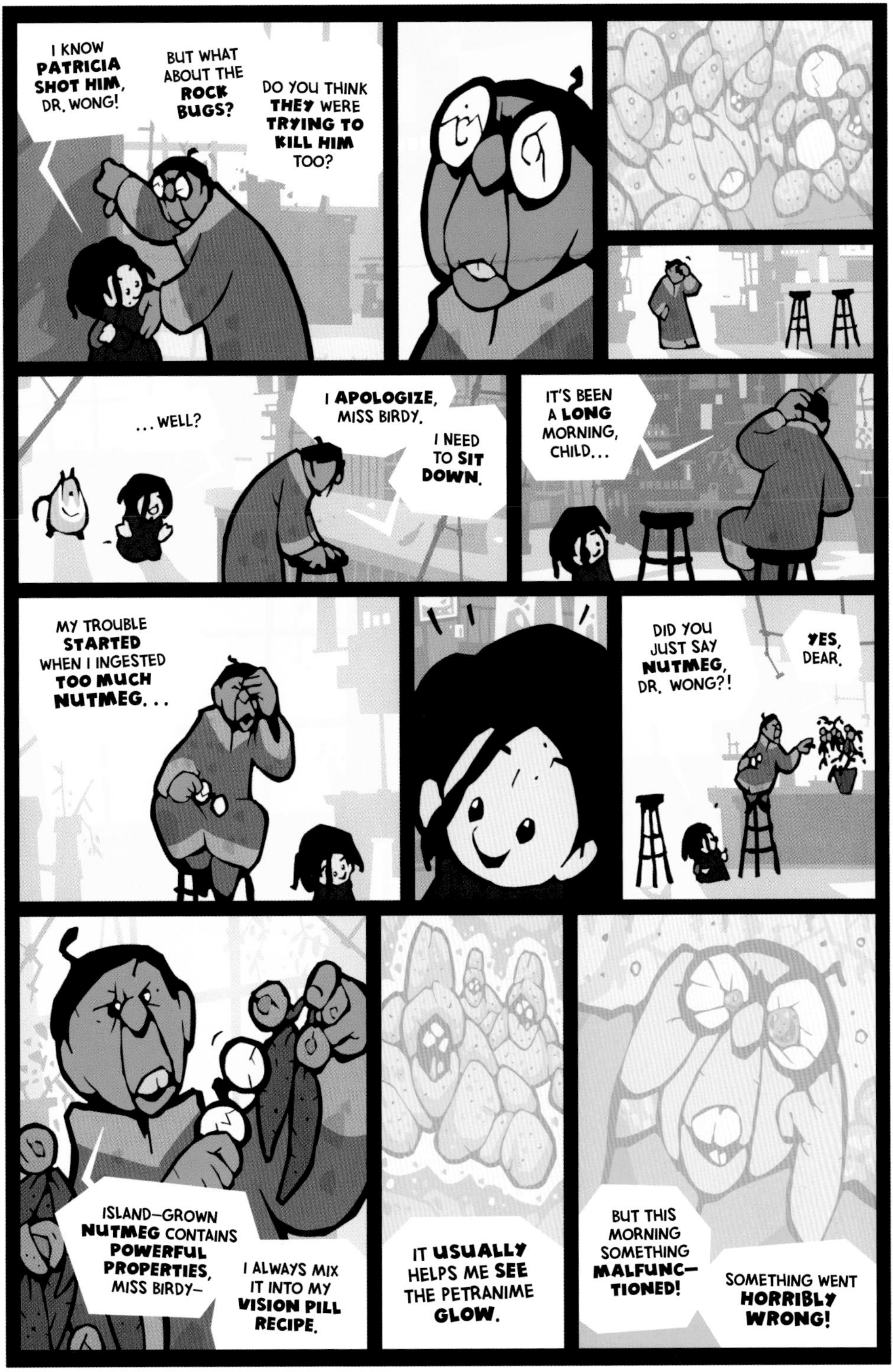
I KNOW PATRICIA SHOT HIM, DR. WONG!
BUT WHAT ABOUT THE ROCK BUGS?
DO YOU THINK THEY WERE TRYING TO KILL HIM TOO?
...WELL?
I APOLOGIZE, MISS BIRDY.
I NEED TO SIT DOWN.
IT'S BEEN A LONG MORNING, CHILD...
MY TROUBLE STARTED WHEN I INGESTED TOO MUCH NUTMEG...
DID YOU JUST SAY NUTMEG, DR. WONG?!
YES, DEAR.
ISLAND–GROWN NUTMEG CONTAINS POWERFUL PROPERTIES, MISS BIRDY–
I ALWAYS MIX IT INTO MY VISION PILL RECIPE.
IT USUALLY HELPS ME SEE THE PETRANIME GLOW.
BUT THIS MORNING SOMETHING MALFUNC–TIONED!
SOMETHING WENT HORRIBLY WRONG!

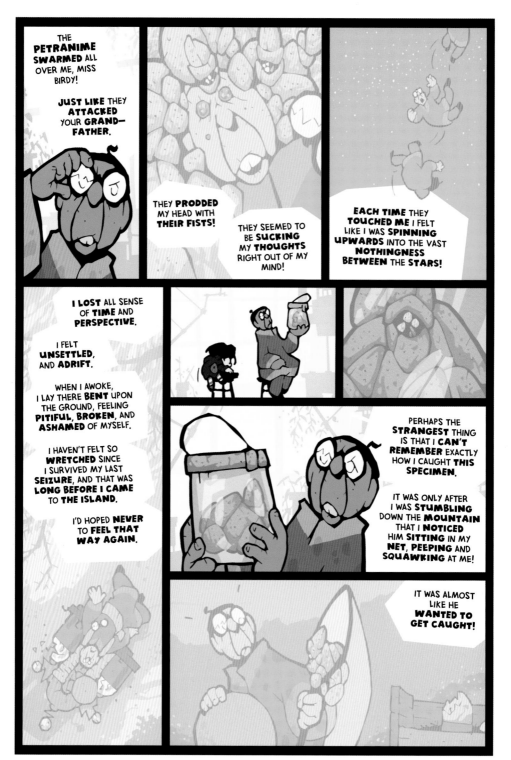

THE **PETRANIME SWARMED** ALL OVER ME, MISS BIRDY!

JUST LIKE THEY **ATTACKED** YOUR **GRAND— FATHER.**

THEY **PRODDED** MY HEAD WITH **THEIR FISTS!**

THEY SEEMED TO BE **SUCKING** MY **THOUGHTS** RIGHT OUT OF MY MIND!

EACH TIME THEY **TOUCHED ME** I FELT LIKE I WAS **SPINNING UPWARDS** INTO THE VAST **NOTHINGNESS BETWEEN** THE **STARS!**

I LOST ALL SENSE OF **TIME** AND **PERSPECTIVE.**

I FELT **UNSETTLED,** AND **ADRIFT.**

WHEN I AWOKE, I LAY THERE **BENT** UPON THE GROUND, FEELING **PITIFUL, BROKEN,** AND **ASHAMED** OF MYSELF.

I HAVEN'T FELT SO **WRETCHED** SINCE I SURVIVED MY LAST **SEIZURE,** AND THAT WAS **LONG BEFORE I CAME** TO **THE ISLAND.**

I'D HOPED **NEVER** TO **FEEL THAT WAY** AGAIN.

PERHAPS THE **STRANGEST** THING IS THAT I **CAN'T REMEMBER** EXACTLY HOW I CAUGHT **THIS SPECIMEN.**

IT WAS ONLY AFTER I WAS **STUMBLING** DOWN THE **MOUNTAIN** THAT I **NOTICED** HIM **SITTING** IN MY **NET, PEEPING** AND **SQUAWKING** AT ME!

IT WAS ALMOST LIKE HE **WANTED TO GET CAUGHT!**

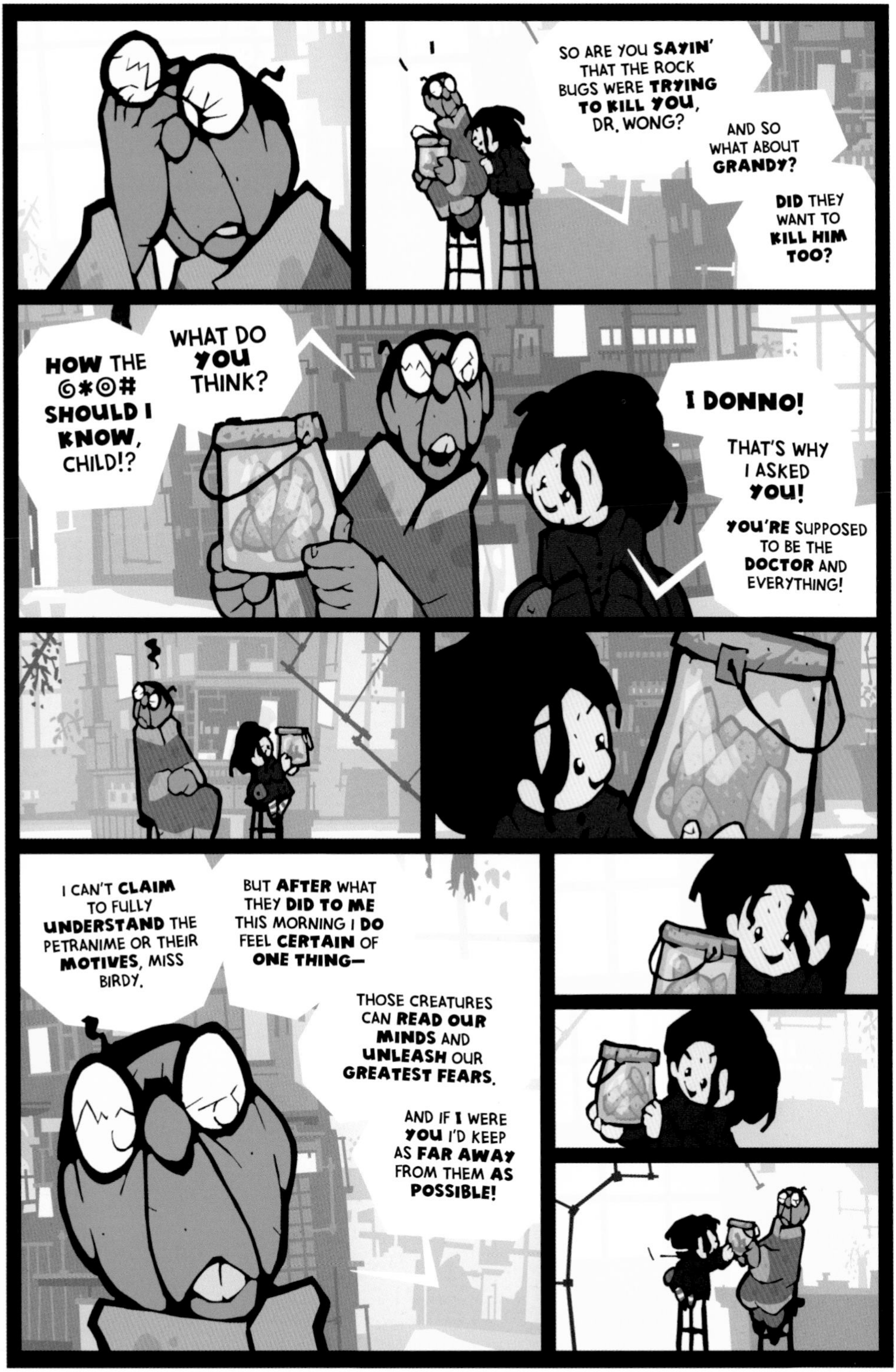
SO ARE YOU SAYIN' THAT THE ROCK BUGS WERE TRYING TO KILL YOU, DR. WONG?
AND SO WHAT ABOUT GRANDY?
DID THEY WANT TO KILL HIM TOO?
HOW THE ©*@# SHOULD I KNOW, CHILD!?
WHAT DO YOU THINK?
I DONNO!
THAT'S WHY I ASKED YOU!
YOU'RE SUPPOSED TO BE THE DOCTOR AND EVERYTHING!
I CAN'T CLAIM TO FULLY UNDERSTAND THE PETRANIME OR THEIR MOTIVES, MISS BIRDY.
BUT AFTER WHAT THEY DID TO ME THIS MORNING I DO FEEL CERTAIN OF ONE THING—
THOSE CREATURES CAN READ OUR MINDS AND UNLEASH OUR GREATEST FEARS.
AND IF I WERE YOU I'D KEEP AS FAR AWAY FROM THEM AS POSSIBLE!

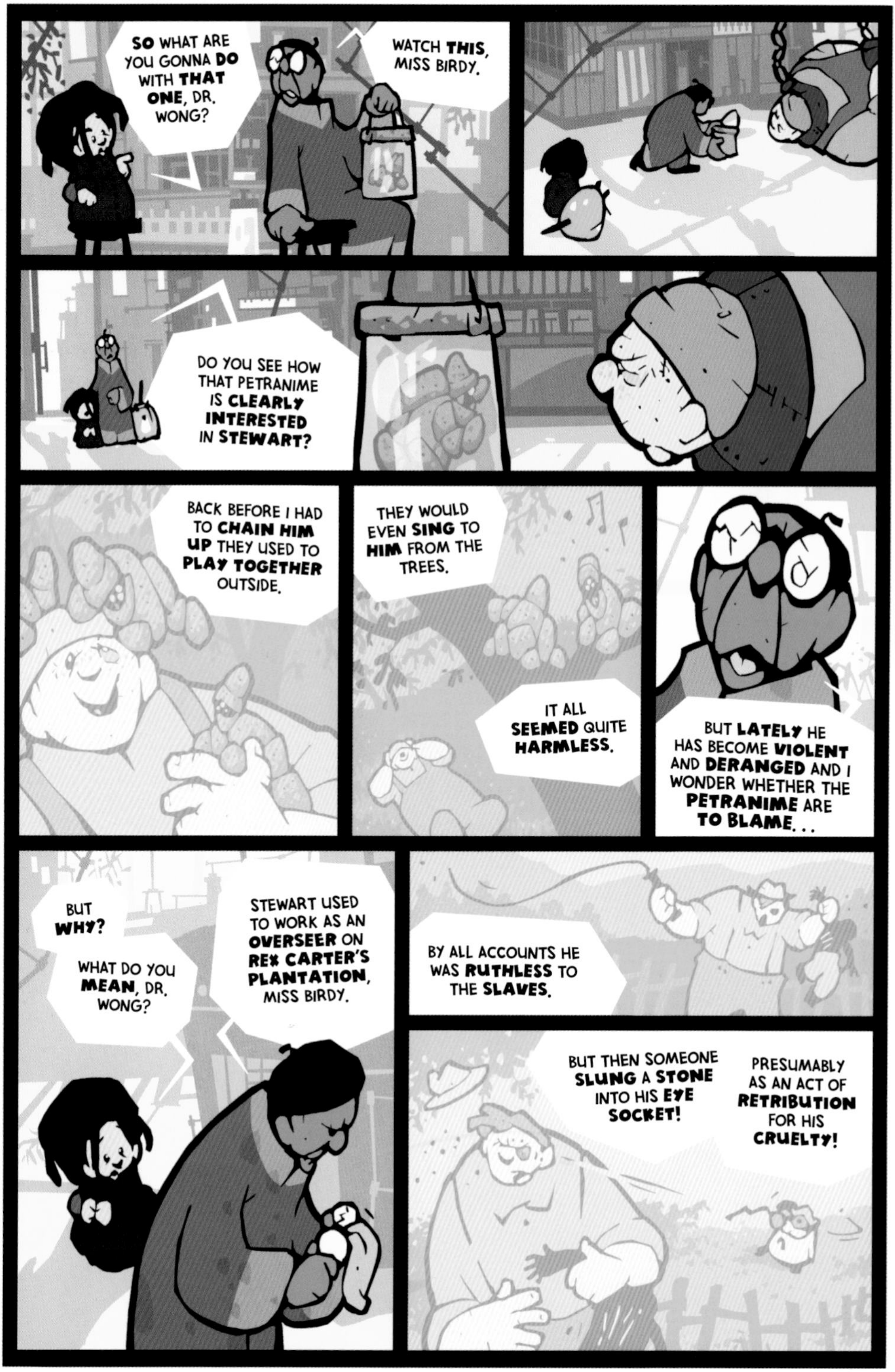
SO WHAT ARE YOU GONNA DO WITH THAT ONE, DR. WONG?
WATCH THIS, MISS BIRDY.
DO YOU SEE HOW THAT PETRANIME IS CLEARLY INTERESTED IN STEWART?
BACK BEFORE I HAD TO CHAIN HIM UP THEY USED TO PLAY TOGETHER OUTSIDE.
THEY WOULD EVEN SING TO HIM FROM THE TREES.
IT ALL SEEMED QUITE HARMLESS.
BUT LATELY HE HAS BECOME VIOLENT AND DERANGED AND I WONDER WHETHER THE PETRANIME ARE TO BLAME. . .
BUT WHY?
WHAT DO YOU MEAN, DR. WONG?
STEWART USED TO WORK AS AN OVERSEER ON REX CARTER'S PLANTATION, MISS BIRDY.
BY ALL ACCOUNTS HE WAS RUTHLESS TO THE SLAVES.
BUT THEN SOMEONE SLUNG A STONE INTO HIS EYE SOCKET!
PRESUMABLY AS AN ACT OF RETRIBUTION FOR HIS CRUELTY!

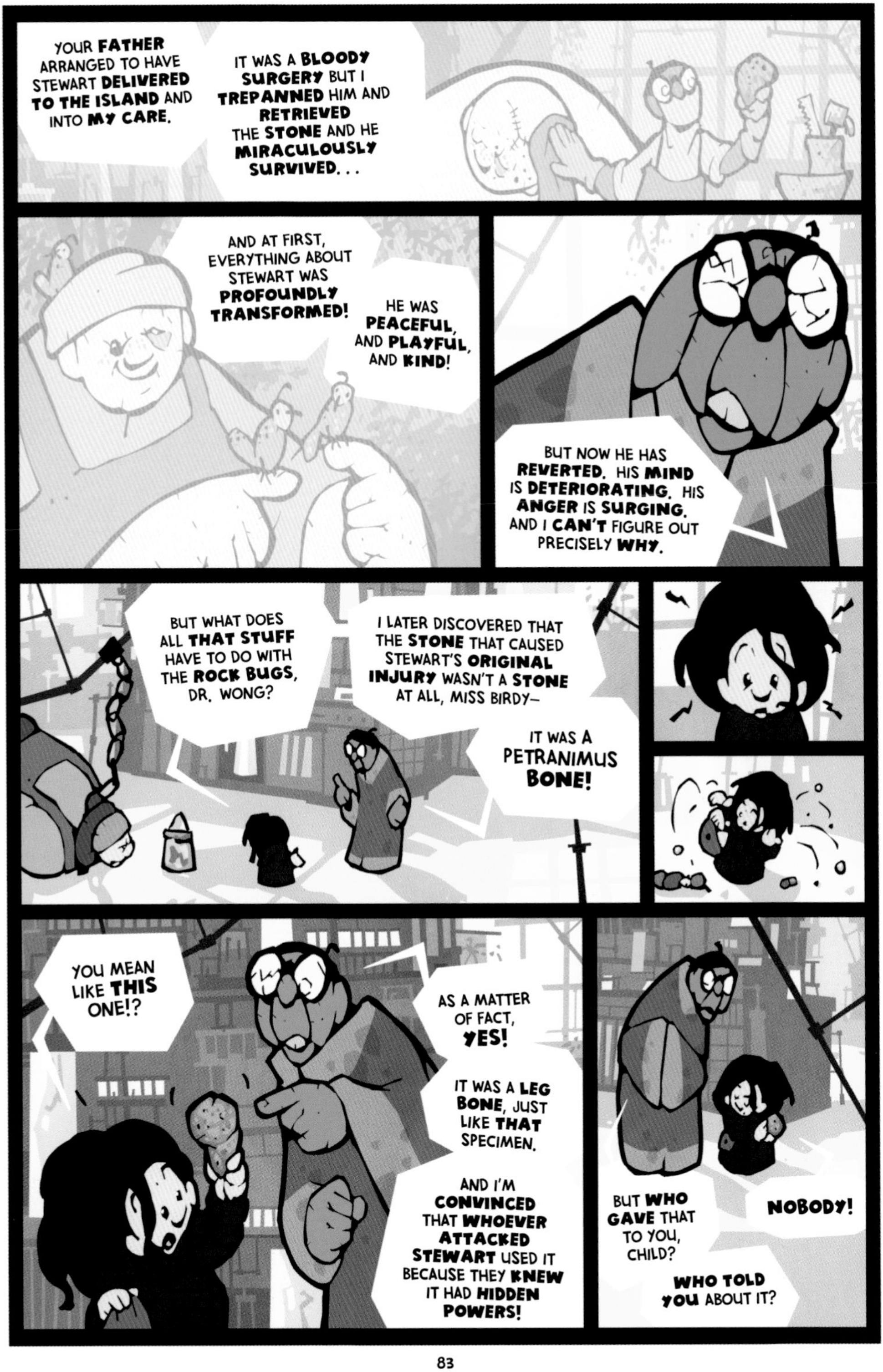
YOUR FATHER ARRANGED TO HAVE STEWART DELIVERED TO THE ISLAND AND INTO MY CARE.
IT WAS A BLOODY SURGERY BUT I TREPANNED HIM AND RETRIEVED THE STONE AND HE MIRACULOUSLY SURVIVED. . .
AND AT FIRST, EVERYTHING ABOUT STEWART WAS PROFOUNDLY TRANSFORMED!
HE WAS PEACEFUL, AND PLAYFUL, AND KIND!
BUT NOW HE HAS REVERTED. HIS MIND IS DETERIORATING. HIS ANGER IS SURGING. AND I CAN'T FIGURE OUT PRECISELY WHY.
BUT WHAT DOES ALL THAT STUFF HAVE TO DO WITH THE ROCK BUGS, DR. WONG?
I LATER DISCOVERED THAT THE STONE THAT CAUSED STEWART'S ORIGINAL INJURY WASN'T A STONE AT ALL, MISS BIRDY–
IT WAS A PETRANIMUS BONE!
YOU MEAN LIKE THIS ONE!?
AS A MATTER OF FACT, YES!
IT WAS A LEG BONE, JUST LIKE THAT SPECIMEN.
AND I'M CONVINCED THAT WHOEVER ATTACKED STEWART USED IT BECAUSE THEY KNEW IT HAD HIDDEN POWERS!
BUT WHO GAVE THAT TO YOU, CHILD?
WHO TOLD YOU ABOUT IT?
NOBODY!

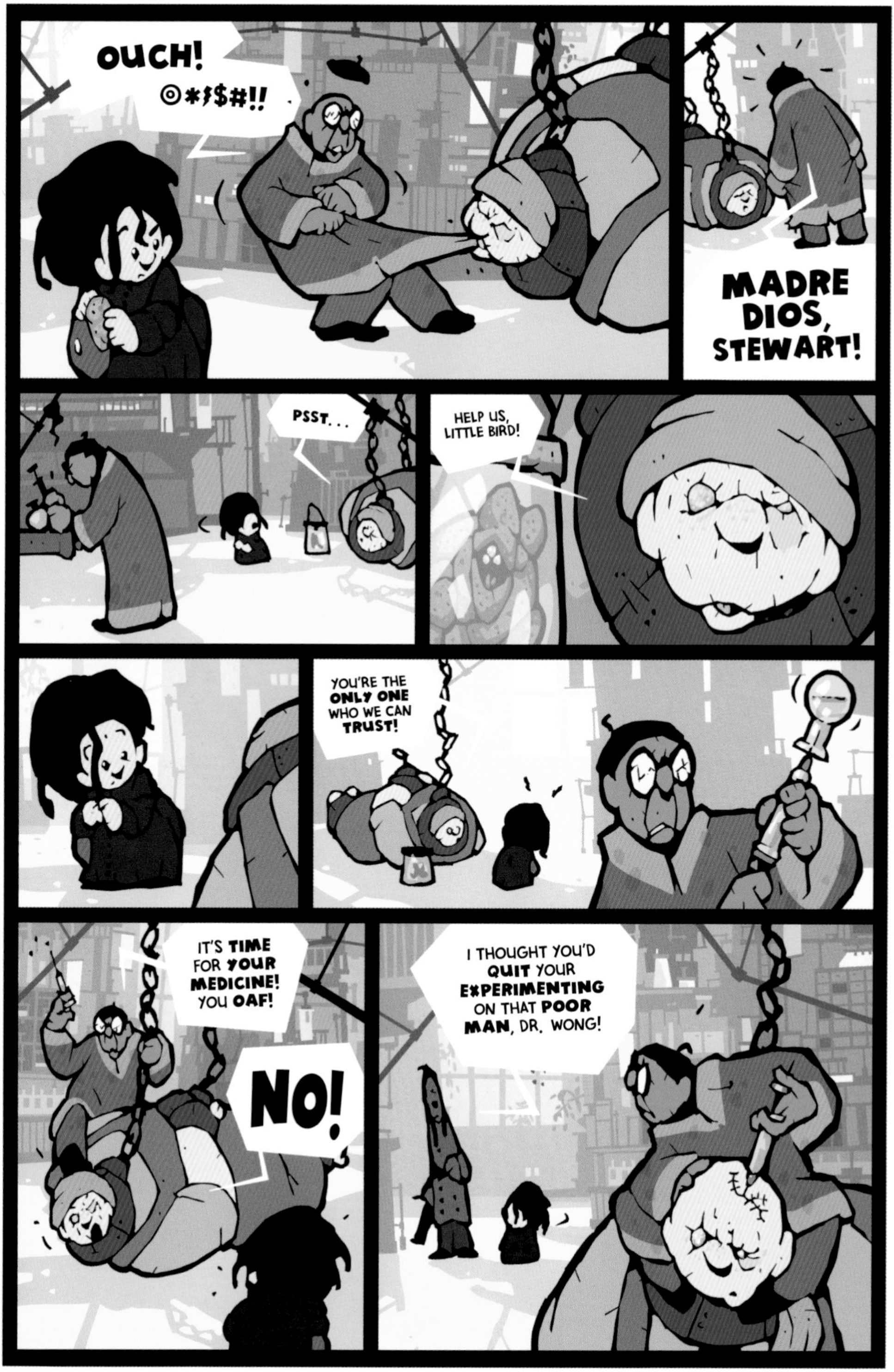
OUCH!
©*$#!!
MADRE DIOS, STEWART!
PSST...
HELP US, LITTLE BIRD!
YOU'RE THE ONLY ONE WHO WE CAN TRUST!
IT'S TIME FOR YOUR MEDICINE! YOU OAF!
NO!
I THOUGHT YOU'D QUIT YOUR EXPERIMENTING ON THAT POOR MAN, DR. WONG!

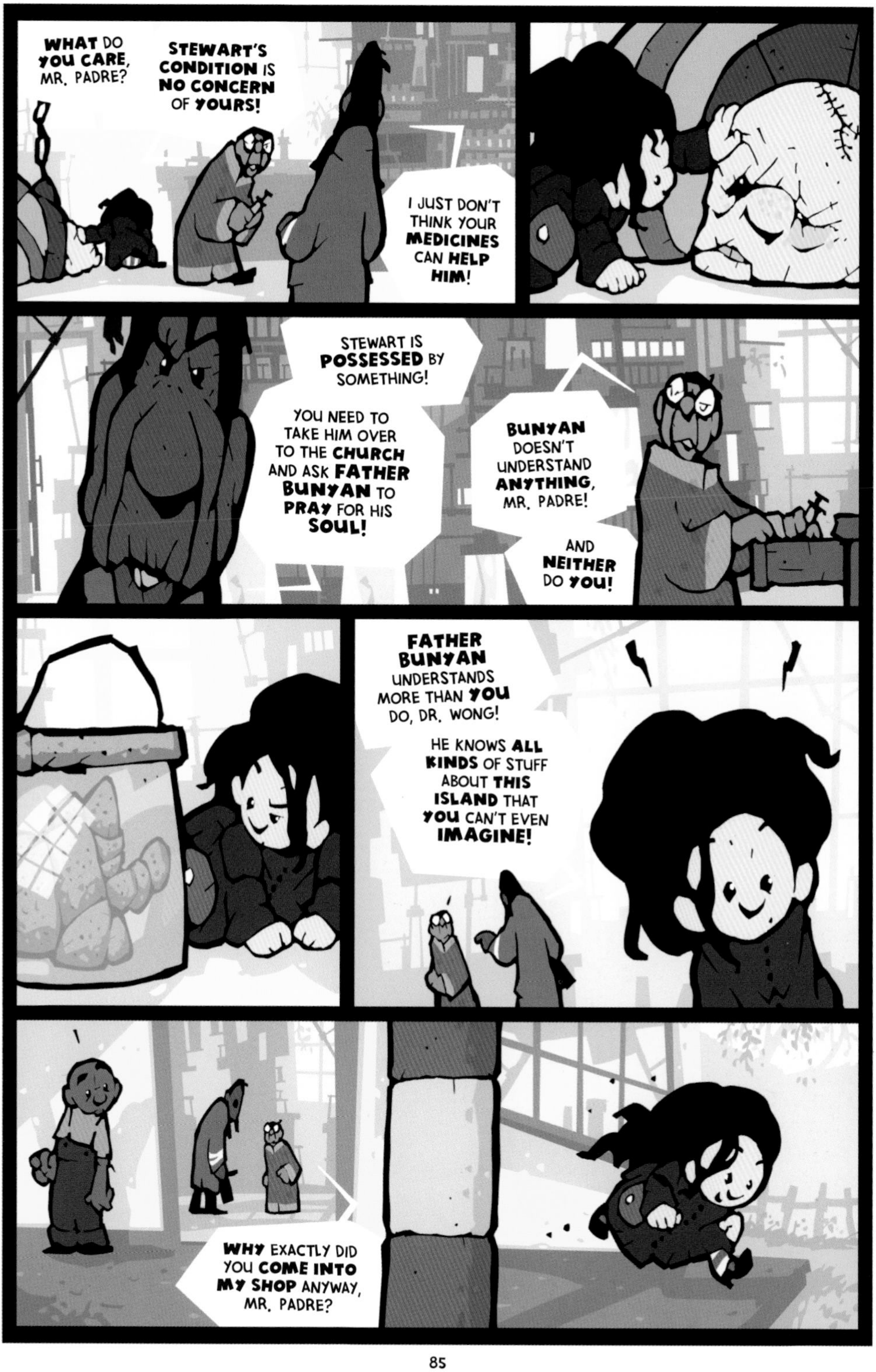
WHAT DO YOU CARE, MR. PADRE?
STEWART'S CONDITION IS NO CONCERN OF YOURS!
I JUST DON'T THINK YOUR MEDICINES CAN HELP HIM!
STEWART IS POSSESSED BY SOMETHING!
YOU NEED TO TAKE HIM OVER TO THE CHURCH AND ASK FATHER BUNYAN TO PRAY FOR HIS SOUL!
BUNYAN DOESN'T UNDERSTAND ANYTHING, MR. PADRE!
AND NEITHER DO YOU!
FATHER BUNYAN UNDERSTANDS MORE THAN YOU DO, DR. WONG!
HE KNOWS ALL KINDS OF STUFF ABOUT THIS ISLAND THAT YOU CAN'T EVEN IMAGINE!
WHY EXACTLY DID YOU COME INTO MY SHOP ANYWAY, MR. PADRE?

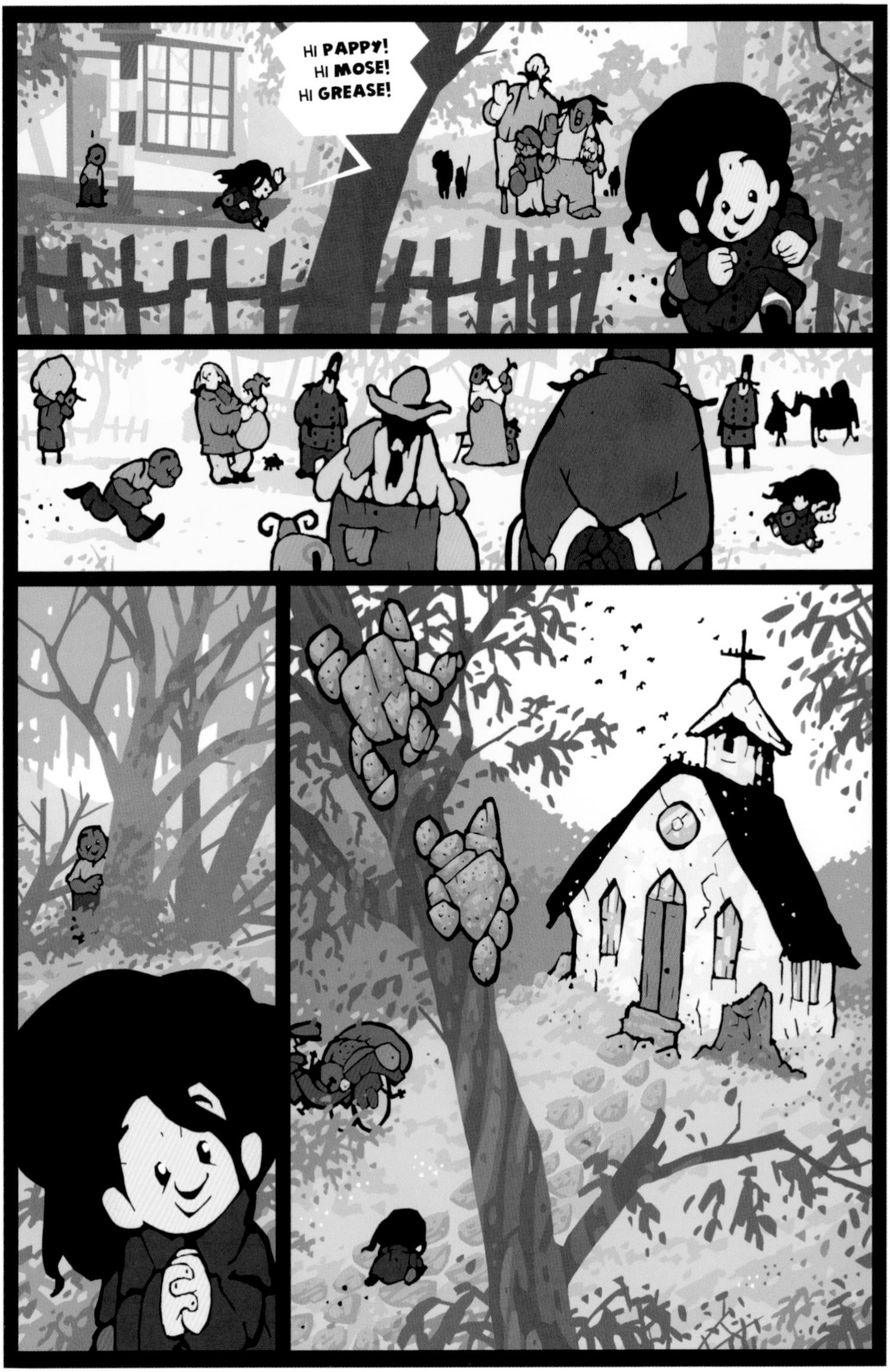
HI PAPPY!
HI MOSE!
HI GREASE!

CHAPTER SIX
❧ Attraction & Revulsion ❧

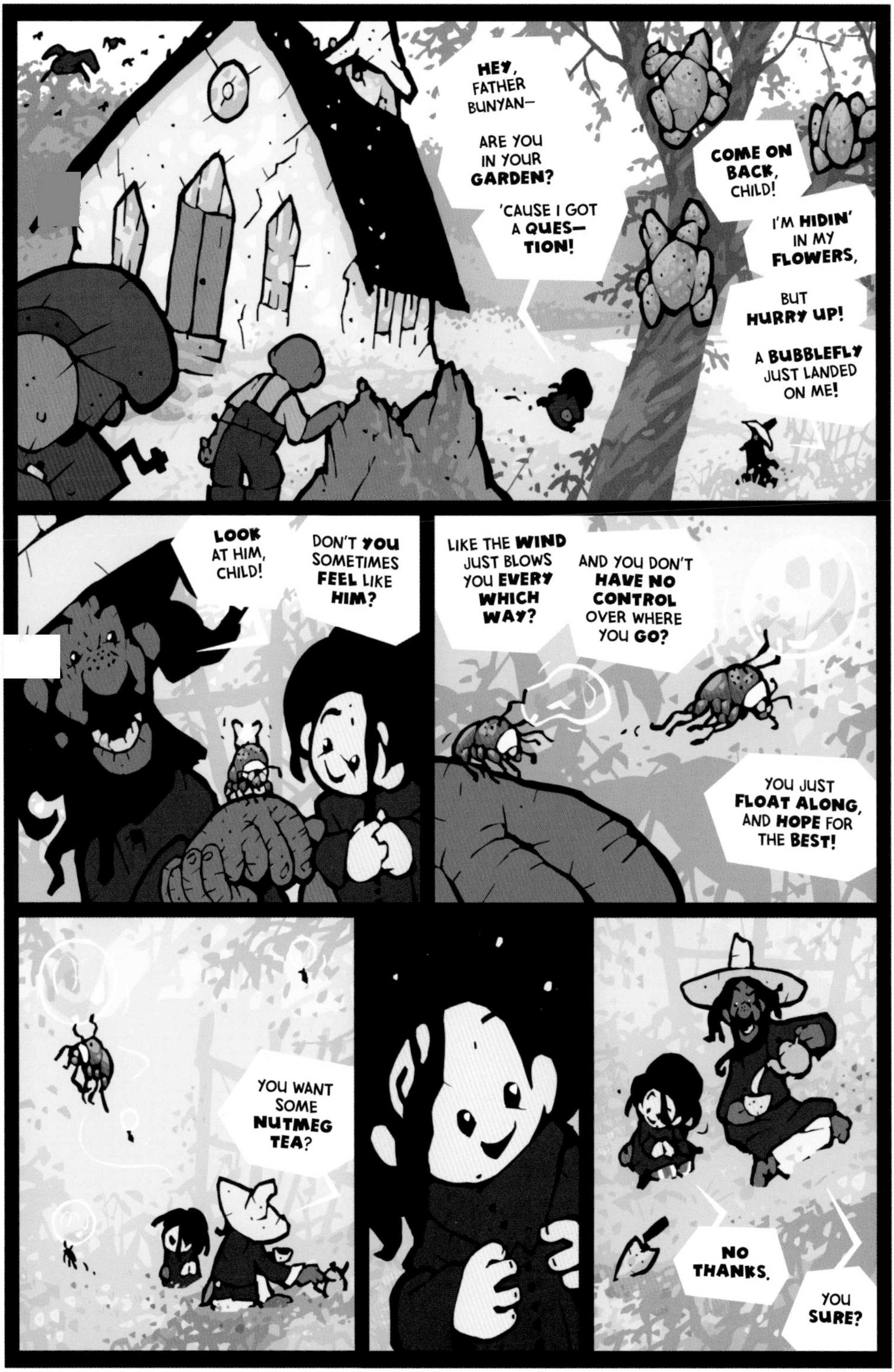
HEY, FATHER BUNYAN—
ARE YOU IN YOUR GARDEN?
'CAUSE I GOT A QUES— TION!
COME ON BACK, CHILD!
I'M HIDIN' IN MY FLOWERS,
BUT HURRY UP!
A BUBBLEFLY JUST LANDED ON ME!
LOOK AT HIM, CHILD!
DON'T YOU SOMETIMES FEEL LIKE HIM?
LIKE THE WIND JUST BLOWS YOU EVERY WHICH WAY?
AND YOU DON'T HAVE NO CONTROL OVER WHERE YOU GO?
YOU JUST FLOAT ALONG, AND HOPE FOR THE BEST!
YOU WANT SOME NUTMEG TEA?
NO THANKS.
YOU SURE?

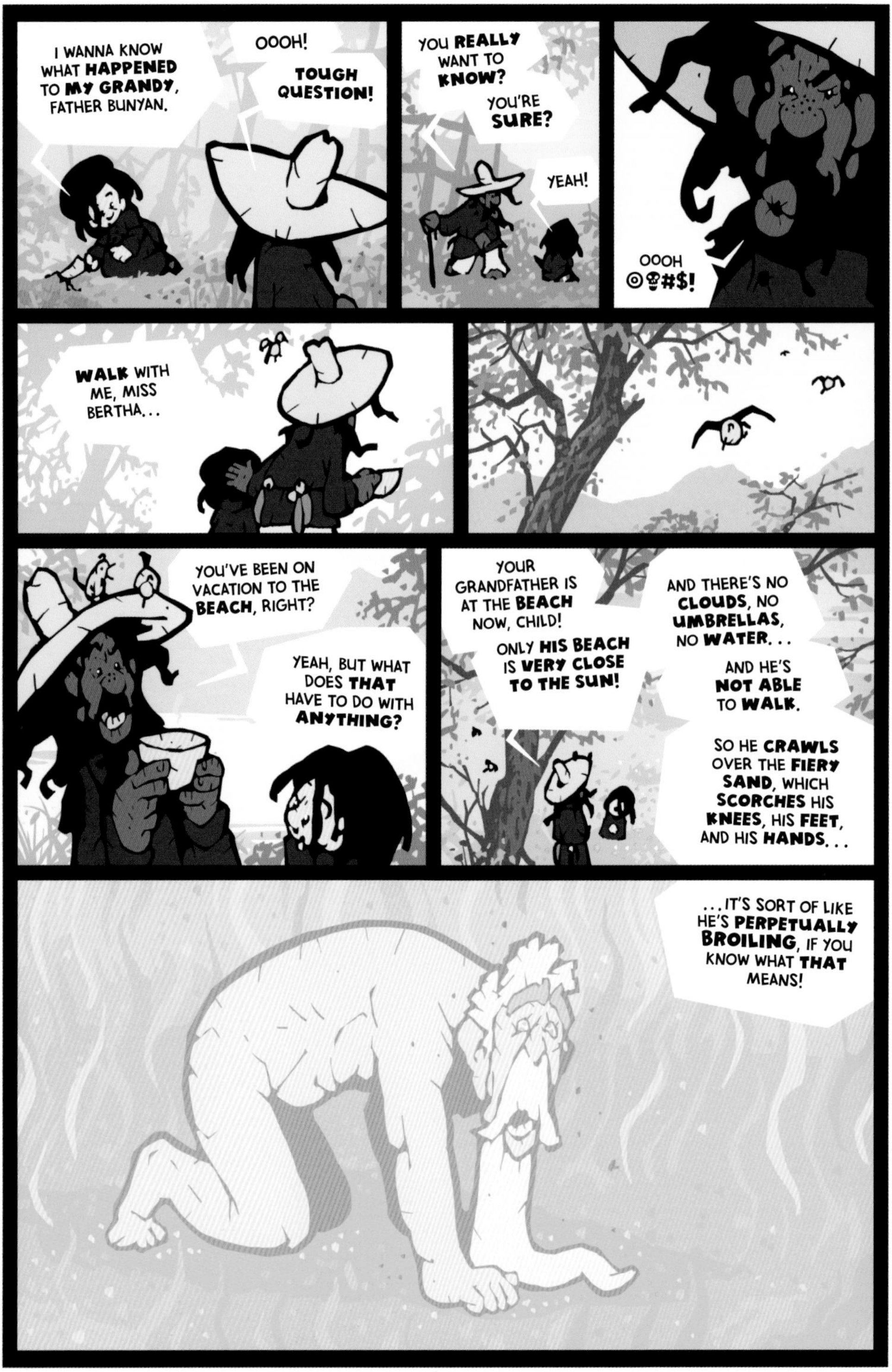

I WANNA KNOW WHAT HAPPENED TO MY GRANDY, FATHER BUNYAN.
OOOH!
TOUGH QUESTION!
YOU REALLY WANT TO KNOW?
YOU'RE SURE?
YEAH!
OOOH @☠#$!
WALK WITH ME, MISS BERTHA...
YOU'VE BEEN ON VACATION TO THE BEACH, RIGHT?
YEAH, BUT WHAT DOES THAT HAVE TO DO WITH ANYTHING?
YOUR GRANDFATHER IS AT THE BEACH NOW, CHILD!
ONLY HIS BEACH IS VERY CLOSE TO THE SUN!
AND THERE'S NO CLOUDS, NO UMBRELLAS, NO WATER...
AND HE'S NOT ABLE TO WALK.
SO HE CRAWLS OVER THE FIERY SAND, WHICH SCORCHES HIS KNEES, HIS FEET, AND HIS HANDS...
...IT'S SORT OF LIKE HE'S PERPETUALLY BROILING, IF YOU KNOW WHAT THAT MEANS!

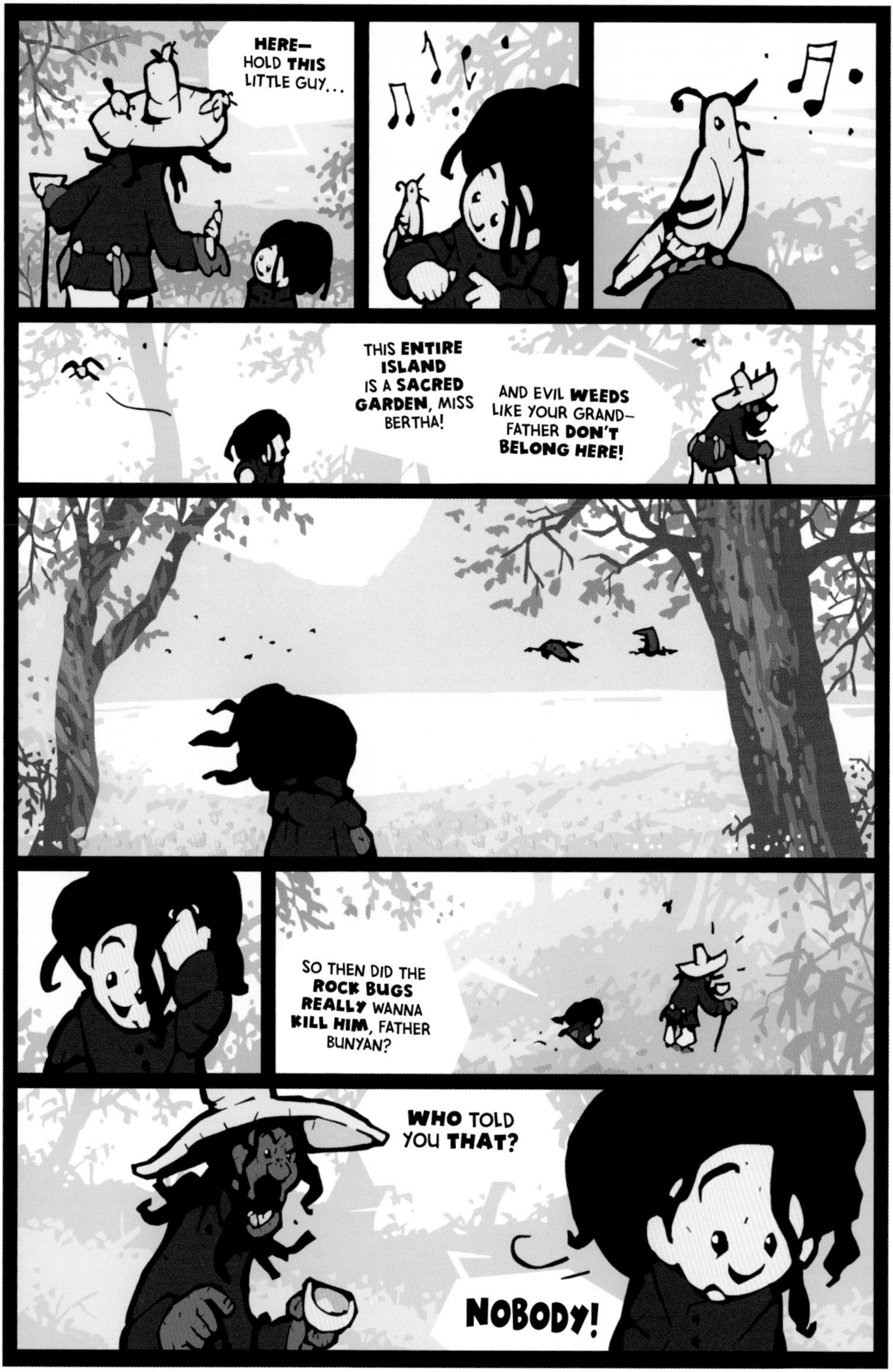
HERE— HOLD THIS LITTLE GUY...
THIS ENTIRE ISLAND IS A SACRED GARDEN, MISS BERTHA!
AND EVIL WEEDS LIKE YOUR GRAND-FATHER DON'T BELONG HERE!
SO THEN DID THE ROCK BUGS REALLY WANNA KILL HIM, FATHER BUNYAN?
WHO TOLD YOU THAT?
NOBODY!

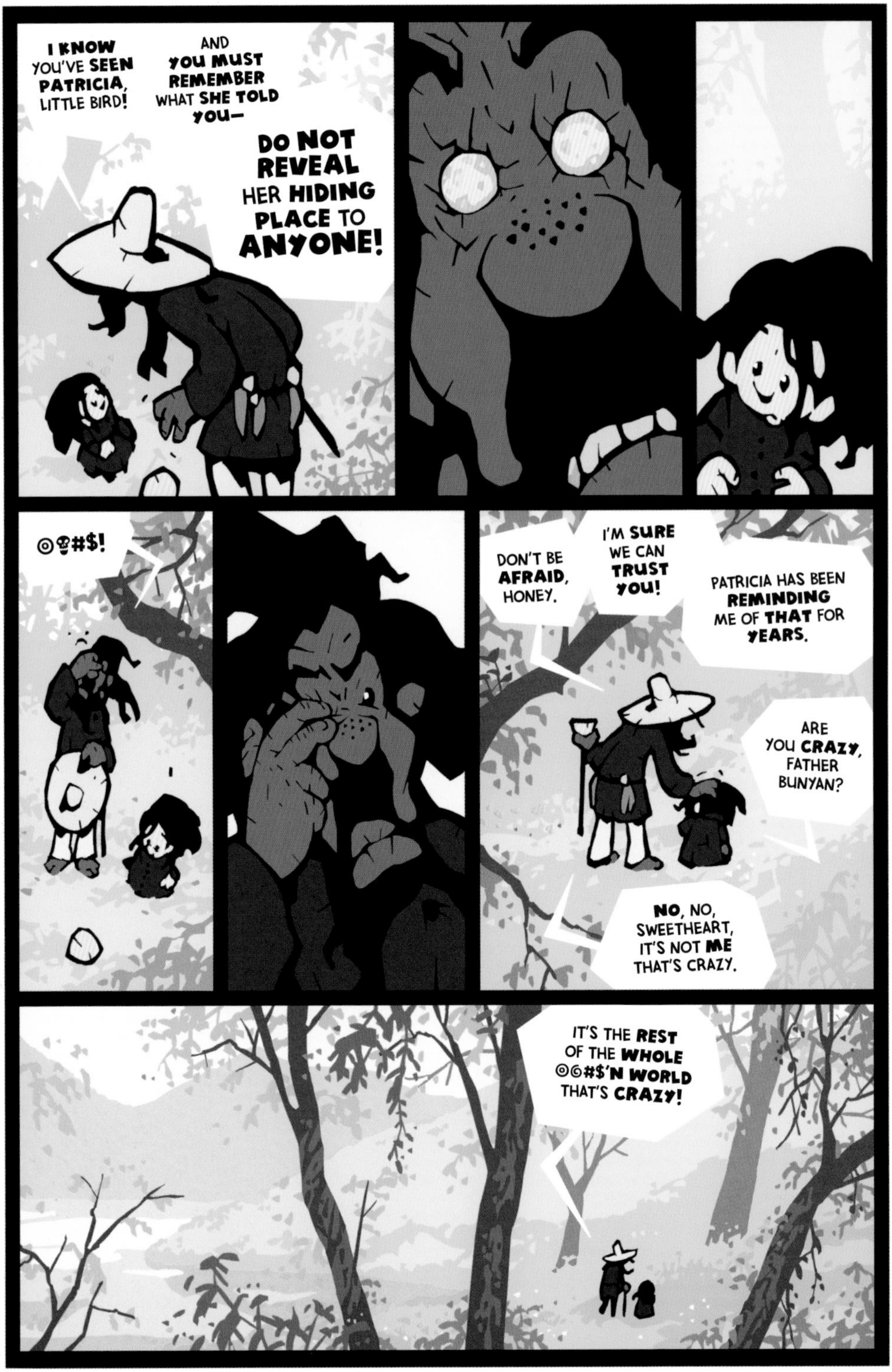

I KNOW YOU'VE SEEN PATRICIA, LITTLE BIRD!
AND YOU MUST REMEMBER WHAT SHE TOLD YOU—
DO NOT REVEAL HER HIDING PLACE TO ANYONE!
@#$!
DON'T BE AFRAID, HONEY.
I'M SURE WE CAN TRUST YOU!
PATRICIA HAS BEEN REMINDING ME OF THAT FOR YEARS.
ARE YOU CRAZY, FATHER BUNYAN?
NO, NO, SWEETHEART, IT'S NOT ME THAT'S CRAZY.
IT'S THE REST OF THE WHOLE @#$'N WORLD THAT'S CRAZY!

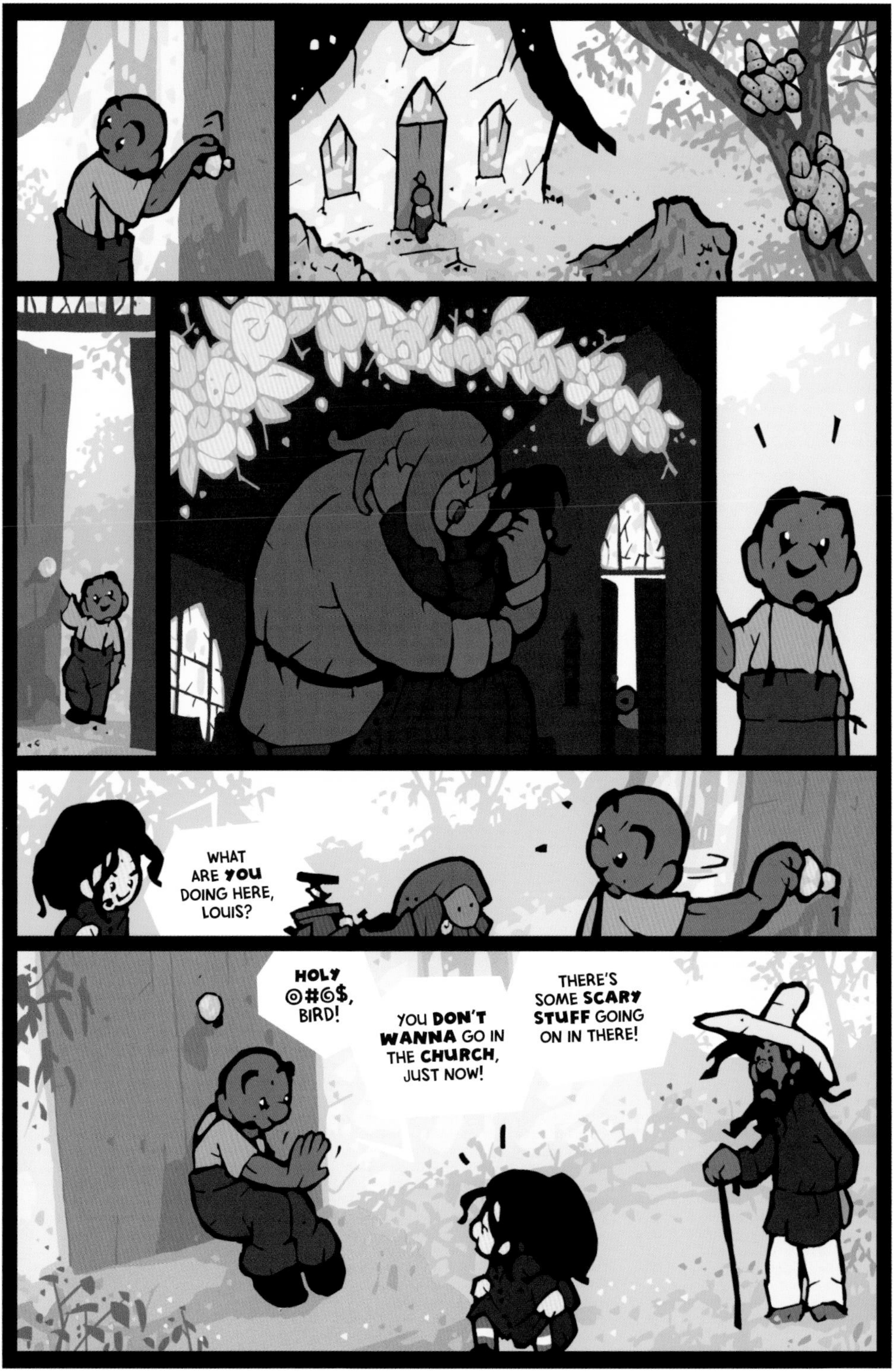
WHAT ARE YOU DOING HERE, LOUIS?
HOLY @#6$, BIRD!
YOU DON'T WANNA GO IN THE CHURCH, JUST NOW!
THERE'S SOME SCARY STUFF GOING ON IN THERE!

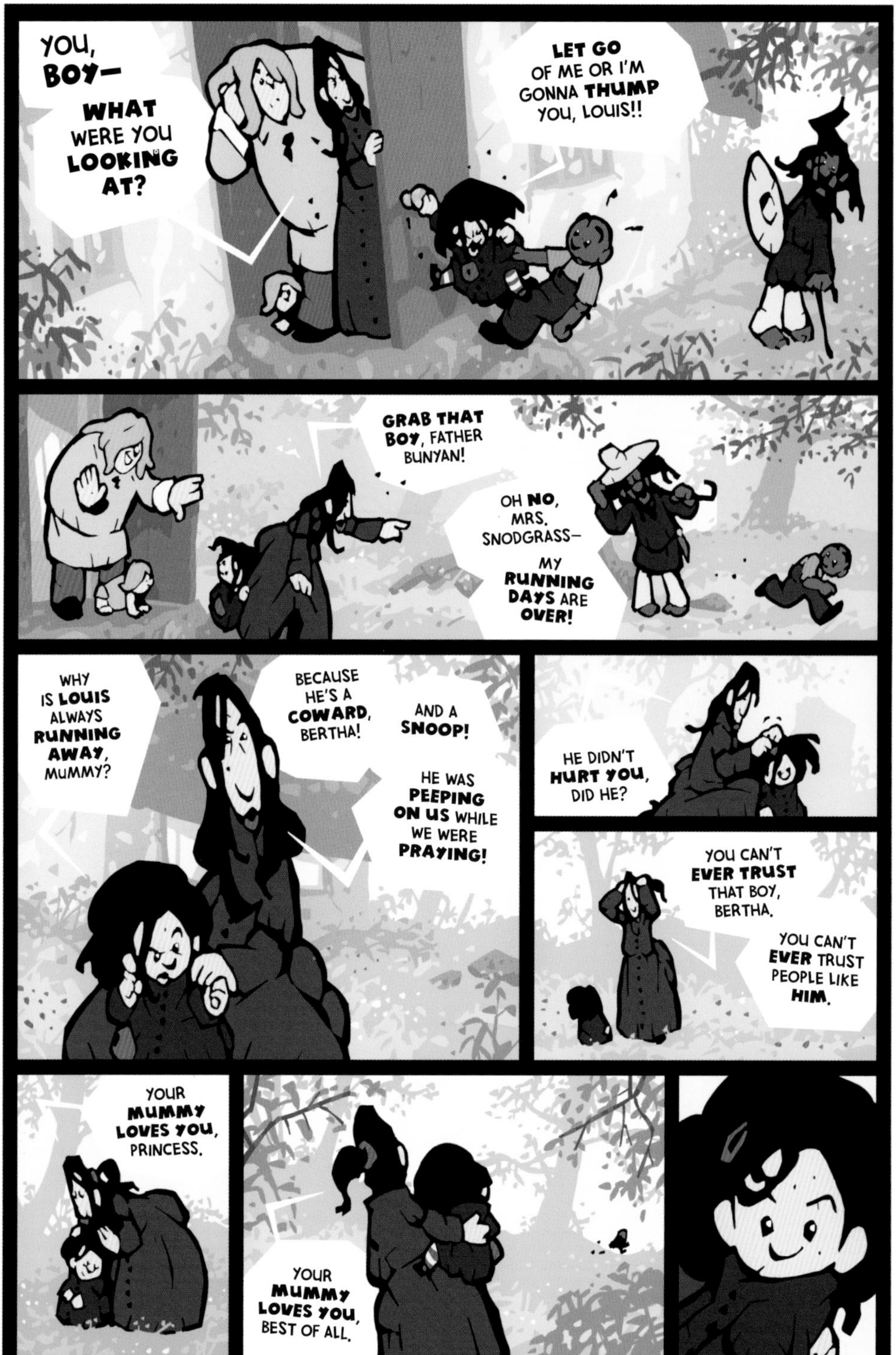
YOU, BOY— WHAT WERE YOU LOOKING AT?
LET GO OF ME OR I'M GONNA THUMP YOU, LOUIS!!
GRAB THAT BOY, FATHER BUNYAN!
OH NO, MRS. SNODGRASS—
MY RUNNING DAYS ARE OVER!
WHY IS LOUIS ALWAYS RUNNING AWAY, MUMMY?
BECAUSE HE'S A COWARD, BERTHA!
AND A SNOOP!
HE WAS PEEPING ON US WHILE WE WERE PRAYING!
HE DIDN'T HURT YOU, DID HE?
YOU CAN'T EVER TRUST THAT BOY, BERTHA.
YOU CAN'T EVER TRUST PEOPLE LIKE HIM.
YOUR MUMMY LOVES YOU, PRINCESS.
YOUR MUMMY LOVES YOU, BEST OF ALL.

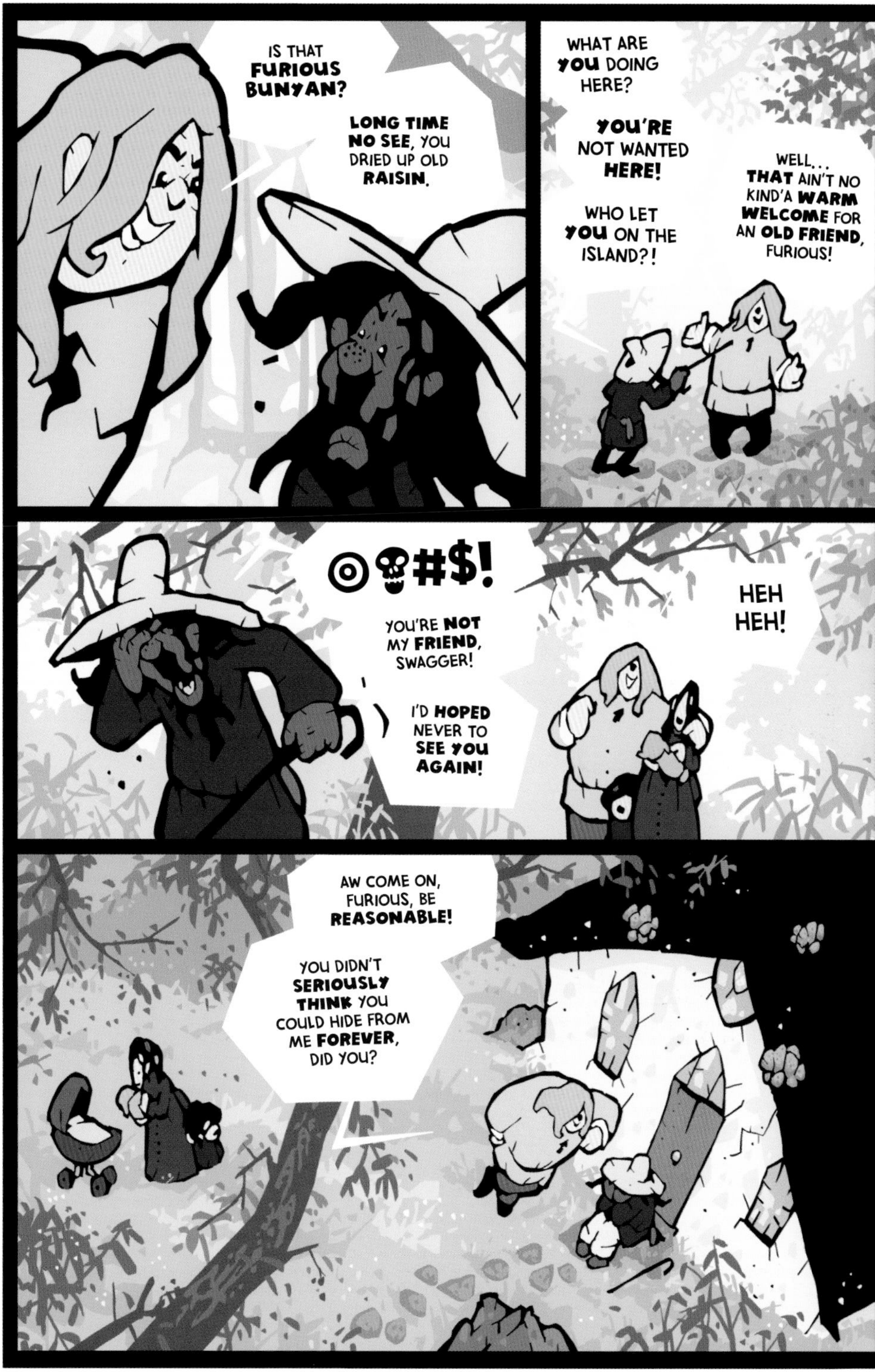
IS THAT FURIOUS BUNYAN?
LONG TIME NO SEE, YOU DRIED UP OLD RAISIN.
WHAT ARE YOU DOING HERE?
YOU'RE NOT WANTED HERE!
WHO LET YOU ON THE ISLAND?!
WELL... THAT AIN'T NO KIND'A WARM WELCOME FOR AN OLD FRIEND, FURIOUS!
#$!
YOU'RE NOT MY FRIEND, SWAGGER!
I'D HOPED NEVER TO SEE YOU AGAIN!
HEH HEH!
AW COME ON, FURIOUS, BE REASONABLE!
YOU DIDN'T SERIOUSLY THINK YOU COULD HIDE FROM ME FOREVER, DID YOU?

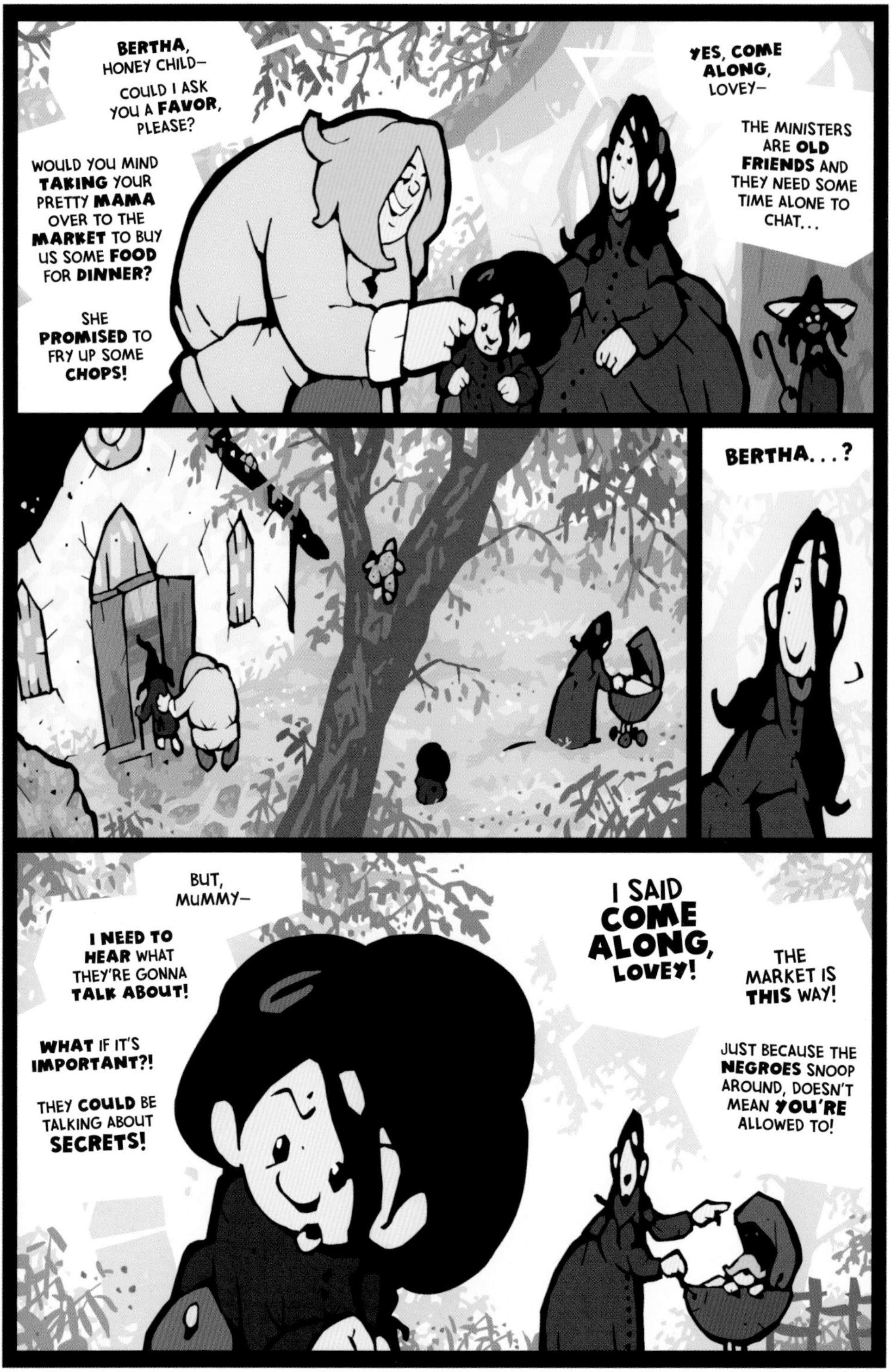
BERTHA, HONEY CHILD—
COULD I ASK YOU A FAVOR, PLEASE?
WOULD YOU MIND TAKING YOUR PRETTY MAMA OVER TO THE MARKET TO BUY US SOME FOOD FOR DINNER?
SHE PROMISED TO FRY UP SOME CHOPS!
YES, COME ALONG, LOVEY—
THE MINISTERS ARE OLD FRIENDS AND THEY NEED SOME TIME ALONE TO CHAT...
BERTHA...?
BUT, MUMMY—
I NEED TO HEAR WHAT THEY'RE GONNA TALK ABOUT!
WHAT IF IT'S IMPORTANT?!
THEY COULD BE TALKING ABOUT SECRETS!
I SAID COME ALONG, LOVEY!
THE MARKET IS THIS WAY!
JUST BECAUSE THE NEGROES SNOOP AROUND, DOESN'T MEAN YOU'RE ALLOWED TO!

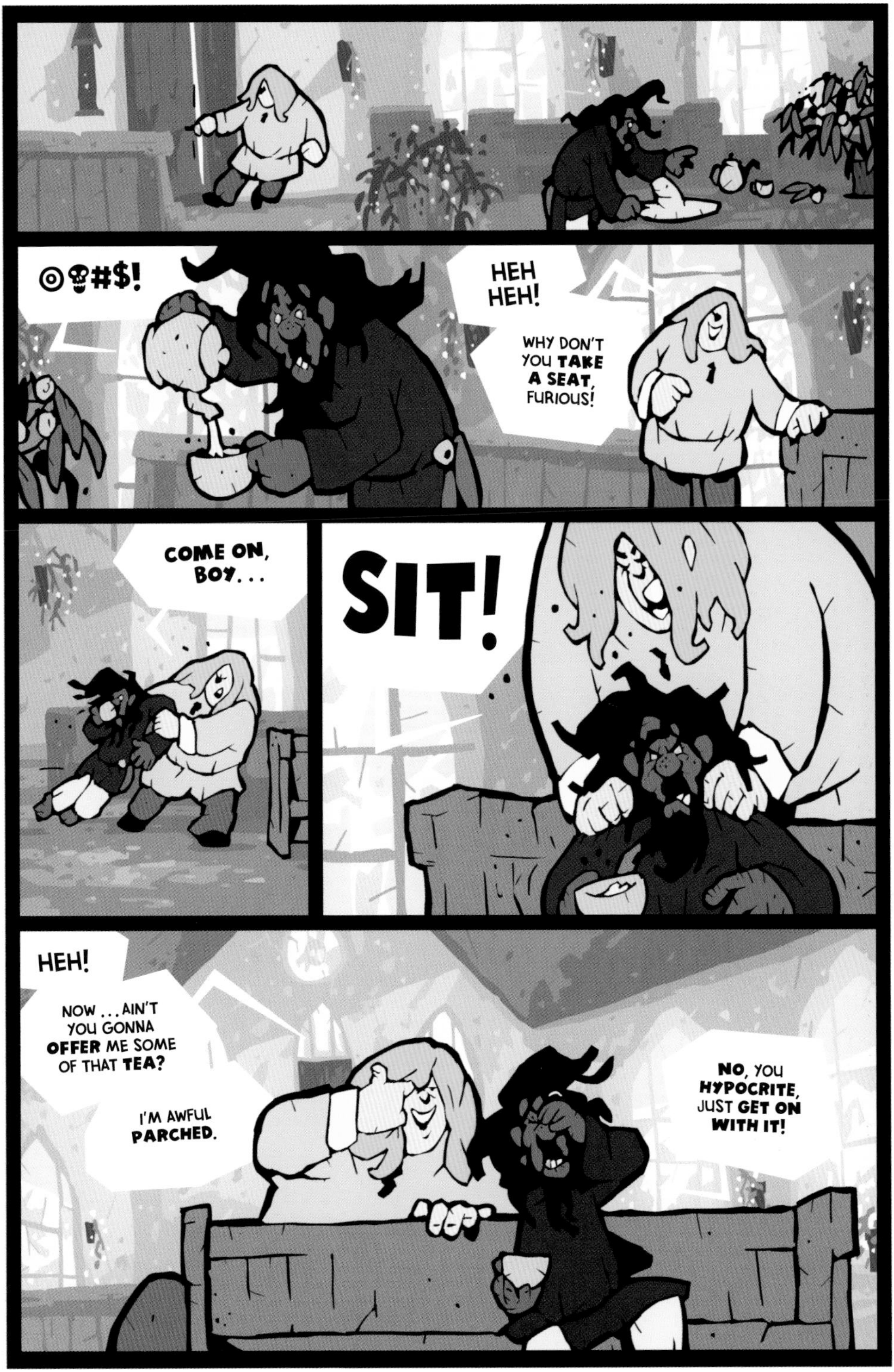
@💀#$!
HEH HEH!
WHY DON'T YOU TAKE A SEAT, FURIOUS!
COME ON, BOY...
SIT!
HEH!
NOW ... AIN'T YOU GONNA OFFER ME SOME OF THAT TEA?
I'M AWFUL PARCHED.
NO, YOU HYPOCRITE, JUST GET ON WITH IT!

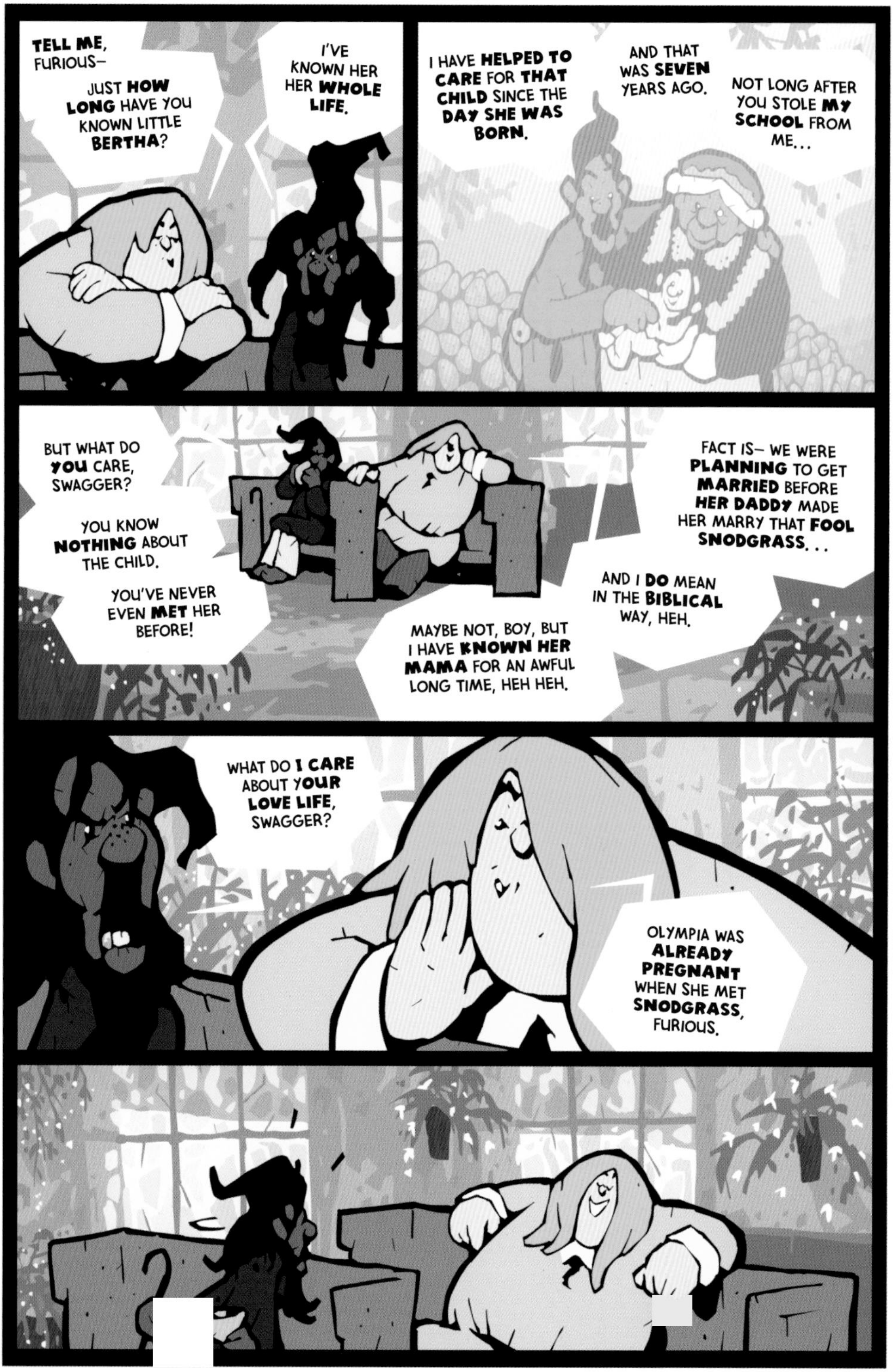

TELL ME, FURIOUS—
JUST HOW LONG HAVE YOU KNOWN LITTLE BERTHA?
I'VE KNOWN HER HER WHOLE LIFE.
I HAVE HELPED TO CARE FOR THAT CHILD SINCE THE DAY SHE WAS BORN.
AND THAT WAS SEVEN YEARS AGO.
NOT LONG AFTER YOU STOLE MY SCHOOL FROM ME...
BUT WHAT DO YOU CARE, SWAGGER?
YOU KNOW NOTHING ABOUT THE CHILD.
YOU'VE NEVER EVEN MET HER BEFORE!
MAYBE NOT, BOY, BUT I HAVE KNOWN HER MAMA FOR AN AWFUL LONG TIME, HEH HEH.
FACT IS— WE WERE PLANNING TO GET MARRIED BEFORE HER DADDY MADE HER MARRY THAT FOOL SNODGRASS...
AND I DO MEAN IN THE BIBLICAL WAY, HEH.
WHAT DO I CARE ABOUT YOUR LOVE LIFE, SWAGGER?
OLYMPIA WAS ALREADY PREGNANT WHEN SHE MET SNODGRASS, FURIOUS.

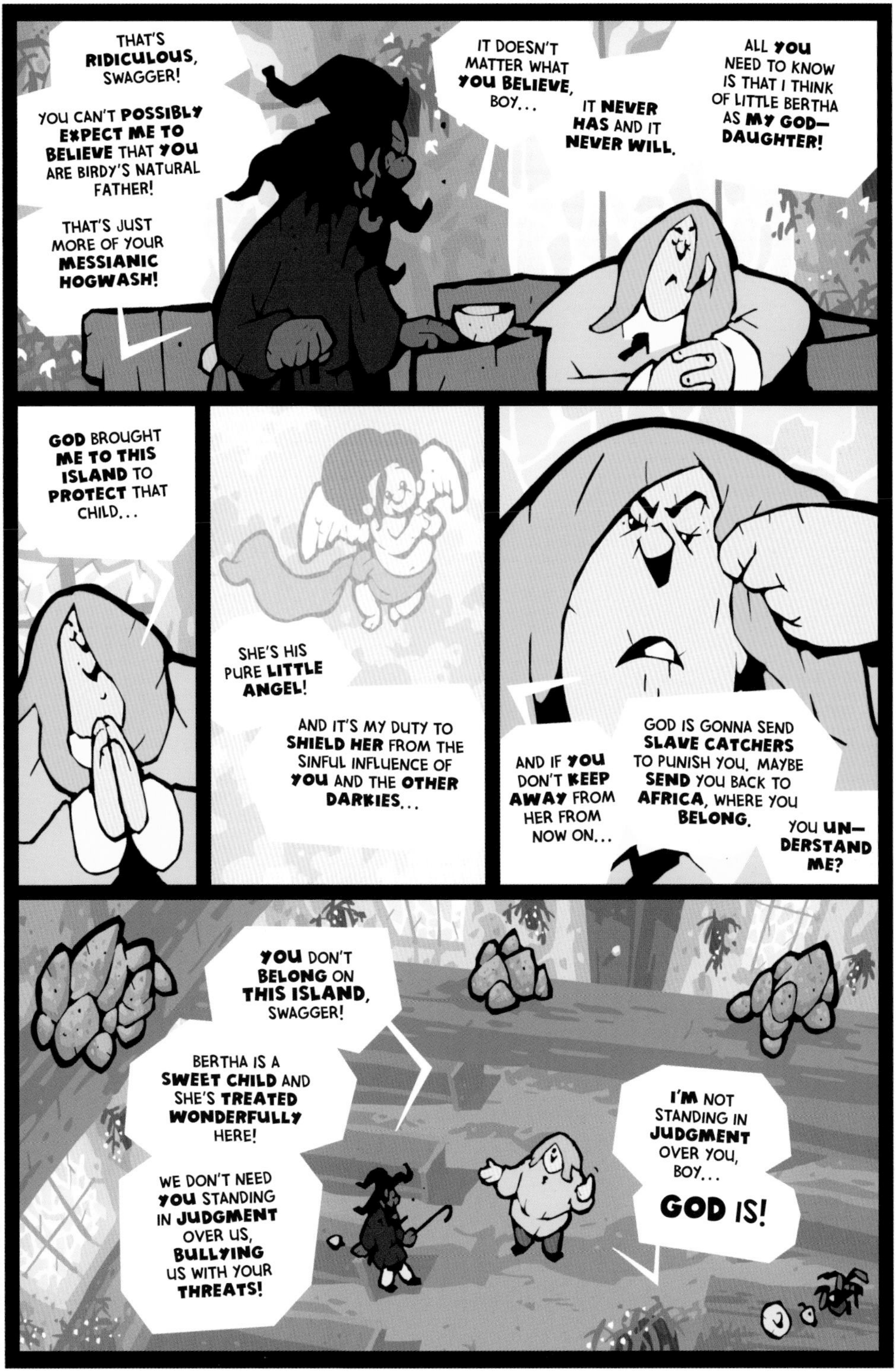
THAT'S RIDICULOUS, SWAGGER!
YOU CAN'T POSSIBLY EXPECT ME TO BELIEVE THAT YOU ARE BIRDY'S NATURAL FATHER!
THAT'S JUST MORE OF YOUR MESSIANIC HOGWASH!
IT DOESN'T MATTER WHAT YOU BELIEVE, BOY...
IT NEVER HAS AND IT NEVER WILL.
ALL YOU NEED TO KNOW IS THAT I THINK OF LITTLE BERTHA AS MY GOD-DAUGHTER!
GOD BROUGHT ME TO THIS ISLAND TO PROTECT THAT CHILD...
SHE'S HIS PURE LITTLE ANGEL!
AND IT'S MY DUTY TO SHIELD HER FROM THE SINFUL INFLUENCE OF YOU AND THE OTHER DARKIES...
AND IF YOU DON'T KEEP AWAY FROM HER FROM NOW ON...
GOD IS GONNA SEND SLAVE CATCHERS TO PUNISH YOU. MAYBE SEND YOU BACK TO AFRICA, WHERE YOU BELONG.
YOU UNDERSTAND ME?
YOU DON'T BELONG ON THIS ISLAND, SWAGGER!
BERTHA IS A SWEET CHILD AND SHE'S TREATED WONDERFULLY HERE!
WE DON'T NEED YOU STANDING IN JUDGMENT OVER US, BULLYING US WITH YOUR THREATS!
I'M NOT STANDING IN JUDGMENT OVER YOU, BOY...
GOD IS!

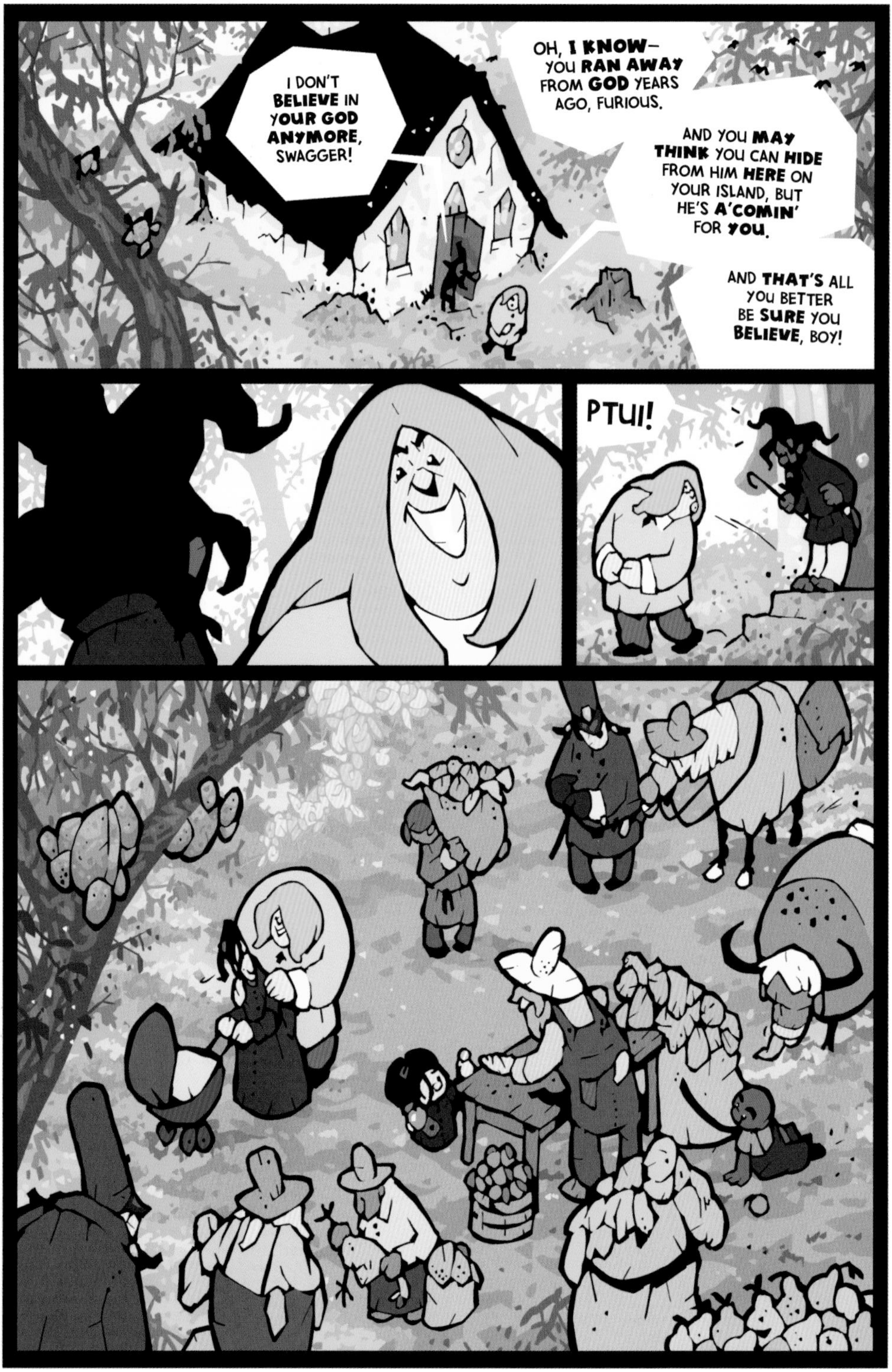
I DON'T BELIEVE IN YOUR GOD ANYMORE, SWAGGER!
OH, I KNOW— YOU RAN AWAY FROM GOD YEARS AGO, FURIOUS.
AND YOU MAY THINK YOU CAN HIDE FROM HIM HERE ON YOUR ISLAND, BUT HE'S A'COMIN' FOR YOU.
AND THAT'S ALL YOU BETTER BE SURE YOU BELIEVE, BOY!
PTUI!

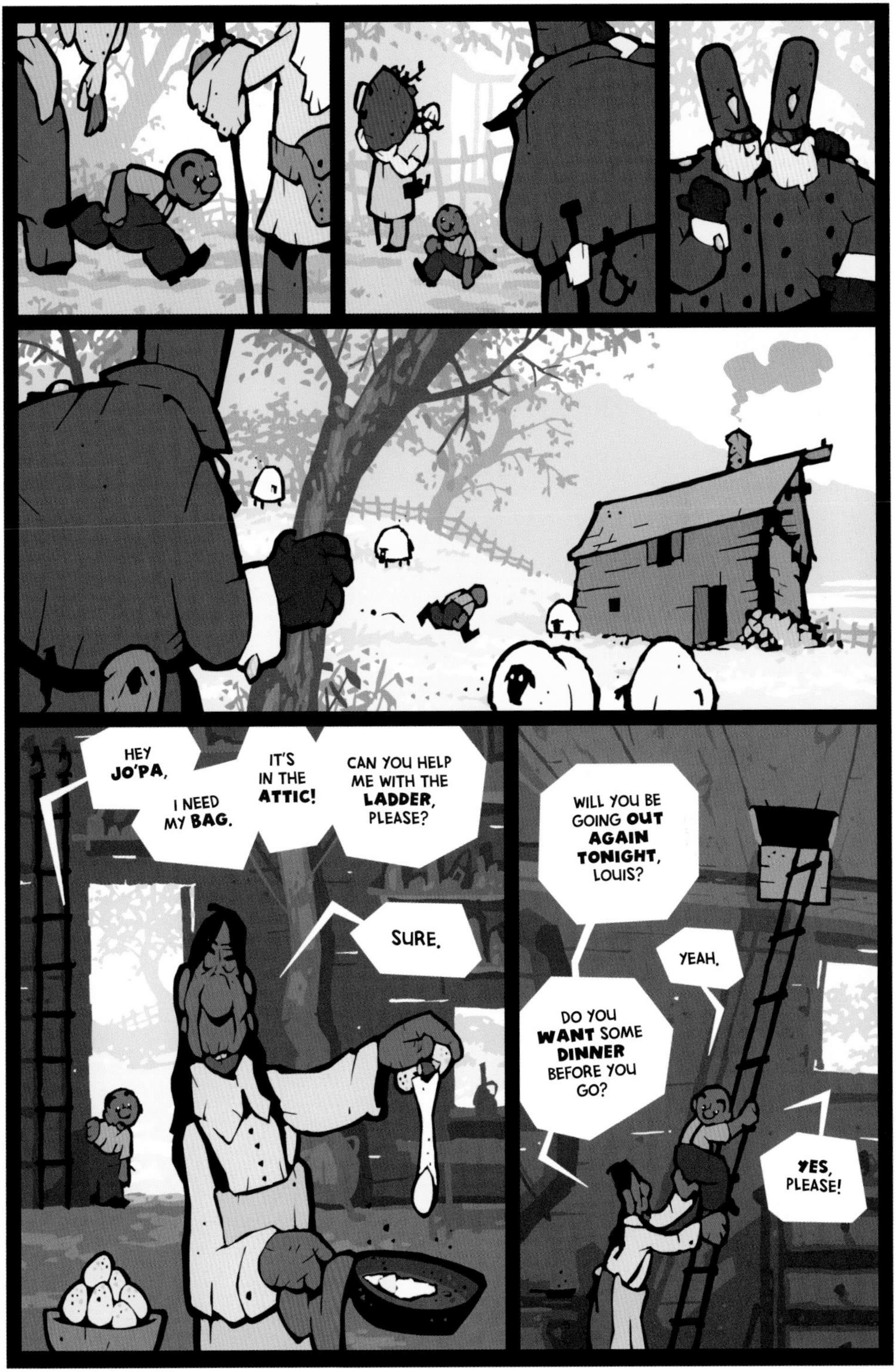
HEY JO'PA,
I NEED MY BAG.
IT'S IN THE ATTIC!
CAN YOU HELP ME WITH THE LADDER, PLEASE?
SURE.
WILL YOU BE GOING OUT AGAIN TONIGHT, LOUIS?
YEAH.
DO YOU WANT SOME DINNER BEFORE YOU GO?
YES, PLEASE!

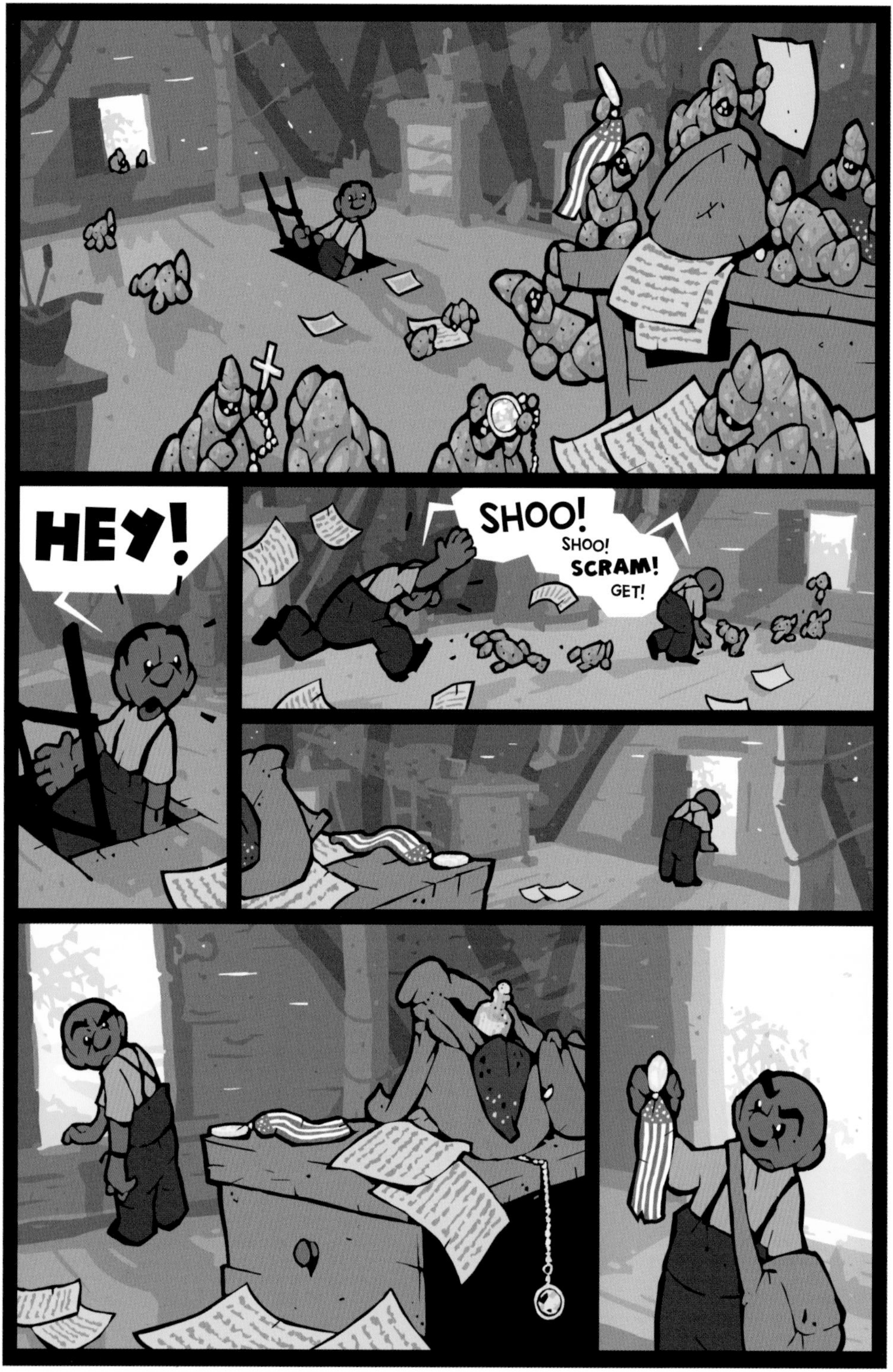
HEY!
SHOO!
SHOO!
SCRAM!
GET!

CHAPTER SEVEN
❧ *Bedtime* STORIES ❧

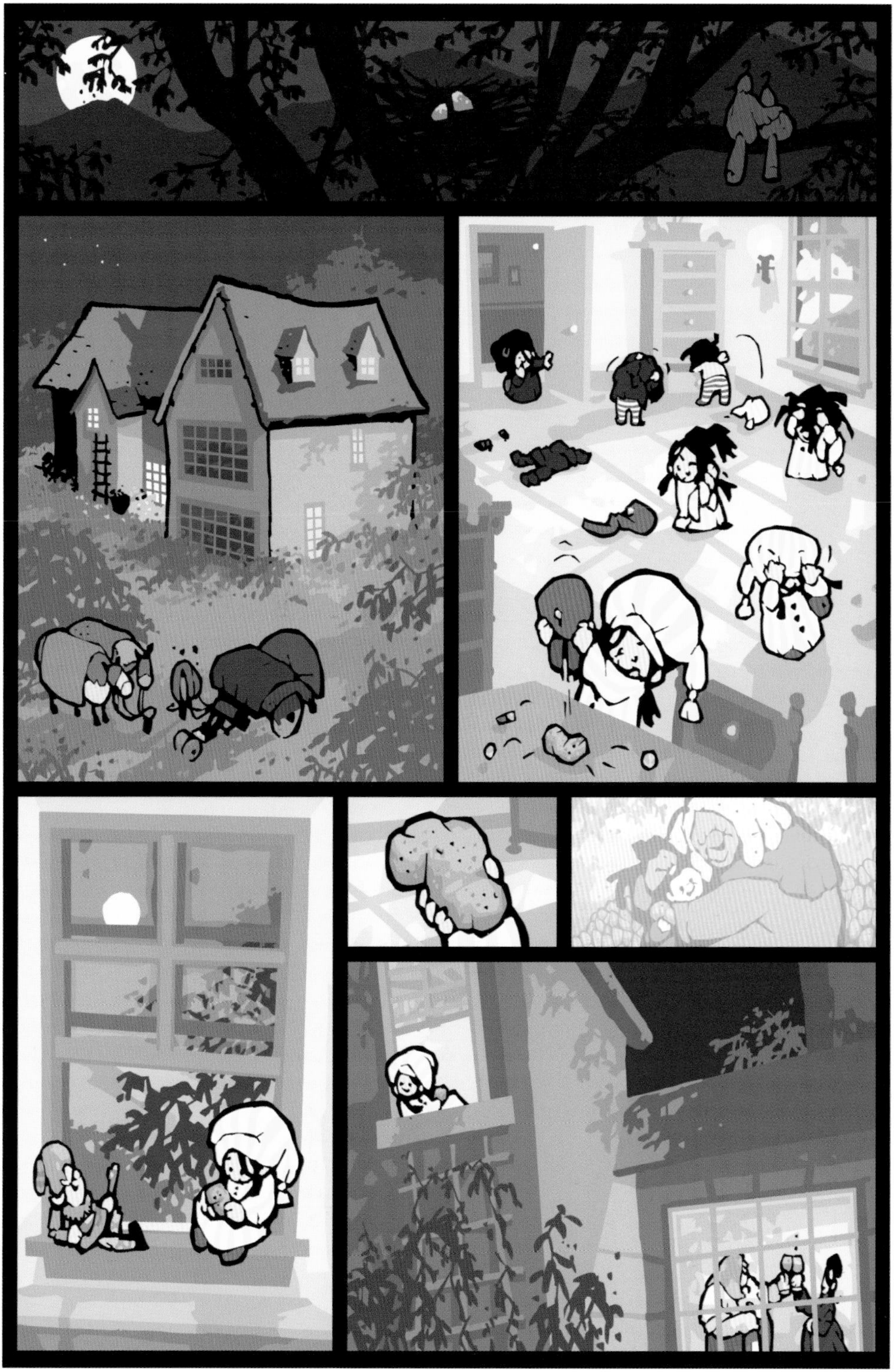

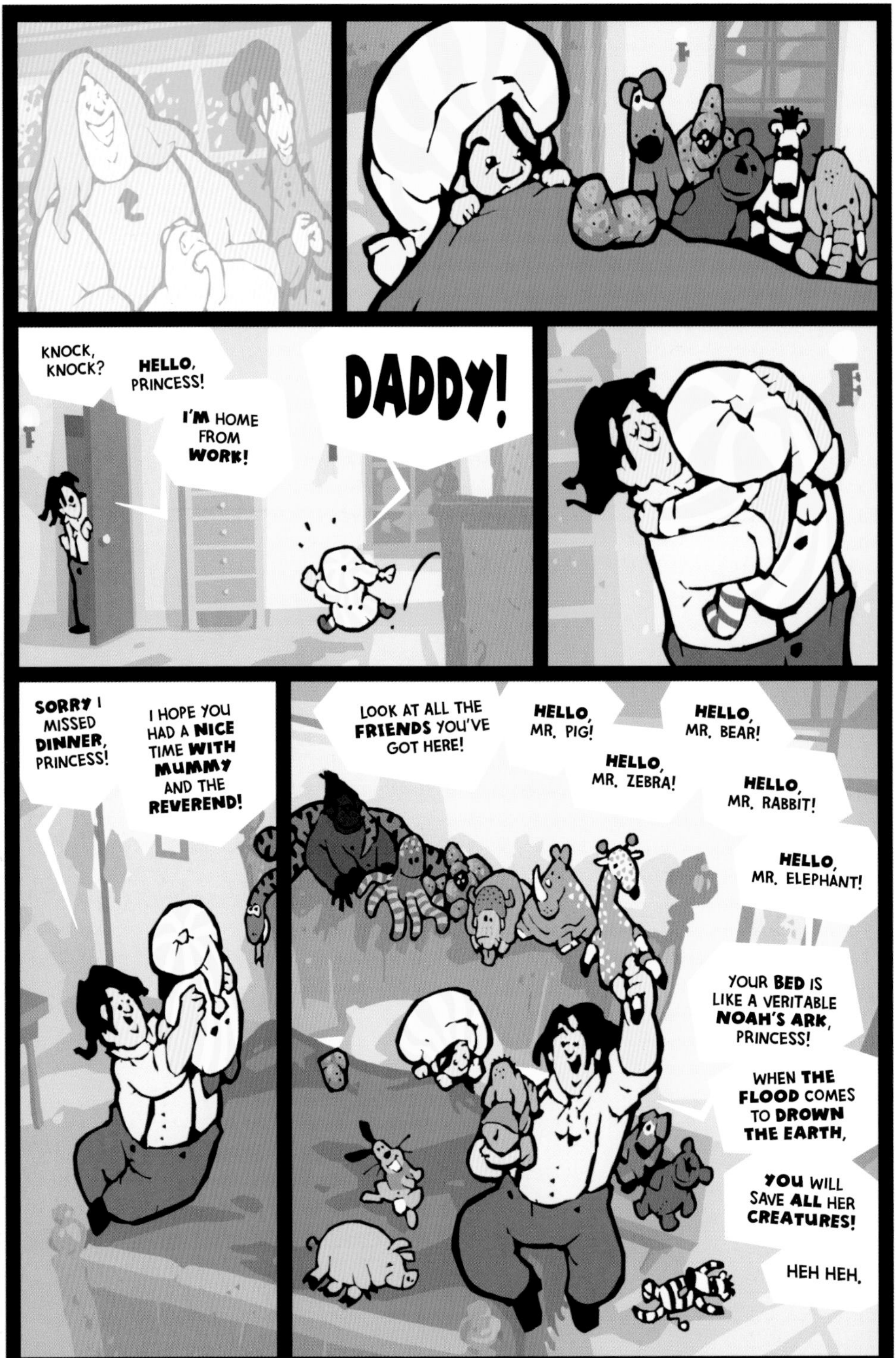
KNOCK, KNOCK?
HELLO, PRINCESS!
I'M HOME FROM WORK!
DADDY!
SORRY I MISSED DINNER, PRINCESS!
I HOPE YOU HAD A NICE TIME WITH MUMMY AND THE REVEREND!
LOOK AT ALL THE FRIENDS YOU'VE GOT HERE!
HELLO, MR. PIG!
HELLO, MR. BEAR!
HELLO, MR. ZEBRA!
HELLO, MR. RABBIT!
HELLO, MR. ELEPHANT!
YOUR BED IS LIKE A VERITABLE NOAH'S ARK, PRINCESS!
WHEN THE FLOOD COMES TO DROWN THE EARTH,
YOU WILL SAVE ALL HER CREATURES!
HEH HEH.

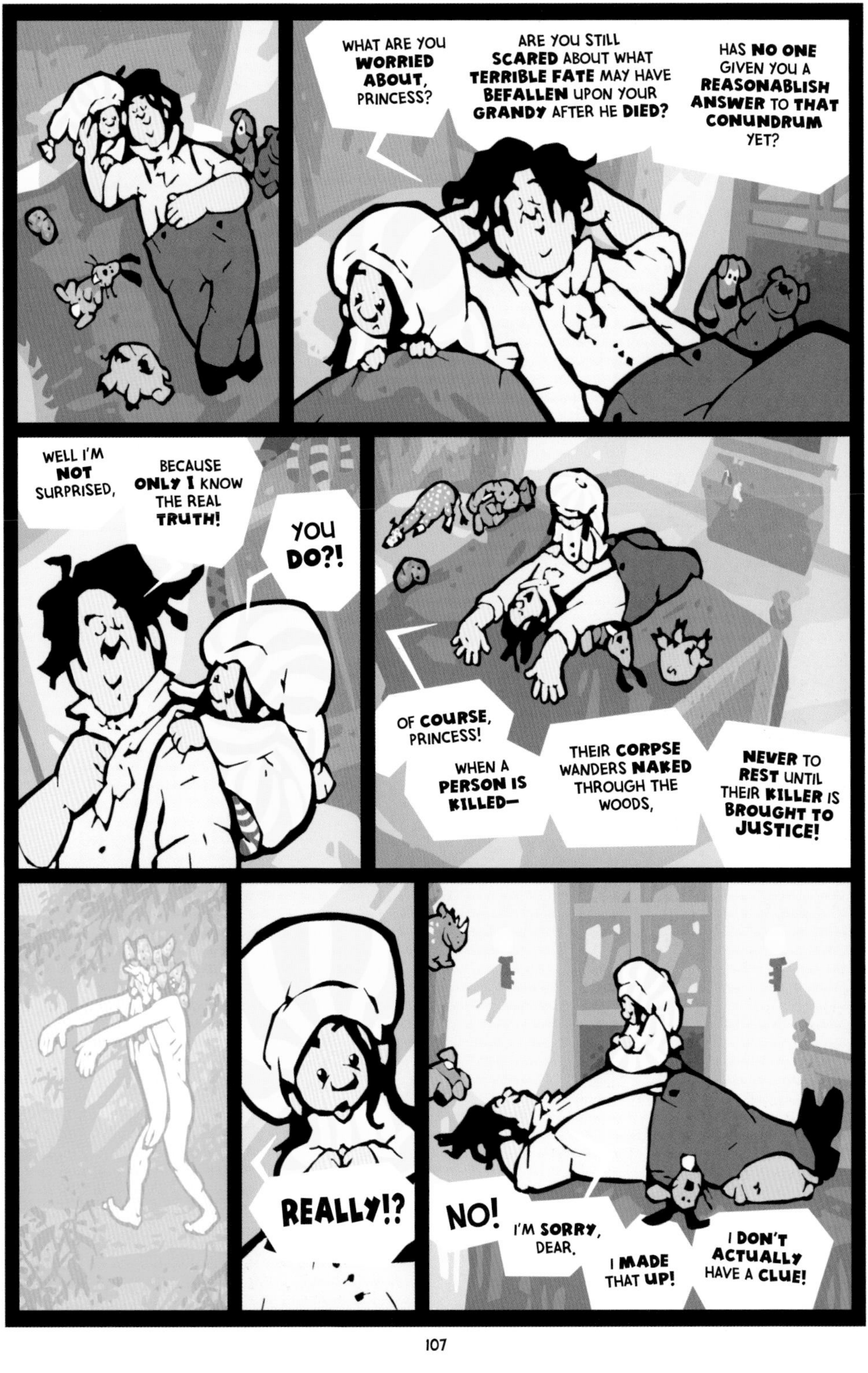
WHAT ARE YOU **WORRIED ABOUT**, PRINCESS?
ARE YOU STILL **SCARED** ABOUT WHAT **TERRIBLE FATE** MAY HAVE **BEFALLEN** UPON YOUR **GRANDY** AFTER HE **DIED?**
HAS **NO ONE** GIVEN YOU A **REASONABLISH ANSWER** TO **THAT CONUNDRUM** YET?
WELL I'M **NOT** SURPRISED,
BECAUSE **ONLY I** KNOW THE REAL **TRUTH!**
YOU **DO?!**
OF **COURSE**, PRINCESS!
WHEN A **PERSON IS KILLED—**
THEIR **CORPSE** WANDERS **NAKED** THROUGH THE WOODS,
NEVER TO **REST** UNTIL THEIR **KILLER** IS **BROUGHT TO JUSTICE!**
REALLY!?
NO!
I'M **SORRY**, DEAR.
I **MADE** THAT **UP!**
I **DON'T ACTUALLY** HAVE A **CLUE!**

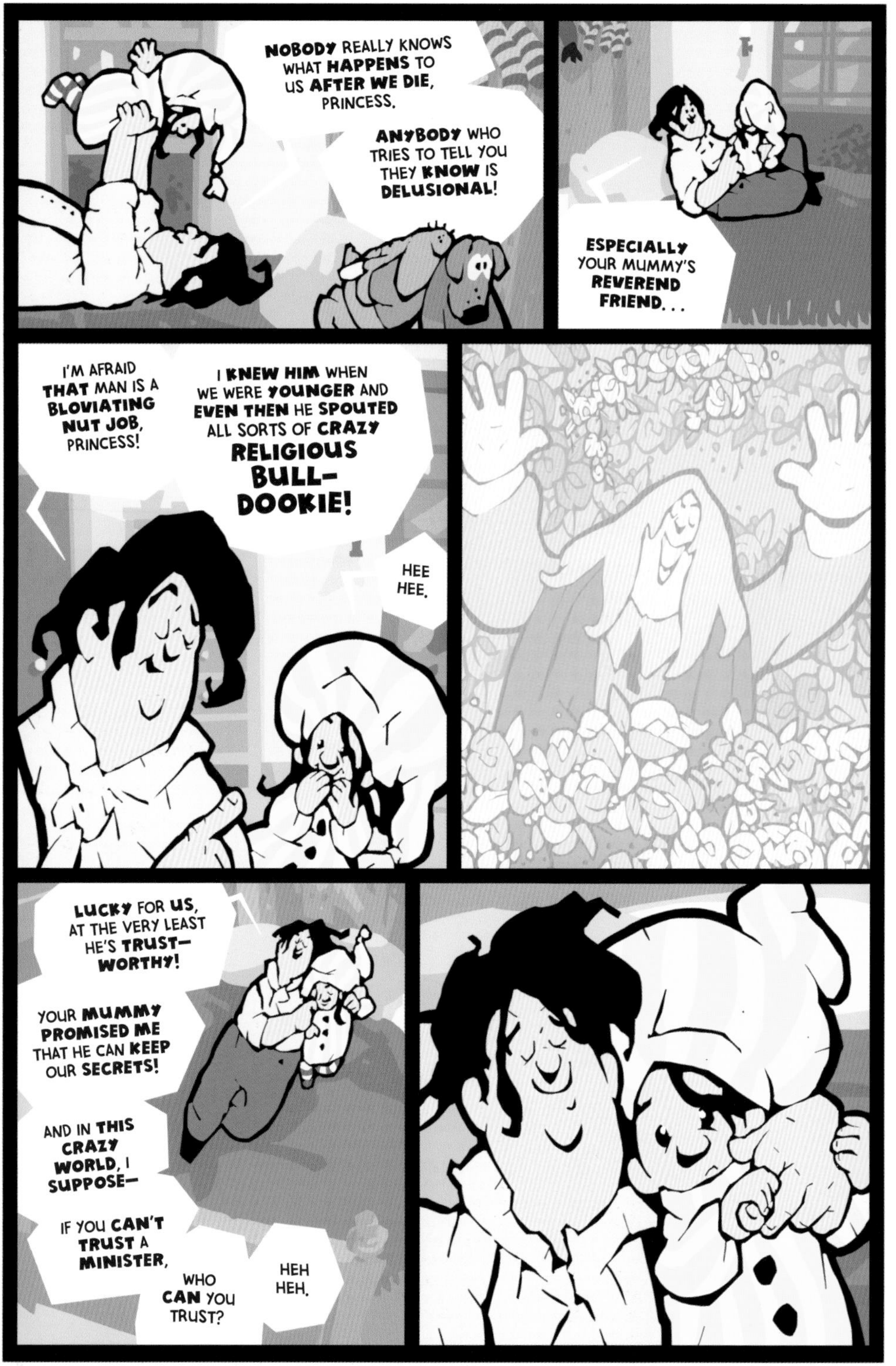
NOBODY REALLY KNOWS WHAT HAPPENS TO US AFTER WE DIE, PRINCESS.
ANYBODY WHO TRIES TO TELL YOU THEY KNOW IS DELUSIONAL!
ESPECIALLY YOUR MUMMY'S REVEREND FRIEND...
I'M AFRAID THAT MAN IS A BLOVIATING NUT JOB, PRINCESS!
I KNEW HIM WHEN WE WERE YOUNGER AND EVEN THEN HE SPOUTED ALL SORTS OF CRAZY RELIGIOUS BULL-DOOKIE!
HEE HEE.
LUCKY FOR US, AT THE VERY LEAST HE'S TRUST-WORTHY!
YOUR MUMMY PROMISED ME THAT HE CAN KEEP OUR SECRETS!
AND IN THIS CRAZY WORLD, I SUPPOSE—
IF YOU CAN'T TRUST A MINISTER,
WHO CAN YOU TRUST?
HEH HEH.

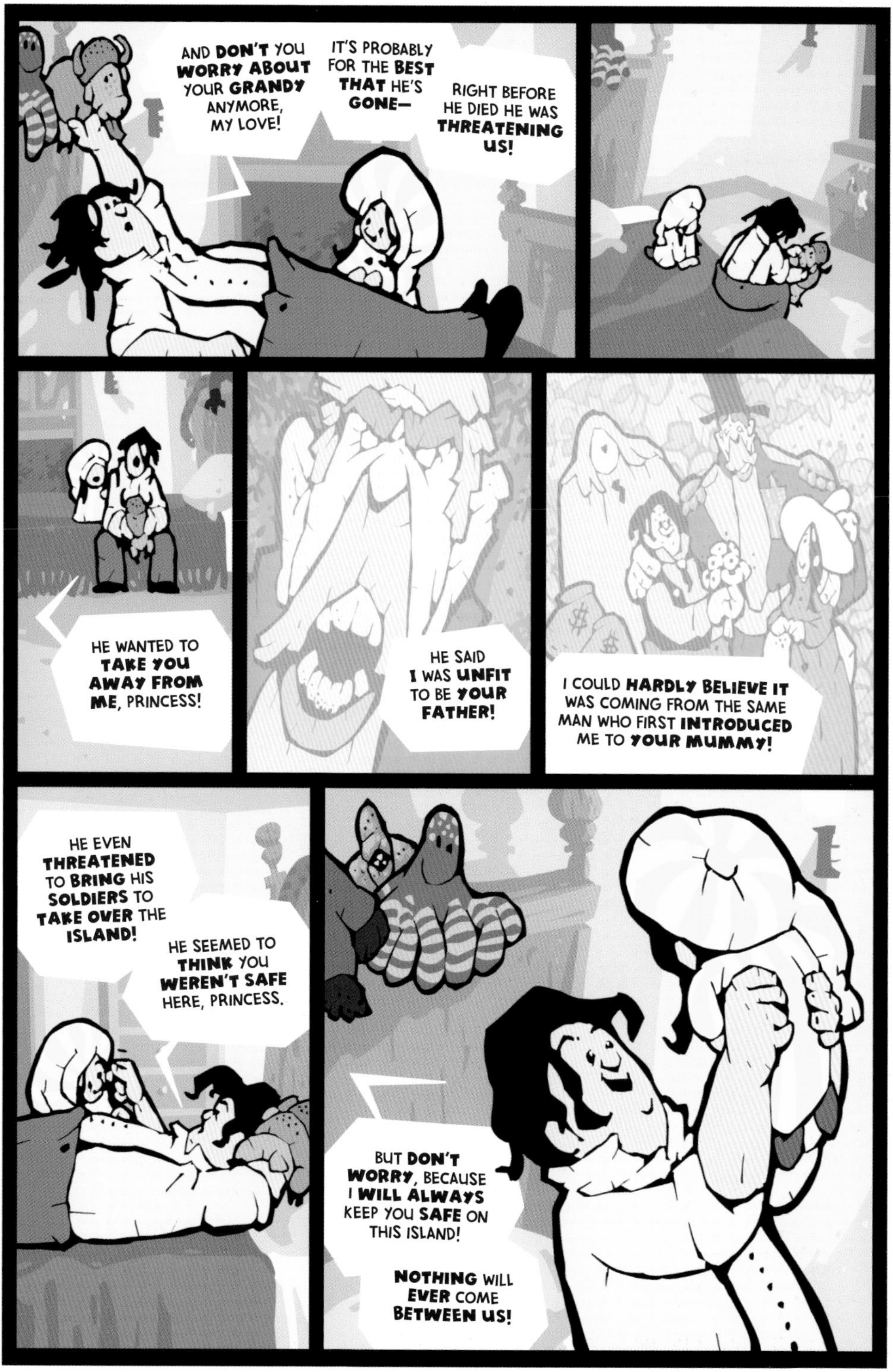
AND DON'T YOU WORRY ABOUT YOUR GRANDY ANYMORE, MY LOVE!
IT'S PROBABLY FOR THE BEST THAT HE'S GONE—
RIGHT BEFORE HE DIED HE WAS THREATENING US!
HE WANTED TO TAKE YOU AWAY FROM ME, PRINCESS!
HE SAID I WAS UNFIT TO BE YOUR FATHER!
I COULD HARDLY BELIEVE IT WAS COMING FROM THE SAME MAN WHO FIRST INTRODUCED ME TO YOUR MUMMY!
HE EVEN THREATENED TO BRING HIS SOLDIERS TO TAKE OVER THE ISLAND!
HE SEEMED TO THINK YOU WEREN'T SAFE HERE, PRINCESS.
BUT DON'T WORRY, BECAUSE I WILL ALWAYS KEEP YOU SAFE ON THIS ISLAND!
NOTHING WILL EVER COME BETWEEN US!

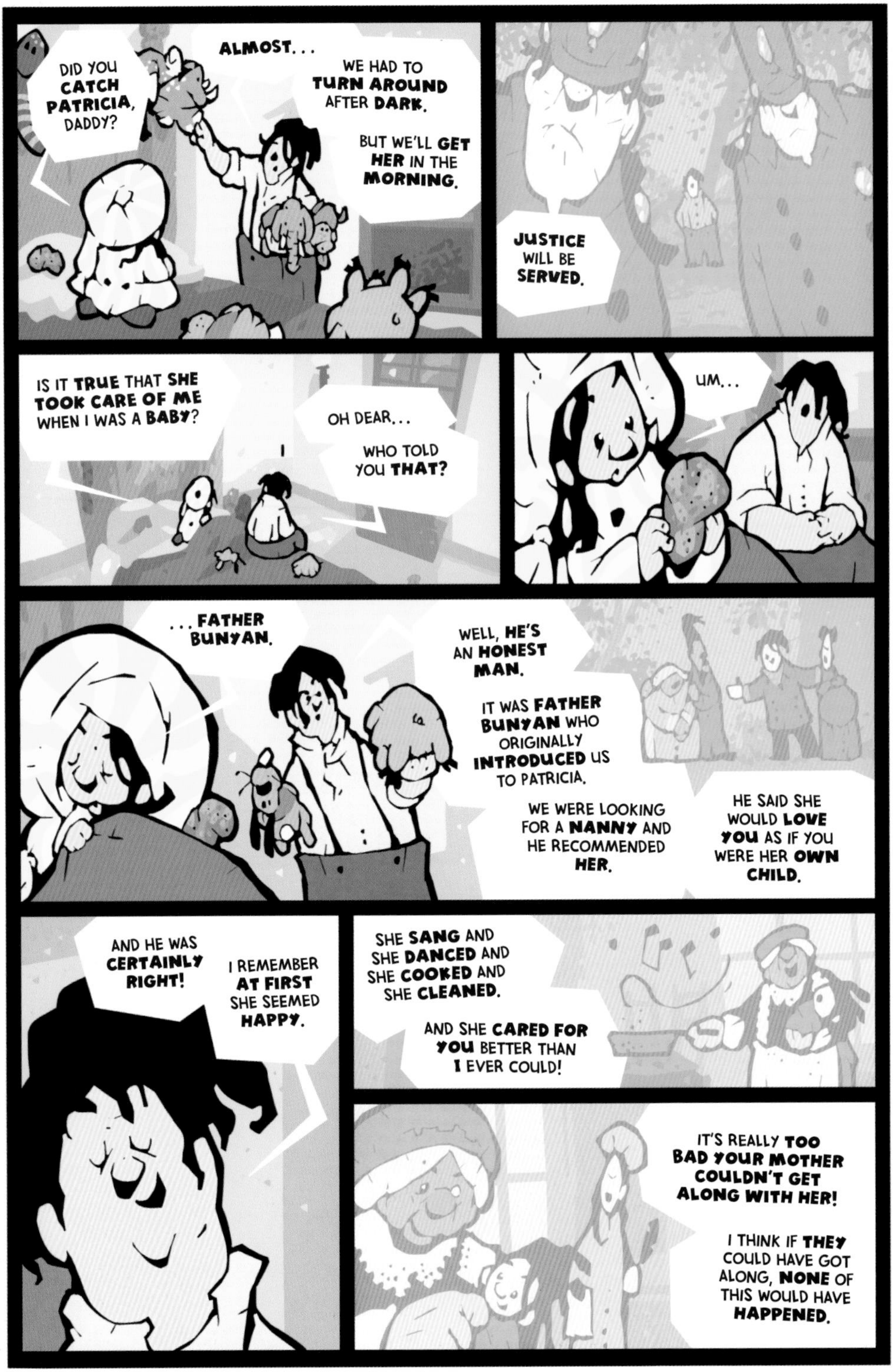
DID YOU CATCH PATRICIA, DADDY?
ALMOST...
WE HAD TO TURN AROUND AFTER DARK.
BUT WE'LL GET HER IN THE MORNING.
JUSTICE WILL BE SERVED.
IS IT TRUE THAT SHE TOOK CARE OF ME WHEN I WAS A BABY?
OH DEAR...
WHO TOLD YOU THAT?
UM...
...FATHER BUNYAN.
WELL, HE'S AN HONEST MAN.
IT WAS FATHER BUNYAN WHO ORIGINALLY INTRODUCED US TO PATRICIA.
WE WERE LOOKING FOR A NANNY AND HE RECOMMENDED HER.
HE SAID SHE WOULD LOVE YOU AS IF YOU WERE HER OWN CHILD.
AND HE WAS CERTAINLY RIGHT!
I REMEMBER AT FIRST SHE SEEMED HAPPY.
SHE SANG AND SHE DANCED AND SHE COOKED AND SHE CLEANED.
AND SHE CARED FOR YOU BETTER THAN I EVER COULD!
IT'S REALLY TOO BAD YOUR MOTHER COULDN'T GET ALONG WITH HER!
I THINK IF THEY COULD HAVE GOT ALONG, NONE OF THIS WOULD HAVE HAPPENED.

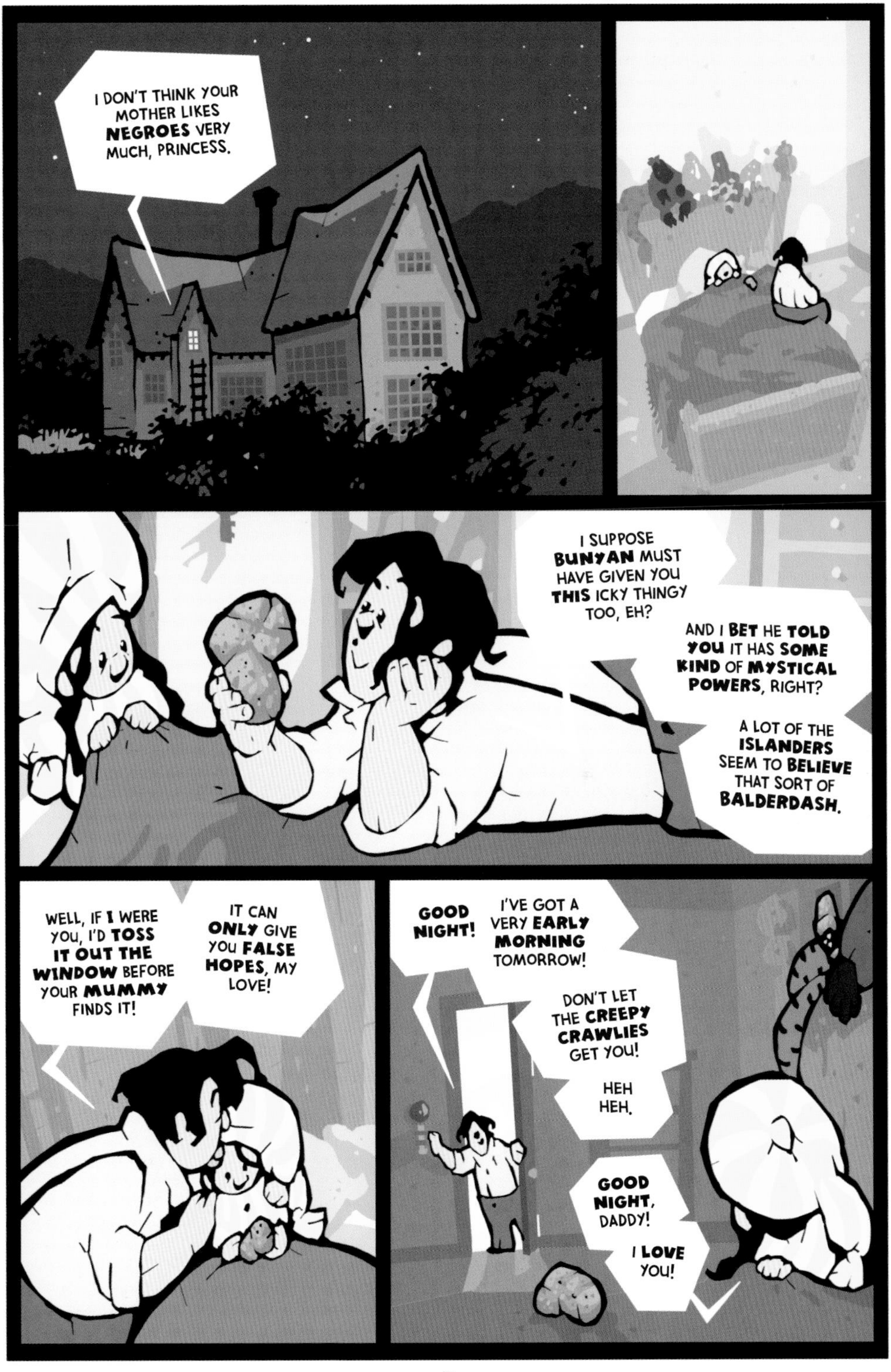

I DON'T THINK YOUR MOTHER LIKES NEGROES VERY MUCH, PRINCESS.
I SUPPOSE BUNYAN MUST HAVE GIVEN YOU THIS ICKY THINGY TOO, EH?
AND I BET HE TOLD YOU IT HAS SOME KIND OF MYSTICAL POWERS, RIGHT?
A LOT OF THE ISLANDERS SEEM TO BELIEVE THAT SORT OF BALDERDASH.
WELL, IF I WERE YOU, I'D TOSS IT OUT THE WINDOW BEFORE YOUR MUMMY FINDS IT!
IT CAN ONLY GIVE YOU FALSE HOPES, MY LOVE!
GOOD NIGHT!
I'VE GOT A VERY EARLY MORNING TOMORROW!
DON'T LET THE CREEPY CRAWLIES GET YOU!
HEH HEH.
GOOD NIGHT, DADDY!
I LOVE YOU!

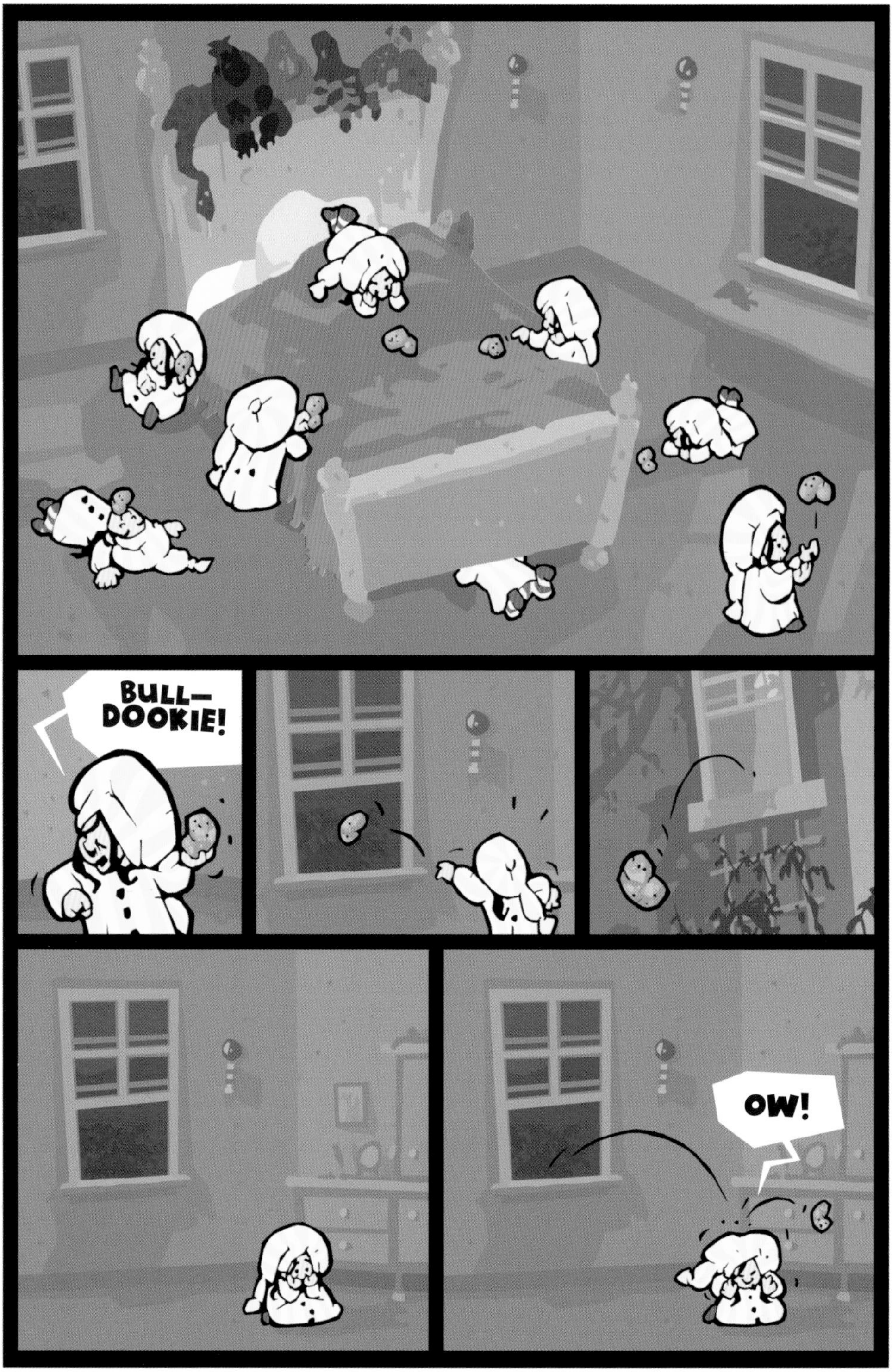
BULL-DOOKIE!
OW!

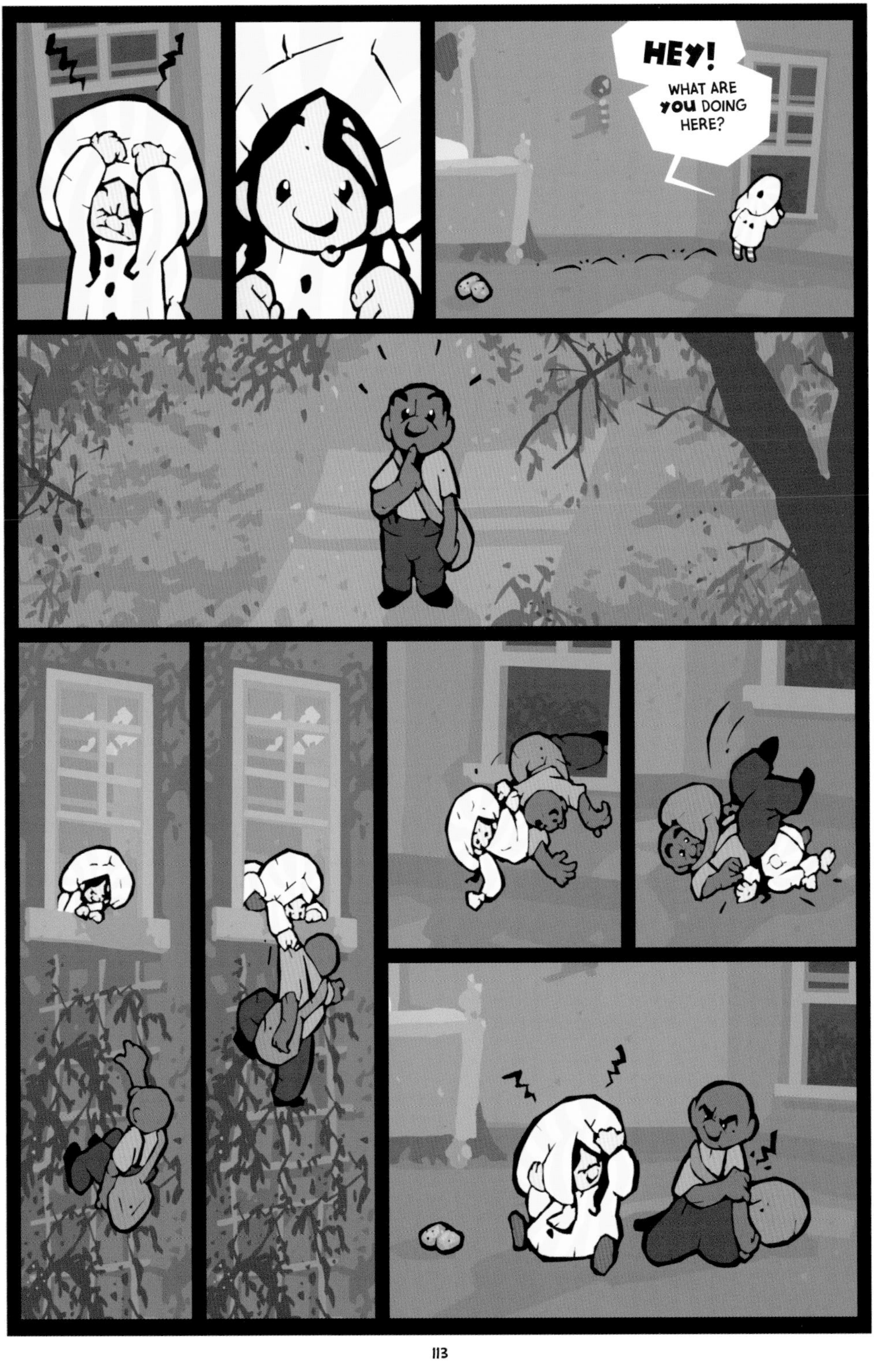
HEY!
WHAT ARE **YOU** DOING HERE?

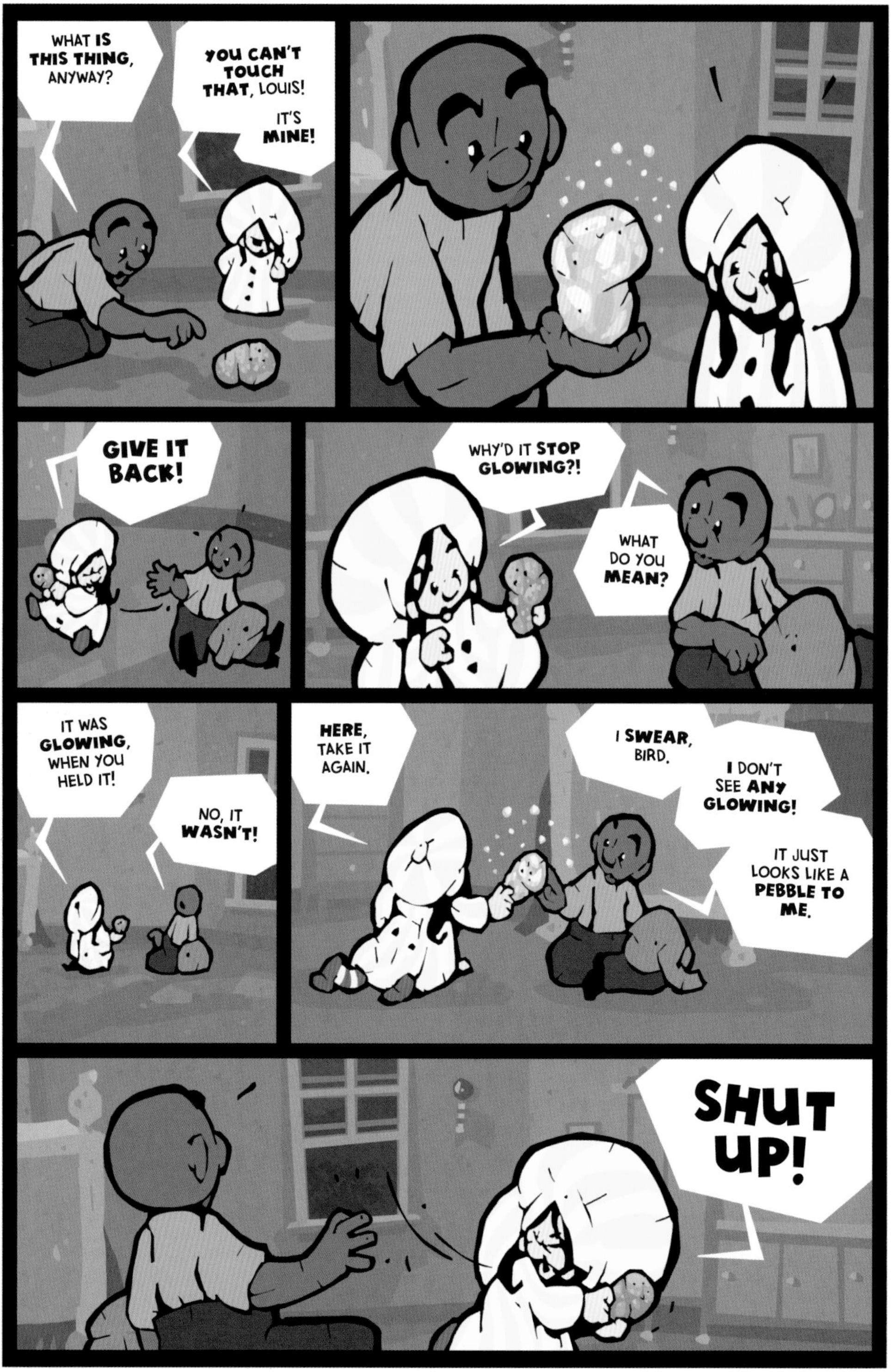
WHAT IS THIS THING, ANYWAY?
YOU CAN'T TOUCH THAT, LOUIS!
IT'S MINE!
GIVE IT BACK!
WHY'D IT STOP GLOWING?!
WHAT DO YOU MEAN?
IT WAS GLOWING, WHEN YOU HELD IT!
NO, IT WASN'T!
HERE, TAKE IT AGAIN.
I SWEAR, BIRD.
I DON'T SEE ANY GLOWING!
IT JUST LOOKS LIKE A PEBBLE TO ME.
SHUT UP!

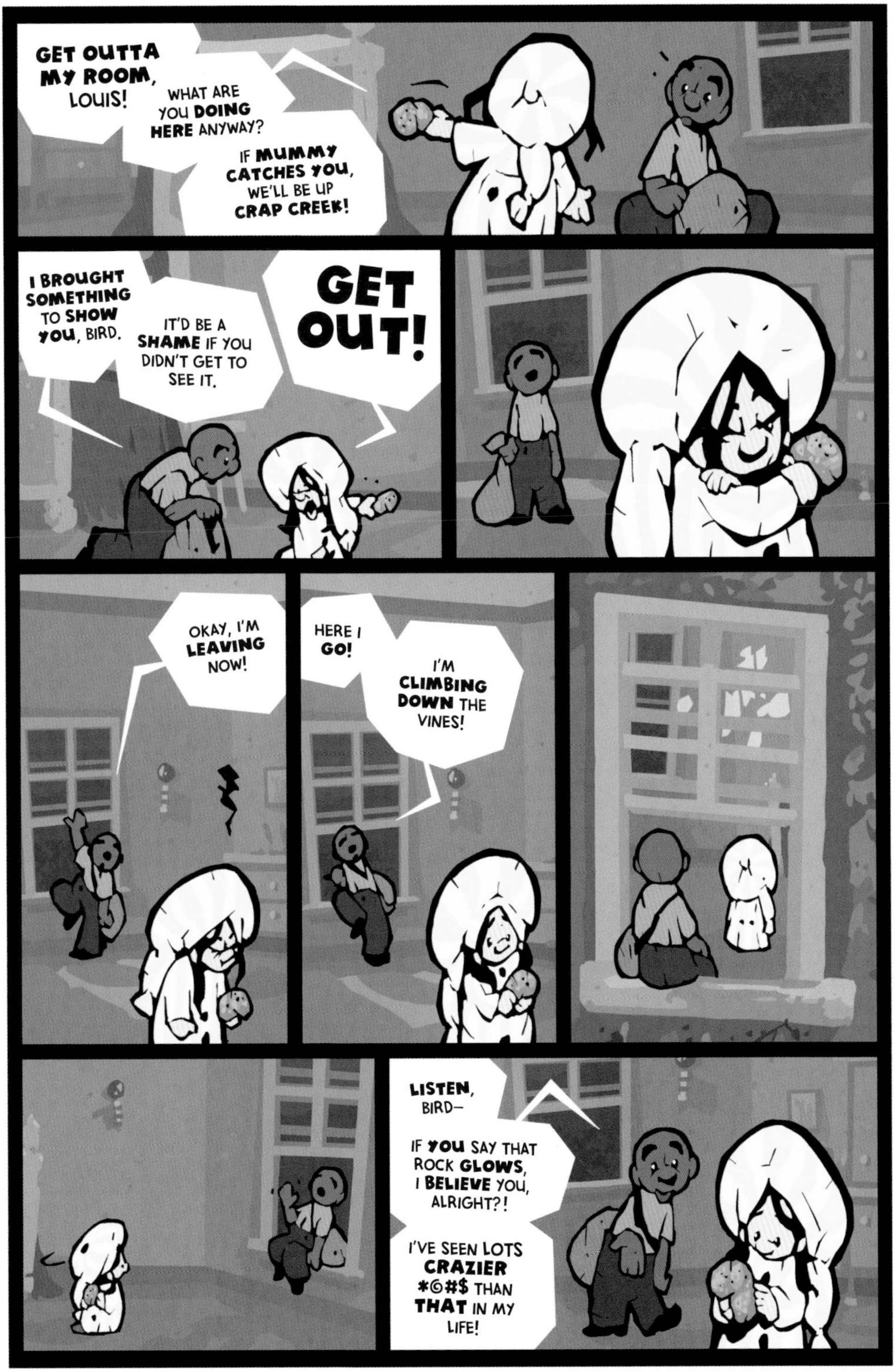
GET OUTTA MY ROOM, LOUIS!
WHAT ARE YOU DOING HERE ANYWAY?
IF MUMMY CATCHES YOU, WE'LL BE UP CRAP CREEK!
I BROUGHT SOMETHING TO SHOW YOU, BIRD.
IT'D BE A SHAME IF YOU DIDN'T GET TO SEE IT.
GET OUT!
OKAY, I'M LEAVING NOW!
HERE I GO!
I'M CLIMBING DOWN THE VINES!
LISTEN, BIRD—
IF YOU SAY THAT ROCK GLOWS, I BELIEVE YOU, ALRIGHT?!
I'VE SEEN LOTS CRAZIER *@#$ THAN THAT IN MY LIFE!

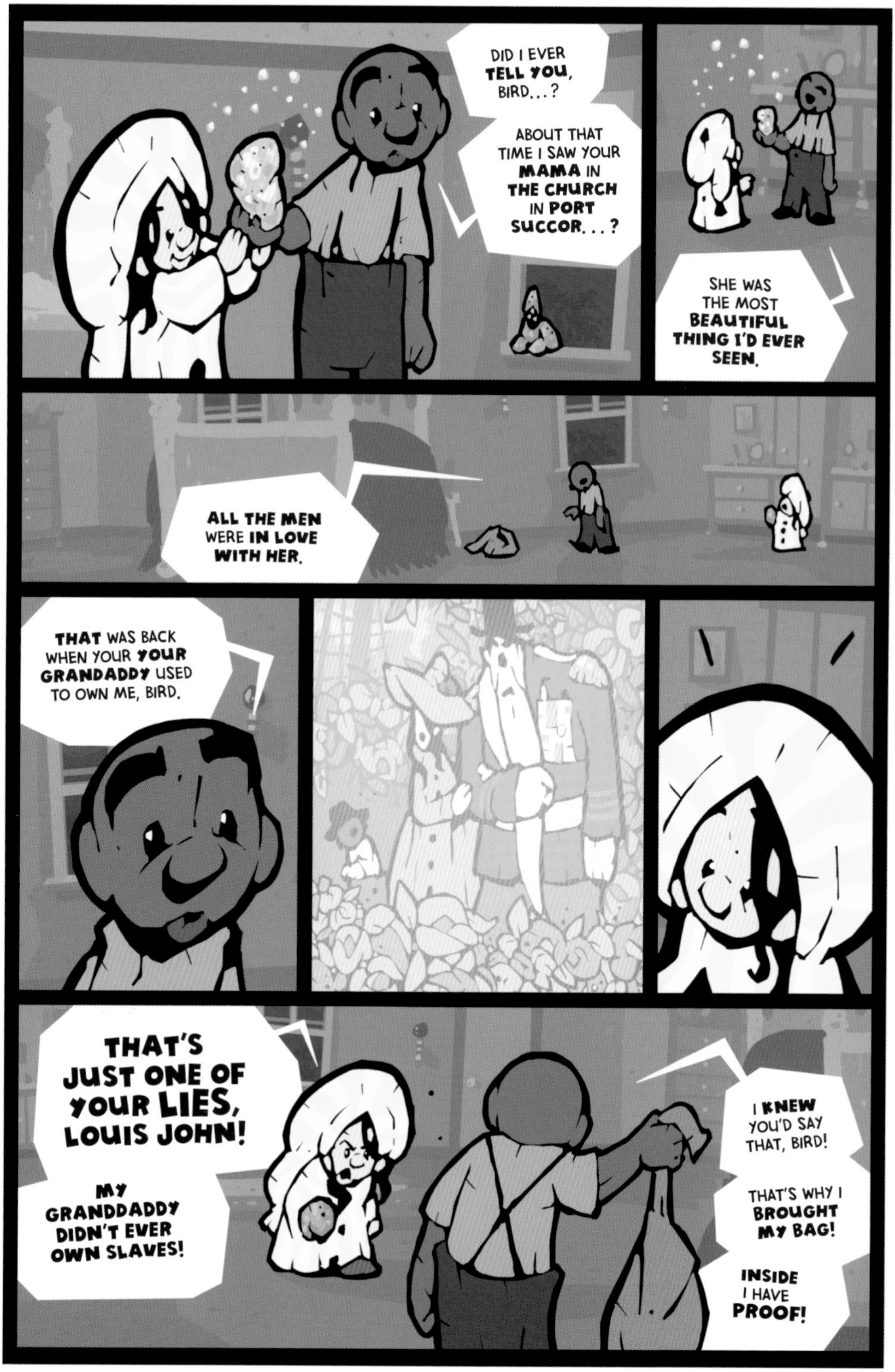
DID I EVER TELL YOU, BIRD...?
ABOUT THAT TIME I SAW YOUR MAMA IN THE CHURCH IN PORT SUCCOR...?
SHE WAS THE MOST BEAUTIFUL THING I'D EVER SEEN.
ALL THE MEN WERE IN LOVE WITH HER.
THAT WAS BACK WHEN YOUR YOUR GRANDADDY USED TO OWN ME, BIRD.
THAT'S JUST ONE OF YOUR LIES, LOUIS JOHN!
MY GRANDDADDY DIDN'T EVER OWN SLAVES!
I KNEW YOU'D SAY THAT, BIRD!
THAT'S WHY I BROUGHT MY BAG!
INSIDE I HAVE PROOF!

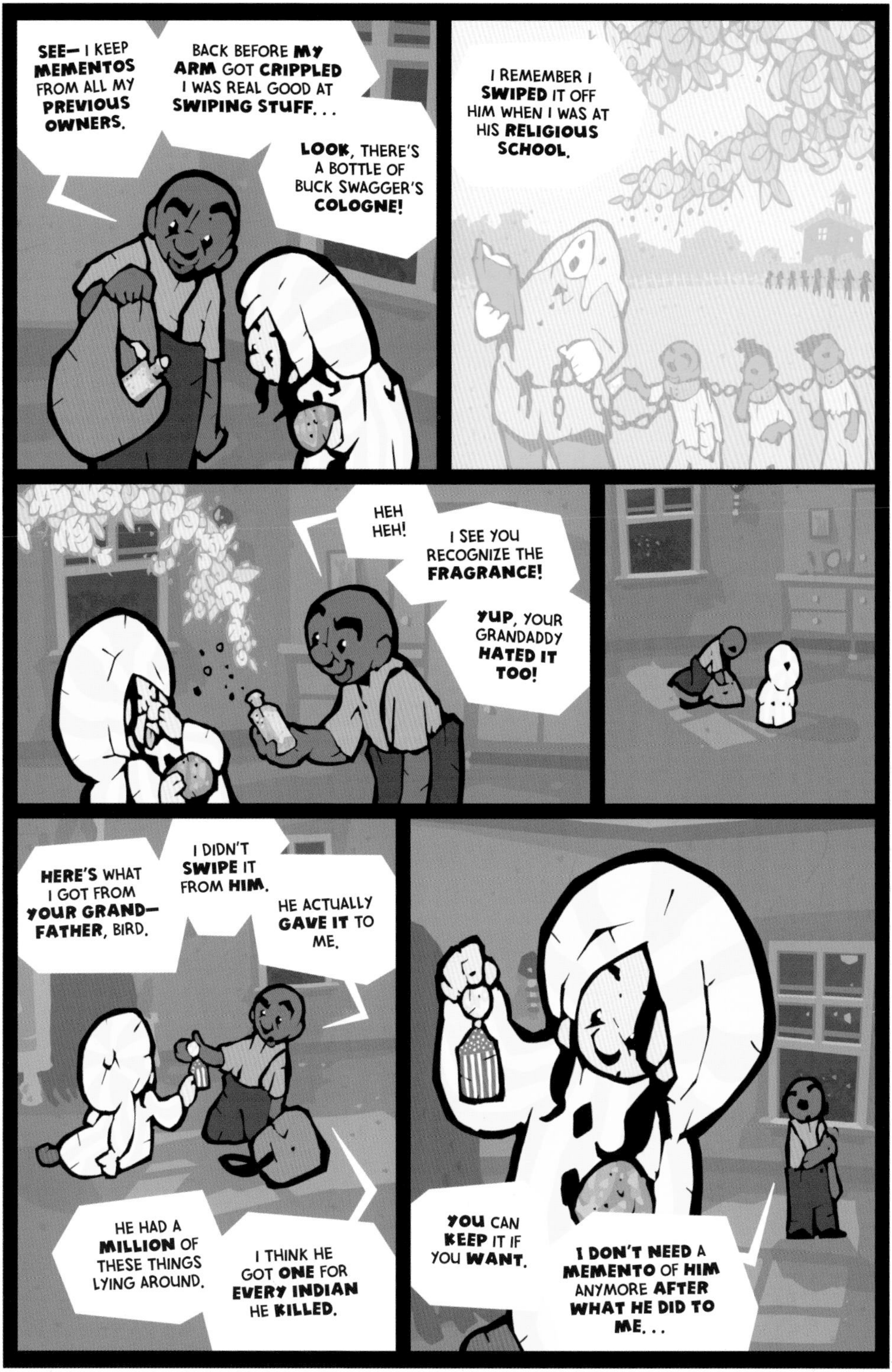
SEE— I KEEP MEMENTOS FROM ALL MY PREVIOUS OWNERS.
BACK BEFORE MY ARM GOT CRIPPLED I WAS REAL GOOD AT SWIPING STUFF. . .
LOOK, THERE'S A BOTTLE OF BUCK SWAGGER'S COLOGNE!
I REMEMBER I SWIPED IT OFF HIM WHEN I WAS AT HIS RELIGIOUS SCHOOL.
HEH HEH!
I SEE YOU RECOGNIZE THE FRAGRANCE!
YUP, YOUR GRANDADDY HATED IT TOO!
HERE'S WHAT I GOT FROM YOUR GRAND-FATHER, BIRD.
I DIDN'T SWIPE IT FROM HIM.
HE ACTUALLY GAVE IT TO ME.
HE HAD A MILLION OF THESE THINGS LYING AROUND.
I THINK HE GOT ONE FOR EVERY INDIAN HE KILLED.
YOU CAN KEEP IT IF YOU WANT.
I DON'T NEED A MEMENTO OF HIM ANYMORE AFTER WHAT HE DID TO ME. . .

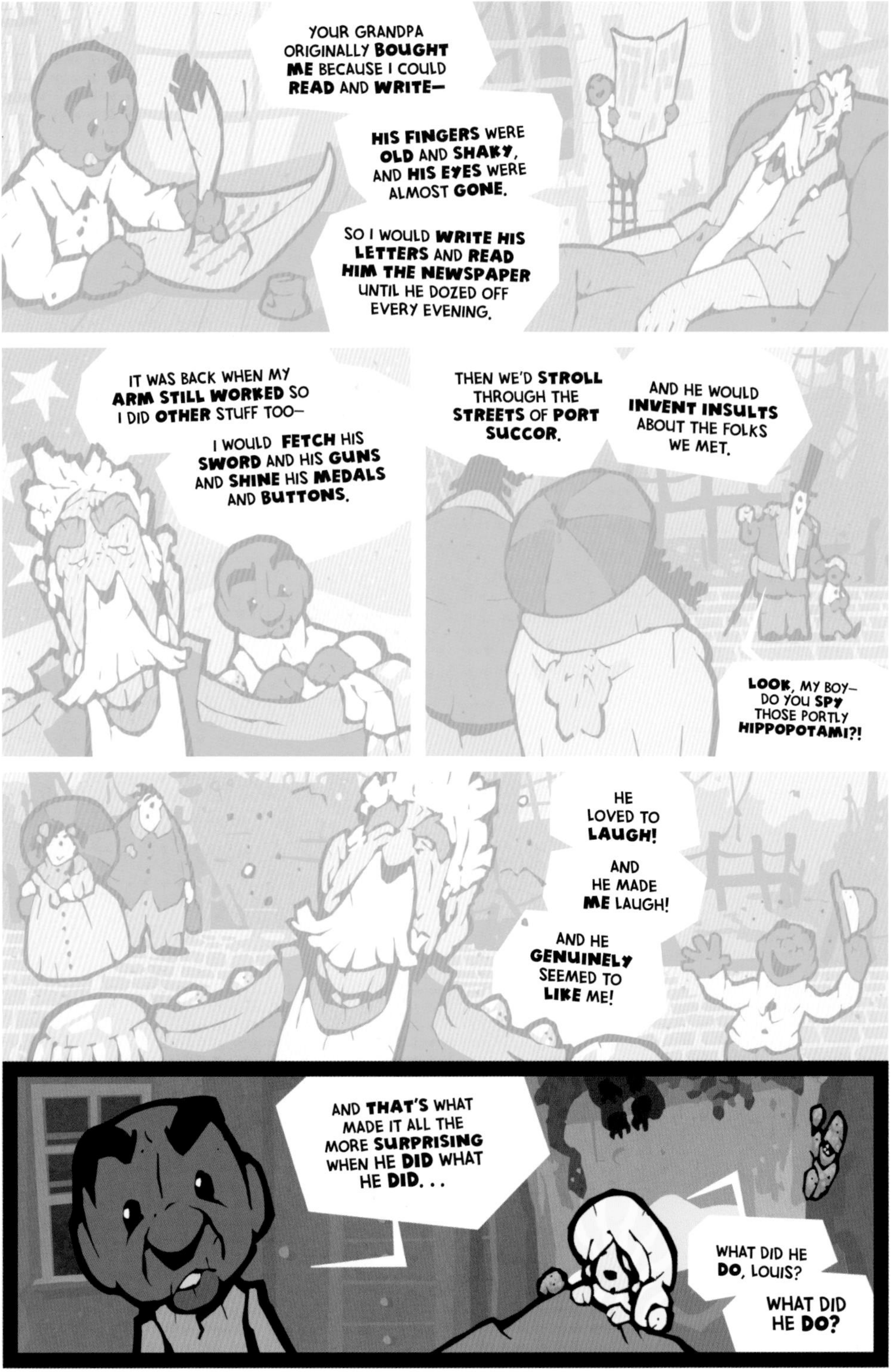
YOUR GRANDPA ORIGINALLY BOUGHT ME BECAUSE I COULD READ AND WRITE—
HIS FINGERS WERE OLD AND SHAKY, AND HIS EYES WERE ALMOST GONE.
SO I WOULD WRITE HIS LETTERS AND READ HIM THE NEWSPAPER UNTIL HE DOZED OFF EVERY EVENING.
IT WAS BACK WHEN MY ARM STILL WORKED SO I DID OTHER STUFF TOO—
I WOULD FETCH HIS SWORD AND HIS GUNS AND SHINE HIS MEDALS AND BUTTONS.
THEN WE'D STROLL THROUGH THE STREETS OF PORT SUCCOR.
AND HE WOULD INVENT INSULTS ABOUT THE FOLKS WE MET.
LOOK, MY BOY— DO YOU SPY THOSE PORTLY HIPPOPOTAMI?!
HE LOVED TO LAUGH!
AND HE MADE ME LAUGH!
AND HE GENUINELY SEEMED TO LIKE ME!
AND THAT'S WHAT MADE IT ALL THE MORE SURPRISING WHEN HE DID WHAT HE DID. . .
WHAT DID HE DO, LOUIS?
WHAT DID HE DO?

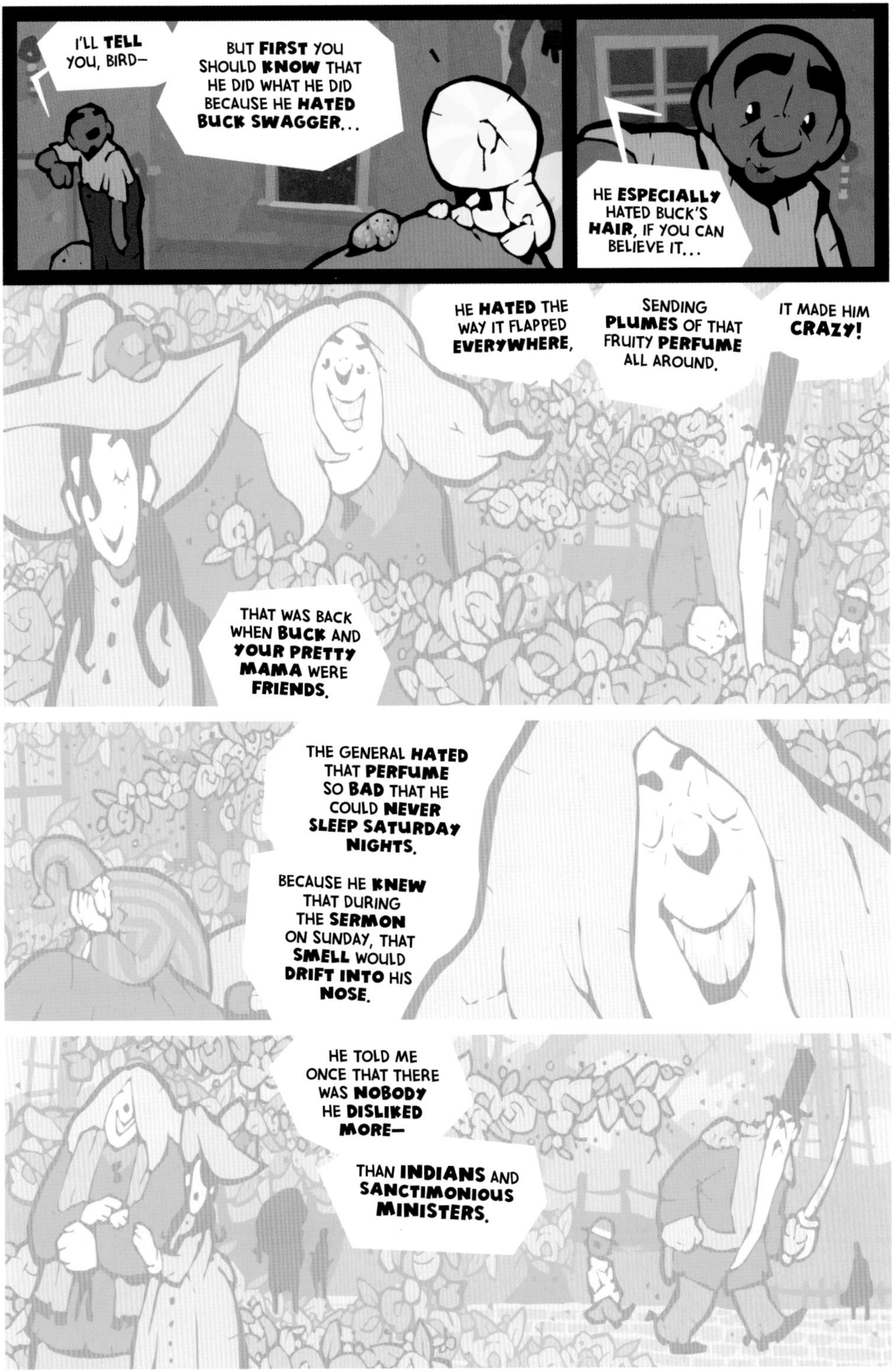
I'LL TELL YOU, BIRD–
BUT FIRST YOU SHOULD KNOW THAT HE DID WHAT HE DID BECAUSE HE HATED BUCK SWAGGER...
HE ESPECIALLY HATED BUCK'S HAIR, IF YOU CAN BELIEVE IT...
HE HATED THE WAY IT FLAPPED EVERYWHERE,
SENDING PLUMES OF THAT FRUITY PERFUME ALL AROUND.
IT MADE HIM CRAZY!
THAT WAS BACK WHEN BUCK AND YOUR PRETTY MAMA WERE FRIENDS.
THE GENERAL HATED THAT PERFUME SO BAD THAT HE COULD NEVER SLEEP SATURDAY NIGHTS.
BECAUSE HE KNEW THAT DURING THE SERMON ON SUNDAY, THAT SMELL WOULD DRIFT INTO HIS NOSE.
HE TOLD ME ONCE THAT THERE WAS NOBODY HE DISLIKED MORE–
THAN INDIANS AND SANCTIMONIOUS MINISTERS.

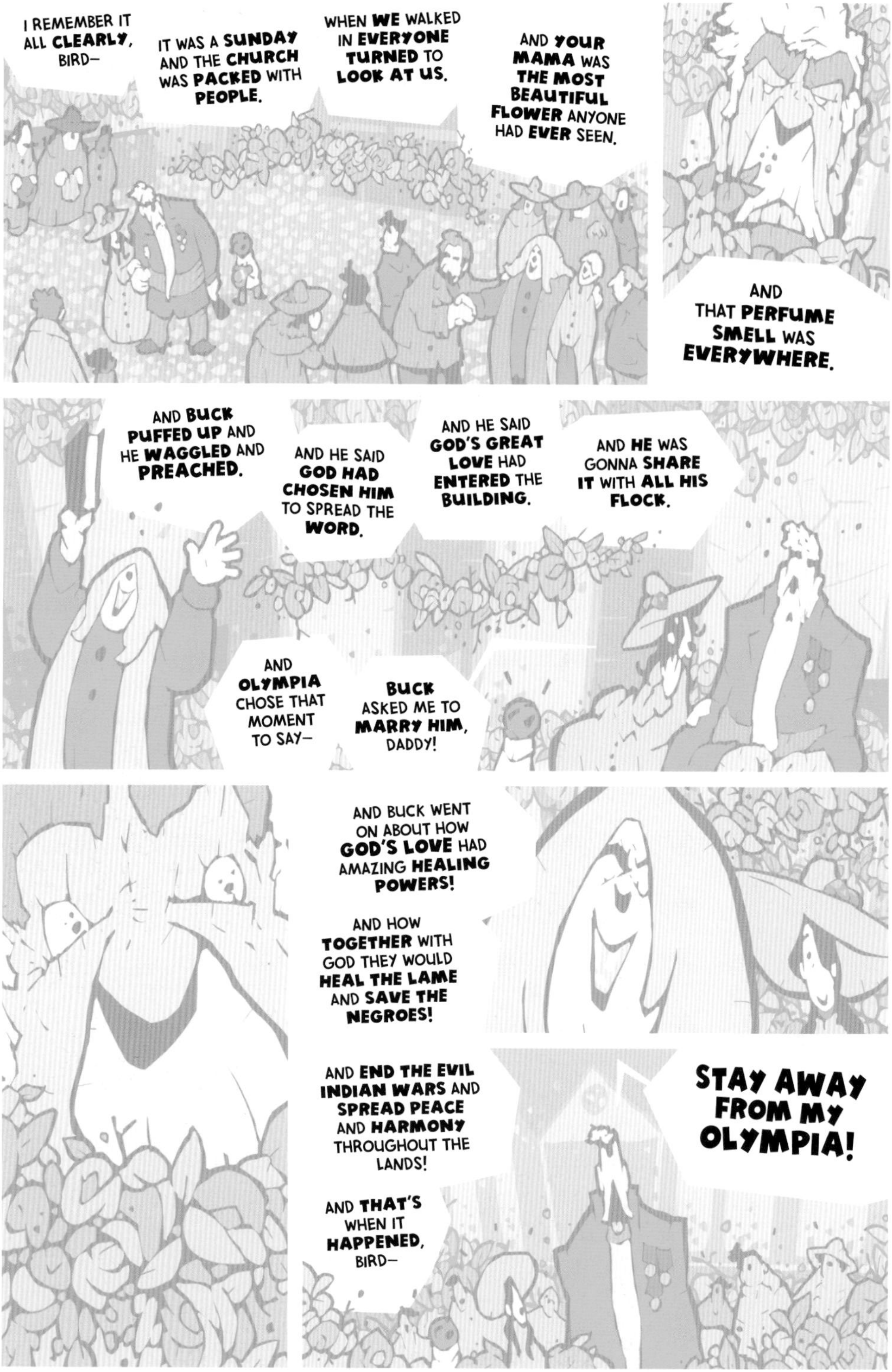
I REMEMBER IT ALL CLEARLY, BIRD—
IT WAS A SUNDAY AND THE CHURCH WAS PACKED WITH PEOPLE.
WHEN WE WALKED IN EVERYONE TURNED TO LOOK AT US.
AND YOUR MAMA WAS THE MOST BEAUTIFUL FLOWER ANYONE HAD EVER SEEN.
AND THAT PERFUME SMELL WAS EVERYWHERE.
AND BUCK PUFFED UP AND HE WAGGLED AND PREACHED.
AND HE SAID GOD HAD CHOSEN HIM TO SPREAD THE WORD.
AND HE SAID GOD'S GREAT LOVE HAD ENTERED THE BUILDING.
AND HE WAS GONNA SHARE IT WITH ALL HIS FLOCK.
AND OLYMPIA CHOSE THAT MOMENT TO SAY—
BUCK ASKED ME TO MARRY HIM, DADDY!
AND BUCK WENT ON ABOUT HOW GOD'S LOVE HAD AMAZING HEALING POWERS!
AND HOW TOGETHER WITH GOD THEY WOULD HEAL THE LAME AND SAVE THE NEGROES!
AND END THE EVIL INDIAN WARS AND SPREAD PEACE AND HARMONY THROUGHOUT THE LANDS!
AND THAT'S WHEN IT HAPPENED, BIRD—
STAY AWAY FROM MY OLYMPIA!

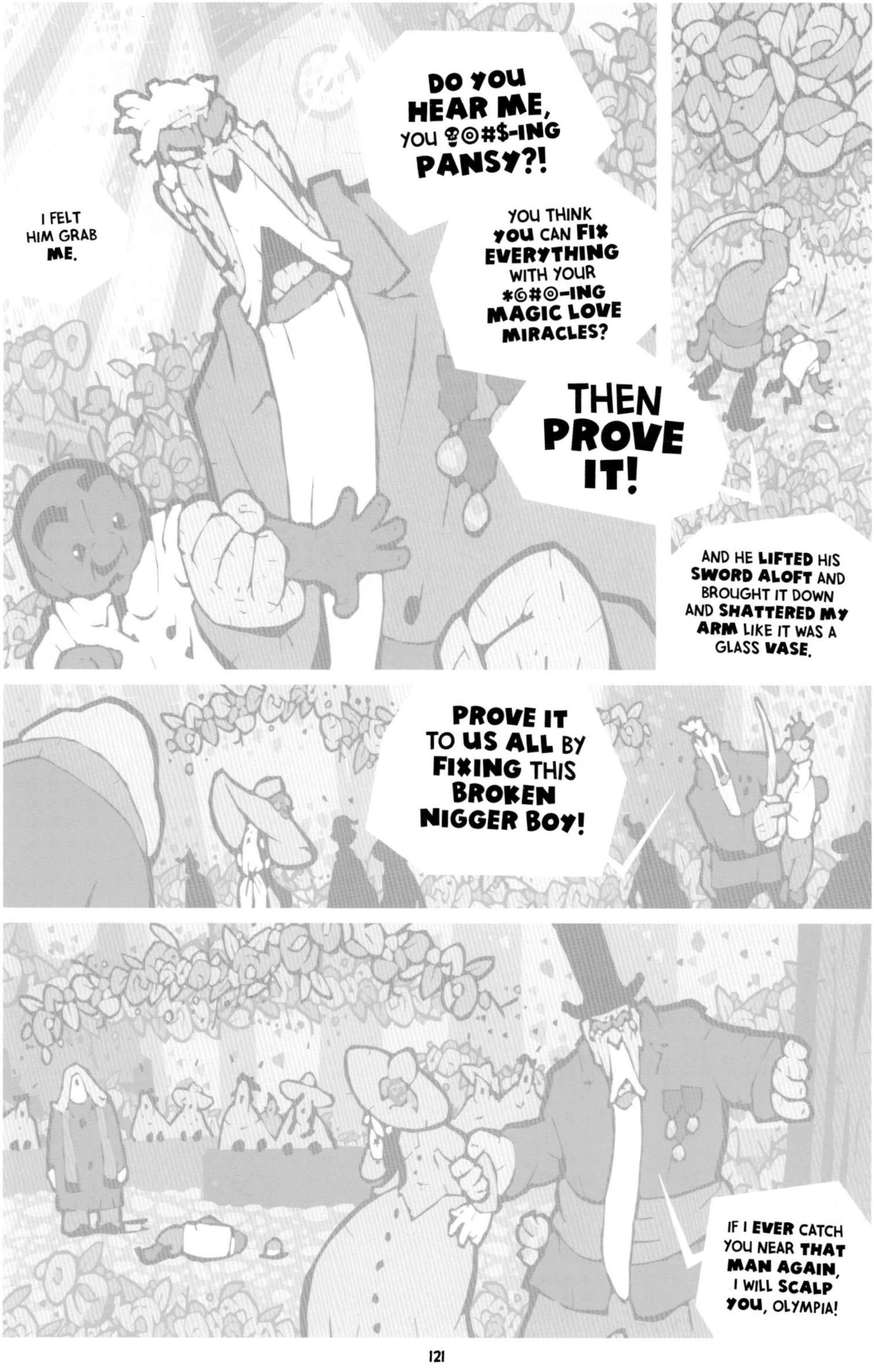
I FELT HIM GRAB ME.
DO YOU HEAR ME, YOU ☠◎#$-ING PANSY?!
YOU THINK YOU CAN FIX EVERYTHING WITH YOUR *©#◎-ING MAGIC LOVE MIRACLES?
THEN PROVE IT!
AND HE LIFTED HIS SWORD ALOFT AND BROUGHT IT DOWN AND SHATTERED MY ARM LIKE IT WAS A GLASS VASE.
PROVE IT TO US ALL BY FIXING THIS BROKEN NIGGER BOY!
IF I EVER CATCH YOU NEAR THAT MAN AGAIN, I WILL SCALP YOU, OLYMPIA!

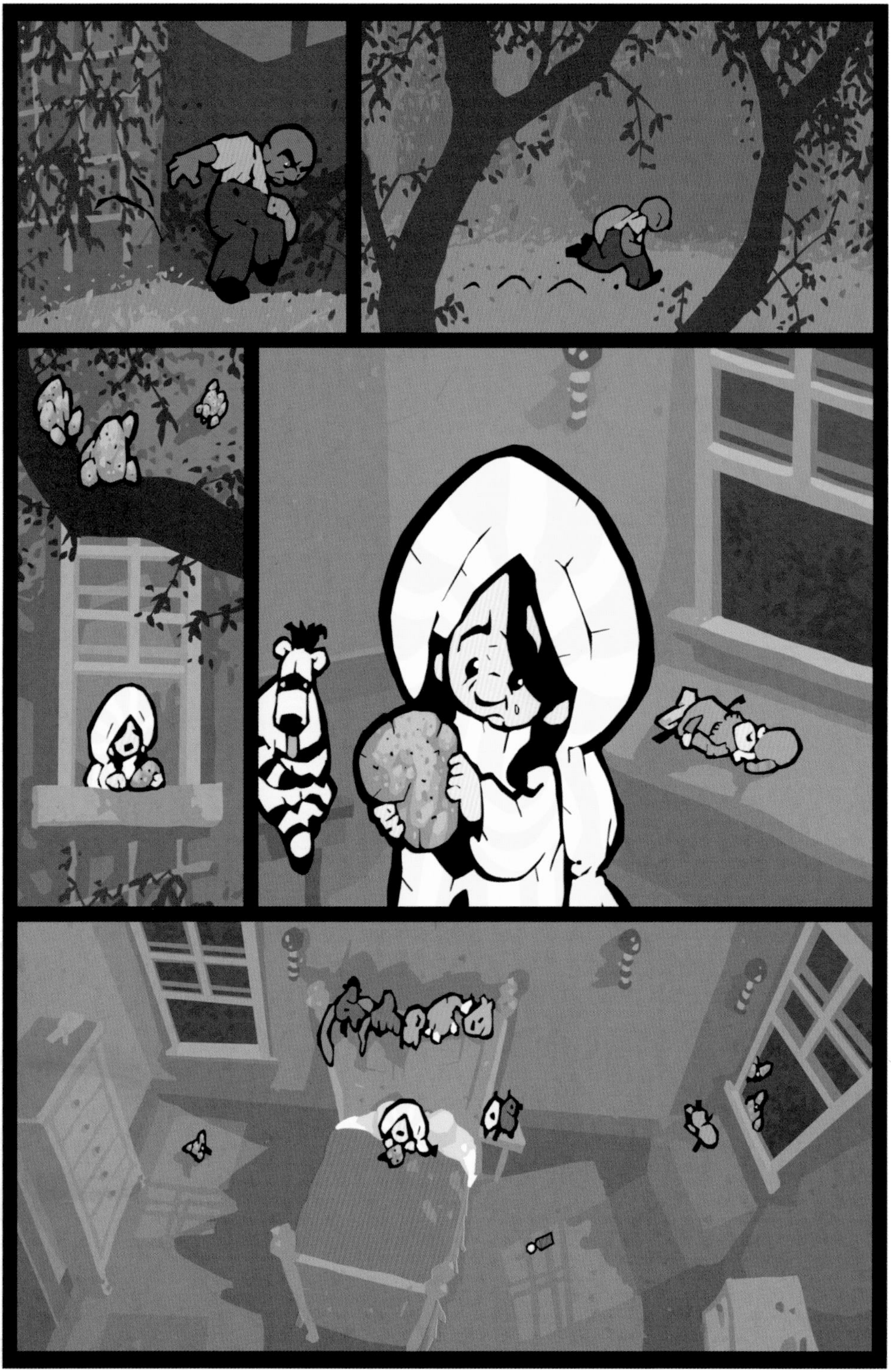

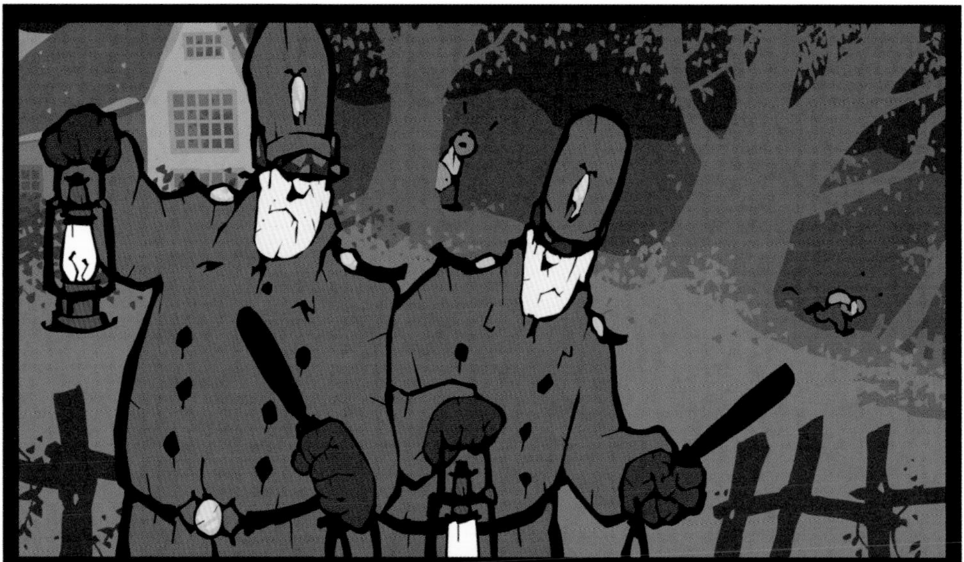

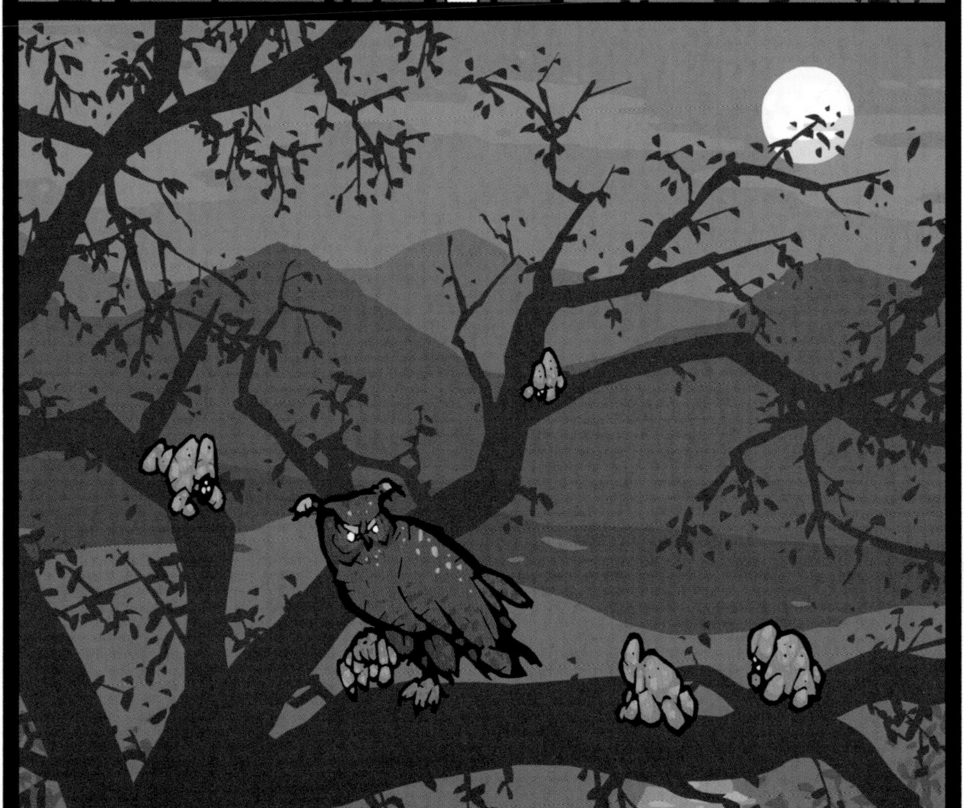

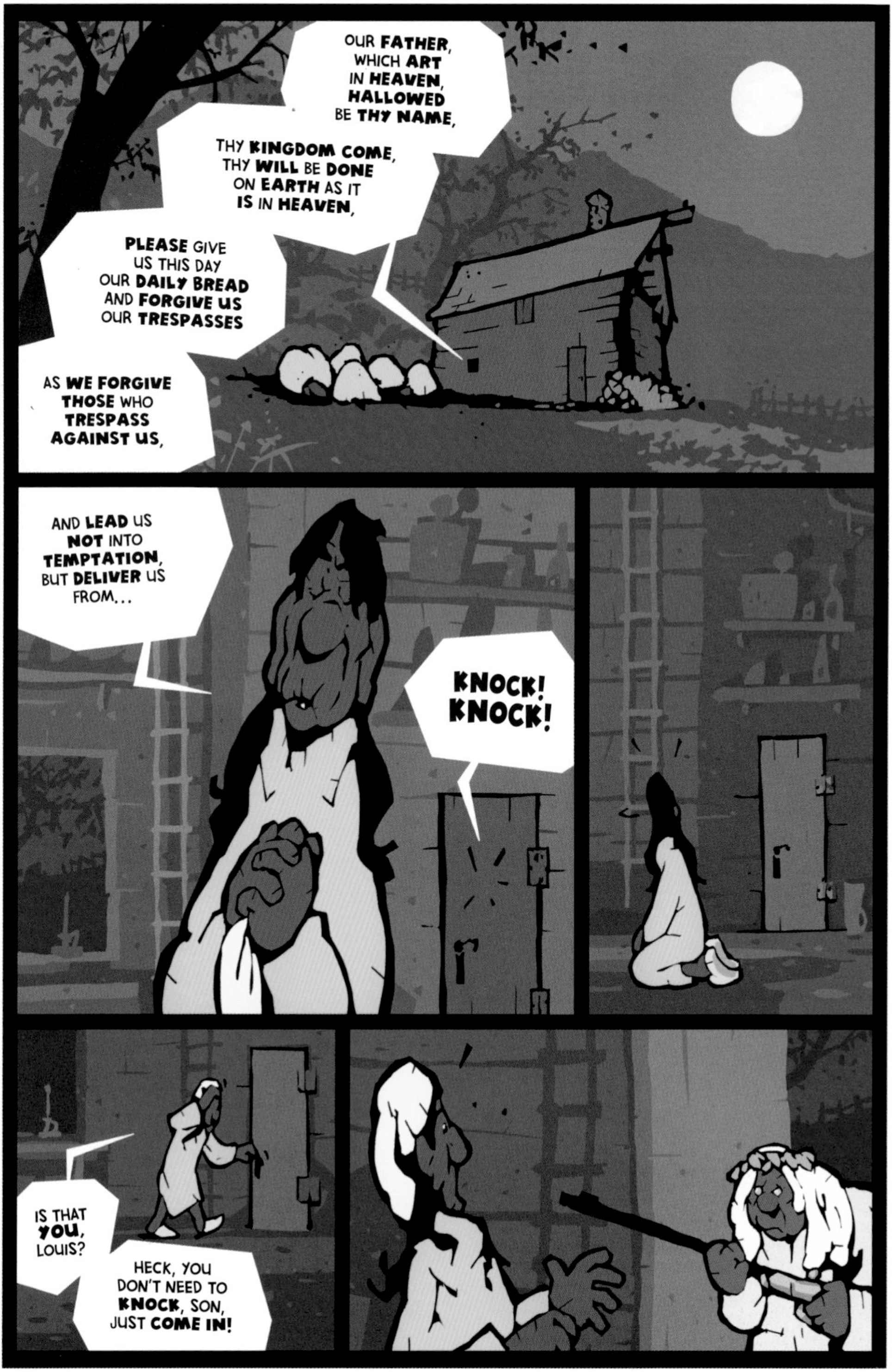
OUR FATHER, WHICH ART IN HEAVEN, HALLOWED BE THY NAME,
THY KINGDOM COME, THY WILL BE DONE ON EARTH AS IT IS IN HEAVEN,
PLEASE GIVE US THIS DAY OUR DAILY BREAD AND FORGIVE US OUR TRESPASSES
AS WE FORGIVE THOSE WHO TRESPASS AGAINST US,
AND LEAD US NOT INTO TEMPTATION, BUT DELIVER US FROM...
KNOCK! KNOCK!
IS THAT YOU, LOUIS?
HECK, YOU DON'T NEED TO KNOCK, SON, JUST COME IN!

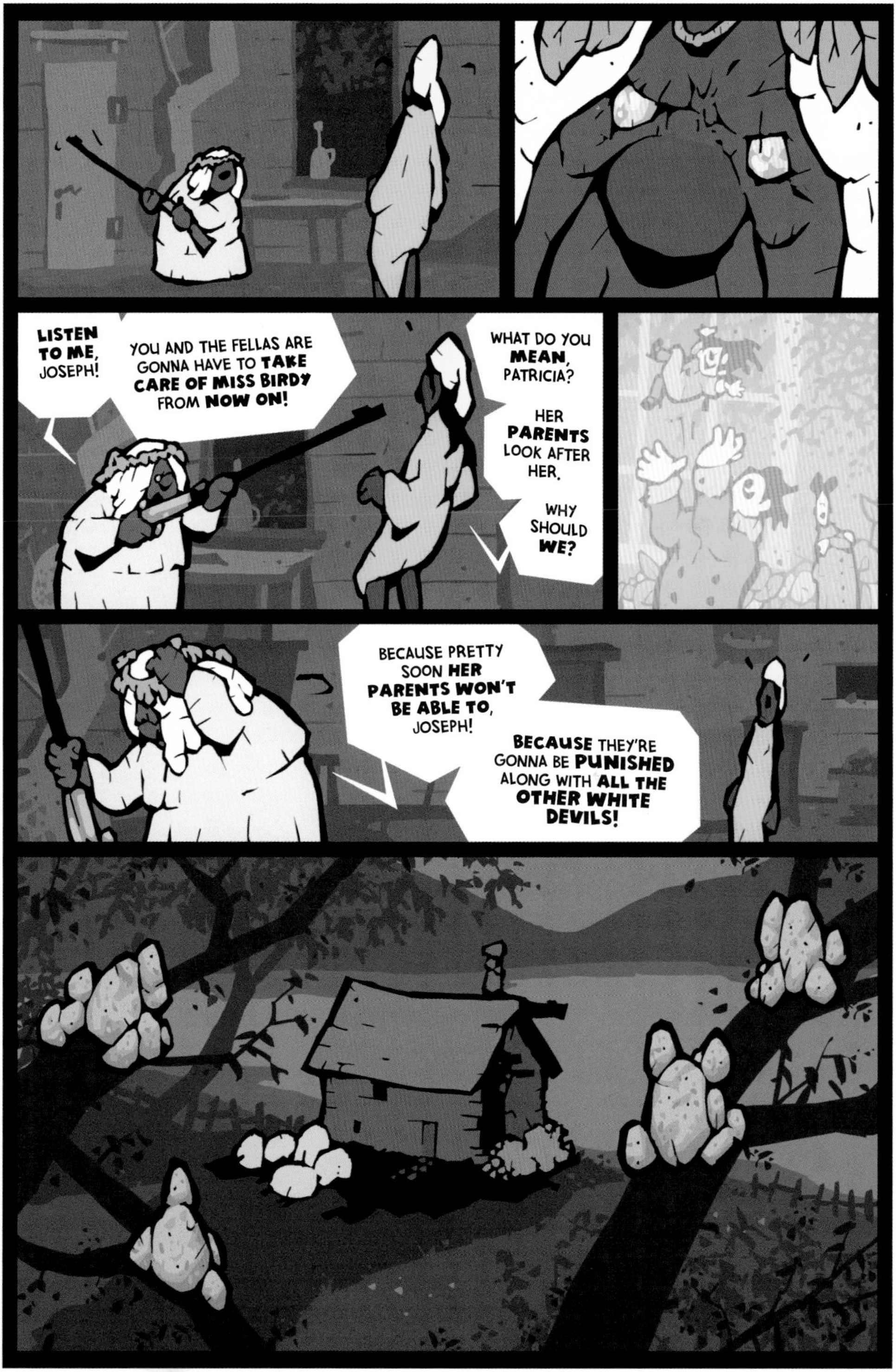
LISTEN TO ME, JOSEPH!
YOU AND THE FELLAS ARE GONNA HAVE TO TAKE CARE OF MISS BIRDY FROM NOW ON!
WHAT DO YOU MEAN, PATRICIA?
HER PARENTS LOOK AFTER HER.
WHY SHOULD WE?
BECAUSE PRETTY SOON HER PARENTS WON'T BE ABLE TO, JOSEPH!
BECAUSE THEY'RE GONNA BE PUNISHED ALONG WITH ALL THE OTHER WHITE DEVILS!

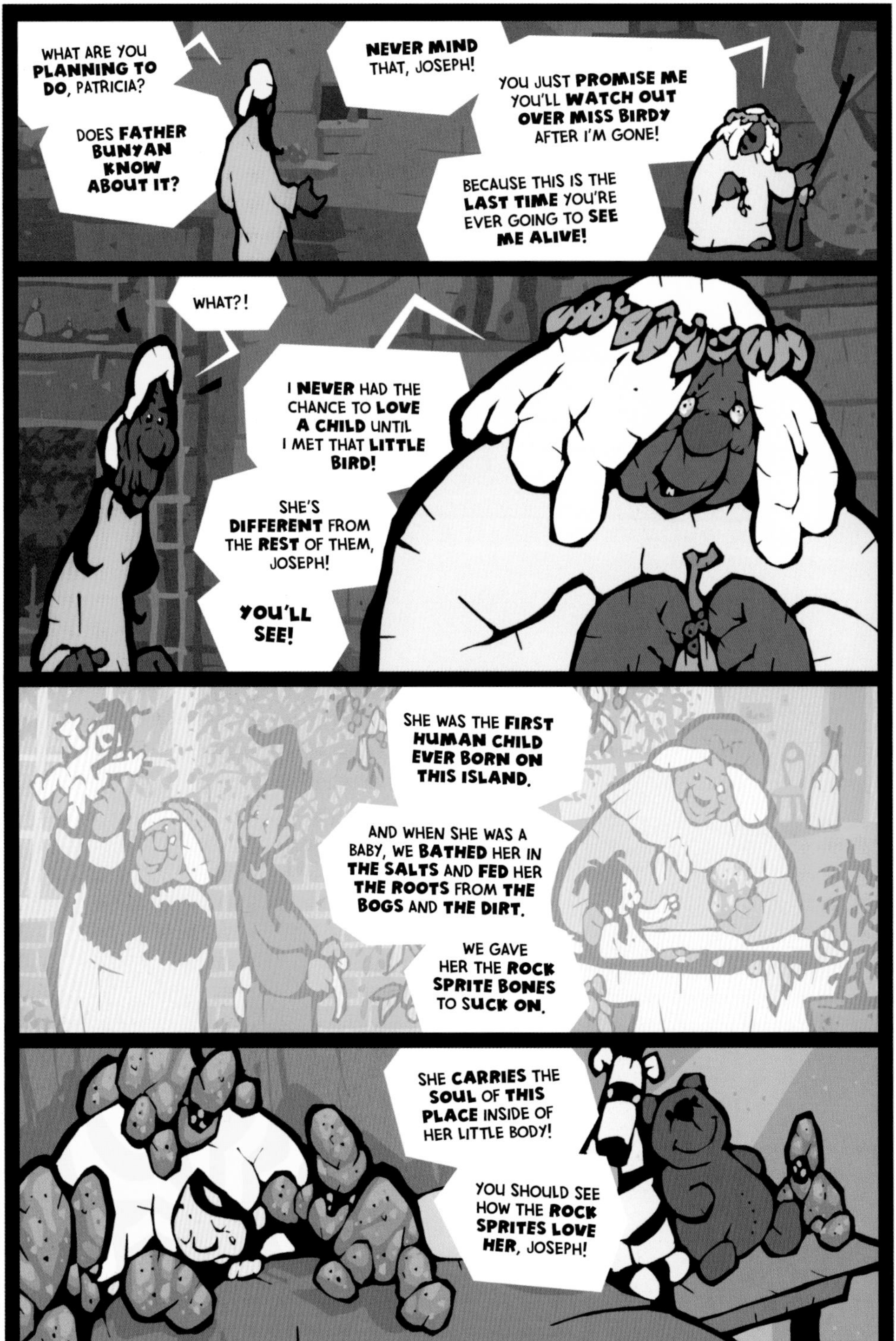
WHAT ARE YOU PLANNING TO DO, PATRICIA?
DOES FATHER BUNYAN KNOW ABOUT IT?
NEVER MIND THAT, JOSEPH!
YOU JUST PROMISE ME YOU'LL WATCH OUT OVER MISS BIRDY AFTER I'M GONE!
BECAUSE THIS IS THE LAST TIME YOU'RE EVER GOING TO SEE ME ALIVE!
WHAT?!
I NEVER HAD THE CHANCE TO LOVE A CHILD UNTIL I MET THAT LITTLE BIRD!
SHE'S DIFFERENT FROM THE REST OF THEM, JOSEPH!
YOU'LL SEE!
SHE WAS THE FIRST HUMAN CHILD EVER BORN ON THIS ISLAND.
AND WHEN SHE WAS A BABY, WE BATHED HER IN THE SALTS AND FED HER THE ROOTS FROM THE BOGS AND THE DIRT.
WE GAVE HER THE ROCK SPRITE BONES TO SUCK ON.
SHE CARRIES THE SOUL OF THIS PLACE INSIDE OF HER LITTLE BODY!
YOU SHOULD SEE HOW THE ROCK SPRITES LOVE HER, JOSEPH!

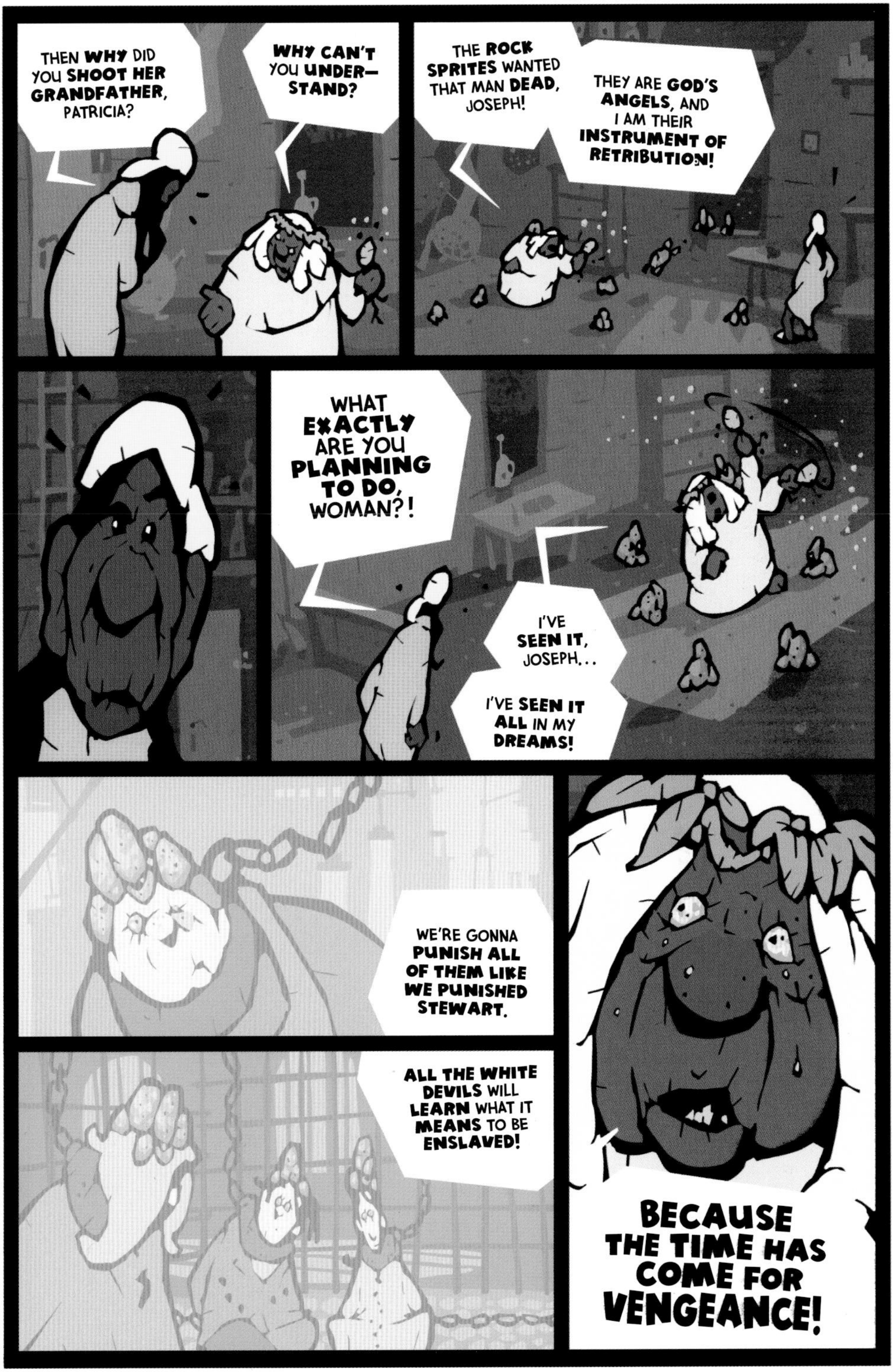
THEN WHY DID YOU SHOOT HER GRANDFATHER, PATRICIA?
WHY CAN'T YOU UNDER-STAND?
THE ROCK SPRITES WANTED THAT MAN DEAD, JOSEPH!
THEY ARE GOD'S ANGELS, AND I AM THEIR INSTRUMENT OF RETRIBUTION!
WHAT EXACTLY ARE YOU PLANNING TO DO, WOMAN?!
I'VE SEEN IT, JOSEPH...
I'VE SEEN IT ALL IN MY DREAMS!
WE'RE GONNA PUNISH ALL OF THEM LIKE WE PUNISHED STEWART.
ALL THE WHITE DEVILS WILL LEARN WHAT IT MEANS TO BE ENSLAVED!
BECAUSE THE TIME HAS COME FOR VENGEANCE!

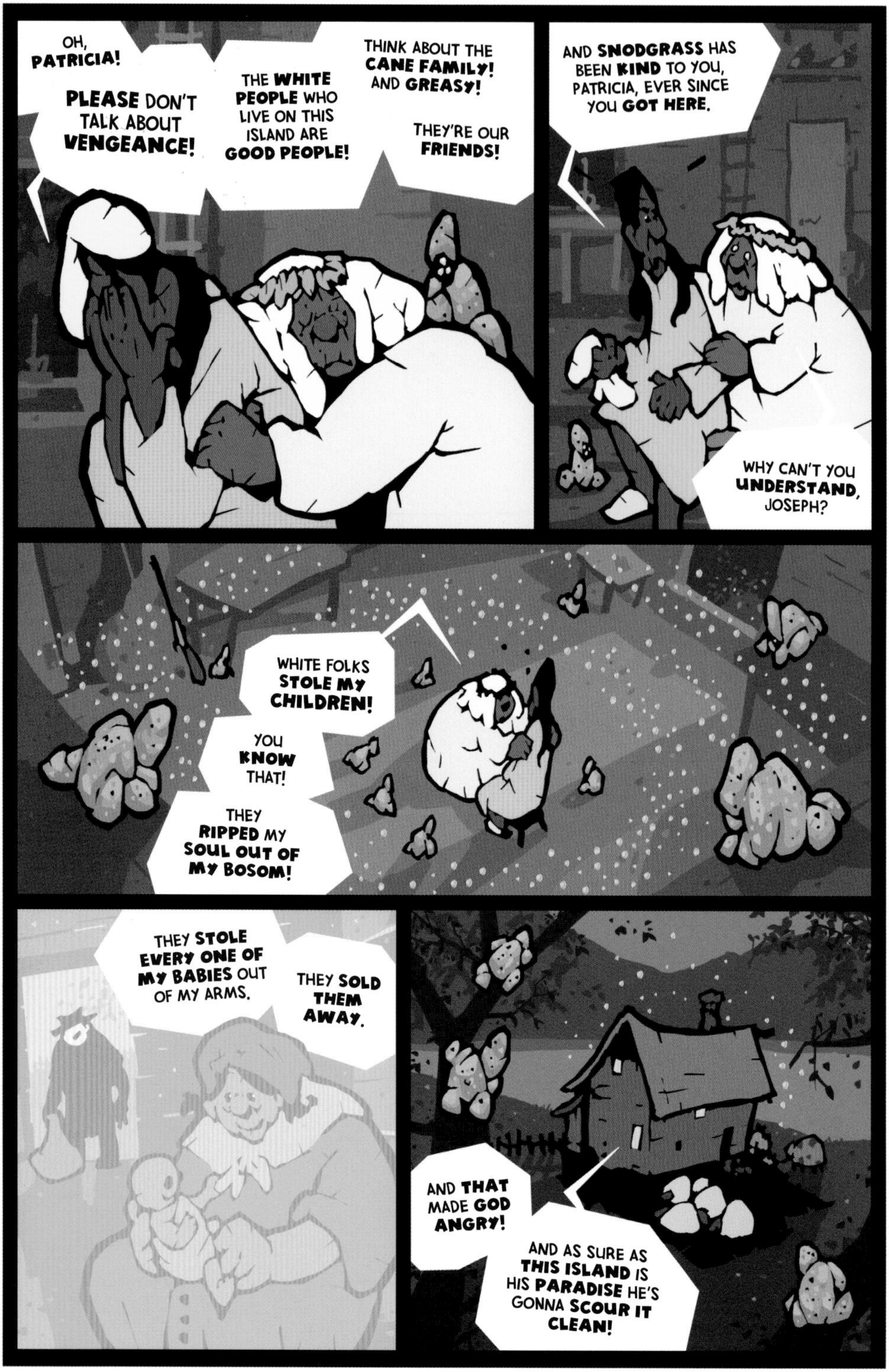
OH, PATRICIA!
PLEASE DON'T TALK ABOUT VENGEANCE!
THE WHITE PEOPLE WHO LIVE ON THIS ISLAND ARE GOOD PEOPLE!
THINK ABOUT THE CANE FAMILY! AND GREASY!
THEY'RE OUR FRIENDS!
AND SNODGRASS HAS BEEN KIND TO YOU, PATRICIA, EVER SINCE YOU GOT HERE.
WHY CAN'T YOU UNDERSTAND, JOSEPH?
WHITE FOLKS STOLE MY CHILDREN!
YOU KNOW THAT!
THEY RIPPED MY SOUL OUT OF MY BOSOM!
THEY STOLE EVERY ONE OF MY BABIES OUT OF MY ARMS.
THEY SOLD THEM AWAY.
AND THAT MADE GOD ANGRY!
AND AS SURE AS THIS ISLAND IS HIS PARADISE HE'S GONNA SCOUR IT CLEAN!

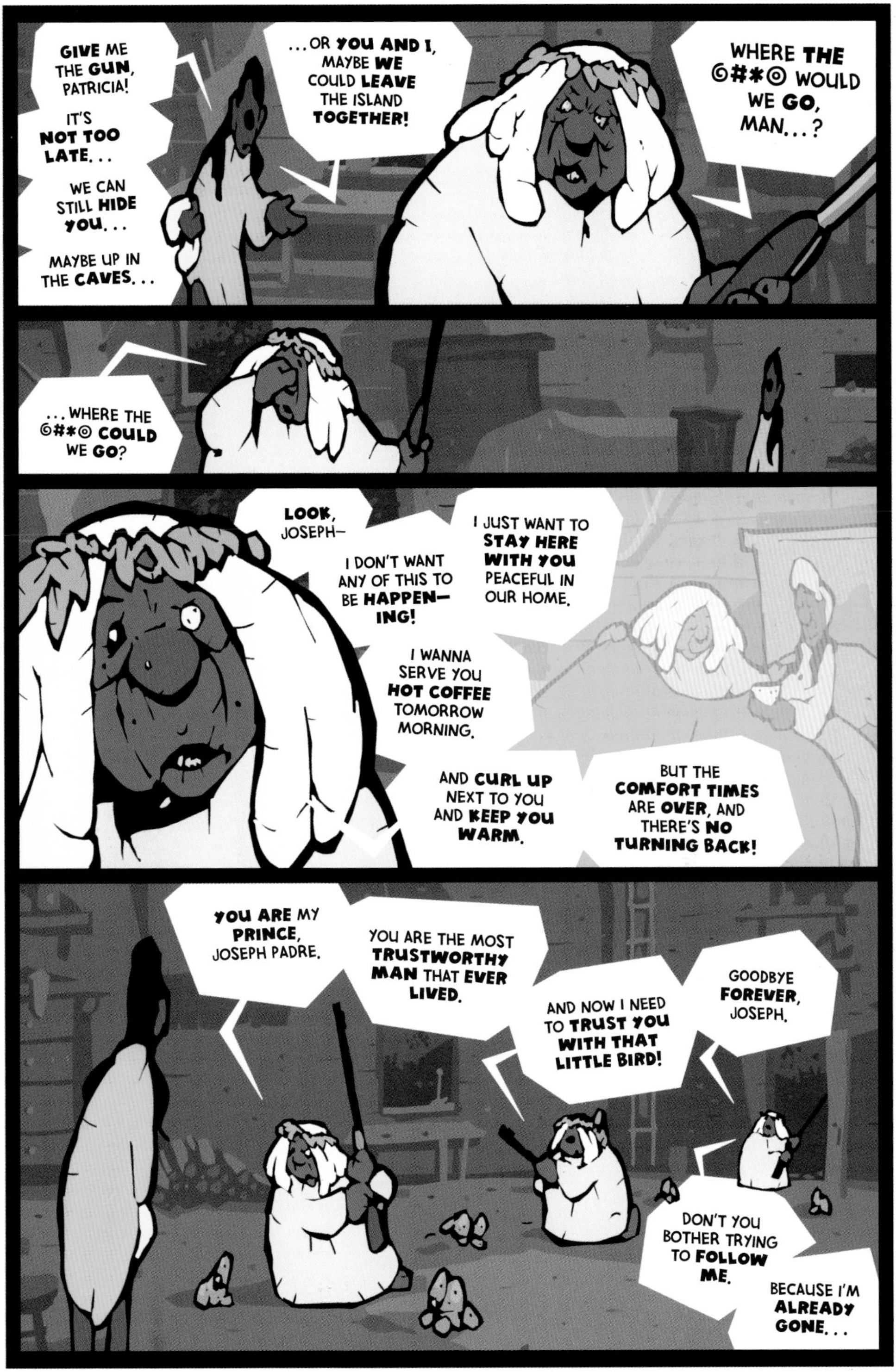
GIVE ME THE GUN, PATRICIA!
IT'S NOT TOO LATE...
WE CAN STILL HIDE YOU...
MAYBE UP IN THE CAVES...
...OR YOU AND I, MAYBE WE COULD LEAVE THE ISLAND TOGETHER!
WHERE THE ©#*◎ WOULD WE GO, MAN...?
...WHERE THE ©#*◎ COULD WE GO?
LOOK, JOSEPH–
I DON'T WANT ANY OF THIS TO BE HAPPEN–ING!
I JUST WANT TO STAY HERE WITH YOU PEACEFUL IN OUR HOME.
I WANNA SERVE YOU HOT COFFEE TOMORROW MORNING.
AND CURL UP NEXT TO YOU AND KEEP YOU WARM.
BUT THE COMFORT TIMES ARE OVER, AND THERE'S NO TURNING BACK!
YOU ARE MY PRINCE, JOSEPH PADRE.
YOU ARE THE MOST TRUSTWORTHY MAN THAT EVER LIVED.
AND NOW I NEED TO TRUST YOU WITH THAT LITTLE BIRD!
GOODBYE FOREVER, JOSEPH.
DON'T YOU BOTHER TRYING TO FOLLOW ME.
BECAUSE I'M ALREADY GONE...

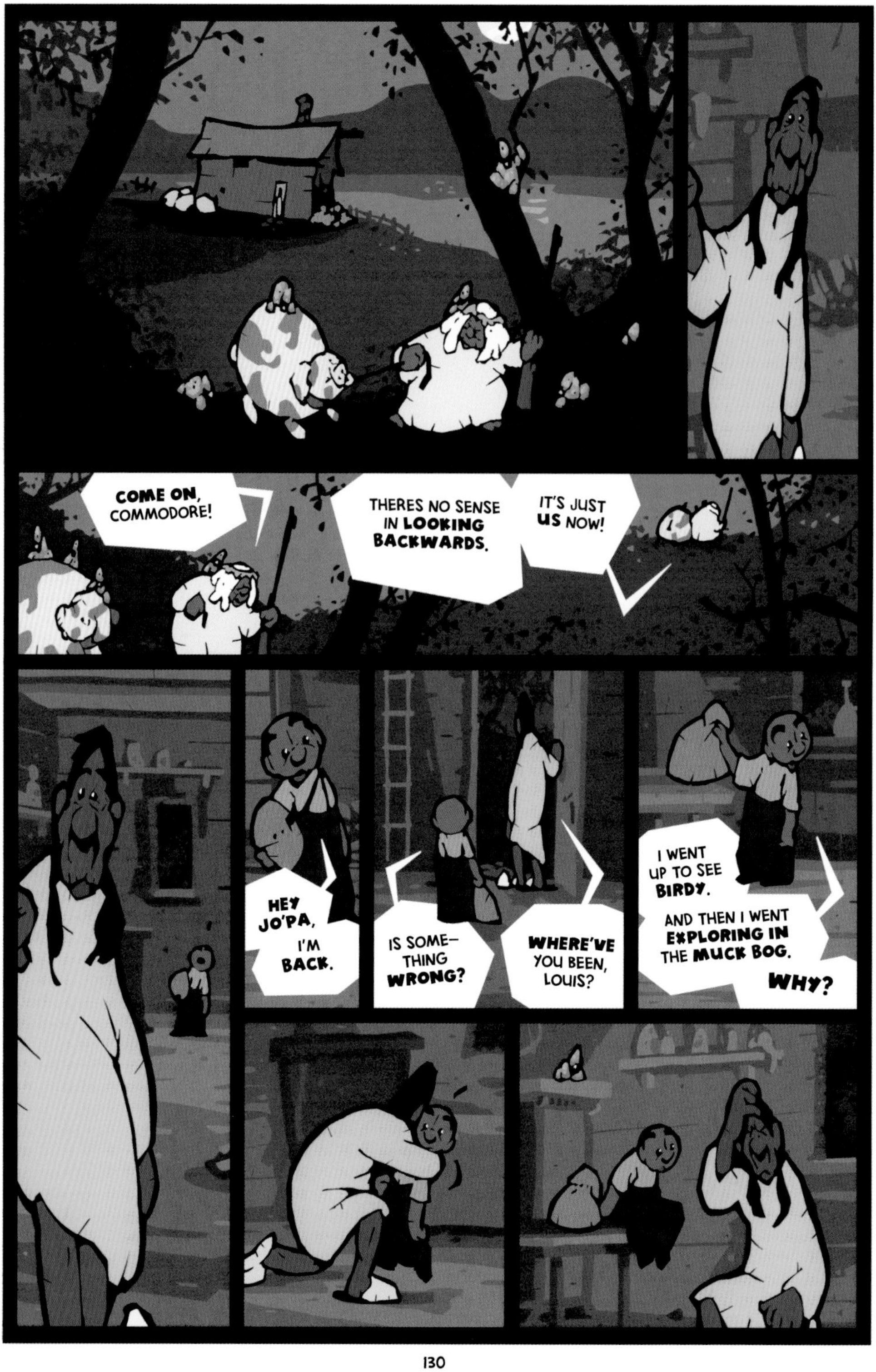
COME ON, COMMODORE!
THERES NO SENSE IN LOOKING BACKWARDS.
IT'S JUST US NOW!
HEY JO'PA, I'M BACK.
IS SOME-THING WRONG?
WHERE'VE YOU BEEN, LOUIS?
I WENT UP TO SEE BIRDY.
AND THEN I WENT EXPLORING IN THE MUCK BOG.
WHY?

CHAPTER EIGHT
An UNEXPECTED *Betrayal*

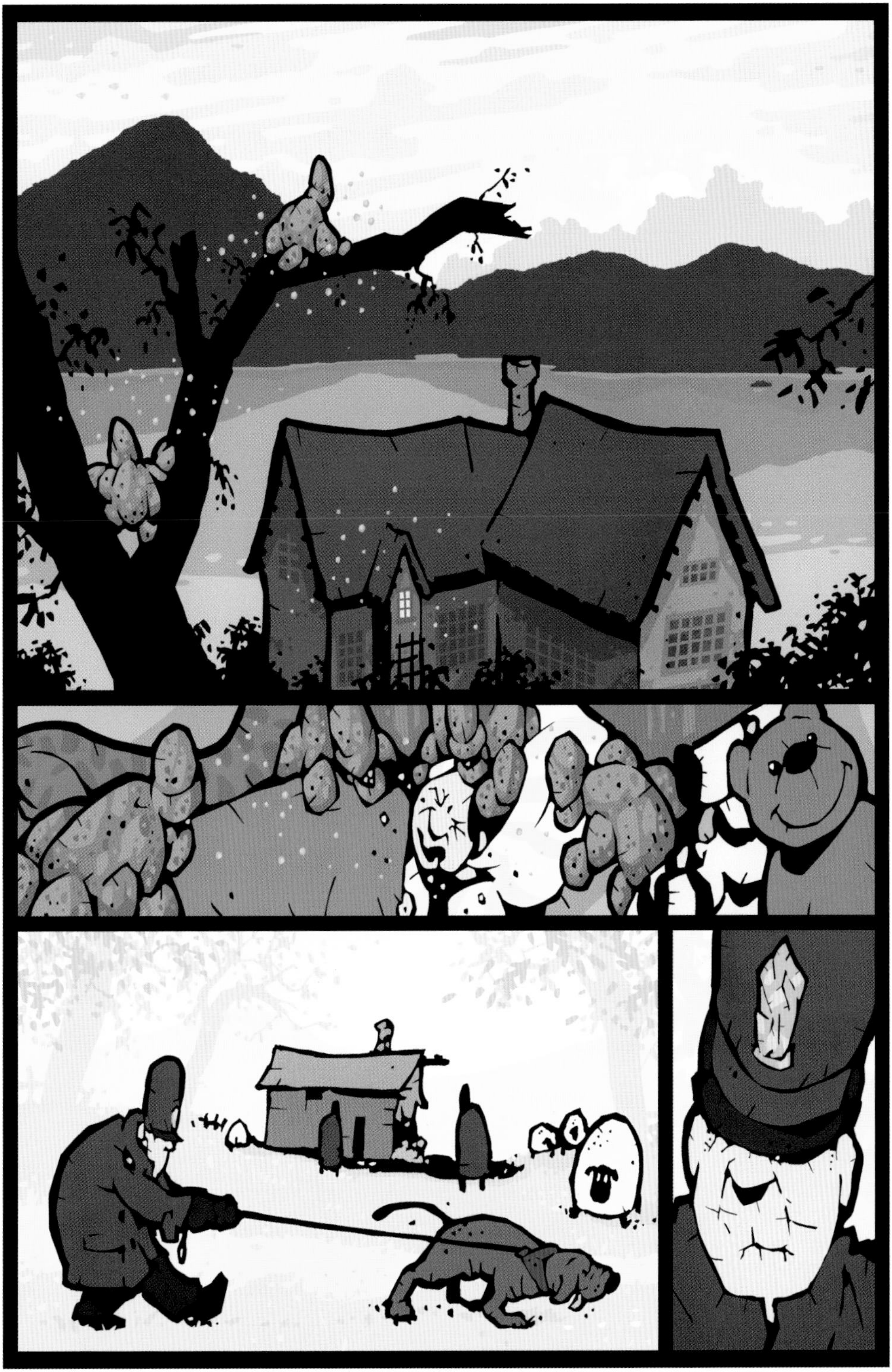

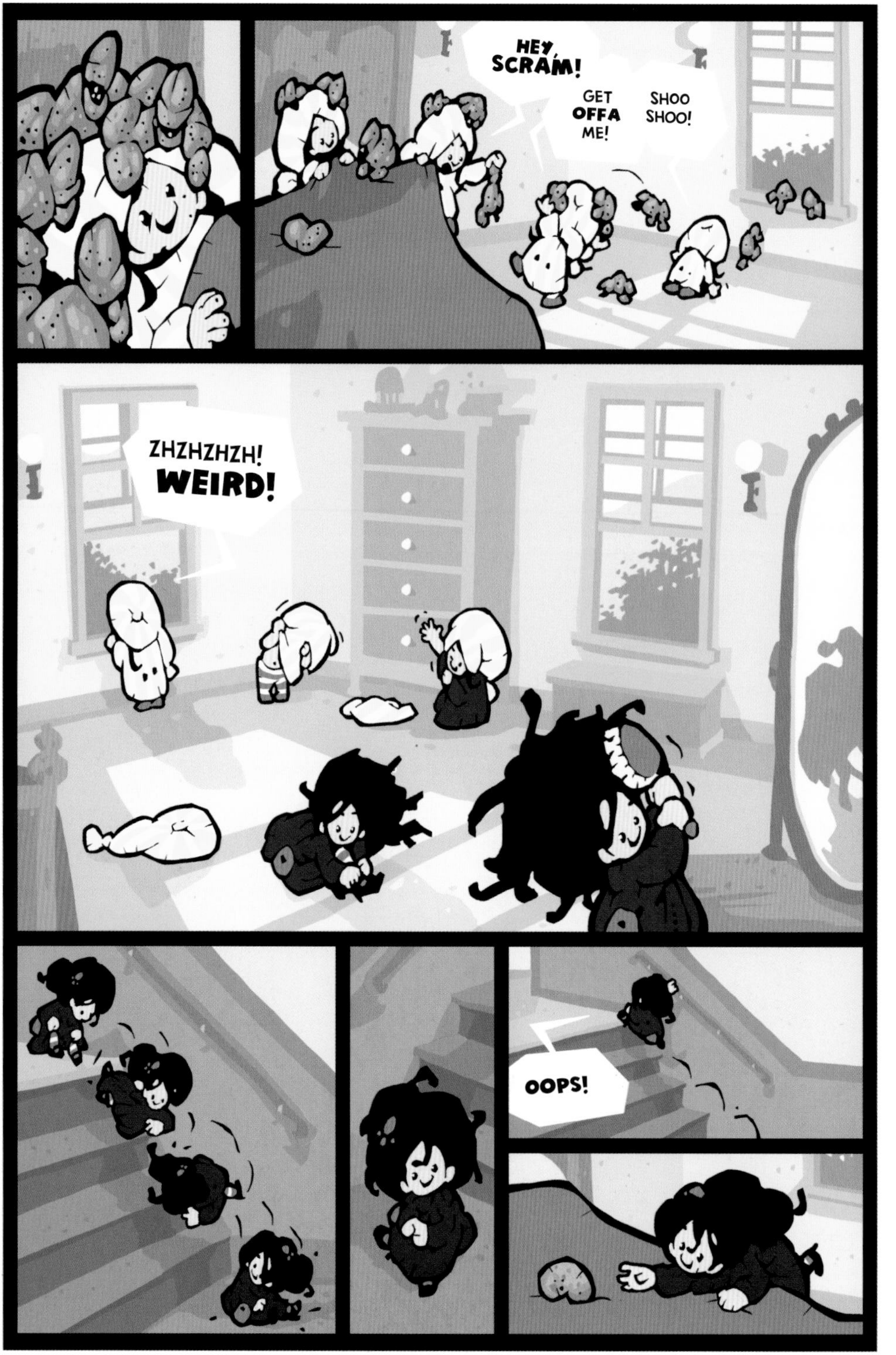
HEY, SCRAM!
GET OFFA ME!
SHOO SHOO!
ZHZHZHZH! WEIRD!
OOPS!

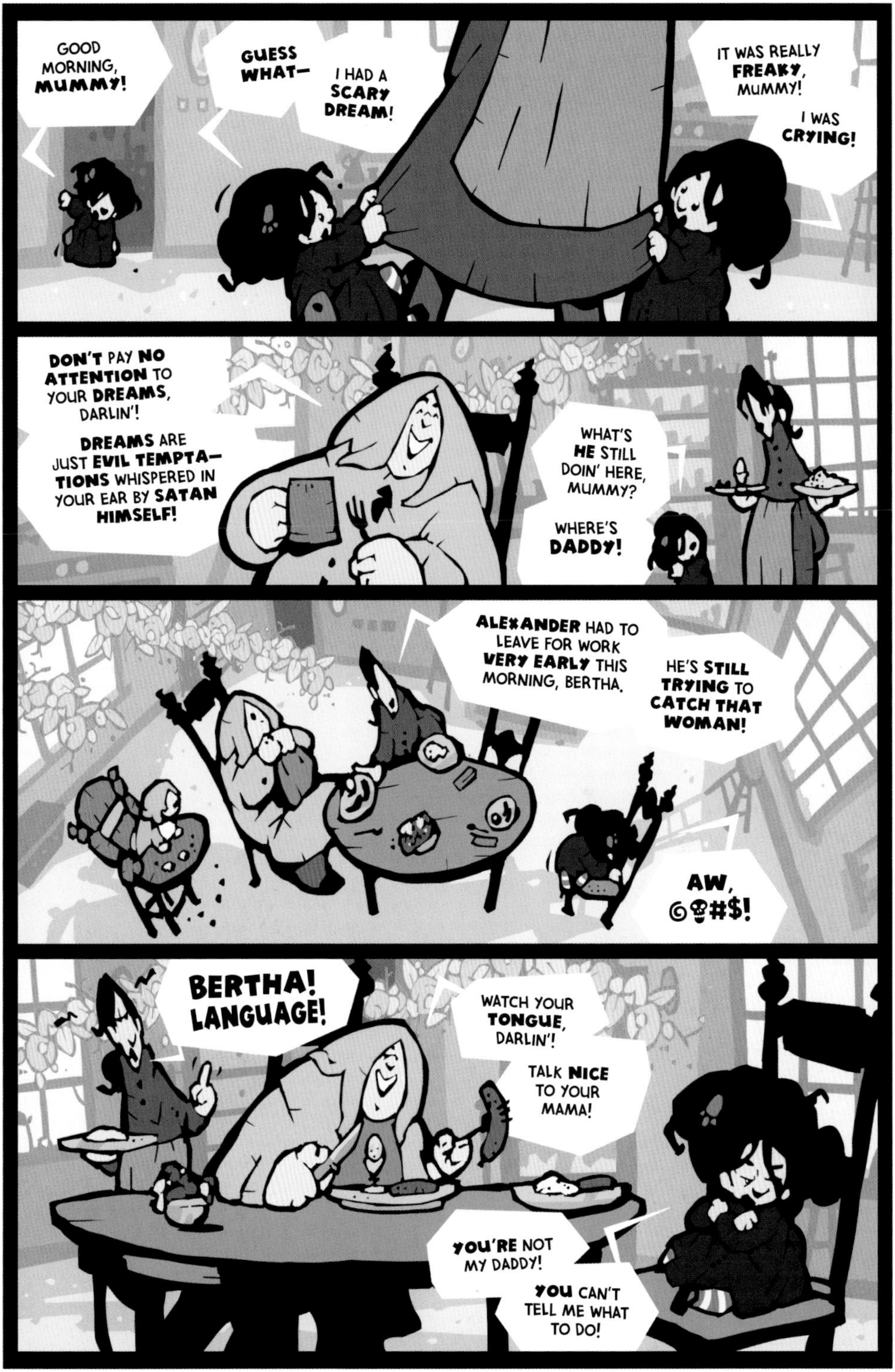
GOOD MORNING, MUMMY!
GUESS WHAT—
I HAD A SCARY DREAM!
IT WAS REALLY FREAKY, MUMMY!
I WAS CRYING!
DON'T PAY NO ATTENTION TO YOUR DREAMS, DARLIN'!
DREAMS ARE JUST EVIL TEMPTATIONS WHISPERED IN YOUR EAR BY SATAN HIMSELF!
WHAT'S HE STILL DOIN' HERE, MUMMY?
WHERE'S DADDY!
ALEXANDER HAD TO LEAVE FOR WORK VERY EARLY THIS MORNING, BERTHA.
HE'S STILL TRYING TO CATCH THAT WOMAN!
AW, @☠#$!
BERTHA! LANGUAGE!
WATCH YOUR TONGUE, DARLIN'!
TALK NICE TO YOUR MAMA!
YOU'RE NOT MY DADDY!
YOU CAN'T TELL ME WHAT TO DO!

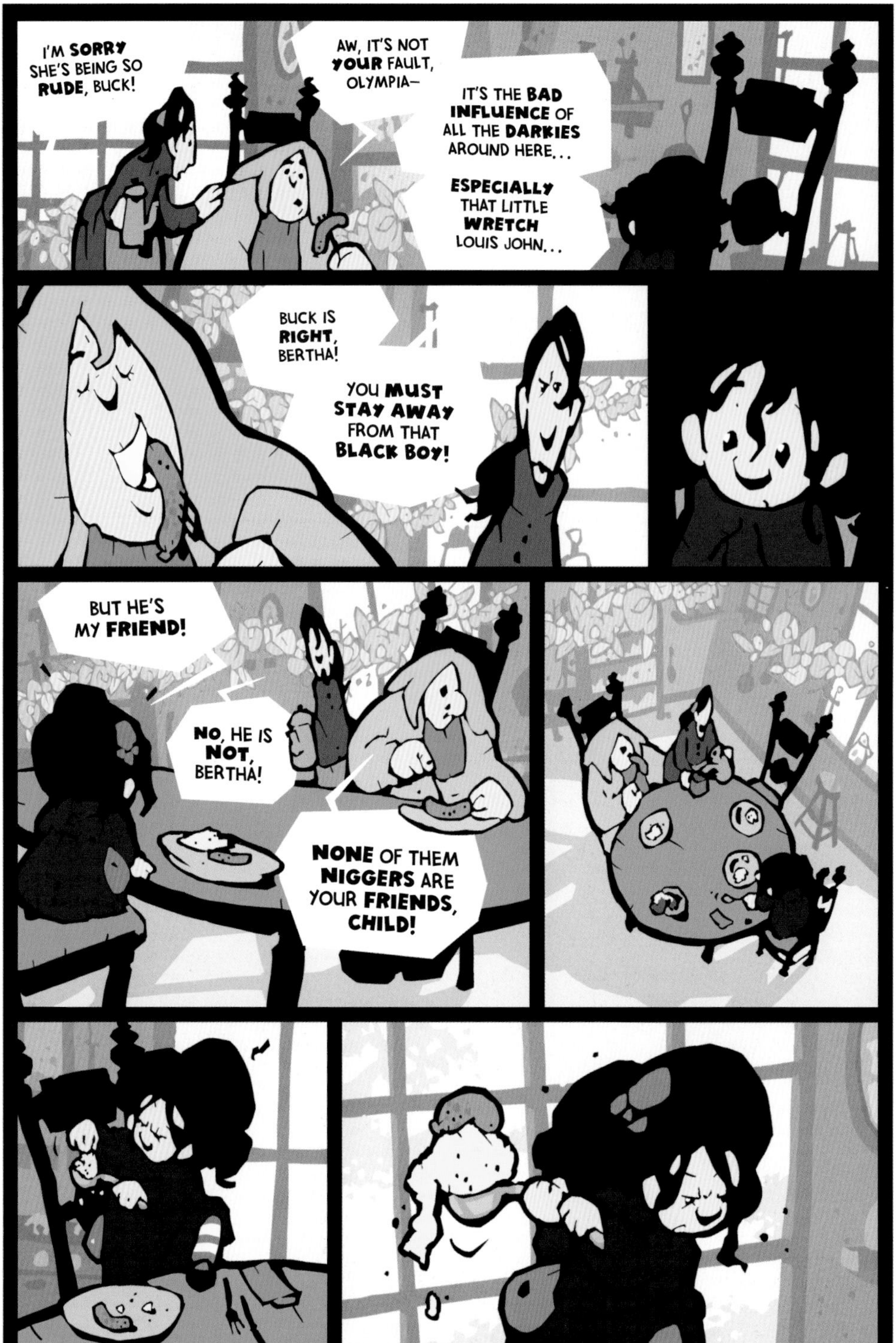
I'M SORRY SHE'S BEING SO RUDE, BUCK!
AW, IT'S NOT YOUR FAULT, OLYMPIA—
IT'S THE BAD INFLUENCE OF ALL THE DARKIES AROUND HERE...
ESPECIALLY THAT LITTLE WRETCH LOUIS JOHN...
BUCK IS RIGHT, BERTHA!
YOU MUST STAY AWAY FROM THAT BLACK BOY!
BUT HE'S MY FRIEND!
NO, HE IS NOT, BERTHA!
NONE OF THEM NIGGERS ARE YOUR FRIENDS, CHILD!

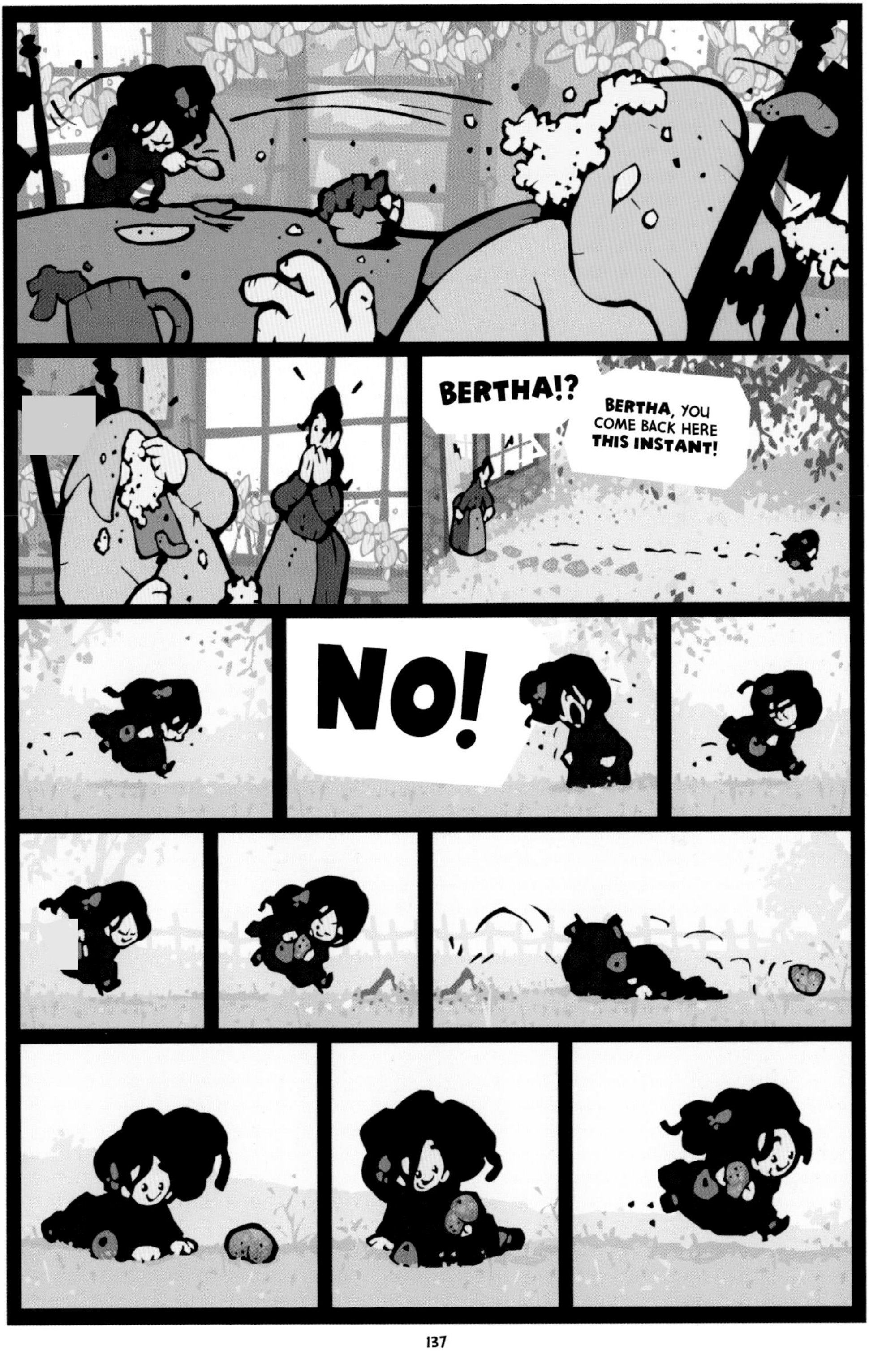
BERTHA!?
BERTHA, YOU COME BACK HERE THIS INSTANT!
NO!

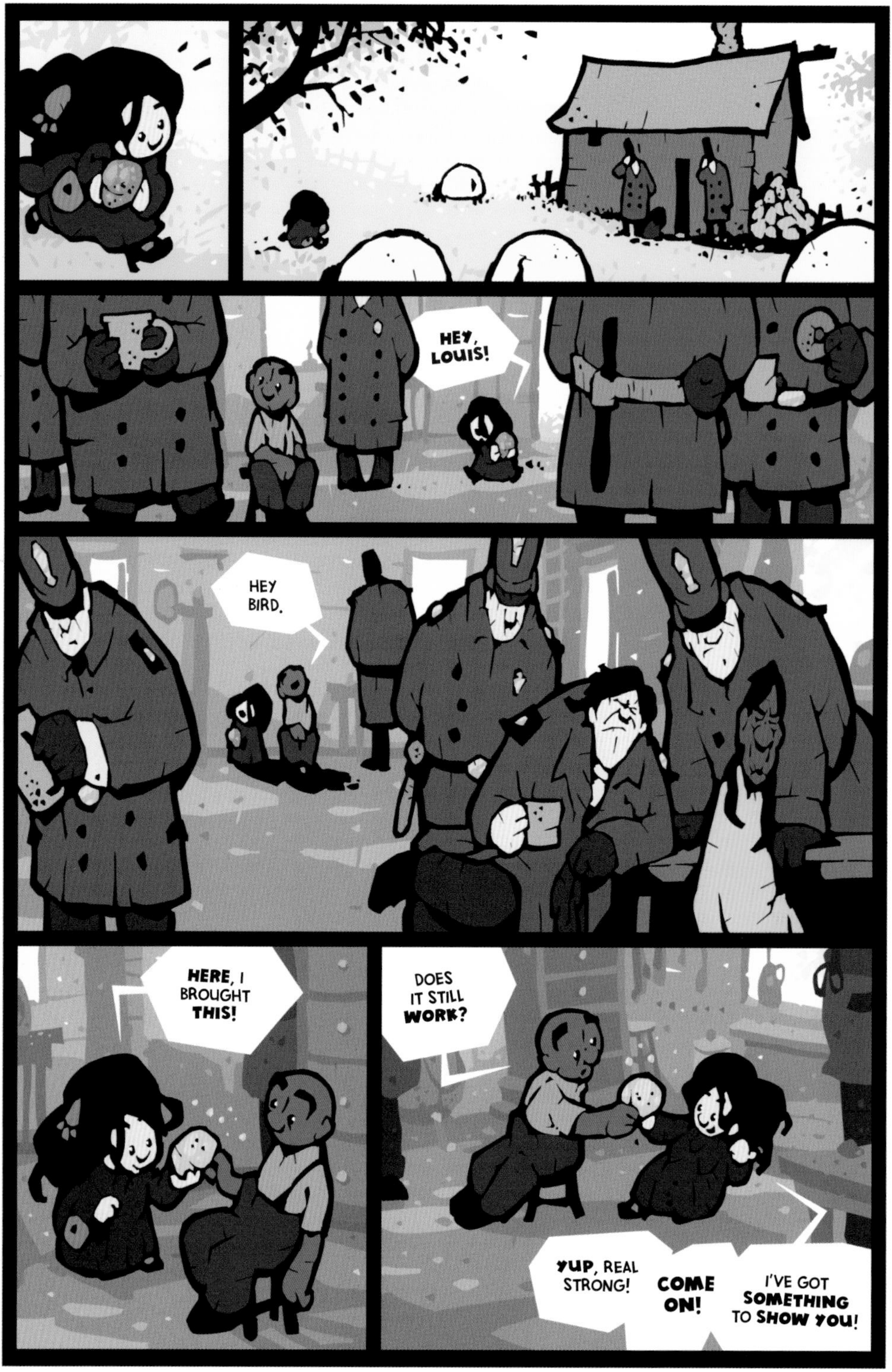
HEY, LOUIS!
HEY BIRD.
HERE, I BROUGHT THIS!
DOES IT STILL WORK?
YUP, REAL STRONG!
COME ON!
I'VE GOT SOMETHING TO SHOW YOU!

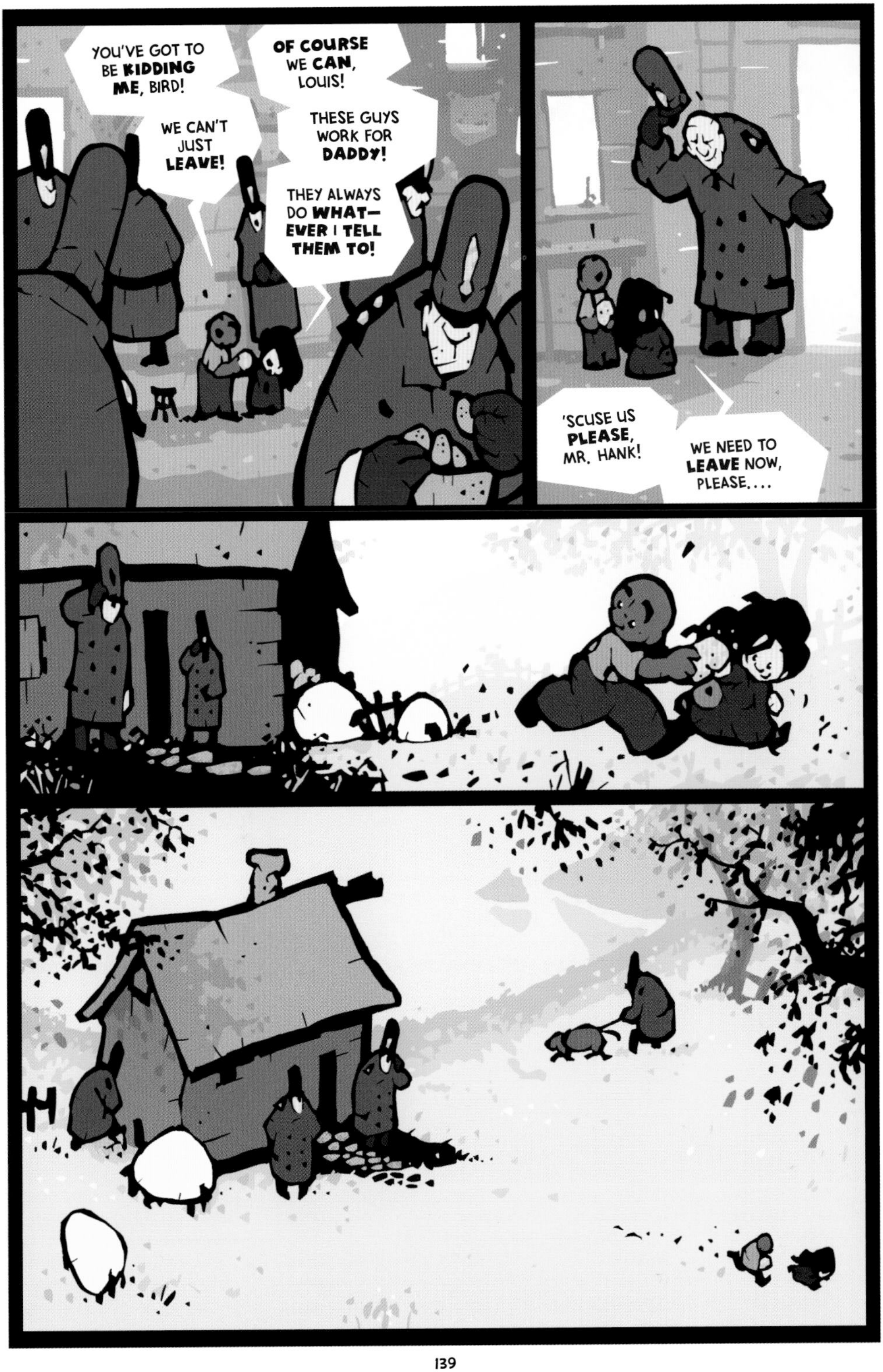
YOU'VE GOT TO BE KIDDING ME, BIRD!
WE CAN'T JUST LEAVE!
OF COURSE WE CAN, LOUIS!
THESE GUYS WORK FOR DADDY!
THEY ALWAYS DO WHAT-EVER I TELL THEM TO!
'SCUSE US PLEASE, MR. HANK!
WE NEED TO LEAVE NOW, PLEASE....

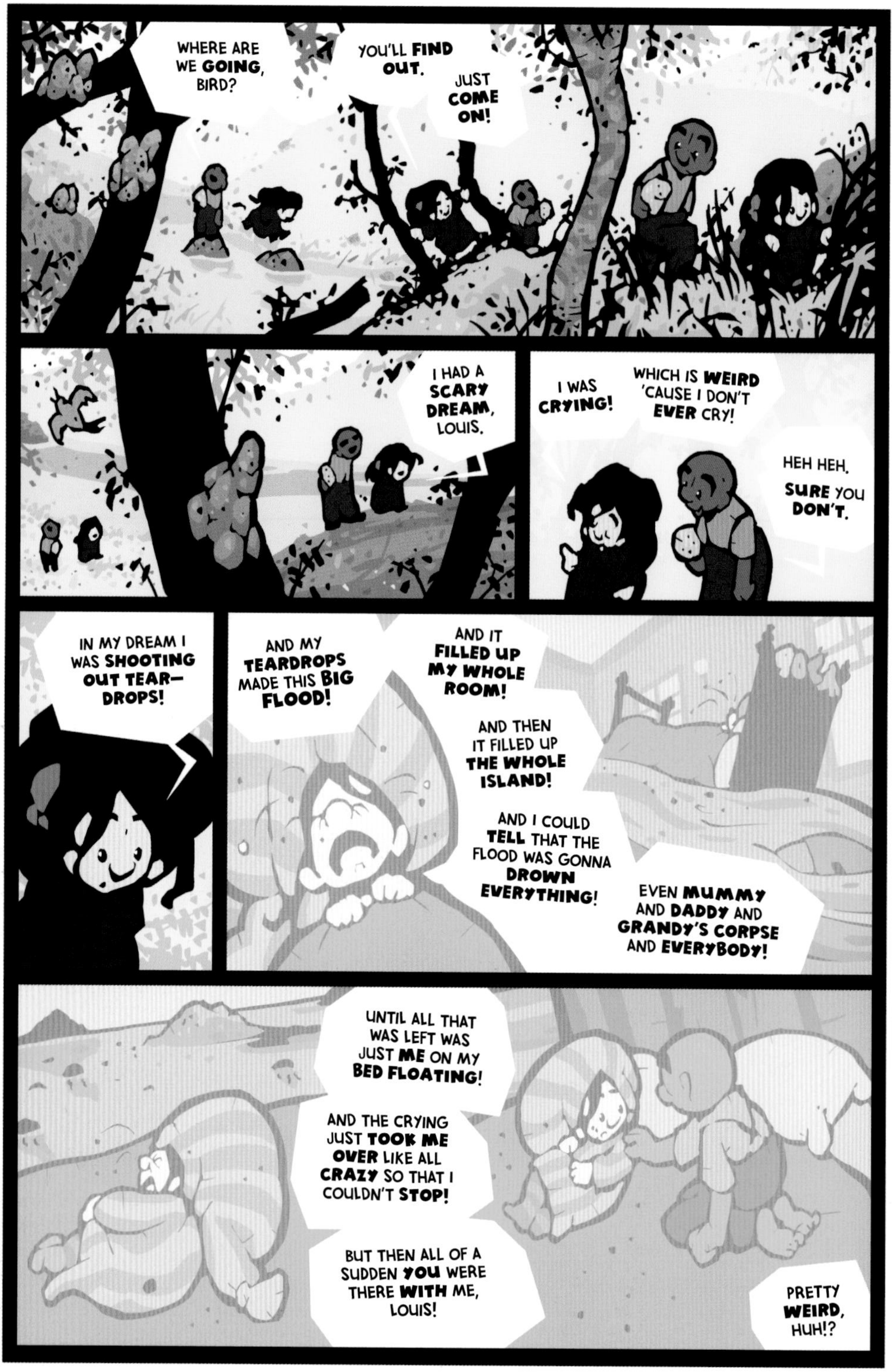
WHERE ARE WE GOING, BIRD?
YOU'LL FIND OUT.
JUST COME ON!
I HAD A SCARY DREAM, LOUIS.
I WAS CRYING!
WHICH IS WEIRD 'CAUSE I DON'T EVER CRY!
HEH HEH.
SURE YOU DON'T.
IN MY DREAM I WAS SHOOTING OUT TEAR-DROPS!
AND MY TEARDROPS MADE THIS BIG FLOOD!
AND IT FILLED UP MY WHOLE ROOM!
AND THEN IT FILLED UP THE WHOLE ISLAND!
AND I COULD TELL THAT THE FLOOD WAS GONNA DROWN EVERYTHING!
EVEN MUMMY AND DADDY AND GRANDY'S CORPSE AND EVERYBODY!
UNTIL ALL THAT WAS LEFT WAS JUST ME ON MY BED FLOATING!
AND THE CRYING JUST TOOK ME OVER LIKE ALL CRAZY SO THAT I COULDN'T STOP!
BUT THEN ALL OF A SUDDEN YOU WERE THERE WITH ME, LOUIS!
PRETTY WEIRD, HUH!?

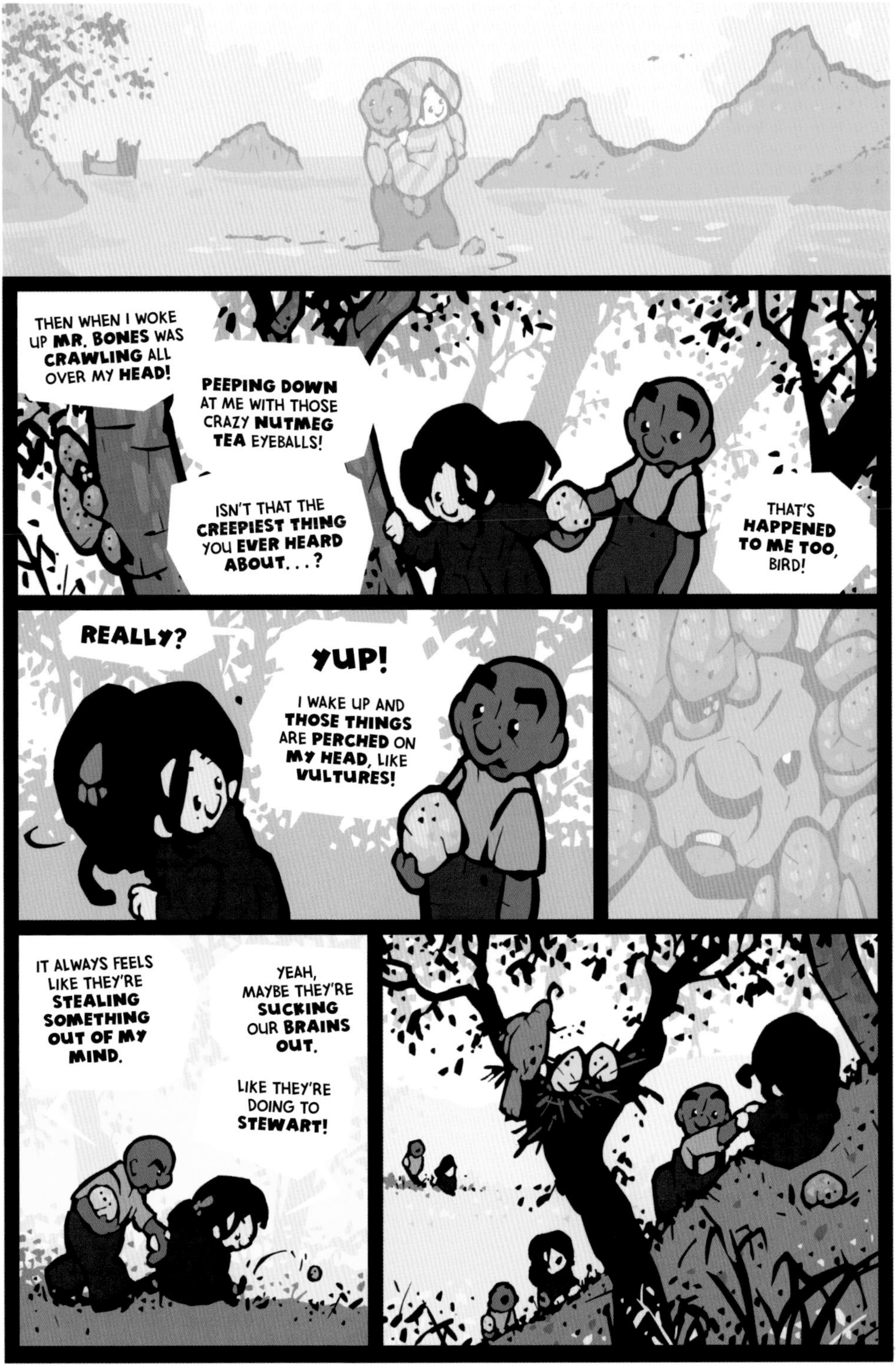
THEN WHEN I WOKE UP MR. BONES WAS CRAWLING ALL OVER MY HEAD!
PEEPING DOWN AT ME WITH THOSE CRAZY NUTMEG TEA EYEBALLS!
ISN'T THAT THE CREEPIEST THING YOU EVER HEARD ABOUT. . . ?
THAT'S HAPPENED TO ME TOO, BIRD!
REALLY?
YUP!
I WAKE UP AND THOSE THINGS ARE PERCHED ON MY HEAD, LIKE VULTURES!
IT ALWAYS FEELS LIKE THEY'RE STEALING SOMETHING OUT OF MY MIND.
YEAH, MAYBE THEY'RE SUCKING OUR BRAINS OUT.
LIKE THEY'RE DOING TO STEWART!

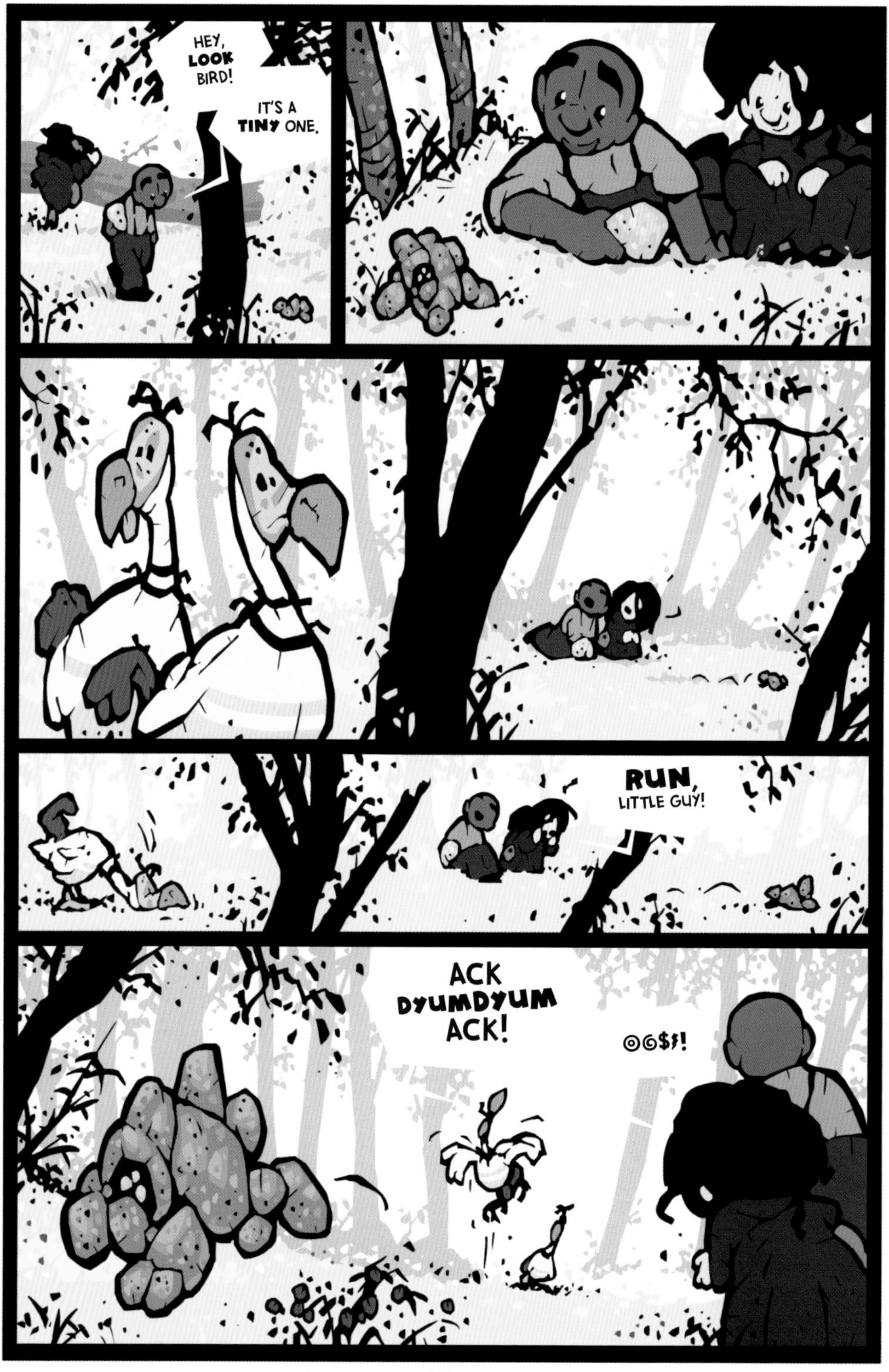
HEY, LOOK BIRD!
IT'S A TINY ONE.
RUN, LITTLE GUY!
ACK DYUMDYUM ACK!
@@$#!

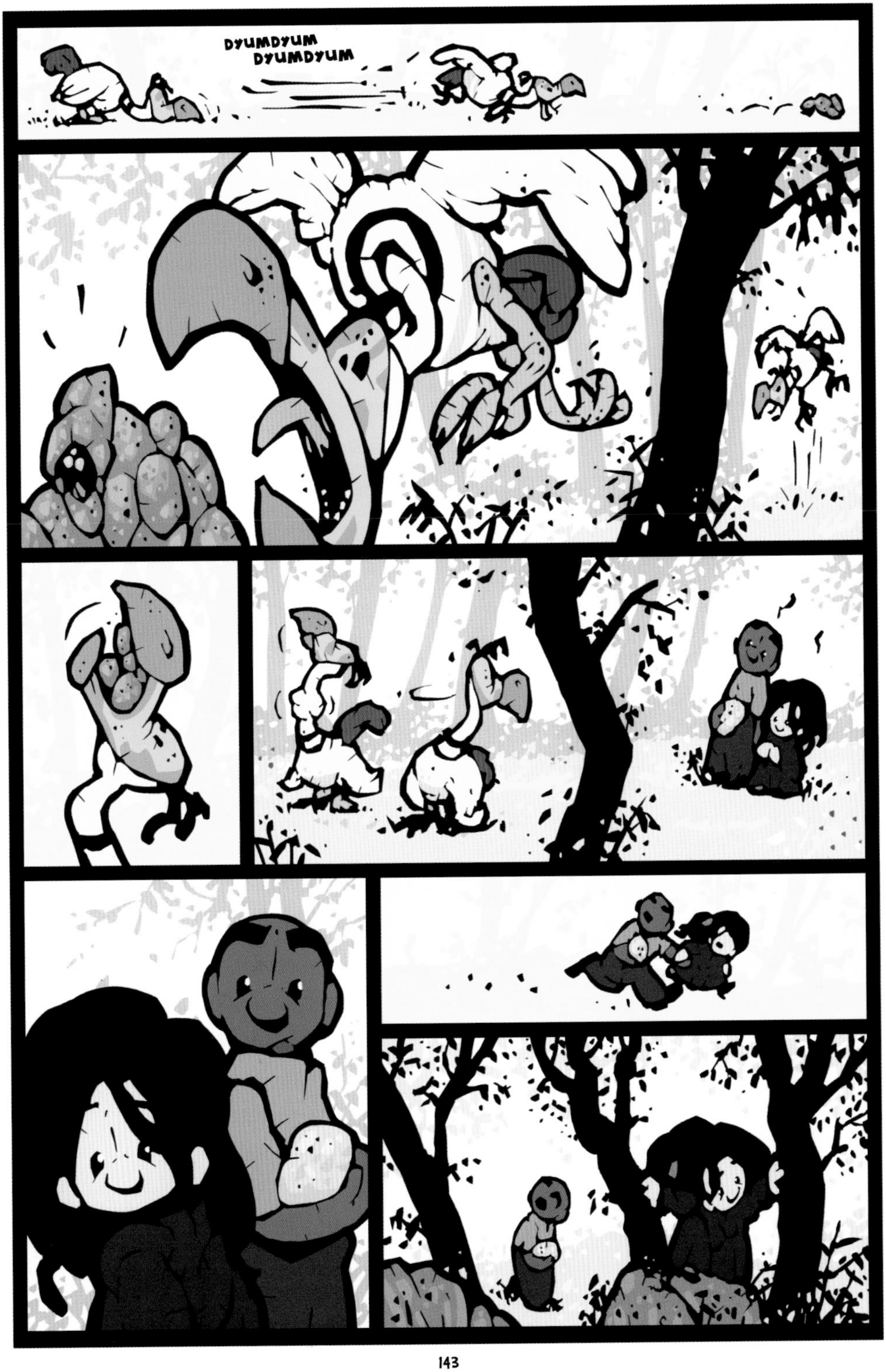
DYUMDYUM
DYUMDYUM

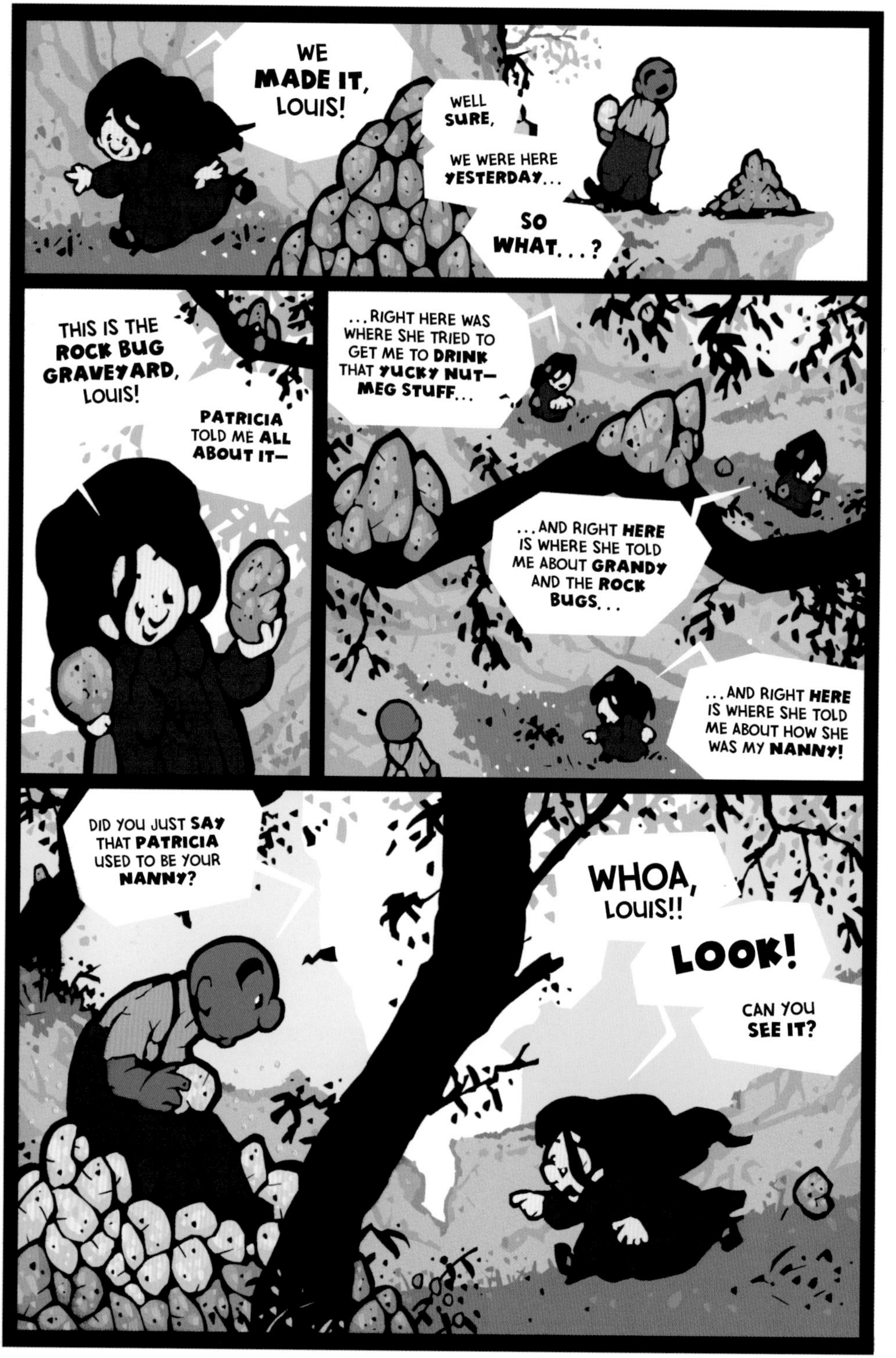
WE MADE IT, LOUIS!
WELL SURE,
WE WERE HERE YESTERDAY...
SO WHAT...?
THIS IS THE ROCK BUG GRAVEYARD, LOUIS!
PATRICIA TOLD ME ALL ABOUT IT—
...RIGHT HERE WAS WHERE SHE TRIED TO GET ME TO DRINK THAT YUCKY NUT-MEG STUFF...
...AND RIGHT HERE IS WHERE SHE TOLD ME ABOUT GRANDY AND THE ROCK BUGS...
...AND RIGHT HERE IS WHERE SHE TOLD ME ABOUT HOW SHE WAS MY NANNY!
DID YOU JUST SAY THAT PATRICIA USED TO BE YOUR NANNY?
WHOA, LOUIS!!
LOOK!
CAN YOU SEE IT?

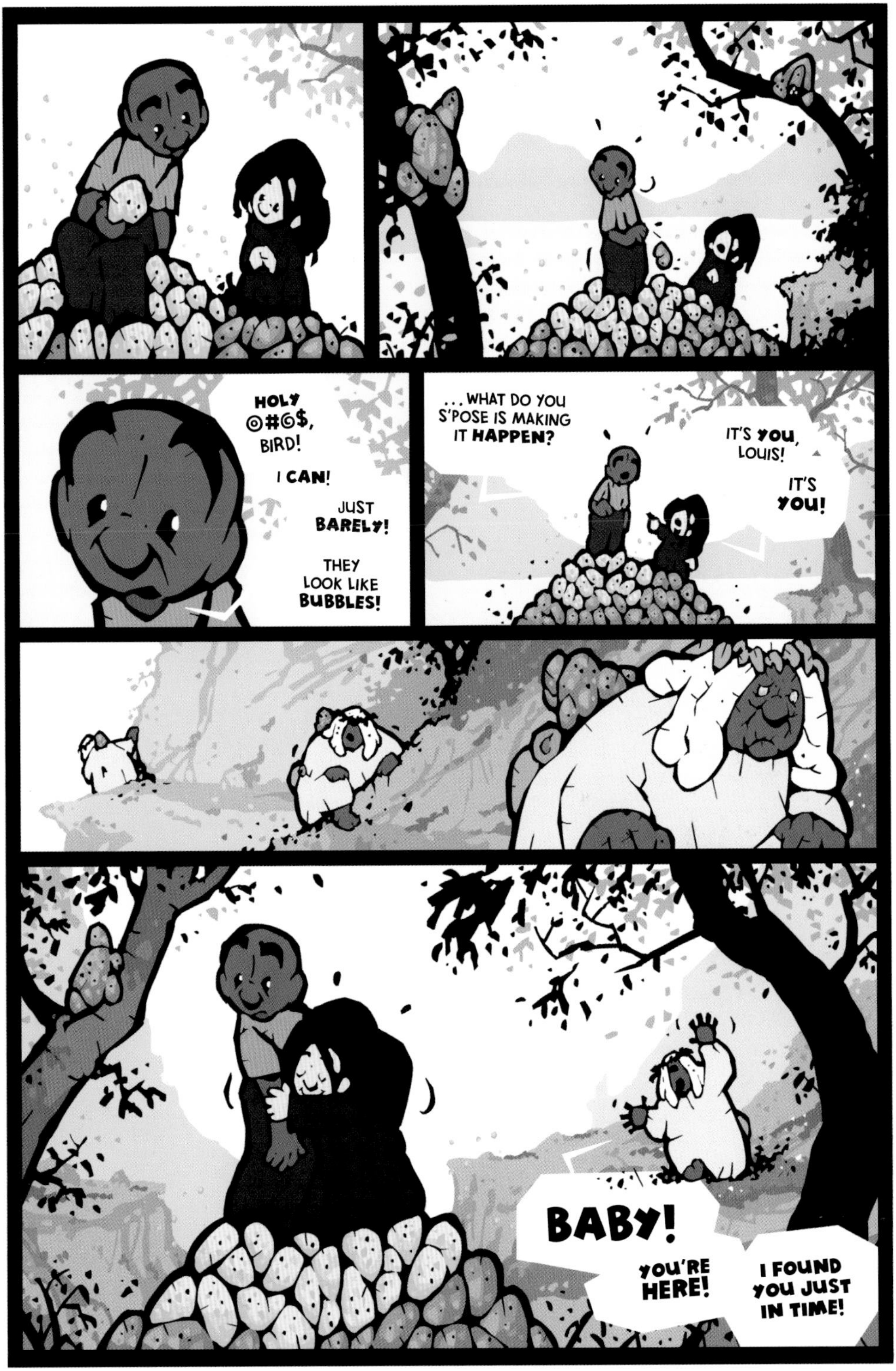
HOLY
@#G$,
BIRD!
I CAN!
JUST
BARELY!
THEY
LOOK LIKE
BUBBLES!
...WHAT DO YOU
S'POSE IS MAKING
IT HAPPEN?
IT'S YOU,
LOUIS!
IT'S
YOU!
BABY!
YOU'RE
HERE!
I FOUND
YOU JUST
IN TIME!

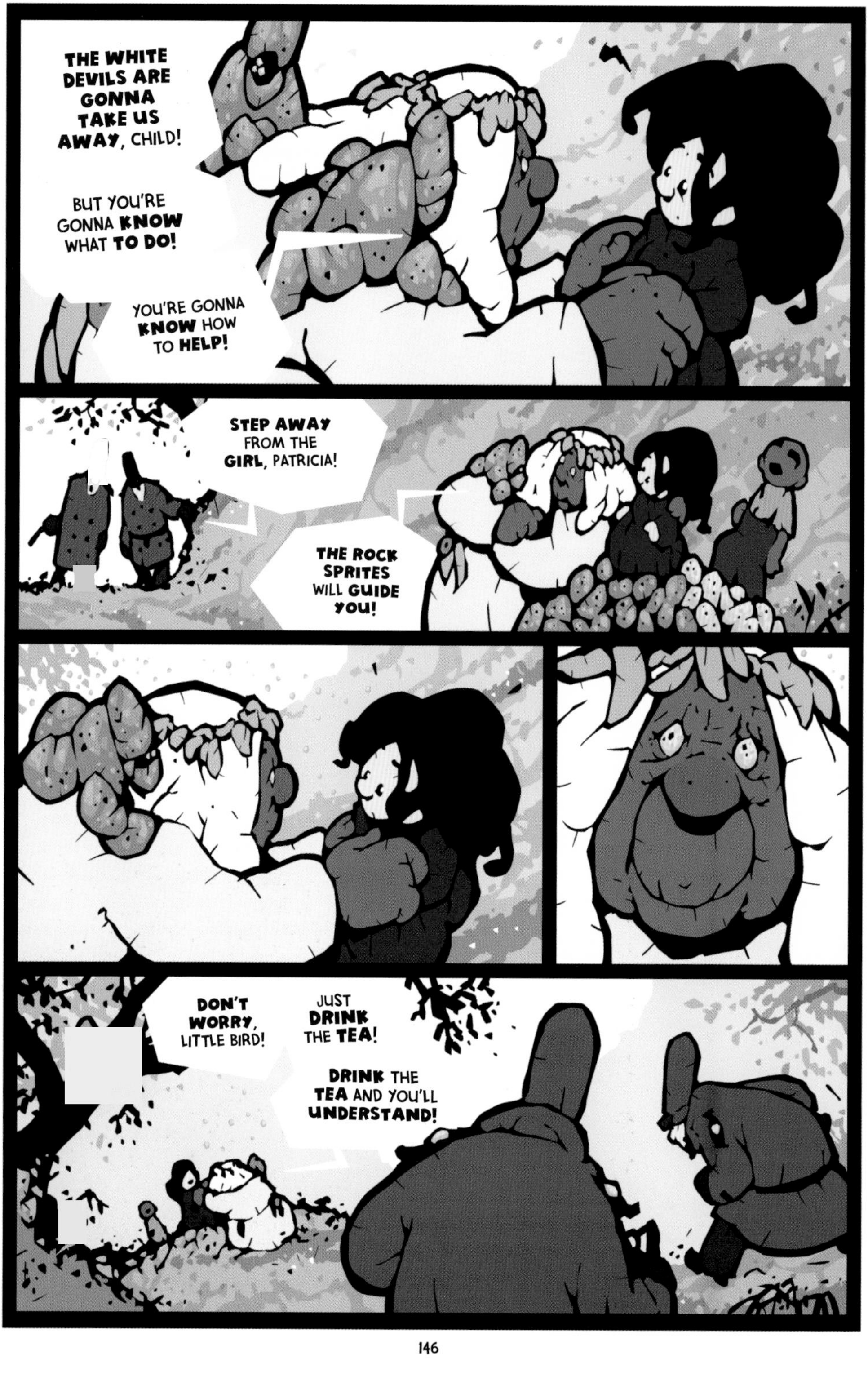
THE WHITE DEVILS ARE GONNA TAKE US AWAY, CHILD!
BUT YOU'RE GONNA KNOW WHAT TO DO!
YOU'RE GONNA KNOW HOW TO HELP!
STEP AWAY FROM THE GIRL, PATRICIA!
THE ROCK SPRITES WILL GUIDE YOU!
DON'T WORRY, LITTLE BIRD!
JUST DRINK THE TEA!
DRINK THE TEA AND YOU'LL UNDERSTAND!

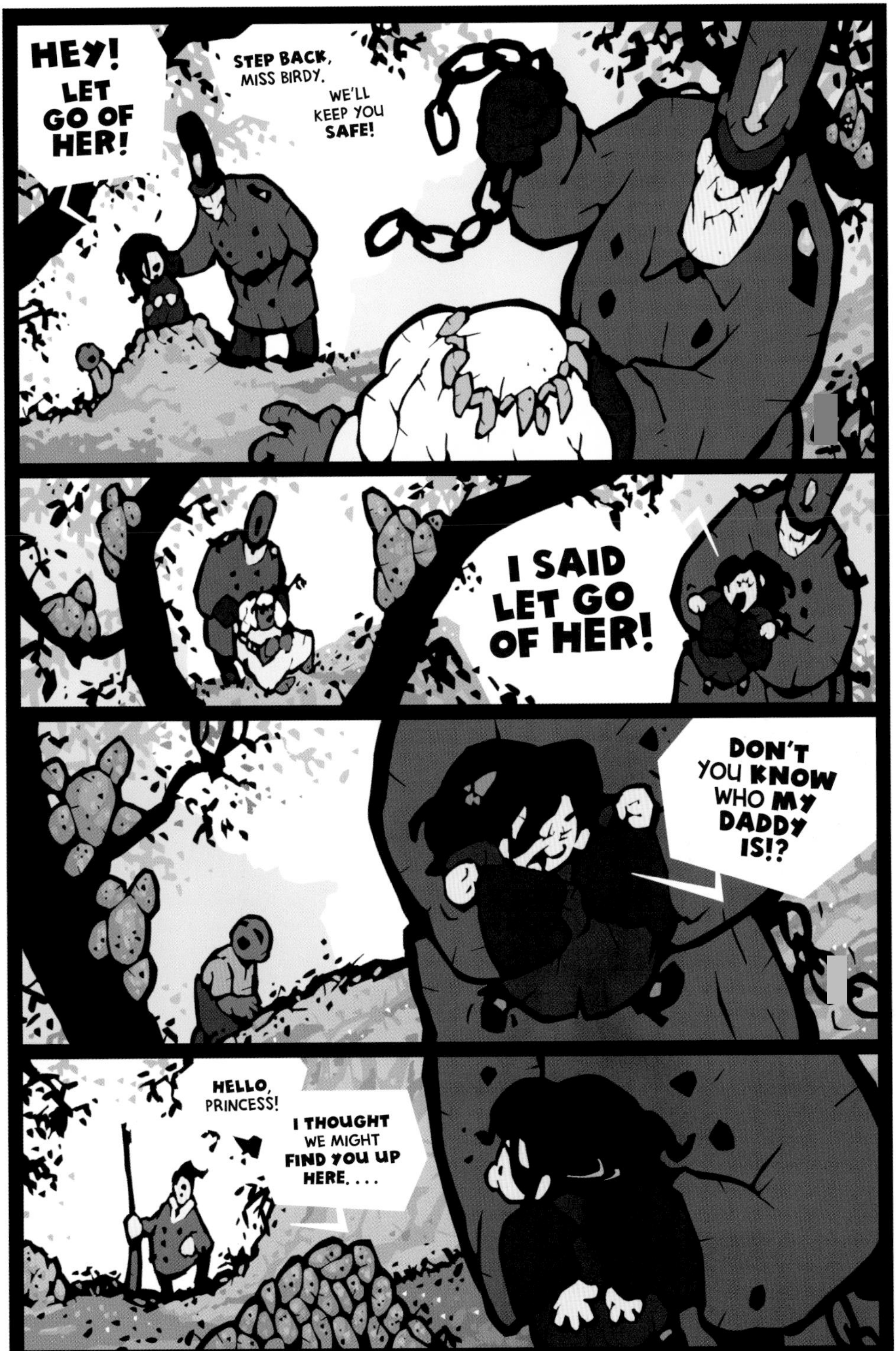
HEY! LET GO OF HER!
STEP BACK, MISS BIRDY.
WE'LL KEEP YOU SAFE!
I SAID LET GO OF HER!
DON'T YOU KNOW WHO MY DADDY IS!?
HELLO, PRINCESS!
I THOUGHT WE MIGHT FIND YOU UP HERE. . . .

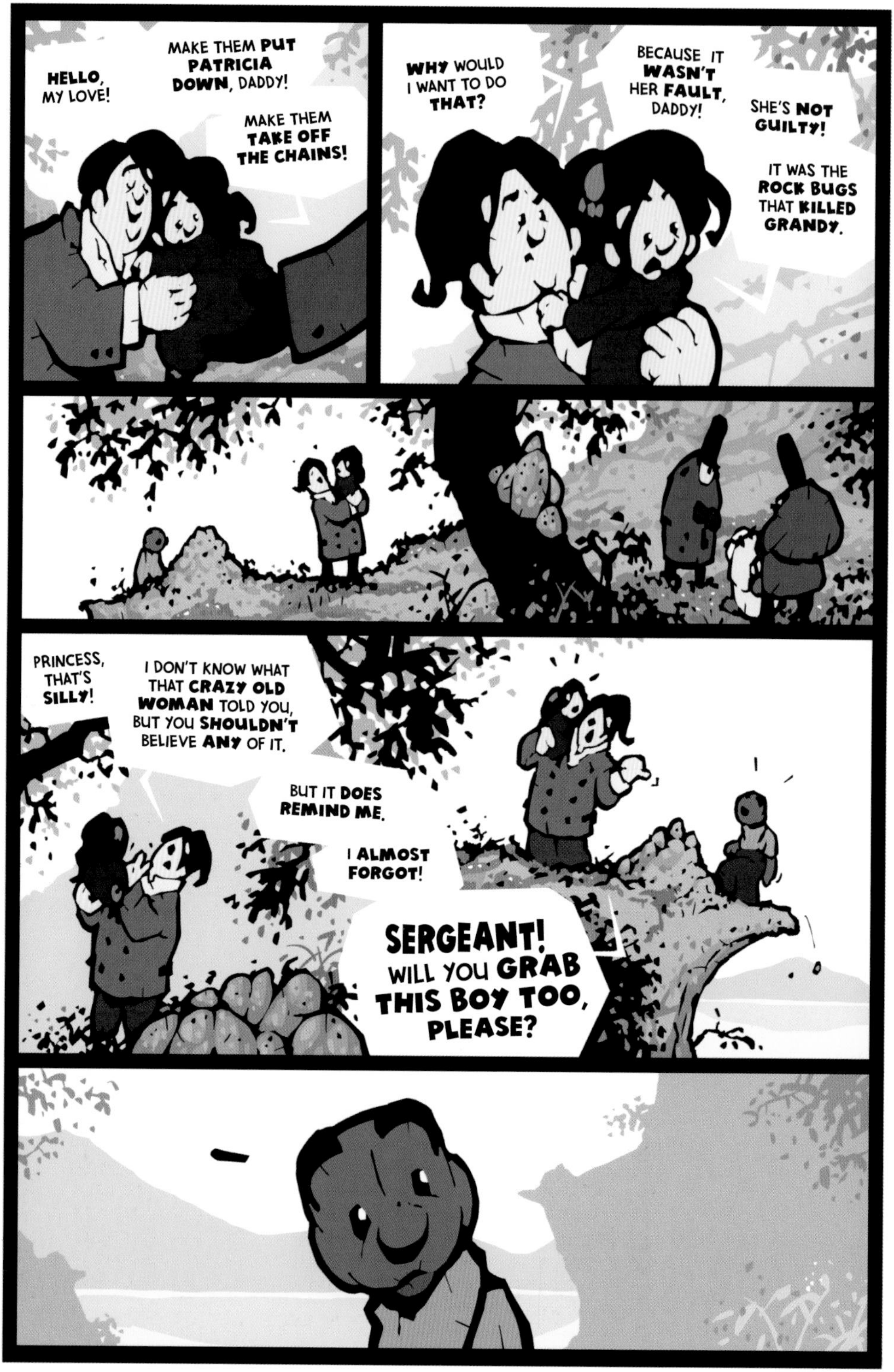
HELLO, MY LOVE!
MAKE THEM PUT PATRICIA DOWN, DADDY!
MAKE THEM TAKE OFF THE CHAINS!
WHY WOULD I WANT TO DO THAT?
BECAUSE IT WASN'T HER FAULT, DADDY!
SHE'S NOT GUILTY!
IT WAS THE ROCK BUGS THAT KILLED GRANDY.
PRINCESS, THAT'S SILLY!
I DON'T KNOW WHAT THAT CRAZY OLD WOMAN TOLD YOU, BUT YOU SHOULDN'T BELIEVE ANY OF IT.
BUT IT DOES REMIND ME.
I ALMOST FORGOT!
SERGEANT! WILL YOU GRAB THIS BOY TOO, PLEASE?

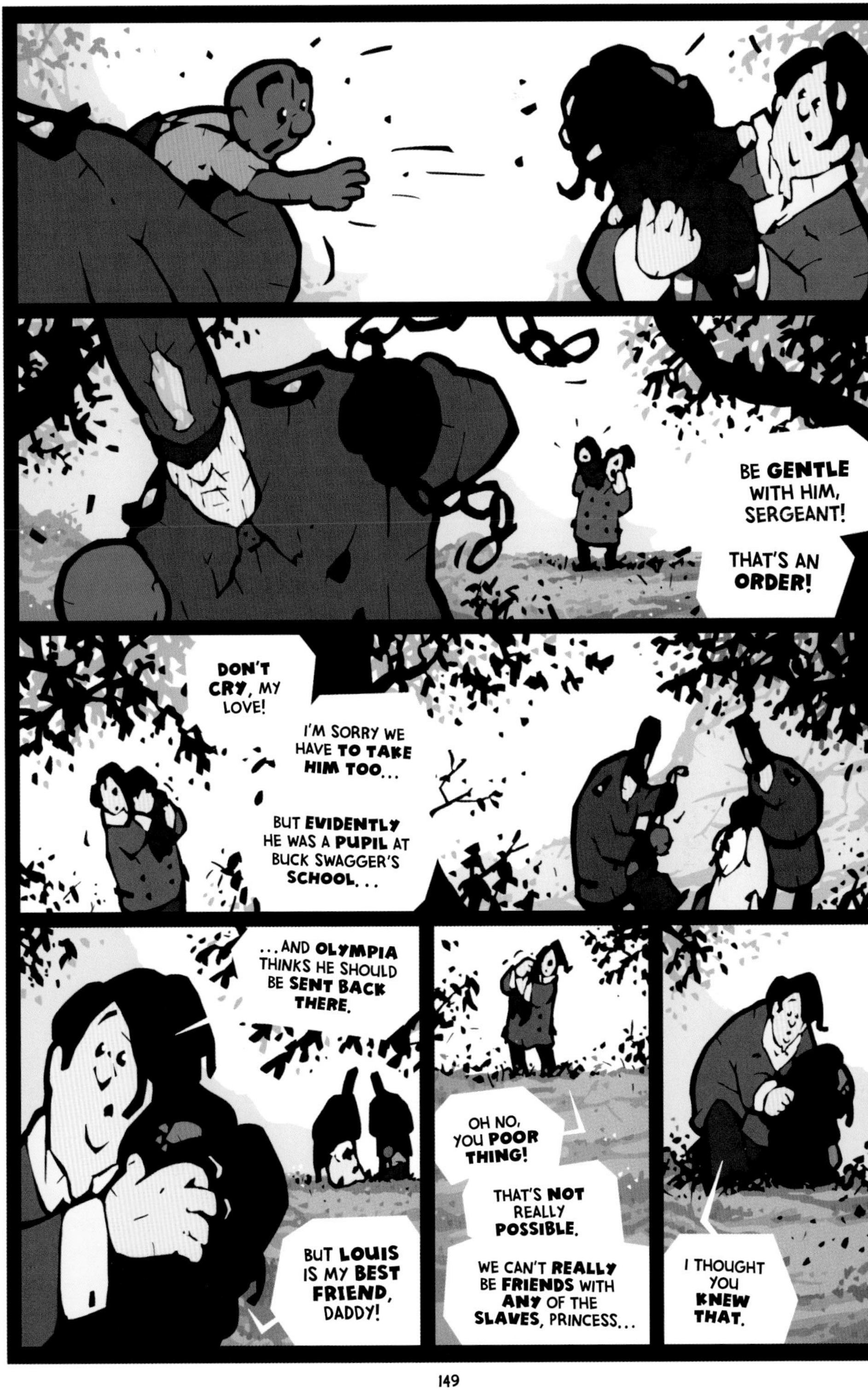
BE GENTLE WITH HIM, SERGEANT!
THAT'S AN ORDER!
DON'T CRY, MY LOVE!
I'M SORRY WE HAVE TO TAKE HIM TOO...
BUT EVIDENTLY HE WAS A PUPIL AT BUCK SWAGGER'S SCHOOL...
...AND OLYMPIA THINKS HE SHOULD BE SENT BACK THERE.
BUT LOUIS IS MY BEST FRIEND, DADDY!
OH NO, YOU POOR THING!
THAT'S NOT REALLY POSSIBLE.
WE CAN'T REALLY BE FRIENDS WITH ANY OF THE SLAVES, PRINCESS...
I THOUGHT YOU KNEW THAT.

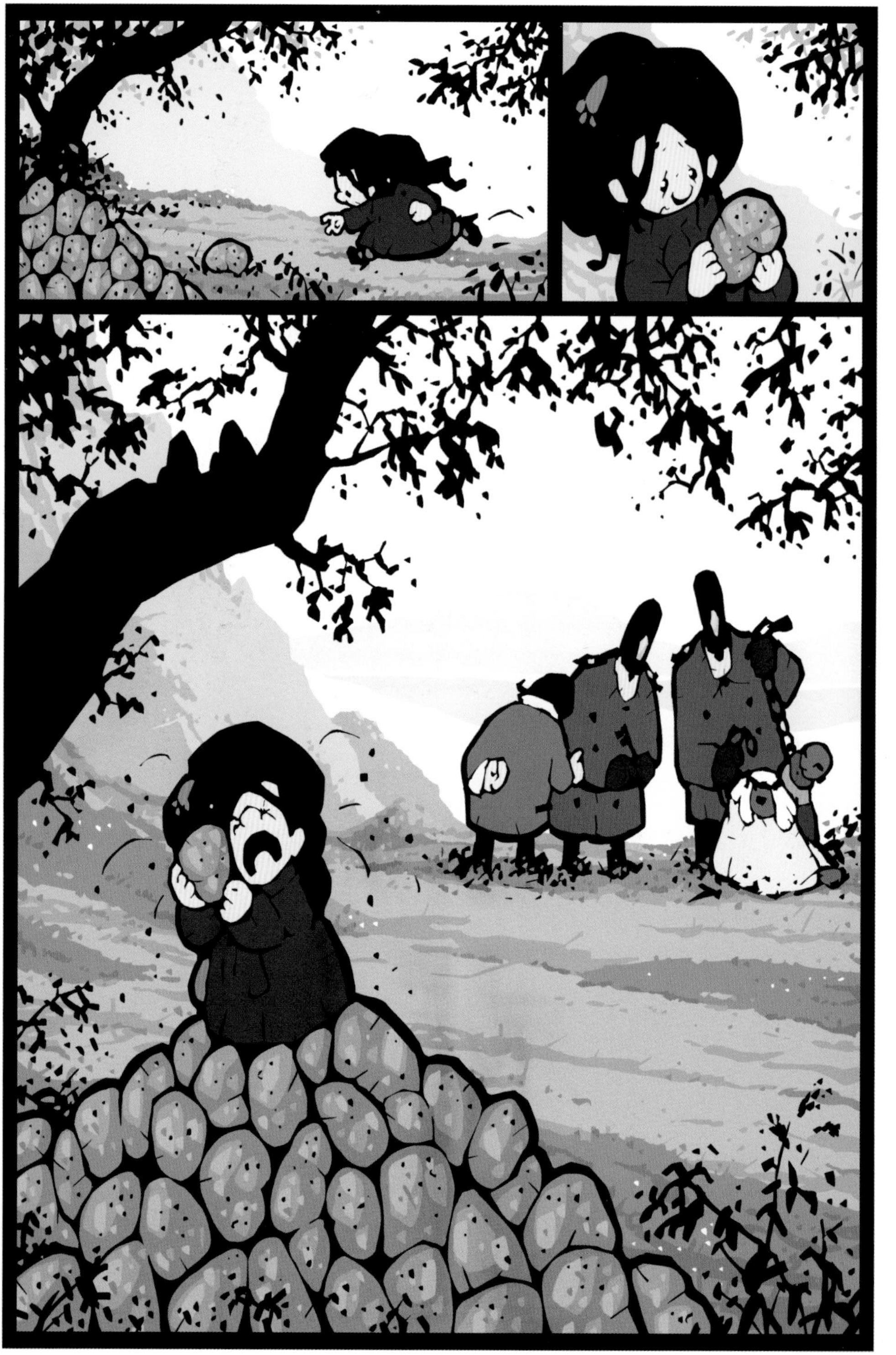

To be CONTINUED...

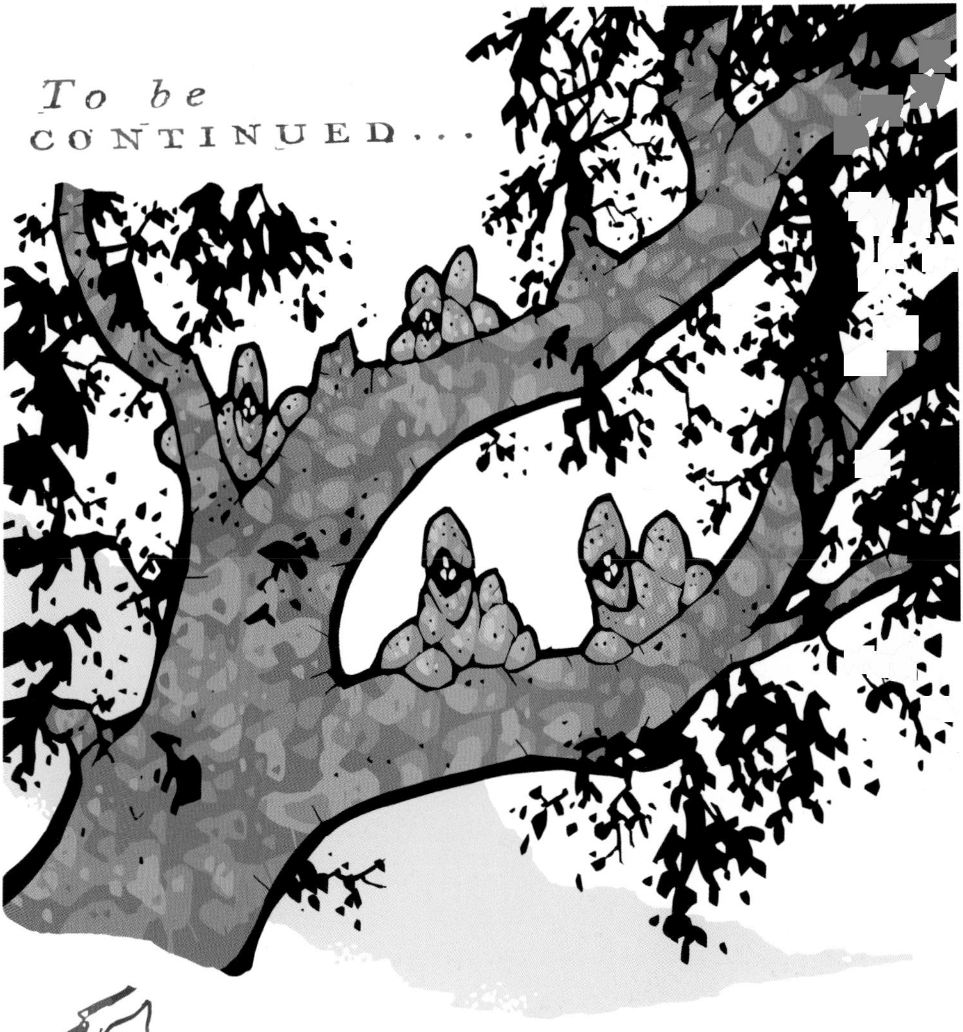

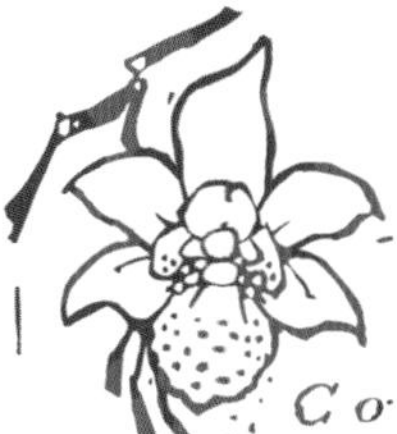

Coming NEXT *Season:* THE LOST COLONY

BOOK NO. 4

Terrible **JUDGMENT**

First Second

New York & London

Published by First Second
First Second is an imprint of Roaring Brook Press, a division of Holtzbrinck Publishing
Holdings Limited Partnership
175 Fifth Avenue, New York, NY 10010

Distributed in Canada by H. B. Fenn and Company Ltd.
Distributed in the United Kingdom by Macmillan Children's Books,
a division of Pan Macmillan.

Cataloging-in-Publication Data is on file at the Library of Congress.

ISBN-13: 978-1-59643-099-0
ISBN-10: 1-59643-099-0

First Second books are available for special promotions and premiums.
For details, contact: Director of Special Markets, Holtzbrinck Publishers.

FIRST

EDITION

First Edition October 2008
Printed in China

10 9 8 7 6 5 4 3 2 1